Where ....,

Chapter 1

Louise Lavender, clad in slim fitting denim jeans, tan boots, and leather jacket to match, leaned against the bar in the lounge of the ferry taking her to Belfast was waiting to be served. The raucous laughter at several table behind her made her sigh with relief that she had booked a cabin. There was no way she would get any sleep with that rowdy lot. Also, the lewd grin from a ginger haired chap with a beard, (her blonde hair and big blue eyes met his approval) made her feel uneasy. If it wasn't for the fact of needing her car and boot load of stuff, she would have taken the plane.

'Can I help you?' A harassed barman had returned from whatever he had been doing, a glob of tomato ketchup was drying on his cream jumper.

'Fish and chips and a pint of Peronni, please,' she ordered, putting the menu on the counter.

'We don't keep that on board,' said ketchup boy, 'we've got Guinness, or cider.'

I'll have a mug of tea, then, can I take it to my cabin?'

'Yes,' he gave her a cheeky grin, 'would you like me to carry the tray?'

'No, thanks,' Louise told him curtly, and added, 'That lot over there,' Louse pointed a finger at one very noisy table, 'are giving me a headache.'

'That's the crowd from Fat gypsy wedding. They're going to County Antrim to film at the Giants Causeway, the marriage service is going to be held there.'

'Interesting,' said Louise with a hint of sarcasm, 'you seem to know a lot about them.'

'I should do,' he sighed, 'they do this crossing every month, exhausting so it is.'

'Ear drum breaking, I'd call it,' she stated, she paid for her meal and when it was loaded onto her tray with a mug of tea, carried it to her cabin.

An hour later, Louise lay on the bed, which was surprisingly comfortable, and re read the letter she had received from the solicitor.

My Dear Miss Lavender,

I write to inform you of the tragic death of your great uncle Arthur, of Clodbury. It is requested that you attend a reading of the will on April 16th in Holglen House, Butterfinney, at 14:00.

I look forward to your attendance, should you not be able to come, it is stated that all proceeds of the will shall go to the local sheep farmers.

Kind regards

Mr Eustace Doherty.

Louise put the letter back in its envelope. She hadn't seen Great Uncle Arthur since she was a teenager ten years ago. Up to that point, she had gone to Clodbury with her parents every summer, spending weeks in the small cottage at the top of the hill, joining forces with cousins to explore the wild beauty of the place. Hours of sunbathing and swimming, and just enjoying the freedom of the country side.

At eighteen, Louise had met Jon, an accountant from London, who had showered her with gifts and affection. Clodbury held unhappy memories for her, and in any case, Jon had preferred to go to Spain instead.

Her parents still went over to Ireland occasionally, filling her in on the gossip and begging her to get in touch with Arthur, he missed her, but Louise couldn't face going back, and used the excuse of wanting to travel further afield, and with her job at a bank, she only had limited holiday entitlement, besides, the pay wasn't good enough to fund two vacations a year.

Louise had been saddened to hear that her great uncle had passed away and had shed a few tears. Her parents had gone over for the funeral, but she had been too busy at work and they wouldn't give her compassionate leave. Often, she wondered what she was doing working for a big company where loyalty wasn't rewarded and she was just a number.

Her parents had been stunned to hear that she had been beckoned to Ireland, her mother especially, Adele Lavender had been close to her uncle Arthur, her mother's younger brother. She was pleased for her daughter, though, Arthur was a canny soul, so there had to be a reason behind it.

Louise was by the doors, ready to exit at 6:30am. She had had a good night's sleep and was ready to start the adventure. It was daunting and exciting, she hadn't seen her Irish family for years, only catching up briefly by email or Facebook. As she drove down the steep ramp leading off the ferry and then heading up the M2 out of Belfast and towards Londonderry, she pondered the look on Jon's face as she told him that she needed to go alone, this was her business and besides, he couldn't afford to take time off from work.

'Where the F is this Clodbury?' Jon had sulked.

'In a remote part of Ireland,' she had told him, letting him know that it wasn't his scene in more ways than one, also, It was a chance to spend some alone time, she had lost her direction in life and needed to find her way.

Chapter 2

Louise could see the high climb of the Glenshane Pass up ahead and wondered worriedly if her small Fiat would make it. She pushed her foot down hard on the accelerator and the car moved like a plane on a runway, practically taking off as she hit full speed. She needn't have worried, the car took the climb in its stride and when she reached the top, she pulled in to an eating place called, the Ponderosa. She remembered stopping here before with her parents. The view from the mountain was spectacular, although a light mist hid some of the vista. She took a deep breath of fresh air and went inside.

A woman greeted her, she had rosy cheeks and a cheery disposition.

'What can I get you, dear?'

'Can I see the menu please,' Louise asked, not knowing what they had on offer.

'Take a seat and I'll go and get you one.'

She sat by the window and admired the view. It was still very early in the morning but she knew the traffic would build up as she neared Derry and the rush hour.

The rosy cheeked woman appeared with a laminated menu, 'can I get you a drink?'

'A pot of tea, please,' said Louise.

'Tea for one or two?'

Louise looked around, trying to spot a mystery guest that she might have overlooked. The woman laughed, 'I meant, you would have more tea in a pot for two.'

'Then I will have a pot for two,' grinned Louise, liking the woman's thinking.

'So, what brings you to these parts? English, aren't you?'

Louise studied the menu before replying, she was starving, 'I'll have the Ulster Special,' she passed rosy cheeks the menu, 'I'm here on family business.'

The breakfast was delicious, fat juicy sausages, white and black pudding, poached eggs, and crispy rashers of bacon, accompanied by a plate of golden toast and creamy butter. Louise was glad of the big pot of tea to wash it all down with.

She paid the bill, made a visit to the Ladies and when she got to the car changed out of the boots, replacing them with comfortable trainers. She sent a quick text to Margaret, telling her she should get to the cottage around ten, after she had stopped at Tesco's in Derry for essentials, like bottles of bleach and bottles of wine. Margaret replied that she would have the kettle boiled and tea pot warmed.

As she approached Bucrania, she wound both windows down and let the salty sea air into the car. Louise couldn't believe how perfect the weather was so early in the morning. A few keen golfers were making their way around the course and the sea was as calm as a sheet of glass. On a whim, she pulled into a wide layby, wound the windows up, switched off the ignition, and got out of the car. The beach was deserted except for one lone dog walker. After a ten-minute brisk walk, the wind chillier than she expected, Louise went back to her car and resumed the journey to Clodbury.

As she approached the village, nerves began to jingle in her belly causing her stomach to cramp. Her hands felt clammy on the steering wheel and she remembered the situation why she had left here, the years seeming like months. She had no worries that people would remember her from that childhood of the years she had spent here. She was a lot thinner and toned for a start, the puppy fat long gone after hours of workouts and running, and her once brown hair was a glorious blonde, cut short to shape her face, emphasising her big blue eyes. Oh yes, Louise was a different person now to the gauche teenager she once was. She refused to think about Gerard, it had taken months of crying into her pillow, she would not go back to that state ever again. Besides, she had Jon now, reliable, dependable and he adored her. The niggling little voice that added boring to the list was firmly quashed.

She drove slowly through the village, noting that not much had changed, apart from a chemist shop that looked relatively new, and the school had been modernised, Margaret had filled her in on some of the changes though, so she wasn't too surprised. She had a little chuckle remembering when she first came to the village and wanted to use the telephone. She couldn't believe that you had to turn a little handle and then got put through to the person sitting at the exchange in the post office. Louise wondered how many calls Mrs Breslin had listened in to. It had been fun to make risqué phone calls knowing that she was being eavesdropped upon. Margaret and Louise had been hysterical with laughter at some of the calls that they had once made. Only Margaret had known about the heartache she had suffered over Gerard Gallagher, but not everything, somethings she couldn't tell her cousin, at least not yet.

With a shudder, Louise forced the memories back in their box and drove towards the cottage. As she reached the crest of the hill near an old church that was said to be haunted, she looked out over the bay, the morning sunlight turning it to an azure blue. It would also be very cold, she thought, driving down the hill, and forking off toward the little road that would take her to Uncle Arthur's cottage. She was amazed at how many new houses had been built in the last few years, and the caravan site had extended to take up both sides of the road.

The road narrowed as she drove towards the cottage and she was pleased to discover that the gate had been left open for her to drive through. As she climbed out of the car, Margaret ran out, her shoulder length dark hair sweeping around her face. As they hugged, Louise realised just how much she had missed her cousin. They had been more like sisters, with only months in the age gap between them. Margaret's mother, Iris, had been Adele's elder sister and had died tragically in a car accident when Margaret was ten. Adele had wanted to take her to England and bring her up as her own, but Brian, Margaret's dad, had refused, he needed her with him.

'So, what do you think this Will is all about?' asked Margaret as she poured tea into mugs and put a homemade fruit cake on a plate.

'I don't have a clue,' sighed Louise, 'even mum was surprised. I guess we will find out soon enough, the appointments at two tomorrow.'

'I know,' Margaret laughed, 'I'm going along as well. Whatever Uncle Arthur has to say, I'm involved too.'

'That's great,' Louise was relieved, she hated the fact that she might be the only one in the family mentioned in the Will.

'We can have lunch in Donath and then walk down to the office.'

Louise was delighted with the cottage; her uncle had kept it in pristine condition. Margaret gave her a tour, there was a wet room, two double bedrooms, a kitchen cum dining room and a large lounge which looked out over the bay. The furniture was old but comfortable and the range Louise remembered from her childhood was still in working order. There were ten acres of land surrounding the cottage and another four below the road, nearest the beach, a neighbour was using it to graze his sheep. Louise wondered who would take it over, it was a shame that Arthur didn't have children of his own to pass it down to.

The girls tidied the kitchen, put on their coats, and set off down the rough track that led to the beach.

'So, how's your love life?' Louise asked, as she cautiously stepped over a large rock covered in seaweed.

'Non-existent,' Margaret sighed, 'since Rory decided to go to Boston, I've spent most of my time either looking after dad or working for the Co-op in Donath.'

'Why didn't you go with Rory?'

'He didn't ask; besides, dad needs me. He might act Mr Independent, but he can't cook or clean.'

'Won't you mean, do you ever get out and have fun?'

'What? Around here?' Margaret laughed, but with little humour.

'What about that night club we used to go to in Bucrania, or the one in Letterkenny?'

'They were knocked down a few years ago, a shopping complex in Letterkenny and an Aldi in Bucrania. There are plenty of pubs in the village, but nowhere to go for a dance, even if I had the time.'

They were half way towards the river, which ran at the bottom of the Beaton Mountain into the sea. The wind was blowing against them, giving them rosy cheeks, and cold hands. In unison, they gathered flat stones and put them in their pockets to skim into the water, something they always did in their youth.

'Do you miss Rory?' Louise asked, thinking that if it had been her, she would have gone to Boston like a shot. She could imagine taking in the sights and then enjoying a trip to Cape Cod. But the dream was only in her head, because the reality of her bank account being in a dismal state meant she would be lucky to have a holiday anywhere exotic.

'Margaret paused to pick up an impressively flat stone, 'at first, but then I realised we were together out of habit more than anything else,' she gave Louise a hug, 'I'm so glad you're here Lou Lou.'

'Me too, I'm just realising how much I've missed you, although I'm curious about the will.'

'I'm curious about the contents in your boot, why have you brought so much stuff with you? Wouldn't it have been easier to fly and hire a car?'

'Yes, and I wish I had done that, with those fat gypsies on board. I thought I would need my duvet, sheets and everything.' Louise sighed and then laughed at the absurdity of it. Arthur's cottage had changed a lot since the last time she had been there.

They skimmed the stones across the churning river, counting the jumps and Louise was delighted that she hadn't lost her touch, winning by six to four. The walk back was a lot easier with the wind in their back.

'Does Ma Duffy still live in the tumble-down cottage?' Louise asked, remembering how scarred they had been of the old woman, believing her to be a witch.

'Yes, she's must be in her eighties now, still as vindictive, and nasty as she always was, no one goes near her.'

'I wonder why she's so bitter and twisted,' Louise pondered, 'we always tried to be nice to her.'

'There were rumours,' Margaret said, linking her arm through Louise's, 'lost love and all that bull. She's never been married, or had kids, as far as we know anyway.'

'Maybe she was abandoned as a baby, left to bring herself up in that cottage,' they both laughed, knowing that the woman who had been nasty to them as young girls deserved no pity.

Louise had a shower in the new wet room and felt awake and ready to go out.

'I've booked a table at West Bay, it's not been open that long, but the food is said to be delicious,' said Margaret.

'I'm starving,' groaned Louise, she hadn't had anything to eat since breakfast at The Ponderosa and a couple of Kimberley biscuits and the cake with a cup of tea when she arrived. She was wearing a pair of slim fitting black trousers and a royal blue silk shirt.

'You look incredible,' said Margaret, 'I bet nobody recognises.'

'That's what I'm hoping.' She planned to hear the reading of the will and then return to her life in England. Jon had already sent her a text asking when she would be back.

'You look pretty stunning yourself,' Margaret was wearing a beautiful deep red dress that complimented her colouring, and a pair of matching strappy shoes with very high heels. Her glossy dark hair cascaded around her slim shoulders.

The food at West Bay was everything their reputation had promised, and more. The sea food was freshly caught and the sauce it was cooked in was creamy and rich.

'I'll have to run ten miles tomorrow,' Louise stated and meant it.

'Just enjoy,' sighed Margaret dreamily, savouring the succulent prawns in white wine.

The desert was a concoction of fruit, meringue, and cream.

'It's called, Eton Bliss,' Margaret told her, 'and it lives up to its title. It's a good job we didn't have a starter.'

The restaurant was full of visitors to the area and Louise was thankful that she didn't recognise anyone. She wasn't in the mood for making small talk or explaining where she had been for the last eleven years. They did attract a lot of admiring glances and one bold chap came over to chance his luck with the attractive duo.

'Where ye from?' he'd asked, cheekily.

'Sarth Landon,' Louise drawled. 'We're staying with Ma Duffy over the Bent.'

'Ye don't mean that ole witch?' his voice trembled.

'The very one,' grinned Margaret, playing along. 'She's got something cooking on the range in a big round pan, looks like one of those cauldron thingies. Would you like to come back with us for a bit of craic?'

'Erm,' he backed away, slowly but banging into tables, 'sorry, I've got to go.'

'Make sure you wash your hands afterwards,' Louise laughed.

They were still laughing when they pulled up outside Arthur's Cottage. A sensor light came on, activated by their movement, making it easier to find their way inside.

'Are you sure Uncle Brian doesn't mind you staying here for a few days?' Louise asked as she kicked her high heels off and bent to rub her feet. They needed a bit of TLC and a paddle in the sea might perk them up a bit.

'Of course, not, I think he quite likes a bit of space,' Margaret laughed, knowing how her dad liked to watch his favourite programs in peace and hated it when Margaret tried to tell him about her day. 'Which room do you want? I've made them both up, one's an en-suite and the other is close to the bathroom.'

'I'll have the en- suite,' Louise grinned, 'it will save me disturbing you when I have to get up several times in the night after all that lager.'

Margaret was cooking bacon and eggs, Louise could smell the delicious aroma as she slowly awoke from a deep slumber. She had gone to sleep as soon as her head had touched the pillow, the previous day had been a long one, especially with the long journey across the sea. She had a shower and wearing a bathrobe and a towel turban style, she went to join her cousin for breakfast.

'I hope you're hungry,' Margaret said as Louise sat down at the rustic table in the centre of what was now the new kitchen. 'I thought it would set us up for a few hours, and then we can have lunch in Donath late afternoon.'

'Good idea,' sighed Louise as she took a sip from a mug of tea, 'I'm nervous, I don't know why Uncle Arthur wanted me there and not mum.'

'I'm curious,' Margaret stated, 'I used to do Uncle's shopping every Friday and give him a lift now and again, yet he never mentioned a Will, but, why would he?'

'Well, we'll find out at two o'clock, after this lot I think we should go for a walk. The sun's shining and I want to have a paddle.'

The water was extremely cold but bliss to Louise's feet, they walked along the sea's edge for a few minutes, dried their feet and after putting on slip-on pumps, they walked up to the road, enjoying the heat of the sun. Margaret pointed out some of the new houses, giving Louise a bit of information on them.

'An English woman lives there,' Margaret waved her hand towards the two-story house with four windows facing towards the road, the back had a panoramic view of the beach, and the view would be stunning. 'She spends half her time here and the other in Warwickshire. She doesn't mix with the locals, and I think she does all her shopping in the North. Someone said her name's Karen.'

'Have you met her?' Louise was curious about this mystery woman.

'I haven't actually met her, but I saw her once, she looked to be in her mid to late-thirties, very well dressed, by that I mean high fashion, blonde shoulder length hair and she was driving a bright green Audi, purchased in the UK.'

They continued walking up the hill, towards the cottage, some of the houses belonged to people Louise knew when they were teenagers or young adults. They veered towards a beaten track, leading to what was called the back beach, by the locals. It was full of pot holes where Lorries had once driven to collect gravel from the pit. At the very end of the road, a small track led across the green to a shambling run-down cottage, Louise remembered it well from all those summers of long ago. She shivered as the sun sneaked behind a cloud and cast the bright day into a grey one. Aggie Duffy had been a vindictive, bitter woman, who Louise thought had always been old.

Louise remembered a day in June years ago, it had been a hot day and she had gone down to the beach with Margaret and a few boys, she had been around fourteen and very shy. The sea had been deliciously warm and they had all plunged in, the boys in swimming shorts and the girls in bikinis. Ma Duffy, as they had called her, had called them the most disgusting names, whores, jezebels, and so many other words that Louise had never heard of. She had run up to the cottage, Margaret close behind, sobbing with a towel clutched tightly around her body. Mrs Lavender had stormed down to the beach, found the woman, and warned her that should she go near the kids again, Adele would go to the police. Aggie had never uttered a word since, but her black beady eyes glared at her whenever their paths crossed. Seeing the ruined cottage now, reminded Louise just how much those hateful words had affected her. For years, she refused to wear a bikini, she had felt too exposed, and it was only through talking it through with close friends that she realised that Aggie had the problem, and Louise realised they were right, Aggie always wore long black dresses and a black shawl draped around her. A raven of doom, or a crow, Louise could never decide.

A tendril of black smoke drifted from the chimney darkening the grey sky and Louise shivered, pulling her scarf tighter around her neck.

'Let's go back and get a cuppa,' Louise linked her arm through Margaret's, she felt uncomfortable around the cottage and a feeling of unease gave her goose bumps, she wanted the past to stay where it belonged, not stirred, and prodded back into the future. She began to think she had made a mistake coming back here, the door to her memories was slowly opening and she had to keep it closed, she had lived through the pain once, she couldn't face it a second time.

Chapter 3

Margaret was gripping Louise's arm so hard that she would have bruises the next day.

'Can you repeat that, please, *Mr Doherty*?'

Louise was too stunned to say anything, she had a job keeping her mouth from gaping, and Margaret was asking the questions, giving her a chance to let it all sink in.

'Your Uncle Arthur has left the cottage, the land and all monies to be split equally between you, Miss Margaret Grant, and you, Miss Louise Lavender.'

'But what about our other cousins?' stated Margaret, 'and Lou's mum.'

'The terms of the will are very straight forward and rigid,' said Eustace Doherty.

'But,' Louise managed to say, 'you said if I didn't come over, everything would be left to the sheep farmers.'

Eustace laughed, 'Arthur had a wicked sense of humour, and he knew you wouldn't come over unless he added a little white lie.'

'Crafty old bugger,' Louise sighed, knowing how right he had been.

Eustace was enjoying the exchange, he hadn't had so much fun since Old Brigid passed away and left her money to a son that had been a deep dark secret, her daughter had been furious, but what could she expect when she had done nothing to help her mother in the last years of her life. Much like Arthur, he had doted on his two favourite nieces, and looked on them as the daughters he had never had.

'Are there terms and conditions for the cottage and the land? Asked Louise, 'I mean, can we rent it out, sell it, rent the land, sell the land?'

'I'm glad you asked that,' said Eustace, stroking his snow-white beard. Louise thought he had a touch of Dumbledore about him.

'Tell us,' Margaret looked over at Louise, 'what are the terms and conditions?'

'I've got my secretary, Theresa, to type a copy up for you both,' Eustace shuffled some papers on his desk, there were so many piles of files that Louise wondered how he found any space to do any work.

'Stop procrastinating,' she said, 'we need to know where we stand. Can we sell the cottage?'

'Erm,' Eustace looked out of the window, 'looks like it might rain,' he stated, 'clouds are grey.'

'Are you going to break into song,' Louise sighed, 'There may be troubles ahead, that kind of thing.'

'Oh, well, I'm not a very good singer, although I was in the church choir for a while, they threw me out when they realised. It was their own fault, asking for a solo performance.'

Margaret sat forward,' Okay, out with it, just say it fast, what don't you want to tell us? We can't sit here all day, I haven't brought an umbrella.'

'It might be better if you took the list home and read the terms. Then if you have any questions, ask Miss Green.'

'Miss Green?' they chorused.

'Theresa,' Eustace got up and rubbed his leg, 'it's a bit stiff, sure sign of rain.'

'For F's sake,' spat Louise, 'tell us now, before I lose the will to live.'

Eustace sat back down and stroked his beard, 'I did tell Arthur that he was playing god with your lives, so don't blame me.'

'Are you a man or a mouse?' asked Margaret.

'Most definitely a mouse, my dear,' he chuckled. He took a deep breath and began.

'Rule one. The cottage must not be sold for two years.

Rule two. You must both live in the cottage and create a business of your choice. Funds are available to you both and planning permission has been obtained to extend or build on.

Rule three. Do not under any circumstances let Darius Denton near the property, the gun is in the back room if he should darken the door,' Eustace coughed and took a sip of water from a glass perched precariously near the edge of his cluttered desk. 'I don't recommend you shooting Denton,' Eustace grinned.

'Rule four. If after two years you both discover that you can't make a success of the business, you have permission to sell and donate all monies remaining to the sheep farmers.'

'Was he joking?' Louse asked.

'Treat it more like a challenge,' he smiled gently.

'But, I can't live here,' she said, 'my life is in England, my boyfriend is there and so is my job.'

'You hate your job,' said Margaret, 'and Jonathan is not the right person for you.'

'Whose side are you on,' Louise demanded, 'I can't live here, it's impossible. Let the bloody sheep farmers have it.'

'Wait,' Margaret shouted as Louise opened the door, preparing to leave. 'How much money is in the account?

Eustace flicked through a pile of papers, obviously, he hadn't mastered the art of spreadsheets and filing in the cloud. 'Twenty million, six hundred and fifty thousand pounds, forty-five pence.'

'What?' screeched Louise coming back into the room and taking her seat next to Margaret.

'Where did he get all that money from? He was always saying he had no money.'

'I don't suppose he would mind if I told you,' smiled Eustace. 'Arthur liked to dabble.'

'In paint?' asked Margaret, she was dumbfounded. She had always bought him groceries, a loaf of bread, a pot of jam or a pint of milk because she felt sorry for the old boy.

'Stocks and shares,' Eustace told them. 'He had a good eye for the market, in fact, he tried to show me the tricks of his trade, but I don't have the first clue about computers.'

'I can see that,' said Louise cheekily.

'Take the paperwork away with you,' he told them, getting to his feet. The girls took that as their cue to leave.

They travelled the short distance from Butterfinney to Donath in silence. Louise was wondering how to get out of the situation without letting Margaret down, Margaret was musing how her dad would react to the news. Louise slowed down when a tractor pulled out of a side gate in front of her, just before the road forked off to Donath. She held the palm of her hand on the horn, sending the sheep in the nearby field scampering to the bottom end. A woman on a horse glared at her, and it took all her willpower not to stick her fingers up at her. She would be glad to escape from the country.

Chapter 4

Louise had made hot chocolate and marshmallows, they were sitting by the range flicking through the pages of Uncle Arthurs photo album. There were pictures of Louise as a baby, Adele the proud mother, standing by her uncle.

Arthur must have missed his niece terribly when she upped roots and moved to the UK in search of a bigger world than the one she grew up in. There were some that Adele had sent over to show him her new life, Louise knew that her mum had often begged Arthur to go over for a visit, had even decorated a room especially for him, but he would never travel far from his home place.

Louise reached over and took her mug of chocolate from the corner of the range, knocking the album to the floor.

'Oops, sorry,' she bent to pick up the dog-eared album and noticed a larger photo had fallen out and fluttered to land near Margaret's slipper clad foot. She picked it up and as she studied the picture, her stomach clenched, so tightly that she thought she might bring up the lunch they had enjoyed at Donarth.

'What's wrong, Lou? You've gone as white as a sheet.'

Wordlessly, Louise passed the photograph over to her cousin.

'What was Arthur doing with a photograph of you and Gerard?' Margaret exclaimed, studying it closely. From the snap shot, you could see how close the couple were, they only had eyes for each other, and Margaret could never understand what had happened between them, she was only told the basic facts, betrayal and lies leaving Louise heartbroken and fleeing to England.

'I didn't even know it existed,' Louise said quietly, memories had flooded into her mind and pain had shattered her heart. The box she had filed away in her subconscious had sprung open, leaving her vulnerable and raw. There was no way she could stay here, it was impossible.

'I'll leave at the weekend,' she told Margaret, 'Maybe Uncle Brian will move in and help you spend the money.'

'But, Lou, you know the terms of the will, we both have to make a go of it. I know Gerard hurt you badly, but that was over ten years ago, you were only kids. Besides,' she took Louise's hands, 'he lives miles away, what are the chances of you bumping into him?'

'There's my job and Jon, remember.'

'Ask Jon to come over, give your notice in.'

'I don't belong here,' Louise sighed, 'how can we build a business? I don't want to be a bloody farmer.'

'Nor do I,' Margaret raised her voice, 'how many people get the opportunity that we have? Think positive for a change, you used to be so fun loving, what's happened to you, Lou?'

'I've grown up,' she took her mug of chocolate into the kitchen and poured what was left down the sink. 'I'm going for a walk.'

Although it had been sunny in the afternoon, it had turned windy and chilly now it was early evening. But Louise didn't care, even though her eyes streamed and her ears hurt, she welcomed the pain, hoping to numb her feelings altogether, she had buried the memories deep, only her mother knew how badly she had been scarred, but now they had resurfaced and she couldn't bare it. Sobs shook her body and her eyes were now shedding tears, she wanted to wail like a banshee, let it all out, but she didn't know who could be lurking behind a sand dune. Suddenly, she was gripped from behind, and held tight. Louise turned her face into her cousin's shoulder and sobbed as if her heart would break.

Arm in arm, they carried on the familiar route across the beach, towards the river. The tide was almost in, and they had to clamber up the small pebbles to avoid getting their shoes wet. The sound of the waves crashing on the rocks slowly soothed Louise, and just before they reached the end of the beach, she took a tissue out of her coat pocket, blew her nose loudly and managed a small smile.

'Thanks Margaret, I know I'm a drama queen.'

'Not at all,' she hugged her arm close, 'I can't force you into staying, and if that's what you need to do, I won't stand in your way.'

'I don't see how I can stay,' Louise told her sadly.

Fresh hot chocolate two hours later, they were sitting curled up in chairs on either side of the range. Margaret was wearing a pink, fluffy, onesie reading a book and Louise was in a track suit, checking her phone for messages.

'Jon asks when I'm coming home.'

'Tell him, never,' laughed Margaret.

'I'm telling him, the weekend,' sighed Louise. 'I don't want to leave you, but my life is over there.'

'Yep, home is where your heart is,' Margaret muttered. Just then, there was a loud knock on the front door.

'Who the hell is that now at this time of the night?' Margaret uncurled her body, put her book on a small table by her chair, and went to find out who was disturbing their peace.

Louise could hear raised voices and went to discover who had ruined their evening.

'Oh, little Lou,' sneered the burly, man standing on their doorstep. Louise didn't recognise him, overweight, slovenly dressed with yellow teeth, a tell-tale sign that he smoked a lot.

'What do you want, Darius?' asked Margaret, keeping the door slightly ajar.

Louise thought of her Uncles remark in the will about the gun and wondered fleetingly whether she should get it out of the cupboard.

'I wanna buy the farm,' he slurred.

'It's not for sale,' Louise stated, 'and if you don't clear off, I'll fire a pellet up your back side.'

'It's not a pellet gun,' chuckled Margaret, 'it's a double barrel sawn off shotgun.'

Darius Denton stumbled away, towards the gate, 'I'll be back.'

'Don't say you haven't been warned, 'Louise told him.

Louise slept fitfully, her dreams vivid and weird. First, Eustace had appeared as Merlin the wizard, and she had a massive sword in her hand, a leprechaun was at her feet chanting that it was the sword of Excalibur. Then rainbows had shone in the sky, vivid and intense, wonderful violet, wild indigo, red, orange all the colours merging and as she followed it along a path of yellow bricks, she saw in the distance a man with jet black hair, beckoning her forward to dig, and they did, finding pots of gold at the end of each one, my names Sir Galahad, the handsome man told her, his grin making her tremble. But my friends call me Gerard. Then Louise was awake and sobbing into the pillow.

Louise looked dreadful the next morning, her eyes were swollen and dark shadows circled them.

'You look like you've been in a fight with a panda,' Margaret told her, giving her a brief hug, and passing her a steaming mug of tea with two sugars.

'Thanks,' Louise took a sip and held the mug with both hands, needing the warmth. 'I had a weird dream about Gerard and leprechauns.'

'A twist on Gulliver's travels,' Margaret giggled, trying to make her cousin smile.

'You could say that,' Louise picked up her mobile and checked the numerous texts that Jon had sent. 'He wants to know what route I'm taking,' she sighed. 'I'm going to tell him I'll be back Sunday night, I'll get the ten thirty ferry from Belfast.'

'If you're sure,' Margaret put her mug down and went into the kitchen to start breakfast. She didn't really know what had gone on between Louise and Gerard, she had only been told snippets from Adele. Louise had refused to mention him in emails and phone calls. She hadn't seen him in years, in fact it was just before his eighteenth birthday when they had held a party in the square. He had appeared moody and withdrawn, and when Margaret tried to talk to him he was sharp, telling her to leave him alone and he was going to live in Boston with his uncle. She had heard over the grapevine, also known as the village gossip that he had returned to help his dad run the farm in Burnyfute.

She carried in two plates full of fluffy scrambled eggs and golden-brown toast dripping with pure butter.

'After we've eaten, we are going to write a list of why you should leave and why you should stay,' Margaret told her firmly.

Louise bit into the toast and refused to answer.

'Okay,' Margaret had the pen poised, 'Reasons to stay, one, we have our own place, and enough money to start any business we choose.'

Louise sighed, 'Reason to leave, my fiancé, my job at the bank, my flat and my friends in Oxford.'

'Give Jon a ring and explain, you can't turn your back on the chance of a lifetime.'

'It's not just that and you know it, I could bump into Gerard.'

'But you are grownups now, you might not even recognise him, look at Darius Denton,' she laughed, and up to a point she was right. The last time Louise had seen him he was slim with a mop of red curly hair, she remembered that he had freckles all over his face and arms and they use to tease him when they met him on the beach in skimpy shorts, his skin burnt bright red with not a hope of it turning to the golden brown the girls always obtained.

'Fancy a drive into Derry? We can stock up on essentials, meaning more wine. We could invite some of the girls around for a catch up, Mairead, Teresa and Geraldine for a start. I can say hello and goodbye at the same time.'

'Why don't we buy a convertible,' Margaret said with a grin, 'we can afford it. We could tour around the coast for a bit, Margaret and Louise,'

Louise caught the image in her mind, why shouldn't they do just that? The warm breeze lifting their hair, caressing their faces as they sped along in dark glasses and sun hats. But this was the Atlantic Way, not the Pacific Highway.

'I'll think about it,' Louise pondered, meaning it. The weather would have to be taken into consideration, but the idea sounded very tempting. 'I still have to get back to Jon and my job,' she added.

'I fancy a massage,' Margaret exclaimed 'a new Spa has opened up in Craigend, my friend, Jan, works there. I'll see if she can fit us in this afternoon.'

'It's a bit short notice, but I wouldn't mind the muscles in my back massaged,' Louise sighed, her body felt tense after everything that had gone on these past few days. Although she had to admit, she had been tense when she left the flat in Oxford, Jon had been in one of his black moods when there was no reasoning with him. He didn't understand why she had to come over to Ireland when there were such things as emails and telephones, and so what if her great uncle had left his pittance to sheep farmers, surely, she couldn't begrudge the poor buggers new wellies.

Jan had been happy to fit them both in for the full works, they were having a quiet spell in the salon and readily booked them in. Margaret offered to drive, and Louise sat back and enjoyed the view as they meandered along country roads and then onto the coast road, with numerous signs heralding The Atlantic Way. Margaret wound the windows down and laughed as the cold wind whipped her hair around her face, but she quickly wound them back up when a lorry was coming the other way and for a second she couldn't see with hair over her eyes.

'I've gone off the soft top idea,' screamed Louise in fear. 'You're crazy.'

'Sorry, although it was exhilarating, wasn't it?'

'No, terrorising I would call it, are we nearly there?' she wanted to get out of the car in one piece and her legs were shaking badly after the near miss, the sound of the lorry's horn still echoed in her ears.

'Nearly there, don't worry, I'll drive safely.' Margaret slowed down and drove with more caution; the fright had scared her more than she was letting on. She turned left and took a gravel road, following the sign posts to, The Beaten Track Spa and Health Farm. The impressive tall gates were closed and Margaret spoke into an intercom to let them know that they had an appointment. The gates swung open, and they carried on for another half a mile up a narrow road that led into the car park.

'Are you sure it's a Spa and not a prison?' Louise glanced up to one of the bedrooms on the upper storey, she was sure she could see railings and a face peering out between the bars. The building did not fill her with joy as a Spa should, it was grey brick, concrete and tarmac, there were no fancy lawns or pretty flowers, she shivered and followed Margaret through to the reception, a woman moved forward to greet them, she was a large lady and the white coat she was wearing pulled tight over her wide girth, her fair hair was plaited and shaped around her ears, in a parody of one of those Dutch dolls.

'Hello, my name is Greta, welcome to the sanctuary.'

'Thank you, Greta, we have an appointment with Jan,' Margaret smiled, but it looked fixed. Louise began to back away towards the exit and if she had to, she intended to run along that road and through those wrought iron gates.

'Yes,' she smiled thinly, 'she is expecting you, follow me, please.'

Margaret could see that Louise was trying to escape, 'Come on,' she whispered, 'Jan's waiting.'

Louise reluctantly followed her along a dimly lit corridor, Greta stopped at one of the rooms, saying, 'Miss Jan is in there, enjoy.' Greta smiled, but it was more menacing than reassuring.

'What the hell is this place?' Louise muttered as they walked into a surprisingly large salon.

Jan, she was in her early twenties with short curly very dark hair and olive skin, was sitting on a small stool, gazing out into the courtyard, she got up when they closed the door behind them.

'I'm so glad to see you,' she hugged Margaret and shook Louise's hand.

The salon was all chrome and glass, a bed was over against a far wall with a screen to its side, two hard backed chairs were on the opposite wall, but there were no magazines in view. The place had a clinical feel to it rather than a soothing place to relax, it was more like a dentist waiting room, Louise thought.

'Who's going first?' Jan asked, she moved towards the bed and prepared it with one towel at the bottom and another one folded, ready to pull over the client.

'You go first,' Louise sat down as Margaret went behind the now drawn screen, it was dark brown and opaque.

'You look nervous,' Jan smiled at Louise as she waited for Margaret to get ready.

'I'm still recovering from meeting Greta,' Louise replied, meaning it.

'I know what you mean, she scares the bejaysus out of me.'

'Why do people come here?' Louise was curious, if she wanted a pamper day, this would be the last place she would have chosen.

'Most of our clientele have serious weight issues,' Jan explained, 'the staff are all well qualified, and we get good results, although I'm employed to do the massages, facials and nails, the luxury clients, Greta calls them.'

'That explains the bars on the windows,' Louise laughed, derisively.

'It had to be done, some of the inmates, I mean, patients, were escaping and going to either the pub or chip shop. They weren't losing weight and threatened to sue.'

'Ready,' Margaret gave a muffled shout, she was laying on her tummy with her face through a hole in the bed.

It was a long hour as Louise sat and waited for the treatment to finish. She couldn't get a signal on her phone, and had to pass the time playing angry birds. She was in two minds whether to have a massage, she felt on edge and nervy. She had just decided not to bother, when Margaret appeared, her face shiny and red from the facial.

'Take a seat and drink a pint of water,' Jan looked at Louise, 'are you ready?'

'No, you're all right, I'll give it a miss.'

'Too late,' Margaret beamed, 'I've already paid, get in there and take your top off.'

Reluctantly, Louise did, but as Jan massaged oil into her back, she was glad she hadn't backed out, it was just what she needed, or Jan was kneading, pun intended, as the muscles around her neck and shoulder were teased and pummelled into submission.

'You're in knots,' Jan mused, 'I bet you sit at a desk most of the day.'

'Yep, bent over a sodding computer.'

'Maybe you should change your job.'

'It's all I know, data input and spreadsheets, I'm not very career minded.'

'Mm, well watch your posture when you're sitting at your desk, and I'd suggest going for a swim in the week, ideally the sea, but it's a bit chilly now.'

'Chilly? It's freezing. Have you got a swimming pool nearby?'

'We don't have one here, I've asked for one, but I'm just a minion.'

'You don't look like one,' Louise laughed, thinking of the yellow, funny characters.

'Yes, well, I feel like one, Greta is certainly Despicable me.' They both giggled, Louise liked Jan, and if she lived here, she had a feeling that they would become good mates.

'I feel so relaxed,' Louise collapsed into the chair next to Margaret.

'It's a good job that I'm driving,' Margaret laughed.

'Oh, hell, I forgot that, I feel tense again.'

Margaret shoved her arm, just as she was about to take a sip of water, some of it slopped onto Louise's blouse.

'You're a nightmare,' Louise told her sternly, knowing that it was a waste of time.

They were sitting in the Cranky Pot having a bar meal and sipping cider, they had decided to have a night out instead of sitting by the range. A band was due to start followed by a quiz and it was full, some people standing around the bar, Louise didn't recognise any of them.

'I've booked to go back on Sunday,' Louise knew it was time to sort things out at home. She didn't see how she could stay here any longer, Jon was sending texts every hour, bombarding her with messages to make her feel guilty.

'If you must, Margaret sighed, she knew it was pointless asking her to stay any longer, Louise had made her mind up, she had always been stubborn and nothing had changed over the years.

'I'll come back,' Louise reassured her, 'and I won't leave it so long next time.'

'What about the farm and money?'

'It's not going anywhere, let Edward use the fields for now to graze his cattle, until we think of something.'

'And if Darius comes back?'

'I'll shoot him in the bum,' Margaret laughed, and then a lively jig was played out on a fiddle and accordion, people got up to dance and someone grabbed her arm, swinging her around until she was dizzy. She was relieved when the music stopped and she could sit down. 'Did I tell you that I don't like cider?'

'You've drunk enough of it,' Margaret giggled, she had drunk three pints of it herself and it was strong stuff.

The group took a break when the quiz started, Margaret and Louise joined another table, two women and a man called Pat, Louise remembered him delivering the post on an old bicycle, he told her had retired four years ago, and played darts to pass the time. The two women, Annie and Bridget were teachers in the village school, they were both in their mid-thirties and were very jolly.

The final question was one that only Louise knew the answer to giving them a win by one point. They were given a free round and continued to sit together when the band started playing again. Tables and chairs were pushed back giving them plenty of space to dance. Margaret pulled Louise up to jive and they were having a great time, twirling around. The music got faster and the twirling was wild, Louise hadn't had so much fun in a long time. Margaret pulled Louise in towards her then twirled her wide, causing Louise to lose her balance and stumble into a man standing at the bar.

Louise turned to face him, 'I'm so sorry, she gasped, sweat pouring down her cheeks and her hair plastered in curls around her head.

'Lou?'

The colour drained from her face and the sweat on her brow felt as though it had turned to ice.

'Gerard, what are you doing here?'

Chapter 5

Gerard took her arm and led her outside, Louise was now completely sober, but the situation felt surreal, for years she had thought about this moment, or meeting him one day, the once love of her life, but not like this, sweating and intoxicated, and not in control.

'I can't believe you're here,' there were a few benches in the pub garden, he sat on the one by a wooden archway that had once been used for weddings, and gently tugged her arm so that she sat next to him.

'How long have you been over? God, it's good to see you.'

Louise pulled her arm out of his grasp, 'I'm going home on Sunday,' she told him, 'my boyfriend is missing me.'

'You're not married then?' Louise thought she heard a note of relief in his voice, but put it down to imagination.

'Not yet,' she forced her eyes to take in his face, he hadn't changed very much in the eleven years since she had last seen him, the boy had turned into a gorgeous man, devastatingly good looking, heartbreakingly so, in her case.

'What about you? I bet you're married with twelve kids running around,' her tone was bitter, remembering why they had split up, her shattered heart and the unbearable pain that followed.

'No, I only ever loved one woman,' his deep blue eyes pierced hers, penetrating the depths of her soul.

'Well, I'm sure you will be very happy together,' Louise got up and went to find Margaret, she wanted to go home.

'Lou, wait, you can't leave me again, at least leave a contact number.'

Louise hurried ahead, 'Leave me alone,' she shouted over her shoulder.

Margaret was waiting near the door, 'are you, all right?'

'No, can we go now?'

Louise began packing her bag as soon as the heavy door closed behind them.

'Lou, you can't drive in this state. Wait until Sunday, It's only another day. Besides,' she paused, taking in her cousin's pale face and blotchy eyes, 'why do you have to run off like a scalded cat? Okay, so he broke your heart, whatever Gerard did, you've never told me, but I've got over heartache,' Margaret paused for breath, 'remember Shane Wilson? I was devastated when he threw me over for that blonde bimbo, Bride O'Keefe, and Rory, preferring Boston to me.'

'It's not that simple,' Louise sighed heavily, she took a deep breath and sat in the chair at the side of the range.

'Tell me,' Margaret told her gently.

'One day,' Louise wiped her eyes, 'but just know for now that Gerard hurt me very badly. Yes, I've moved on, but I can't go back, and seeing him again tonight proves that.'

'I think he got the message,' Margaret took Louise's hand. 'Stay until Sunday, we can get the girls round like we planned, have a bit of a party. But for now,' she paused, 'we must pretend that you are staying here, that you've had to return to Oxford for some of your stuff.'

'Okay,' Louise agreed.

The girls decided to splurge out on a massive buffet ordered in from a caterer in Buncrania. There were silver plates laden with everything from Indian cuisine, onion Baja's, samosas, a big dish of lamb Balti, to Chinese, prawn crackers, sweet and sour dishes, and basic buffet finger food, sausages, cheese, salad various dips and garlic bread. The side cabinet was stocked with wine, beer, vodka, gin, and cocktail mixers.

'I can't drink too much,' Louise sighed rather sadly, 'I've got to drive home tomorrow, although I've amended the time, I'm getting the evening ferry.'

It was a fantastic night, Margaret had brought a cd player from home, although she felt home here at Uncle Arthur's now, and they played music ranging from Ed Sheeran to James Blunt, even throwing in a bit of One Direction and Little Mix.

Six friends had come together, to say hello and goodbye to Louise, although, as promised to Margaret, she said she would return when she had sorted things out in Oxford. She had told the story so many times, that she was beginning to believe it herself. Louise loved the cosiness of it all, the closeness with these women that she hadn't had for years, and just for a Nano second, she wondered what it would be like if she did stay and explore her options here.

'I've missed you, Lou,' Mairead Devlin had told her warmly. 'Please hurry back.'

'I'll try,' Louise had crossed her fingers, hating to lie to her friend. It was bitter sweet remembering the long summers they had all spent together, causing mischief and mayhem, but working hard on the farms, turning turf and hay.

Mary, Ann, and Bernadette, three sisters who lived at a neighbouring farm had been constant companions, they often went to the dances put on especially for the teenagers, they were all married now, and Ann had two children.

'I haven't had this much fun in years,' Mary laughed, enjoying the time away from cleaning up after her husband, who was not only a farmer, but also a mechanic.

'It's been a great night,' Kathleen was also married and expecting her first baby, she was nominated as the driver for the 5 women that lived near her.

Betty, Mairead's cousin, was sitting quietly by the range nursing a large glass of red wine. She had been playing golf most of the day and was enjoying the banter.

'Are you all right, hunni?' Louise asked, as she perched on the arm of the chair.

'Just a bit tired,' Betty smiled, 'the golf course was busy today, and a load of bigwigs arrived in their private helicopter. They thought they owned the place.'

Mairead, hearing the conversation, laughed, 'they do silly. It was in the paper yesterday. Tycoons from Texas, or something like that.'

'Oh,' Betty blushed, 'so that's why they had American accents.'

'The music is a bit loud,' Louise said worriedly, thinking how Jon would be banging on the walls by now.

'It's not as if the neighbours can complain,' Margaret giggled in response.

'Because you don't have any,' they all chorused, and got to their feet.

The three sisters were the last to leave, they were staying with their mum Sadie for the night.

'It's been a great night,' Louise sighed, 'I'm glad I stayed a bit longer.'

'But not long enough,' Margaret had tears streaming down her cheeks.

"You've had too much to drink,' Louise gave her a hug. 'Goodnight, I'll see you in the morning.'

Chapter 6

The following morning, Louise went for a ten-mile run, across the back beach, through fields and over fences then a brisk run across the front beach as far as the river and then back again the same way. On her return, Margaret was cooking breakfast and when Louise returned after a badly needed shower, had it dished up with a pot of tea brewed to perfection.

'It's like the last supper,' Margaret said balefully.

'I'll be back,' Louise said, and meant it, she could fly into Derry for quick weekends and someone could pick her up.

They had a late lunch in Donath, and Louise picked up presents for her parents, Jack, her young brother, and Jon.

'How is Jack?' Margaret asked, 'you haven't mentioned him much, it was a bit of a shock when we heard Adele had given birth.'

'Not as shocked as her,' Louise said ruefully. 'Anyway, Jack is great, growing up fast. He'll be ten next month.'

'You should bring him over.'

'Yes, maybe. Let's go and get some lunch, after the fiasco on the boat coming over I think I'll go straight to my cabin this time with a good book.'

It was a very teary goodbye between the cousins, both were crying, and as Louise drove misty eyed down the road, Margaret watched her, openly sobbing. She stood at the door watching until the red car had disappeared, and only then did she go inside and collapse in a ball of misery in the chair Louise had been using since her arrival a few days ago, she couldn't imagine how she was going to cope without her.

Louise stopped in the village of Clodbury to blow her nose and wipe her eyes, part of her wanted to stay, but the other part knew it wasn't possible. Her life, her world, was in Oxford. The roads were quiet, it was out of season for the many tourists that flocked to the beach, and it was a beautiful Sunday afternoon, a perfect time for the three-hour drive to Belfast, yet Louise didn't want to sing along to the radio as she usually did.

It was just after ten when Louise turned the key in the lock to the flat she shared with Jon, he had gone to work, and as she had known, the flat was spotless. The granite work tops were gleaming and the cooker looked like it had just been delivered. Most women would be over joyed to find their home pristine after a few days away, but Louise felt irritated, and she knew that wasn't rational, just a stray sock lurking at the side of the sofa would be endearing. She filled the shiny kettle with water from the shiny tap and took a mug from the cupboard. While she waited for it to boil, she took her case through to the bedroom. She hung up and put away her clothes, all in regimental order, just how Jon liked it. She then put the empty case in the top of the wardrobe in the spare room.

The fridge was full of essentials, Louise made a cheese omelette while the tea brewed and then phoned Adele, filling her in on Uncle Arthur's will and then asking about Jack. Her mother's response was to hurry around as soon as possible, she needed to speak to her.

'What's wrong?' Louise asked as soon as she went into Adele's kitchen.

'Wait until we're sitting down,' Adele said gently, and Louise could feel a trickle of fear travel up her spine.

'You are okay, aren't you?'

'Yes, look go and sit down and I'll carry the tray through, you can grab that box of cream cakes out of the fridge.'

Louise perched on the edge of the beige leather sofa, the cream flan was on the plate untouched, and she couldn't eat a thing until she knew what was going on with her mother.

'Stop looking so worried, darling,' Adele took a sip of tea and placed the cup on its saucer. She was a great fan of bone china and was adamant that tea tasted better in her elegant cups.

'I can't help it,' Louise stated, 'I've had a nerve wracking few days in Ireland and now you have to tell me something. It feels as though I'm mixed up in a drama, the epic rise and fall of Louise Lavender.'

'Your dad has been offered a year's contract to work in Canada,' Adele began. 'It isn't only the one place, though, otherwise we could take Jack, we will be travelling thousands of miles and it's not fair on his schooling.'

Louise could feel her mouth go dry, 'What do you mean? You can't leave him here, it would confuse him.'

'We've been talking,' Adele continued, 'it's time he knew the truth, he's old enough now, and we really cannot leave it any longer, in fact, your dad wanted to tell him two years ago.'

'But Mum, he can't know, how can I explain? And what about Jon?'

'Louise, my dear, it's not about you anymore, it's about Jack and what's best for him.'

Louise knew that she was right, she had closed her mind to the truth for so long and had lived the lie so convincingly that she believed it as the truth. Margaret had asked where the old Lou had gone, and the truth was she was in hiding, from the truth, from being hurt again, from taking any kind of risk, always playing safe, but life is not meant to be lived that way.

'He will hate me mum,' tears were sliding down her cheeks.

'Who? Jack or Jon?'

'Jack of course, his sister has let him down big time.'

'Do you want to tell Jon before Jack? It's hard for us too, but your dad needs this job, it's a new adventure for the both of us,' her face was animated, and her eyes were bright, Louise had never given any thought about her mother having a life, but with stark clarity, she realised her parents were young, both good looking and fit. Her mother especially so, with dark auburn hair and green eyes, she could have been a model in her youth.

'I'm sorry Mum, for not appreciating what you have both done, for taking it all for granted.'

'Jack is a joy, we love him to bits, it isn't easy on any of us, and maybe we should have been honest from the start.'

'I was just a kid, confused and hurt, you gave me the lifeline I needed. I saw him, you know.' She didn't have to say who, and as Louise gazed at the school photograph of Jack, she could see the striking resemblance. It had always been there, but she had refused to acknowledge it.

'Oh,' said Adele in surprise, 'accidental or on purpose?'

'What do you think?' Louise said angrily. 'I was dreading seeing him again, why do you think I haven't been back all these years?'

'Calm down, it was a long time ago, besides, don't you think he has a right to know?'

'Definitely not. Anyway, the Will poses a problem. We can't sell up or use the money.'

'Subject nicely changed, but getting back to the topic in hand, we will need to tell Jack within the next two days.'

Louise felt as though she was sliding down a helter skelter, lurching from side to side and banging her head on the way down. She promised Adele that she would tell Jon, he would be hurt that she had kept the secret all this time, but hopefully he would understand why. She couldn't imagine how Jack would react and she wasn't sure he should be told, at least not now, he was still too young.

Jon took the revelation far worse than Louise could have expected, 'I don't get it,' he ranted, 'we've been together, how long? Nine years! And in all that time you didn't think to tell me that your brother is not really your brother, but your son.'

'My parents were bringing him up as their own, it was easier not to say anything.'

'The way I see it, you have had it easy, poor Jack thinks his grandparents are his real parents and have covered the cost of his upbringing.'

'Of course, bring it down to money,' Louise shouted, 'never mind the emotion.'

'Emotion? What's that supposed to mean?'

'Leave it Jon, I can't take much more today,' Louise went into the spare room and cried into the pillow. The next morning Jon had gone to work before she had gotten out of the shower.

Every muscle ached, she didn't know if it was tension, stress or sleeping funny, but she was going to have a massage before she tackled the confession to Jack. A new spa centre had just opened on the outskirts of town and they had a free spot within the hour. She threw a costume and towel into a sports bag and set off for the half hour trip to The Everglades, an impressive hotel with beautiful grounds.

Louise's first impression was that it was nothing like the spa in Ireland, there were no iron gates, and the driveway was beige gravel snaking up through the grounds, well-kept lawns with flower beds, where the tulips and pansies were a riot of colour. The friendly receptionist gave her a thick towelling robe and mule slippers in the same material, and passed her a gold key card to use for the lockers.

As she swam length after length, Louise thought about her son and how it had been so hard to refuse to acknowledge him as her son as she should have done, but the truth was, she didn't want to confuse the lad. He thought Adele was his mother, and had accepted the idea that Louise was his older sister. She had been tempted to tell him the truth over the years, when he was a chubby toddler, with dark curly hair and big blue eyes, she wanted to hug him and take him home with her, but the thought of upsetting him had always held her back. The thought of upsetting Jon was also an issue, she should have told him from the beginning of their relationship, but she had kept quiet, and now she had to face the truth, she was a coward, no escaping that fact. Gerard had destroyed an integral part of her, by his rejection, he had shattered her heart and soul, but now she was older and wiser, wasn't she? She knew she would have to be strong now, she had no choice.

As the masseur eased the muscles in her neck and shoulders, she came up with an idea, and the more she thought about it, the more the seed grew and blossomed. She sipped a glass of water as she looked out of the window, the full body massage had been amazing, and her body was relaxed and revitalised. Before she changed back into her clothes, Louise asked for a guided tour of the spa.

There was an enormous studio that, as the young girl giving her the tour explained, was used for classes, Pilates, yoga, Zumba, and salsa. Through an adjoining door was a state of the art gymnasium, the music was loud and bouncy and people worked up a sweat on the tread mill and cross trainers. There were weights of all sizes and big blue cushioned mats covered a quarter of the floor space.

They moved on to a sauna and Jacuzzi area, both were near the swimming pool. Louise was impressed with the uniform the staff wore, shiny black and gold leggings and yellow tunic style tops for the women and dark blue tops for the men.

Six treatment rooms, nails, facials, massages, she was informed, lined a long corridor which led outside into the grounds, an outside pool was covered until early June. Finally, they arrived at the restaurant, the menu was adapted for those on a healthy diet. Each segment fed the germ of idea swirling around in her brain, she was impatient to share it, but first, she had to speak to her parents.

'You haven't told Jack, yet have you?' Louise was sitting across the kitchen table from Adele.'

'No, why? It's got to be done, Lou, we have put it off long enough.'

'I've got a plan, I haven't told Jon yet, but I've decided anyway. I'll take Jack to Ireland for a year, we can bond, get to know each other properly, and then I will tell him the truth.'

'Mm, sounds good in practice,' sighed Adele, 'but what if Jon doesn't want to go, or if he doesn't accept Jack?'

'I'm ready to face the bridges, mum' she replied, her voice was confident and for the first time in years, felt the glimmer of a spark in her heart.

Chapter 7

Jon was not having it, in fact he told her categorically that 1, he wasn't going to live in the arse of beyond, and 2, he could never accept that Jack was her son, he would always be her kid brother, it had registered in his brain that that was the case, and it could not be changed.

'Besides,' he added pompously, 'number 3, you have a job here, and how are you going to afford a new son aged 10?'

Louise hadn't told him about the inheritance, there hadn't seemed the point, she had planned to stay in Oxford, but now, well, it was a whole new adventure. She felt the tiny spark throb and grow. She studied Jon, taking in his short, perfectly cut brown hair, pristine white polo shirt and carefully creased beige chinos. She had loved him, in the way she would love a dear friend, but not in the way a relationship should be, and she would miss him, he had been so good to her over the years, treating her like a child, but that had been the problem, she hadn't needed to grow up and face the obstacles that life threw at you. He had protected and sheltered her from conflict, and if she was brutally honest, he had been controlling and manipulating.

She took a deep breath, 'I'm taking Jack to Ireland next week, I'll tell the bank tomorrow that I'm taking a leave of absence, maybe they will keep my job open for a year, maybe they won't, but it doesn't matter.'

'You can't go,' he ordered, 'what about me and our life here?'

'Come with me,' she said, 'join our adventure.'

'Grow up Louise, life is not an adventure and to a place called Clodbury? I don't even know where the F that is.'

'Jon,' she said sadly, 'I feel sorry for you.' She went up to the spare room and knew that the relationship was over, and although it hurt, her heart was still intact, it wasn't shattered or even bruised. She closed the door and phoned Margaret and her scream of excitement at the news that she was going back, nearly burst her eardrums, but she didn't mind.

'I've got a lot to tell you,' Louise said, 'do you know a good architect?''

'Yes, there's a few in the village, I'll ask around and find out which one is the best, why?'

'I'll tell you when I see you, oh, and I'm bringing Jack so we will need a room for him.'

'Leave it with me, I'll get things sorted. I can't wait to see you, I've missed you, Lou.'

'I've missed you too, and I'm only realising just how much. See you soon,' she hung up and got ready for bed.

Jack sat beside her, his little face very pale and dark circles ringed his blue eyes, he had been distraught at being away from his, 'Mum and Dad' for a whole year. Louise ran a finger gently down his cheek, he jerked it away sharply to look out of the window.

'Are you hungry, Jack?' she asked him gently, 'we could stop at Burger King?'

He refused to answer but it was time they had a break, and the services at Westmoreland was just ahead. It had been not only hectic at preparing their move, but also exhausting and emotional. She realised how hard it was going to be for her parents, Jack had been brought up as their son for all his ten years, and Louise realised that they were going away for a year to Canada to help them come to terms with what had to be done. She understood how painful it was for them, as well as Jack, when he found out the truth. Although they were only in their mid-fifties, there would come a time when the truth would have to come out. Jack was registered as Louise's son, father not named. They all realised that Jack should have been told the truth from the beginning. When he was old enough to understand that his real mother was unable to take care of him because she had an education to get through and then, she needed to save some money because they were older, could give him a better start in life. It had seemed the easiest option, and then the timing was never right. Louise had asked them, why now? It was too blasé to say that they were going to Canada with her father's firm. There was more to it, but she had to let it go, for now at least.

She signalled and drove slowly into the carpark and found a space near the entrance to the services. She looked at the clock on the dashboard and was shocked to see that it was 8.30pm. She hadn't booked the ferry from Carnryan, she knew there would not be a problem at this time of the year to get a space and she could pay on arrival, it gave her the freedom to take her time and stop over if she needed to.

'You must be hungry, Jack. Let's go inside and get some food.'

Reluctantly, he unbuckled his seat belt and climbed out of the car. She grabbed their jackets from the boot and gave a blue fleece to Jack. Put that on, it's cold after being in the warmth of the car.'

She shrugged into her leather jacket and he followed her into the entrance leading to the food court, 'I'll go into the ladies, meet you back here,' she indicated a board advertising all that the Lake District had to offer. After freshening up by splashing cold water on her face, Louise found Jack standing where she had asked.

'Right, what do you fancy?' she held his arm and led him to the food counter, where she ordered a cheese and bean jacket potato and burger and fries for Jack.

'Can I have a strawberry milkshake?' he asked.

Louise smiled, glad that he had said a few words, the first since leaving her parents' house, 'of course you can and when we get into Scotland and find somewhere to stay for the night, you can phone Adele.'

'You mean Mum,' he stated solemnly. Louise gave him a small nod, she couldn't call Adele his mother from now on, the fabrication had to end.

They found a small guesthouse in Black Craig, it was a good job she had phoned and booked a bed, because it was after 10pm when she pulled into the yard in front of the bed and breakfast. She could have gone straight to the ferry, they only had a short journey ahead, but that would mean arriving in the middle of the night, and as much as Margaret wouldn't have minded, it would be a horrible journey at the other end in the dark. Jack's head was resting against the door on a rolled-up blanket. He had demolished the burger and fries, followed by the milkshake, despite not wanting to engage in conversation with, in his eyes, the bossy older sister.

She asked Jack to ring the bell, and the door was answered by a small, white haired lady wearing a bright red cardigan and a long black skirt.

'You must be Louise and Jack,' she pulled the door open, 'come on in, I'll show you to your room.'

Louise was delighted with the room, it was spacious with a double bed along one side of the wall with a chest of drawers next to it, a lamp and clock sat on top, and bunk beds on the other, a television was mounted on the wall. The en- suite was old fashioned, a big bath with a shower hanging over it, with a glass screen fitted, but it was clean and served its purpose. She gave the toiletry bag to Jack, and after he had washed and cleaned his teeth, he put on pyjamas and she tucked him into the bottom bunk. He was asleep by the time she had showered.

It took her an age to get to sleep, the trauma of the last few days lay heavily on her mind, and she wondered for the umpteenth time if she was doing the right thing, maybe she should have stayed in Oxford, she could have stopped in her parents' house with Jack. But then the other voice, the stronger one from the new Lou, demanded that she should be confident about the decision, it was the only one possible under the circumstances. Adele had been in floods of tears as Jack was ushered into the red fiesta, the son she had brought up from a baby was going away, and it was at that moment, as Louise considered her mother's ravaged face, that she realised this sacrifice was for her and eventually, Jack. The job in Canada had come along at the right moment for Adele to make the painful decision to hand Jack over to his real mother. Louise promised herself, before dropping off into a deep sleep, that one day, she would make it up to all of them.

The sun was peeking through the curtains and the aroma of frying breakfast, wafted into their room as Louise slowly opened her eyes to greet the beginning of their new life. Jack, sensing that she was awake, sat up in bed and rubbed his eyes.

'You have the first shower,' she told him, 'I'll sort out clothes and then you can have a quick chat to Adele before they catch their flight,' She pretended that she didn't see the tears slide down his cheeks and the drop of his bottom lip. She wanted to give him a big hug, but it was too soon and out of character, she had always put up a barrier towards her son, it was the only way she could cope with the situation.

The breakfast was enormous and delicious, Jack had a bowl of rice crispies followed by bacon, egg, sausages and beans, Louise started with grapefruit and scrambled egg on toast, and they also had orange juice and a big pot of tea to wash it down. Mrs Andrews, the very efficient land lady, held a wealth of knowledge of the area and impulsively, Louise booked them in for an extra night, they could explore the surrounding area and give Margaret a chance to sort out the room for Jack.

They walked for miles, climbing hills and across the moors and after stopping for a quick sandwich, they walked along the cliff edge, and took deep breaths of the sea air, a buzzard soared over head and Jack watched it in fascination. The views were spectacular, and she took a few photographs with her phone, including Jack in the shots, she would send them to her parents later.

They had a meal in a cosy little restaurant and when they arrived back at the Argyle guest house, they were rosy cheeked and pleasantly tired. Louise didn't have any problem getting to sleep and the next morning after showers and a hearty breakfast, they waved goodbye to Mrs Andrews and set off for the short journey to Carnryan where they were catching the ferry to Larne.

There were no fat gypsy weddings on the ferry, just lorry drivers and families and the short journey passed quickly, they even went up on the deck, watching as land came into view. The sun was still shining, and Louise hoped it would stay that way for a few days. Jack was enjoying the trip and managed to give her a few smiles. They were just driving up the steep climb of the Glenshane pass when Jack asked, 'It is only for a year Lou, Mum and dad will take me back then.'

Louise touched his arm, 'They haven't abandoned you, Jack. Look on this year as an adventure, it's going to be fun, and you can keep in touch with Adele in Canada, they are having an adventure too.'

'I wish I was on their adventure,' he turned his head to look out of the window, they were at the top now and the views were stunning, but Louise felt as though she had made small progress, he was young, he would come around.

They stopped for breakfast in a shopping centre and filled a trolley with goodies, Jack insisted on his favourite breakfast cereal and biscuits, the wine was compulsory, she had a feeling they would be going through bottles of it by the weekend.

Jack was impressed with the view of the beach as they rounded the corner at Faun and into Lisfannon. The tide was out and the sweep of the beach looked tantalising in the afternoon sun.

'We'll go down to our beach,' she promised, 'we're not that far now.'

Margaret was waiting at the gate; her face flushed with excitement, screaming in delight at the return of her favourite cousin and younger brother. Jack grudgingly endured the hug before asking if he could go to the bathroom.

'He's so cute,' Margaret told her as she linked arms with Louise.

'Yes, he is,' Louise said proudly, 'you don't mind him coming, do you?'

'Of course not, I've put him in the small bedroom for now and we can share. I can't wait until you fill me in on your big idea.'

'First, I promised Jack a paddle, are you coming?'

They unpacked the car, grabbed towels, put on shorts, and then headed down the rough track that led down to the beach. After spreading out a large blanket, Louise covered Jack in sun cream and then he ran off into the sea, jumping over the waves while the cousins caught up on what had happened over the past few days since she had been in Oxford.

'Old Aggie has been spreading rumours,' Margaret rubbed cream into her shoulder, the sun was at its strongest and there were no clouds for it to hide behind.

'What's the old bat said this time?' Louise remembered how much trouble the old woman had caused over the years.

'That we were selling the farm and land to Darius Denton.'

'What!' Louise screamed, causing Jack to turn around and look anxiously at her.

'She's evil that one,' Margaret said darkly.

'If we were selling,' said Louise, and Margaret looked at her with a frown, 'it would not be to him, but we are not selling, we have big plans for our property.'

Margaret grinned, 'tell me more.'

'I will, when Jack is in bed and we can chat in private.'

So, when Jack was sound asleep after a few hours on the beach, a take away from the Chinese in the village and a warm bubble bath, they sat either side of the range in the big armchairs with a glass of red wine each and the bottle of merlot sitting on a small table in the middle of them, it was nearly empty.

'So, tell me,' Margaret had waited patiently, only asking the barest details, but now she was ready to hear the plans Louise had in mind for their inheritance.

'Remember that ghastly spa you took me to?'

'Well, the massage wasn't ghastly, I thought you enjoyed it,' Margaret looked hurt.

'What I mean,' she grinned, 'the place itself. It wasn't exactly welcoming, was it? The ambience was more suited to one of those old work houses.'

'It's to keep the guests escaping to the chippy,' Margaret told her sharply, 'Jan explained that.'

'Okay, let's go back to basics. A health farm with an in-house dietician, doctor and qualified staff, the guests will want to stay longer and not escape. They will pay a lot of money to stay here.'

'They won't be able to escape anywhere up here,' Margaret laughed, 'if they jogged into the village they would burn calories they might have consumed.'

'Does that mean it's a no?' Louise felt deflated, all the enthusiasm that had spurred her on these past few days, coping with the emotion of taking Jack from her parents, it was all too much. She burst into tears, sobbing into her hands in despair.

'Lou, what's going on? There's more going on here than a health centre.'

'Spa centre, retreat, whatever,' she spluttered through her tears. 'Anyway, if it's a no, I'll have to make other plans.'

'It's not yes or no at this stage, we need to talk about it. Explain your vision,' Margaret passed her a box of tissues.

So Louise told her about the place she had visited in Oxford, how relaxing it was, leading her to have her vision, a retreat for people to escape the rat race for a few days of pampering, or if they were recovering from illness.

'Okay, it sounds good so far, but it's going to take some time to get planning permission, what do we do until then and what happens if we don't get it?'

Louise blew her nose, 'We are not going to be negative for a start. Did you get the list of architects?'

'Yes, we can get someone out here to talk things through,' Margaret filled their glasses, draining the bottle, and then went over to the window and from her vantage point she watched the waves crashing onto the rocks. A stir of excitement was beginning to grow in her gut. The place had potential, and she knew if they worked as a team, they could make a go of it. She also knew that if her answer was in the negative, Lou would leave and never return, she couldn't face that. Now her cousin was back in her life, she didn't want to lose her again.

They had to wait a week before Finn Killian, the best architect in the village, could come out and make notes.

'You want another bedroom added to the cottage,' he quickly sketched the outline of the cottage and planned extension.

'Yes, and en suite,' Margaret explained, ', we would like all the bedrooms to be en suite.'

'That should be grand,' said Finn, 'the problem might be getting planning permission for the main build.' He flipped the page of his A4 pad, and sketched interior rooms and exterior walls, while the girls looked on in awe.

Louise grinned, her vision was taking place.

He worked in silence as Margaret plied him with endless cups of tea and slices of homemade cherry cake.

'Do you design gardens?' Lou joked.

'No, but I know someone that does,' Finn said, as he sketched a high wall and gate. 'Sean Donegan, you can see some of his work around Buncrania and Letterkenny.'

'I'm thinking tall trees and smooth lawns, oh, and loads of pretty flowers.'

Finn chuckled, 'I've got a bean in my pocket if you want to swap it for a cow.'

'I didn't say I wanted an ogre,' Louise laughed.

The door opened, and Jack entered the kitchen, he threw his bag and coat on the floor and flopped down on one of the armchairs.

'How was school,' Louise asked him as she placed a glass of milk and some of the cake on a plate, and then picked up his bag and coat, hanging them on the back of the door.

He had settled in surprisingly well after the first two days. The local lads had taken him under their wings, and he had spent most of his time outdoors playing football, he wasn't allowed down the beach without an adult. He spoke most evenings to Adele via the iPad, and the tears were not flowing as freely, much to Louise's relief.

'Yeh, it was all right, can I go out in a bit?'

'An hour,' Louise looked at her watch, 'we're going out for dinner, where do you fancy?' They hadn't had a chance to cook anything and they were both impatient for Finn to finish what he could today. Margaret was as excited as Louise now about their new venture. They stayed up until the small hours, discussing what staff they would need and what qualifications they would need to get. They were planning to attend an open day to find out what worked around Jack.

'Can we have Chinese?' he asked with a grin.

'Okay, but we can't make a habit of it, all that salt is bad for you.'

'You sound like my mum,' he moaned, before ramming a biscuit in his mouth and washing it down with a large gulp of milk. Louise could feel her cheeks go pink. Adele had begged her to tell him the truth, but she had to get the timing right, it was far too soon.

Finn promised to get things started, he would input his sketches on the computer and then seek the permission they would need, first for the cottage to be extended and then the new build. On screen, both buildings looked amazing, and Louise felt a shiver of excitement, it was really going to happen, she had a good feeling about it.

Luckily there was a new council in place that were lenient towards buildings and the drawings were passed swiftly. A surveyor had visited to see the lay of the land, and once satisfied that it would not interfere or mar the skyline, he happily passed both sets. By now, it was the beginning of June, Louise and Jack had been there for over a month and the big change was about to begin. Louise had also noticed a change in her cousin, especially when Finn was around, with his blonde curly hair and blue eyes, he had captured her imagination, as well as her heart.

'He is gorgeous,' Margaret sighed, as they sat side by side in their comfortable chairs by the range.

'If you like that kind of thing,' Louise giggled, ducking the cushion Margaret threw at her. 'I've been thinking.'

'Oh, no, now what?' Margaret laughed, wondering what else her cousin had in store for them.

'The school holidays will be starting soon,' she began, and then Margaret interrupted her, 'don't tell me you're taking Jack back to Oxford?'

'No, of course, not, there isn't anything there for me now,' and she meant it. Jon had been cold and distant when they had left for Ireland, and she had wondered why she had stayed with him for so long. 'Anyway, it's going to be a building site around here, even the cottage will be knocked about, with dust everywhere, so, I was thinking, why don't we take Jack on holiday, a long holiday, and when we get back at least the cottage will be finished if we get the right men on the job.'

'I like that plan,' Margaret smiled, 'Patrick, Betty Grant's son, is a great builder, we could ask him, and see if he can put a crew together.'

'Great, where shall we go?'

'We can ask Jack in the morning; your little brother might have an idea or two.' Margaret got up and stretched, 'bed time I think, we've got a lot to do tomorrow.'

'Goodnight,' Louise said, feeling guilty that she hadn't yet told Margaret the truth about Jack, but how could she when she had barely got used to living the truth herself?

Chapter 8

Jack chose Disney World, he had heard friends talking about the rides and everything and it seemed magical to him. Louise knew that once the business got started, there wouldn't be much time for holidays, at least until they had staff they could trust. She was also relived that she had thought to pack their passports and with both under the name of Lavender would rouse no suspicion from Jack or Margaret.

'Dad will keep an eye on things here,' said Margaret, 'it might keep him out of mischief.'

Louise couldn't imagine Brian getting up to any kinds of mischief, in fact, a bit of naughtiness would do him good. 'We will find him a job when we're up and running,' they had decided to compile a list while they were away. They both had a lot to learn, but they were willing to work hard and make a go of it.

A week later, Jack had finished school for the summer, the builders were ready to start and Brian was ensconced in the cottage, promising to keep an eye on the workers. He intended to stay there and had asked a neighbour to help him with the farm. It was the first time he had taken a break since his wife had passed away, and it felt alien to him.

He gave them a lift to Belfast airport where they were catching a flight to Manchester, staying the night at a hotel and then continuing their journey to Orlando early the following morning. The girls had decided to splurge some of their inheritance, they had booked 2 weeks at a Disney resort hotel with all the passes to the parks, 2 weeks at Clearwater, and then they had hired a car for 2 weeks to go down to the Everglades and have an adventure.

With every passing day they spent together, the bond between Jack and Louise grew stronger, and Margaret was an important part of the group. They spent hours laughing and screaming on the rides, enjoyed the attractions at Epcot and the magic of Animal Kingdom and they left the best for last, Magic Kingdom. Universal studios and sea world were also explored with gusto and it was a relief to spend the next two weeks relaxing on a beach so white, it could be mistaken for snow and swim in water so clear that stingrays drifted past their legs on their daily sweep of the sea. It was a taste of paradise. Jack blossomed, his skin was a golden brown emphasizing his bright blue eyes, so like his mother's. Sometimes she would catch Margaret gazing at him quizzically, as if she had a question she wanted to ask, but didn't want to say the words. At these times, Louise wanted to tell her, but the timing wasn't right, and she couldn't spoil the holiday. One day everyone would know the truth.

Jack spoke to Adele every night, and it was a lot easier now that the time zone was the same while they were in Florida, Jack had begged her to visit them in Florida, but Louise and Adele agreed that it would be a massive set back and make it harder when he was eventually told the truth. Adele was excited about the spa retreat and begged to be their first guest.

'Of course, auntie,' Margaret had joked one night as they all spoke on facetime, 'we can practice on you, you can be our guinea pig.'

Adele was thrilled to see how well Jack was, sun kissed and happy. She told them about Canada and what an amazing country it was, and the girls promised to visit one day, when their business was up and running and they could leave it in trusted hands.

They took it in turns to drive, Jack was thrilled with the car, a luxury convertible in canary yellow. They took him to the space centre before going on towards Cocoa beach and Fort Lauderdale. It was easy to get rooms on the way, there was always a motel with neon vacancy signs in the window. They booked two nights in Miami in a hotel that overlooked the massive beach, and then they explored the Everglades, taking a motor trip among the rushes. Jack loved every moment and kept his eyes peeled for alligators. Soon they were down to their last few days and decided to go back to Orlando and have a spot of retail therapy. Jack was treated to new jeans, trainers and tee shirts and was quiet as they waited for their return flight.

'We will come back one day,' Louise told him, 'have you had a good time?'

'Yes, I wish we could stay here.'

Margaret laughed, 'so do I pet, but it's all make believe, but when we get back its going to be one big adventure, and you will have your very own bedroom.'

On the flight back to Manchester, Jack had fallen asleep with his head resting on Louise's shoulder, she didn't notice the quizzical look Margaret gave her as she ran a gentle finger down his cheek and gazed at him with such love in her eyes that Margaret felt a tug of recognition. This was the look a mother would give her child, not her kid brother. The proverbial penny had dropped, no wonder Louise had returned to Ireland with Jack, he was at an age to know the truth, but obviously, that hadn't happened yet, and Margaret was in no doubt who Jack's father was.

Chapter 9

They were impressed with the progress made to not only their cottage, but also the foundation for the new build. Jack was delighted with his bedroom, it was a good size and the builders had fitted not only wardrobes and cupboards, but also shelving for his game console and a gaming chair was set up ready for Jack's use. The boy was ecstatic with it all, even when he had been warned that he would be limited during the week to the time spent in there. What thrilled him the most was that due to the superfast WIFI, he could facetime his 'parents' through the massive television they had installed, and Lou had overheard the conversation with one of the builders when he had thought she was out of ear shot,

'He's one lucky wain, I didn't even have a pot to piss in when I was a kid,' Eamon Joe Murphy had sniffed.

'I know what ye mean, Eamon Joe, we walked to school in our bare feet,' Martin Mackie shook his carrot top head, 'wains these days don't know they're born, in the good old days we had it so much simpler.'

Lou had struggled not to laugh at their exaggeration, they were proper characters, full of the folk lore of Clodbury, and the men had done a great job on the house, she guessed they were only happy when they were having a good moan.

Jack settled in well at the village school and had made friends not only at school, but with the local lads, so it was a shock to Louise when he ran in one afternoon tears streaking his cheeks and his shoulders shaking where he was trying not to sob his little heart out.

'What's happened?' Louise demanded, 'tell me and I'll go and sort them out.'

'That old woman who always wears that long black cloak,' he spluttered, 'she waved a stick at me and told me to go back to where I come from.'

Louise was livid, 'where is she now?'

'She was on the beach picking up sticks, Tommy Casey called her a witch and that's when she shouted at me.'

'Wait there,' she told him, and grabbing a cardigan from the back of the chair, she went to have a word with Aggie Duffy. If she could have shot the old crone with the shotgun they kept locked in the cupboard, she would have done. She would not do to her son what she had once done to her, making her feel worthless.

Aggie was sitting on a rock with a scruffy mongrel at her feet, she turned to face Louise as she approached and the malice in the crones eyes made her gasp.

'Don't you ever talk to Jack like that again,' Louise kept her voice even and cold.

'Don't tell me what to do, Miss England,' the crone spat viciously.

'I'm warning you, if you go near him, speak to him, or have any contact, you will be sorry, you miserable old bat.'

Aggie cackled, 'Are you scared that I'll put a spell on you?'

'No, I'm scared that I will do you serious harm and I wouldn't like to do time for it, although the guards would probably give me a reward. Just stay away from my brother.'

'Brother? You don't fool me.'

'I don't wish to fool you, I'm deadly serious,' Louise told her ominously.

Margaret was in the kitchen when she returned to the cottage, her face red with rage and shoulders shaking with fury,

'Where's that gun?' she opened a couple of cupboard doors and slammed them shut when she didn't find it.

'Calm down, Lou, what's happened?'

'That evil crone Aggie has had a go at Jack, I'm not having him put up with her vicious tongue.'

'If I thought it would help,' sighed Margaret, 'I'd get you the gun, but it won't, you know that. Take her out and there will be another one to take her place, you can't shoot everyone in Clodbury.'

Louise managed a weak smile and sat at the table, 'I know, and I couldn't really shoot her, not today anyway.'

'Do you know what time it is?' grinned Margaret.

'I should feed Jack, so it must be around 4.'

'I was thinking it was wine time,' Margaret frowned.

'Give it a couple of hours, a cup of tea will do for now.'

Jack had cheered up by the time he was served his favourite dinner of fish fingers, creamy mashed potatoes, with mushy peas, followed by jelly and ice-cream. He had a shower and played on his X box for his allotted hour as it was a school night. Only then, did Louise agree to get the wine out.

Margaret had decided that this was the night for the skeleton to come out of the closet. It was pointless keeping up the charade when she had already guessed. They were sitting by the range, each curled up in the fat armchairs that they had both agreed to replace at some stage. Margaret filled both glasses with a gorgeous red she had bought from a wine shop in the north.

'You look serious,' Lou took a sip of wine, 'what's up?'

'I need to talk to you about something, well, not need, but,'

'For heaven's sake, just spit it out,' sighed Louise.

'I know, well, I've guessed,' why wouldn't the words come out? Margaret took a large gulp of wine and waited for the spirit to kick in.

'Know what? London is the capital of England?' Louise laughed but stopped when she saw the worried expression on her cousin's face.

'I've guessed about Jack,' Margaret whispered, not wanting the boy to hear.

'How?' Louise could feel her cheeks burn, not with embarrassment, but guilt that she hadn't confided in Margaret.

'On the flight back from Orlando, I've been so blind,' Margaret took a large gulp of wine, showing how foolish she felt.

'I should have told you, at the beginning, but mum persuaded me to keep mum, ha, pardon the pun. As the years passed and I didn't come back, there didn't seem a point.'

'When are you going to tell him?'

'It's all about timing, but he's missing mum and dad, and he will be devastated by the truth. Mum wants me to tell him soon, that's why dad took the job in Canada, she said it's time to come clean.'

'And Gerard? When are you going to tell him?'

'Never,' Louise spat, 'he will never find out, he doesn't need to know.'

'Is that fair?' Margaret asked gently. 'On either of them?'

'Gerard wasn't fair to me when he went off with that tart from Buncrania. I was going to tell him that night, instead he broke my heart.'

'Well, I'm here for both of you,' Margaret filled their glasses, 'the call is yours.'

Then the subject was dropped, at least for the time being. Jack would have to be told soon, it was only right that the boy knew the truth before he was much older.

Chapter 10

The building began to take shape once the foundations were all set. Louise and Margaret both decided it would be a good idea to take a business course during the hours Jack was at school, and as luck would have it, classes were being held in Donath community centre for people wanting to start up a business. It was tailor made for them, informing them how to hire and fire staff, keeping the accounts up to date and spreadsheets for salaries and everything else.

It was tough going at first, both struggling with who would be their creditors, what column should hold the debits, but after a few sessions, it all fell into place. They would need a purchase ledger, and the figures would all have to be input on a spreadsheet.

Weeks passed, and their spa hotel took shape. It had two stories and once the roof had been erected, they hired plumbers, plasterers, and electricians. It was great fun but very hard work, and they loved every moment of it. Their dream was becoming reality.

Louise's parents were due back from Canada in just under four months, time was running out for her to be honest with Jack. He had settled well into the village school and had made a group of close friends, but he insisted on skyping his parents every night and begged them to hurry back. Adele had warned Louise that she couldn't put off telling Jack the truth and they were thinking of extending their time in Canada for a further six months. Louise decided that the coming weekend would be the decisive moment.

Saturday arrived with a beautiful sunny day, the sky was a bright shade of blue that echoed on the stillness of the calm sea. Jack was out playing football with his friends, leaving Louise and Margaret to cook his favourite biscuits and cakes. Louise was rehearsing what she would say to Jack, softening the blow, but letting him know that he was much loved by all of them.

The door swung open with such force that both women jumped, startled, and then the angry sounds of Jack screaming and crying that Aggie the witch was a liar, as he burst into the kitchen, the beauty of the day ruined as a dark shadow descended. Louise felt dread hit her stomach, and a feeling of foreboding made her voice shake, as she asked him what had happened.

'Aggie the witch said that I was your dirty little bastard, what does she mean?'

Any colour in Louise's cheeks vanished, she grabbed the hard back of the kitchen chair and slowly sank down on to it. Margaret filled a glass with cold water, passed it to her and then left the kitchen, Lou needed to explain, and she could be no part in it.

The tender words and careful explanation were too late in coming, Louise had no choice but to be brutally honest, yet finding a way to cause as little pain as possible to her son. She could kill Aggie bloody Duffy!

'Sit down, Jack,' Louise pulled a chair out, and poured a glass of milk, the table had been set for the special treat they had planned. Reluctantly he sat, but ignored the proffered milk.

'Why did the witch say that?' he demanded, 'she always picks on me, and its Billy that calls her names, I never do.' Jack fought back an angry sob at the injustice of it, Louise took his hand.

'Many years ago, I used to come here on holiday,' she began, 'Old Aggie was a bitter woman back then, and she often said horrible things to me and made me cry.'

Jack slowly nodded his head, and took a sip of milk, 'I thought she was telling lies,' he sighed.

'She is a horrible woman, especially to call you such a hateful word. But I need you to be brave and listen to me,' she kept his hand in hers, 'I was a teenager the last time I came to stay here in Uncle Arthur's cottage. 'We would go to the local hotel, Margaret and other cousins, they had dances with live bands, and we had a great time. One night I met Gerard. He was my first love and we spent every moment together. But before I could tell him some important news, he told me he was going to America to work for his uncle. He promised he would come back to me, but I knew he was lying.'

'How?' asked Jack with the innocence children have.

'He was dancing with another girl, and I could tell he liked her a lot. So, I kept my secret and went home to mum and dad.'

'Did you tell them the secret?'

'Yes, and they were wonderful. You see,' she smiled into his eyes, 'the secret was that I was having a baby. You.'

'No, that can't be right,' he pulled his hand away and jumped out of the chair, sending it crashing down onto the floor.

'We agreed that they would bring you up until you were old enough to know the truth and give me a chance to finish my education. We should have told you sooner, but they love you so much. It's been heart-breaking for them to leave you, but it was time for you to know the truth.'

'Liar,' he screamed at her, 'You're my sister, not my mum. I hate you,' he ran from the kitchen and Louise heard the slam of his bedroom door.

Margaret put an arm around her shoulders, 'it was never going to be easy. No matter how sweet the words.'

'I know, but it has made it worse, hearing those utterings from the deranged crone,' Louise blew her nose.

'I went over to see her,' Margaret put the chair upright and sat down, 'her sister Ellen is up from the Glenties, she doesn't speak a word of English.'

'I remember her,' Louise sniffed, 'she was as strange as Aggie. Is her hair the same?'

'Yes,' Margaret pulled a face, 'it's still pure white and so long it reaches her skinny arse.'

Louise couldn't stop a laugh escaping, 'was she wearing a pointy black hat?'

'No, but there were a few black moggies lurking around. I told Aggie that I was going to set the guards on her, but she just cackled and said she isn't breaking a law for speaking the truth.'

'How does she know? You only found out a few weeks ago.'

'She's a witch, they both are.'

'Oh, god. What if Gerard finds out?'

'I told Aggie that she is wrong, that Jack is your brother and if she spreads any more vicious lies, she will be very sorry. Ellen shouted a few words, but I couldn't understand what the feck she was saying.'

'We can only wait then,' Louise sighed, 'Will you go into Jack? He hates me.'

'Sure, I'll ask him if he's hungry. Don't be silly, he doesn't hate you.'

Louise cleared the table, the special cookies were put in an airtight container, hopefully to be consumed by Jack and his friends another day. She felt drained of all emotion, but at least the truth was out in the open. She looked at the clock, it was too early to phone her parents, but she would need to let them know that Jack had found out the truth, before she went to bed.

She tossed and turned all night, unable to get the tragic look on Jack's face out of her mind. What a way for him to find out. She would make the old crone pay dearly and anyone else that got in the way.

Jack was up and eating his breakfast when a dishevelled Louise made her appearance.

'You resemble one of the old scarecrow's Uncle Arthur used to have,' Margaret grinned as she poured out a big mug of tea and passed it to her.

'I feel like a zombie,' Louise replied, 'I'm sorry about Old Aggie,' she said gently to Jack.

'I don't want to talk to you,' he spat angrily.

'Okay, I'll leave you to finish your breakfast,' tears slid down her cheeks as she carried her tea into the bathroom. Margaret touched her arm gently as she passed her.

It was the appearance of Ebee Hedron that broke Jack's sullen silence. Margaret had taken the boy down to the front strand to collect shells for his school project, there was no let up with the silent treatment to Louise and she was heartbroken over it all.

Between them, Jack and Margaret had filled a plastic bag with shells of all shapes and sizes, and agreed that they had enough to decorate a shoe box that they were intending to cover with the shells and varnish it, the idea was to make a treasure chest. Suddenly, Jack gave a shout of pleasure and ran towards a large rock where a man wearing a red bandana and a black patch over his eye sat gazing out to sea.

'Wow, you're a pirate,' Jack gasped, 'a real one. What's your name?'

'Ebee, but I'm not a pirate, me laddo.'

'Oh,' sighed Jack, very disappointed with the fact that the man wasn't a pirate after all.

'Jack, what are you doing?' Margaret had caught up with him, and red faced she turned to apologise to the man.

'He's doing a school project about pirates,' she explained. 'But I must admit, you do look a bit like one,' she laughed, noting the man's attire, striped black and white tee shirt and long cut off shorts. His feet were bare and dangled in the sea. He appeared oriental with tanned skin and dark eyes.

'It's the patch,' he smiled, showing gleaming white teeth. 'I received an injury to my eye, hurt like crazy, but the patch helps.'

'You don't sound as though you're from around here,' Margaret stated the obvious, knowing perfectly well that he wasn't from around the village, she would have known who he was, it was that kind of place.

'No, I'm from Nuneaton,' he grinned. 'I've been doing a job out at Malin Head for that film crew.'

'Not the Star wars mob?'

'Yes,' he grinned, 'the star wars mob, we finished shooting last week, but I got the injury before we went home, I'm taking a bit of a break before joining them next week.'

'Where are you staying?' asked Jack, impatient to be part of the conversation, after all, he had discovered the pirate.

'Jack,' Margaret reprimanded, 'you can't ask questions like that.'

'He's fine,' Ebee ruffled Jacks dark hair. 'I'm not sure yet, lad. Most of the hotels in the area are full.'

'He can stay with us, can't he? Please Margaret. I'll speak to Louise again, Please.'

'That's blackmail, Jack. Besides, Ebee wouldn't want to stay in our humble abode.'

'It's very kind of you, but your aunt is correct, you shouldn't ask strangers into your home, especially pirates.'

'She's not my aunt,' Jack was back into a black mood.

'Would you like a cup of tea?' Margaret asked, she liked this big man and it was the least she could do.

'I'd love one,' he smiled, and so the trio made their way up the sand dune, across the field and into the kitchen where a startled Louise nearly dropped the kettle.

His balk appeared to fill the living area, where they all sat drinking great mugs of tea and the cakes and cookies Jack had refused to eat until now. Ebee was easy to talk to, and he regaled them with stories of life on the road with the camera crew. Jack was enthralled, he loved the fact that his new friend had met some of his heroes in the film industry.

'Did you really meet Luke Skywalker?' he asked, not daring to believe it.

'Yes, the actor that plays him,' Ebee smiled, 'would you like me to introduce you to Mark Hamill?'

'Who?' Jack frowned and they all laughed.

'Is that possible?' Louise didn't like fibbing to her son.

'Of course, he's staying in Butterfinny until next week, then the crew are off to film in New Zealand.'

'Are you going with them?' Margaret asked, with interest.

'Not straight away, but I will be joining them later. My eye has to heal first.'

It was agreed that the big man could stay in Jack's room, while Jack would sleep in with Louise.

'I hate to put you to all this trouble,' he had a worried frown on his smooth brow.

'It's no trouble, I changed the bed this morning so it's all ready for you.'

Ebee was good company, he regaled them with stories of life on the road as a camera man, working in different locations all over the world.

'There's filming going on in Belfast,' Ebee took a sip from his mug, 'an epic fantasy, it looks as though it will be a massive hit.'

'I'm going to be a camera man and make movies,' Jack decided, he had hung on to Ebee's every word, taking it all in. 'Did you really see Batman?'

'I never lie, Jack, it is one of the things I hate most.'

'I'm sorry,' Jack muttered, 'I meant, it must be cool to meet so many super heroes.'

Ebee laughed, 'they are not really super heroes, Jack, and they are just actors performing to entertain an audience. They are based on someone else's imagination, like, for example, the writers of Marvel comics.' Ebee looked at Louise, he hoped he wasn't shattering the lad's dreams.

'Well,' Jack said slowly, 'I might be an actor instead then.'

They all laughed, 'Bedtime,' grinned his mother, 'go and change into your pyjamas while I make you a drink.'

It was just before the ten-o clock news that they heard loud banging on the front door.

'Who the hell is it at this time of night,' Margaret got to her feet, putting her wine on the small table beside the chair. Ebee and Louise heard shouting and hurried to find out what was going on.

Darius Denton was red faced and drunk. 'Sell me the land you bitch,' he slurred. 'I've wanted it for years and that old uncle of yours wouldn't sell it to me.'

'It's not for sale,' Margaret shouted, 'and if you don't get off our land, I'll shoot so many pellets up your arse that the doctor will never get them all out.'

'You wouldn't dare,' he yelled back.

'I wouldn't chance it,' Ebee appeared at the door, 'she's got quite a temper.'

'Who the fuck are you?' Denton looked Ebee up and down, 'you're not from around here.'

'Observant little fella,' Ebee let his gaze wander down to Denton's crotch. 'Did you say you had a gun, Margaret?'

'I'll go and get it,' she looked at Ebee gratefully, and then went inside to get the gun. The problem was, it didn't fire pellets, it used bullets, big fat shiny ones. She put one in the barrel and the rest in her pocket. No one was going to threaten their home, they would die first.

'Little Annie Oakley with her ickle gun,' Denton roared with laughter.

'You talking to me?' Margaret shouted, all the talk about films had stirred her senses.

Louise took up the thread, 'Just ask yourself, Denton. Are you feeling lucky?'

Ebee chuckled, 'You can't buy all this with a fistful of dollars.'

'Shud up the lotta ya. I'll be back.' Denton staggered down the drive and got into his car, not noticing that the three characters were creased up with laughter.

'Oh, my, God,' Louise gasped, gripping her side, 'I've never had so much fun in my life.'

'It killed me when the idiot said he'd be back, who does he think he is, the terminator?' added Margaret.

'He probably will be back,' said Ebee, seriously. 'He could be dangerous.'

'I will shoot him,' Margaret said firmly.

'You'll go to prison,' Ebee frowned. 'Tell the Guarda, let them deal with him.'

Margaret laughed derisively, 'Huh, they wouldn't do anything, he's been getting away with fraud and theft for years, the law is always on his side.'

'He can't get away with threatening two young ladies,' Ebee shook his head. 'It's not like this where I come from.'

'Come inside, we've got a bottle of wine to finish,' said Louise.

'And another to open,' grinned Margaret, 'thanks for your support,' she touched Ebee's arm, 'we appreciate it.'

They resumed their place in the cosy kitchen and as they sipped the wine and nibbled on nuts, Ebee felt at peace, as though he had come home somehow, and suddenly he realised how sick he was of travelling the world and living out of suitcases.

Chapter 11

It was the official day of opening and a small group were gathered for the tour of the hotel and spa. The name of their business was to be Cheyanne, it seemed apt with the holistic and traditional treatments they would be offering. All the rooms were booked, people were going to come from all over Ireland to stay for a few days of rest and rejuvenation. Three masseurs had been hired, along with a nail technician, spray tan operator, a doctor, a psychoanalyst, two fitness trainers and a natural remedy nurse. More would be taken on if needed. As the girls escorted the visitors around their Spa Hotel, they both felt a rush of pride for what they had accomplished. They viewed each room as if they had come to stay, the gleaming treatment rooms on the first floor, all ready for business, bottles of oils lined out along glass shelves, creams and lotions set out up on a tray by the treatment bed.

They had three treatment rooms a tanning booth and a nail bar, with the potential to add more on if required. 'It's impressive,' exclaimed a local reporter who had come along to write a piece for the paper.

'We thought we would use the available land,' said Louise, 'but as you can see, there is still enough ground to let our guests sit out and admire the view.'

'The grounds are amazing,' agreed the reporter, 'you must give me the name of the gardener that did the work. He has captured tranquillity to a fine art.'

On the ground floor was the kitchen, restaurant and café bar with two comfortable lounges, squashy leather reclining chairs and thick carpets on the floor, with a television in one and a music system in the other, where the guests could relax after a meal or treatments. The girls had decided not to put televisions in the bedrooms as the idea was to get away from it all.

The stairs leading to the bedrooms were made of solid mahogany, and gleamed after hours of elbow grease by their newly appointed cleaner, Olga. There were twelve bedrooms, all en suite and a giant hot tub sat in the middle, like the centre of a daisy. Hence the reason that six of the bedrooms had been given names of flowers, Poppy was decorated in shades of red, Rose in pink, Bluebell gorgeous shades of blue, Primrose, the yellow room, Lavender was shades of violet and purple, and a subtle green room representing the leaves and stems. The other six rooms were named after gems, Diamond, Opal, Topaz, Emerald, Sapphire and Ruby.

'All gorgeous of course,' gushed the radio presenter from Buncrania radio, she had curly dark hair and was wearing an enormous pair of glasses with black frames, 'but where is the swimming pool?' she turned to the reporter and smirked, some hotel and spa this is, she thought.

'Well,' Louise began. The presenter sniggered.

'We thought you would never ask,' smiled Margaret, 'if you would like to follow us this way.

The group were led down the stairs, past the first lounge, and then, through a heavy door and down another flight of stairs, these were more serviceable, coated in heavy rubber to prevent anyone slipping on them.

Along the corridor, using the whole width of the building was a swimming pool, Jacuzzi and sauna, the adjoining room held a state of the art gym, with weights, bikes and cross trainers and the usual apparatus, mirrors were fixed along the width of one wall and speakers were in each corner to thump out the beat. The gym led into a studio where they planned to hold classes in the near future.

Four bedrooms were at the other end of the corridor with a small kitchen in the middle.

'For staff,' Margaret explained.

'I must say,' the reporter said, 'the design is unique. I've not come across a building like yours, and it is all made to measure.'

'We love it,' said Louise, linking her arm through Margaret's and took great satisfaction from the stunned expression on the presenter's face.

They all went back to the ground level and Louise ushered them into the café, where they were served drinks of their choice and a selection of snacks.

'Of course, the hotel is aimed at the higher end of the market,' said Margaret while the reporter scribbled furiously in her pad.

'But we have ideas for the land nearest the beach,' continued Louise. 'We have planning permission to erect Yurts, authentic log cabins and two shower blocks. They will cater for the family side of the market. Of course, we will need to think of a shop, crazy golf and that sort of thing.'

'Yes, it's like, how long is a piece of string,' grinned Margaret, 'I mean, our ideas keep coming.'

'Do we get a discount?' asked the presenter, and the reporter poised her pen waiting for the answer.

'Of course,' smiled Margaret sweetly. 'Let our receptionist know when you would like to come and the treatments you require.'

'We just need to take some shots of you both, some outside the hotel, some by the pool and a few more on the beach.' The reporter, Maggie, got to her feet and began to direct their poses.

An hour later they had all gone to write up their notes and begin the advertising campaign. Ebee joined them in the coffee bar for a donut and hot chocolate.

'You've kept out of the way,' Louise stated, frowning at him.

'You didn't need me getting in the way,' Ebee flashed a smile, 'besides, I've been busy plotting the outline for the Yurts.'

It had been a hard nine months getting to this point. Ebee had decided to take a sabbatical, saying he was sick of living out of a suit case. He hadn't filled them in with much history of his life, but it was his business and not theirs. He had his own room in the complex leaving jack to have his room in the cottage back. He had offered his services as a valet parking person and also a concierge, brushing up his knowledge of places of interest to visit. It was Ebee that had suggested the statue in the middle of the roundabout in front of the reception entrance. Cheyenne on a horse, rearing up as if to do battle, with a headdress of many feathers flying out behind, only it was Arthur's face on the statue, a testament to their uncle. The girls both loved it, seeing it as a monument to what they wanted to do with their future with the spa, something that Great uncle Arthur would be proud of. When they had discussed the naming of the spa, Margaret had suggested Arthurs seat, but it had been used before on other landmarks, and it was decided that Cheyenne captured the spirit and essence of what they wanted to do.

Margaret had kept her relationship with Finn on a low simmer, he had worked on most of the building design and had joined the girls for meals on occasions and Finn had built up a solid relationship with Ebee, both having the same sense of fun, fairness and work ethic. They formed part of their core team and Louise had made sure that both had been mentioned during all the interviews. All they had to do now was wait for the clients to arrive and then the adventure could begin.

Chapter 12

A week after the local paper was in circulation, the phone rang off the hook, hen parties and special birthdays, groups of all ages wanted to come along for a few days for a bit of pampering and relaxation. Word of mouth spread out across Ireland from County Cork to County Antrim. They joined forces with Butterfinney golf club to offer lessons and golfing weekends, the local riding school wanted to take part with trekking and rides across the wide sandy beach and the surf club was available to provide not only surfing lessons, but also canoeing and yachting across the bay.

Ebee had been nominated to oversee the crazy golf course, and with input from Jack, it was a pirate theme with eighteen holes and tricky obstacles, a masterpiece had been created. Families from not only the local area, but also across the border in Derry, came in droves, which gave Ebee the idea for a café, separate from the hotel and catering for the day-trippers, snacks, hot drinks and ice-creams, which was ideal when the sun made its presence felt, it proved to be a little gold mine and Ebee was thrilled. He also thought of building chalets along the beach for people to change in, but that would be on hold until the yurts were erected.

'I wonder if we need a bigger car park,' sighed Louise, 'the one at the point and the one below the road are constantly full, Denton will soon spread complaints.' They were sitting outside the cottage on a bench at the gable. It had been a busy day only marred by the car situation.

'Maybe we should put an offer in for one of Sadie's fields,' Margaret wondered, 'we could make her a decent offer and it would be a bit of money in the bank for her. It would also give her and Edward more time and money to visit the boys in America.'

'Mm, definitely worth considering,' Louise got to her feet and took in the view of the neighbouring farms,' why stop at Sadie's? We could expand the whole of the point. Arthur's Point has a good ring to it.'

'Maybe we should tread a bit cautiously,' Margaret knew that they had already spent a hefty sum of their inheritance, and to expand as much as Lou was thinking would mean going to the bank for a loan.

Louise sat down, 'yes, you're right, I'm trying to run before I've learnt to crawl,' she chuckled.

'It's so easy to get carried away,' Margaret took a sip of her fruity red wine, 'we both have the same vision, but we don't want our dream to collapse around us.'

'Can you imagine? I'd have to go back to Oxford,' Louise shuddered. She couldn't believe that this time last year, she couldn't imagine living here, and now there was nowhere else she would rather be.

A shadow fell in front of them and they looked up. Darius Denton stood there, unshaven and grubby, he had holes in his jeans and the red tartan shirt he was wearing was threadbare.

'What do you want, Denton?' Louise sighed, why couldn't this rat leave them alone?

'I've come to offer my services,' he grinned, showing gaps between his yellow stained teeth.

'There is nothing we need help with,' Margaret tried to keep her voice pleasant, mindful that several people were milling about, looking at the spa.

'Get rid of the big guy,' he spat.

'The big guy, as you call him, will get rid of you if you don't take your sorry arse off our land. If you come through the gates or any part of our business, you will get the barrel of the gun up your jacksie,' Louise gave him a wide grin, showing that she was only half joking.

'Words can't hurt me,' he sniggered.

'But the bloody gun will,' Margaret shouted, losing her temper.

'Just you wait,' he threatened, 'the big guy will take a holiday and then I will be back.'

'Clear off,' Louise barked, getting to her feet, 'it would be a waste of time calling for the guards, you're related to most of them. But we will use that gun if we have to. Uncle got it for stray dogs and rats, I think you fit the description of a rat.'

Denton sauntered off, shoulders bowed, but as he got to the gate he yelled at them, 'You'll be sorry.'

Louise held her fingers up as if she was shooting a gun, 'bang, bang,' she shouted, 'and next time it will be the real gun.'

'Oh boy,' Margaret sighed before taking a big gulp of wine, 'what the feck is wrong with him? Has he got a death wish?'

'I feel sorry for Mairead,' Louise said, 'he makes her life a misery, poncing around as if he owns her land and getting away with it. Why are the police so scared of him?'

'I don't know, but he's always got away with stuff. That's why he thought he could breeze in here and take our land.'

'Maybe we shouldn't underestimate him,' Louise shivered and rubbed the Goosebumps on her arms. 'He looked like a rabid dog.'

'Let's go inside and get the dinner sorted, unless you fancy going to that lovely new restaurant,' Margaret grinned.

'What new restaurant?' Louise fumed, not wanting any competition at this stage of the game, even if their restaurant wasn't yet ready.

'Oh, that spectacular one just up from here, walking distance actually so we can have a drink.'

'Funny, I'm sure, but we haven't actually got a chef yet, remember.' Louise frowned, they really needed to find a top-class chef and soon. Bookings for the spa were one thing, but they were having to fob off interest in the soon to be opened restaurant.

'Oh, I forgot to mention that a few people are coming to cook up a feast for us to sample and then we can choose the best chef.' Margaret had a grin like the Cheshire cat.

'Why are you just telling me now?'

'I wanted to surprise you, but Denton has spoilt the evening now. Come on, let's go and tell Ebee and Jack to get ready, we can meet them inside at 7.'

Louise discovered that Margaret had not only been extremely busy decorating the restaurant, but she had also sent out invites to their close friends. They were all dressed up for the occasion, and Mairead, clad in a beautiful blue, low cut evening gown, greeted them at the door with a wide smile.

'You look surprised, Lou,' Mairead took her arm and led her into the centre of the room where a large round table was set for eight people, Jack was already seated but Ebee was sitting on the table opposite, which was also laid for eight people.

'I can't believe Margaret has kept all this quiet. What a lovely surprise.'

'It's her way of thanking you for being here. You mean the world to her.'

Louise felt tears sting her eyes, she turned to give her cousin a hug, but she was at the bar, whispering to the bar man, who she recognised as Finn. Margaret's face was pink when she finally took her seat next to Louise.

'Fancy the barman, do you?' Louse teased. 'I can't believe you've done all this, I love it.' She kissed Margaret's cheek.

'I want it to be a special night, not only to thank you, but also to begin our adventure,' she had just got the words out when a waiter arrived at their table with a bottle in an ice bucket.

'Champagne?' Louise gasped.

'What else can we celebrate with,' Margaret poured them a glass each and filled Jack's glass with orange juice. She lifted her glass and held it towards Louise and Jack, 'To us,' she clinked her glass against the other two and took a sip. 'I don't really like it, but I'm sure I will acquire the taste.'

'Why is Ebee sitting over there with Edward and Sadie? Surely he should be on our table.'

'It's a long story, I'll tell you later,' Margaret explained. 'I did invite a few people, after all, we need to know who can cope with a crowd.'

'True, but where did the chefs come from?' Louise couldn't get her head around it.

'Catering college, of course, duh. They have to start somewhere, so not only do the chefs gain experience, they will also be cheaper than somebody like Rick Stein or Gordon Ramsey.'

'Where are the menus?' Jack asked, 'Do they do chicken nuggets, or chicken tikka?'

'Just be patient, we must wait for everyone to be seated,' Margaret smiled at him, Jack had grown up over the past few months, not only mentally but physically too. His eyes were a piercing blue, made even more striking with his sun kissed skin, and his dark hair was so much like his father's. Margaret guessed he would be breaking a few hearts in years to come, again, just like his father.

After half an hour, the remaining tables were full of friends, neighbours and the press. They were all smiling and drinking and Margaret signalled to Finn to have the menus delivered to the tables.

'It feels a bit strange, sitting on this big table, with empty seats,' Louise said, 'and why is Finn acting as barman?'

'Well, we can't be seen to be mixing with the staff, we're the owners, Margaret stated solemnly, 'and Finn offered, he thought it would be fun and a change from sketching.'

'Rubbish,' Louise was shocked, 'Ebee has been part of our family for most of this year, and we couldn't have done half of it without his help and Finn is an amazing architect.'

'Ah, here are the menus,' Margaret cut her off.

Louise looked up to take the dark green leather menu, 'very posh,' she exclaimed, feeling a bit deflated by her cousin's attitude.

'We hope madam will like what she sees,' said a female voice that Louise recognised.

'Mum!' she screamed, and then noticed her father, Jack was ecstatic, hugging first Adele and then his granddad, Brian was also standing there with a big grin on his face and a lady on his arm.

'Now you see why we have spare seats, and there is an empty space for Ebee if he wants to join us later.'

'I don't know what to say,' Louise had tears streaming down her face.

'We couldn't miss tonight, we are so proud of you both,' Adele also had tears in her eyes.

'Take a seat,' grinned Margaret, the instigator. 'Let's see how our young chefs have performed.'

The starters began with plates of tasters, each chef competing for best flavour and presentation. The menu was varied with a good choice and the dishes were brought out by young men and women from the local catering college. The transition between courses was excellent, and the wine was replenished when required. It was going to be a hard decision on who they would employ, but with the café in the pipeline, they would be able to use a few of the young hopefuls. The dessert dishes were whisked away and everyone was served a liqueur of their choice, the children were invited to try a mocktail.

'It's been incredible,' said Louise. Everything had been perfect, the ambience, and the service and there were no words to describe the delicious food. She had ordered plaice in a light garlic sauce accompanied with cauliflower cheese and new potatoes.

'Once the word gets out, we will have bookings for the restaurant in its own right,' Margaret stated, thoroughly pleased with herself.

'Are you staying with us or at the spa?' Louise asked her parents.

'Margaret has booked us into a lovely suite, we have even tried the hot tub,' Adele smiled at her daughter and ruffled Jack's thick curly dark hair. 'You've grown darling,' she kissed her grandson's cheek.

'What should I call you?' Jack wiped his cheek, 'I mean, I can't call you Mum anymore, can I?'

'Call me what feels comfortable,' Adele took him in her arms and gave him a hug.

'I'll think about it,' he pulled away, but smiled at her.

There had been so many photographs taken that Margaret felt as though her lips had gone numb. The local press had come along to add more to the article already under way, and the promise of a free meal had ensured a full page spread, not only in the local paper, but the county press was also there to be wined, dined and report on the magnificent spa, hotel and soon to be fully fledged holiday resort. The girls were ecstatic with the feedback received from all that had attended their special evening, especially Margaret who had planned the whole thing. Louise was beginning to realise just how talented her cousin was and guessed that old Arthur had known all along. He would be beaming down on them, she was sure of it.

As a special treat, Jack was staying at the hotel with Ebee and he had been promised a full cooked breakfast in the morning.

'It's been money well spent,' sighed Margaret, linking her arm through Louise's as they walked towards their cottage.

'I'm still in shock,' Louise laughed, 'how did you do all that under my nose?'

'Ha, that's for me to know, anyway, you've had a lot going on, dealing with the planning mob and Denton sticking his oar in.'

'Don't mention that bastard,' snarled Louise, 'I wish we could shoot him and throw him in the priest's hole.'

'He's not worth it,' Margaret squeezed her arm.

They walked the rest of the way in contemplative silence, there were so many ideas buzzing around in their heads, yet they were still high on euphoria. They spotted the flashing lights of a guard's car outside the cottage and quickened their steps, something wasn't right.

'Sorry to trouble you,' it was Denton's cousin, Officer Riordan, he didn't look at all sorry.

'Why are you troubling us at such a late hour?' Louise asked him, 'We are tired, it's been a long night.'

'Can I come in?' Riordan asked, 'I need to ask you both some questions.'

'Not until you tell us what it's about,' demanded Louise.

'There's been a murder,' he said, grimly.

Chapter 13

Darius Denton had been discovered amongst the long grass on the sand dunes by a honeymooning couple from Belfast, he had been shot twice in the head and his throat had been cut. Seagulls had scavenged his eyes out, so it wasn't pretty. Whoever had killed him wanted to make sure he was dead. It was hard to determine the exact time of death due to the state of the corpse, but they could tell which gun had been used to shoot him, one of the bullets had been found during the autopsy lodged behind the right empty eye socket, it had been identified as a shot gun.

'You were heard shouting, Miss Lavender, that you wanted to shoot Denton,' Riordan's voice was grim as he stared stony faced at the two bemused women.

'I wanted to shoot the bastard as well,' added Margaret in support. 'I'm not going to cry over his sorry arse, he was a torture, didn't give us a moment's peace.'

'But it wasn't us,' Louise told him, 'If it had been, you would not have found the body.'

'I don't find that helpful or funny,' stated Riordan.

'I don't find it funny that you have ruined a lovely evening,' snapped Margaret, she was extremely tired and wanted to go to bed, trust that bloody Denton to ruin their night.

'Can I see your gun,' sighed Riordan, it was well past his bedtime.

Louise went to get it from the locked cupboard, she had a moment of panic wondering if like in the movies it would be missing. She sighed with relief, it was where they had left it. She took it out, there was no need to remove the bullets; it was never kept loaded. Arthur had taught them both well.

'I will be taking it to forensics,' said Riordan, 'I hope for your sakes it was not the weapon used in the murder.'

'I hope for your sake,' said Margaret, with a coldness of steel in her tone, 'that it's not, because if it is, we will have been framed, and not in a good way.'

'Good night, ladies,' Riordan's voice was heavy. 'I will be in touch.'

'Damn right you will,' said Louise, 'we will want that gun back soon, you never know whose lurking about.' The door closed behind the retreating guard.

'What a nightmare,' Louise and Margaret were drinking hot chocolate by the range, 'I hope they don't try and pin it on us, everyone knew we threated Denton.'

'Don't worry, Lou, it wasn't our gun that killed him. Besides, when could we have murdered him? The only time we left the cottage after Denton left was to go to the hotel.'

'And another thing,' Margaret grinned, 'why would we shoot him twice in the head? We hate the sight of blood and it would've been a waste of a good bullet.'

Louise laughed, feeling some of the tension leaving her body, it was a good job Jack was staying up at the hotel. 'I wonder who told the police we threatened Denton.'

'Probably that old bat, Duffy, she's always hanging around in the shadows.

'Denton had enough enemies, but we have solid alibis, even if we had threatened him on several occasions, we did not do it. Time for bed I think. Tomorrow is going to be a long day.'

Chapter 14

The gun was returned with a caution, they were to get a license in their names and were warned not to threaten anyone with it, even in jest. The bullets used were a different calibre, but was similar in shape and velocity. Louise and Margaret locked the gun solemnly in the cupboard, minus the bullets.

'I have been a bit gung hoe,' Louise sighed, 'I didn't really think about the implications of using it.'

'Same here,' Margaret was realistic, she knew she would use the gun if she had to, if her family were threatened, the gun would make its dramatic appearance again.

'Mum is bringing Jack back in an hour, they are going to have a swim and dad is going to Butterfinney for a game of golf.'

'We need to sort the short list out, too. It's so hard to choose from those excellent young chefs and waiters.' Margaret hated conflict and loathed to hurt some of the promising catering students.

'It was great practice for them,' Louise stated briskly, 'we can put in a good word for all of them. It will put them in good stead for their next assignment.'

Margaret put her hands on her hips and glared at her cousin, 'well, Lou, you have the job of telling the ones that didn't get the job, I'll be the one bearing good news.'

'I don't think so,' Louise spluttered, 'I don't want to be the bad guy.'

'Tough,' said Margaret. 'You've talked yourself into it. Let's draw up the list, the sooner we start the sooner we get it over with.'

After the list was compiled of staff to keep, put on the reserve list, and better luck next time list, they took it in turns to phone them. It was easier than they had expected, some of the hopefuls were planning to move to England or America once they had qualified, so weren't disappointed to be let down gently. Others wanted employment nearer home, leaving the successful chefs delighted that they could live in the hotel and spread their wings. It was agreed that their contracts would cover the hotel and also the up and coming coffee shop, where they would have free reign to experiment on culinary delights. They were invited to come for a formal interview the following week.

Next on their agenda was to find a decent doctor and psychotherapist. They planned to run mind, body and spirit classes. No one else in the area offered the full package and they were determined to keep their spa hotel innovative and exciting. A knock on the door was met by a sigh from the cousins.

'It can't be mum,' said Louise, getting to her feet, 'she would just walk around the back and come in.'

'And it can't be Denton, cos he's dead,' said Margaret. She flipped through the pages of her notebook, making it clear that she wasn't going to answer the door.

Louise was stunned to find Aggie and Ellen standing on the doorstep.

'What do you want?'

'We've come to warn ye,' Aggie spoke while Ellen stood mutely by her side. 'We don't want any devil worshipping going on.'

'What the hell are you going on about?' Louise shouted.

'Lurgen de ba consa,' spluttered Ellen.

'Margaret,' Louise shouted, 'I think you'd better come here.'

'What's going on?' she saw the sisters, one all in black, the other in grey. 'Why are you here?'

'We've come to ask you nicely,' Aggie said, with a menacing tone.

'Gin ganda be seech,' said Ellen.

'What the f is she saying?' Louise looked at Margaret, bemused.

'It's not Irish, I remember some from school,' she looked in Ellen's faded grey eyes and said, 'pog mo thoin.'

'Are you putting a spell on her,' Aggie hissed.

Margaret laughed so hard that she had to grip the side of the door panel, 'clear off,' she spluttered, 'the last person to threaten us ended up with his eyes gouged out by seagulls.'

'We don't want any trouble,' hissed Aggie, 'we want one of the treatments you're offering to the locals, it's only fair, but we still don't want any of that voodoo stuff.'

'I suggest you go up to the hotel and make a booking,' Louise said coldly, 'the receptionist will book you in.'

'Gweeb de longen,' Ellen nodded her head.

'What are you two doing here?' Adele had arrived with Jack and she ushered him inside while she confronted the old women.

'Nought for you to worry about, dearie' said Aggie slyly.

'Gwindon,' Ellen shook her head.

'I thought you were in the psychiatric hospital, Adele asked Ellen, 'when did they let you out?'

'She can't understand you,' said Aggie, 'They damaged her with the electric shock treatment.'

'She was damaged before she went in,' Adele flinched, remembering the past.

'I think we've said all we are going to, so kindly leave and close the gate behind you,' Margaret glared at them and as soon as Adele and Louise had gone into the cottage, she closed the door.

'What's the story with Ellen?' Louise asked her mother as Margaret brewed a big pot of tea and sliced up a chocolate cake.

'I don't want to talk about it,' sighed Adele. 'But she was one of the reasons I went to England.'

The subject was changed and they chatted about the previous night and what a success it had been. Jack was on his X Box, telling his friends about the reunion and planning to meet up later to play football.

'The suite was gorgeous,' smiled Adele, 'are you sure you don't mind us staying a few days? It's good to see Brian so happy.'

'Don't be daft,' grinned Louise, happy to see her parents after so long, 'Jack has a lot of catching up to do, he can fill you in on how well he's doing at school, his place in the hurling team, and all the friends he's made.'

'Oh, he's already done that,' laughed Adele, 'but on a serious note, have you told him about his father, or his father about him?'

'No to both. If he asks, I'll tell him.'

'Gerard or Jack?'

'Jack of course, Gerard doesn't need to know.' Adele and Margaret locked eyes and both shook their heads in mutual agreement. A can of worms was going to be opened one day, but Louise wouldn't be budged.

'Ebee is a great find,' Adele cut a small slice of cake as Jack entered the kitchen.

'I found him,' he looked at Margaret, 'I did, didn't I? Can I have some cake please?'

'You certainly did, and yes, you can have some cake and a glass of milk.'

'Can we go swimming later?' Jack was still struggling on what to call Adele and it meant that he didn't call her anything. It was hard for all of them, he still found it hard to call Louise, Mum, but the word had slipped out more and more over the last few months.

'I'll take you,' Margaret ruffled his hair, 'Your mum and Nan have a lot to talk about, and I need the exercise.' Jack shrugged his shoulders, he didn't mind who took him as long as he could have a swim in the massive pool.

'I've just had a thought,' Louise put down her tea cup, 'we could have swimming lessons during the winter, when the hotel is quieter. For example, an hour every Monday and Wednesday. Obviously, if the hotel is booked solid, the school will have to change their days.'

'What a brilliant idea,' smiled Margaret.

'I can have them too,' she laughed, knowing that Margaret had pulled a blinder the previous night.

'Adele, would you like to help us tomorrow?' Margaret realised that her aunt would be a great judge of character when they interviewed the staff they would need.

'I've just had a brainwave,' Margaret burst into peals of laughter, as she tried to find the words to explain. It was a couple of minutes before she regained her composure while Louise and Adele waited for her to tell them.

'We have Doctor Swain coming for an interview next week,' she spluttered.

'What? Is that old perv still alive?' Louise gasped. 'He won't be working here.'

'Well,' Margaret laughed again, 'imagine if we said he could have a try out, and then got Aggie and Ellen to be his patients.'

'Love it,' Louise screamed. 'And if they complain we kill three birds with one stone.'

'Are you sure?' Adele was concerned, 'they are all nasty. Ellen was going to be a nun at one time, but the convent didn't want her. Be careful.'

'We will,' they chorused.

Margaret took Jack for a swim while Louise had a walk along the beach with Adele. She could tell that her mother was homesick by the tone of her voice.

'Why don't you go back to Oxford if the travelling is getting you down?'

'It's not that simple,' Adele sighed, 'your dad has another four months before he can be released from the contract.'

'Does he like it in Canada?'

'He loves it, but he wants to go home too. We can visit you more then. Jack is growing up so quickly.'

'Yes, and it's been great having him here, I realise now that I should have told him the truth years ago, he was heartbroken when he discovered the truth from witch Aggie.'

'I told you she is dangerous, be careful.'

When they returned to the cottage, everyone was there, waiting to be fed. Margaret had put a massive leg of lamb in the oven, purchased from William's the butcher in the village. The rich aroma filled the kitchen mingling with the vegetables and stuffing.

Louise peeled a mound of potatoes to do a mixture of roast and mash. Louise's dad, Frank was rosy cheeked, but she wasn't sure if it was the round of golf or the cheeky pint he had had at Comskies bar.

'Maybe when you get established, you could give me a job,' Frank chuckled. 'It's been a great day and so peaceful.'

'Hey, you could be one of our masseurs, right Lou?' grinned Margaret.

'Yes, or a head waiter,' Louise replied.

'I'm being serious,' frowned Frank, 'I was talking to a chap at the golf course, you could tie in with Butterfinny, I could arrange coaches to take tourists to play golf, or even trips further afield, like, the Giants Causeway.'

'That's where those fat gypsies get married,' pondered Louise, remembering her trip over many months ago. 'Are you serious, Dad? I mean, once we are established there will be all kinds of things you can do, and the trips sound an excellent idea.'

'And dad will have his sister nearby,' joined Margaret. 'I mean, if you are really serious, at the end of your contract, you could sell up in Oxford and build a house here.'

'Is that possible?' Adele's eyes sparkled at the thought that she could move away from the hustle and bustle of busy cities.

'We would have to check for planning permission,' Louise said, 'but it shouldn't be a problem, we have that plot at the side of the cottage.'

'It would be wonderful, oh, I'm so excited, but would you mind having your parents on your doorstep?'

'Free babysitters? Don't be silly,' Louise giggled.

'I'm not a baby,' Jack complained. 'Are you really coming to live here, near us?' Jack was catching the excitement.

'It's certainly an idea,' said Frank. 'We would have to think very carefully before we commit to anything. I've got a few months left to work on that contract in Ontario.'

The excitement died down as real life nudged it aside, but not only was the food ready, food for thought was also on the table.

Two weeks later, Louise and Margaret were at Belfast airport saying a tearful goodbye to Adele and Frank.

'I'll facetime you when we get to the hotel,' promised Adele.

'It's been good, thanks girls,' Frank hugged his daughter and then his niece, 'we've certainly got a lot to talk about over the next few months.'

'We can test the water,' said Louise, 'get some ideas for planning, and if it's possible, you can design your new house with that amazing architect, Finn Killian.'

Margaret blushed, her relationship with the good looking architect was still a private affair, and she only gave Louise the barest details of their infrequent dates. There just wasn't the time to give her all to the relationship at the present.

They waved until Adele and Frank had passed through into the departure lounge. Their flight was taking them to Heathrow, where they would catch a flight the following day to Canada. They were spending the night at a hotel near Heathrow airport.

'Maybe we should take Jack out there,' Margaret wondered, 'when he breaks up from school. We could do Niagara Falls, and maybe go down to New York, it would be good, we could certainly do with a break.'

'Yes,' agreed Louise, 'but who could we leave in charge?'

The answer was waiting for them when they got back to the cottage. Ebee was sitting on their 2 seater sofa while a blonde lady perched at his side. They got to their feet when Louise and Margaret entered.

'This is Karen,' Ebee had a grin from ear to ear. 'She lives down the road, can you believe it?'

'Er, yes,' said Margaret bemused, 'you're the English lady that lives near the bend.'

'Yes, that's right,' smiled Karen. 'I came up to see if you had any jobs going, I'm sick of travelling into Letterkenny, and then I saw Ebee, can you believe it?'

Louise was equally bemused, 'Ebee works here, and has done for months, so it's not really a surprise that you should meet him.'

'No, I mean, I sound silly, but I know Ebee. We used to work together in Coventry, remember that place?' she shuddered.

'I remember it very well,' Ebee grimaced, 'It was a lucky day for me when I got a job with the film crew.'

Karen held out her hand, 'I'm Karen Brown, we haven't spoken much,' she smiled at Margaret, 'I'm always dashing from one place to another, chasing my tail.'

'What made you come to Clodbury?' Louise asked, 'It's a bit off the beaten track.'

'My dad's sister owns a house here,' Karen explained. 'Her husband is from the area and when he passed away she inherited a bit of land and a holiday home. I'm looking after it while she tours Australia.'

'What type of job were you looking for?' Margaret asked, they had enough therapists to be going along with.

'Reception, assistant manager, that kind of thing,' Karen smiled.

'You don't look like Helga?' Louise laughed.

Margaret joined in, 'no, you certainly don't.'

'Oh, is that a bad thing,' Karen's smile dropped.

'No, it's definitely a good thing,' Louise told her.

'Can you come up for an interview in two hours? We need to grab some lunch and discuss a role that might be suitable.'

'Of course,' Karen agreed, 'shall I come here or the hotel?'

'The hotel, please,' said Margaret, 'Ebee, why don't you take Karen for a coffee? Tell them it's on the house.'

'Can we have a pastry as well?' he grinned.

'Go on then,' laughed Louise, 'you may just have earned it.'

'Could be a god send,' said Louise as she filled the kettle. They hadn't stopped for a break on the way back from Antrim.

'I'm thinking, Housekeeping,' said Margaret.

'Or assistant manager. It will free up some time for us.'

'If she's up to scratch though, can you believe that Karen knows Ebee?'

'Don't you start,' Louise laughed, 'they're like a comedy duo. Maybe we should have entertainment at the weekends.'

'What a great idea,' Margaret screamed.

'I was joking,' Louise rolled her eyes.

'I'm not, though. We could have a live band, disco, like one of those dinner dance things they used to have during the sheepdog trial festival.'

'That's going back a bit, remember the tramps ball? They were great fun.'

'Exactly,' said Margaret, 'We could have tribute bands.'

'I guess we could use the studio for dancing and then the food would be served in the restaurant.'

'Or just move the table around and have the whole thing in the restaurant, we could even have comedians and drag artists.'

'Ebee is such a star,' grinned Louise.

'Isn't he just, and he doesn't even know he gave us this brainwave.'

Chapter 15

Adele's mind was still in Clodbury as they soared through the clouds. Frank was sound asleep beside her, he had ate the in-flight meal, watched a bit of the film and then closed his eyes. Could she really live in Clodbury again? She was a free spirit and had flown the nest as soon as she reached seventeen to travel to England. There was no future in the small village, where everyone knew your business, but worst of all was the two strange women that lived in a ramshackle house near the back beach. Even back then, people had called the sister witches, especially Aggie, but Adele knew to her cost that Ellen was equally vindictive, dangerous even. She had never told anyone about the day she had gone swimming alone, even though her mind told her that she should, because she could have died that day. She often wondered that if she had told someone, then little Siobhan would not have been harmed.

Frank stirred beside her, 'Are we there yet?' he murmured.

'Not quite,' she smiled, 'Shall we have a drink? I fancy a vodka and coke.'

Chapter 16

Karen proved to be a competent typist and receptionist, she was also able to manage the staff being firm yet fair, apart from Ebee who was a law into himself.

'Sorry Karen,' he grinned charmingly, 'I'm my own man, I can't take orders from you.'

'I don't expect you to,' Karen assured him, 'the girls have already said you are your own boss. In fact, they think very highly of you.'

'It's a great opportunity,' he said. 'How are you settling in?'

'I love it,' she smiled, 'there are some quirky people, but that makes it even more interesting. The girls are planning on taking Jack to Canada in the school holidays.'

'Yes, I know, we have a meeting tomorrow morning to discuss how we should run the spa in their absence.'

'Bookings are up, did you hear about the latest plans?'

'The nightclub? Yes a great idea. I'm going to be the bouncer.'

Karen laughed, 'Mr Odd Job, mind you, it's a far cry from Binley.'

'Too right,' he agreed, 'Those days are far behind us. Do you ever hear from the old crowd?'

'Not really, I lost touch when I moved here. I needed a complete break, I don't know what I'm going to do when Aunt Gill comes back from her travels.'

'Cross that bridge,' he shrugged, 'I'll see you later.'

Ebee needed to check on the yurts and cabins; they had been erected but the interior was yet to be installed. Margaret and Louise wanted to see them finished before going on their trip to Canada. The layout was very impressive and resembled a small village. They wanted a shop to serve the basics and were waiting for planning permission to erect a club house. He still couldn't believe that his vision was happening, taking place just as he hoped. It would soon be the end of his sabbatical, but he knew he had no intention of leaving, Clodbury was home and Louise, Margaret and Jack were his family. Sometimes a niggle from his past would prod him, especially at night, but he forced it back down, he was focussing on the here and now, the past must stay buried.

'Good afternoon, Mr Hedron, what do you think?' Seamus Lynch was finishing off the final touches of a log cabin. It was set up for a family of four with two bedrooms, a bathroom and a living kitchenette area. The master bedroom had an enormous king sized bed, a wardrobe and dressing table with soft furnishings in bright red and white. The children's room had bunk beds and a chest of draws. The curtains of heavy cotton, matched the quilt covers and pillow cases, patterned with dolphins, surfers and big waves, the flooring was all durable tiles, warm under foot and easy to sweep clean. It was decided that carpets would collect the sand. The bathroom was a wet room, with a shower, toilet and washbasin.

'It's looking good, simplistic yet cosy.'

'That was the aim,' Seamus stated. 'The yurts will be more basic, campers will have the choice to either cook outdoors or use the cafe. Are you still thinking of putting in hot tubs?'

'I just need to run it past the girls,' Ebee grinned, 'but it is in the plan. It's the timing we need to sort out before they go on holiday.

'Okay, just keep me posted,' Seamus shrugged his broad shoulders and shoved a pen behind his ear.

'The press are coming out again tomorrow to do a final shoot, its taking ages to get into the press,' Ebee groaned.

'Unpredictable,' Seamus explained, 'if a bigger story emerges they go for that and put others on the back burner, I used to work for the Butterfinney Times.'

'Impressive,' Ebee nodded his head, he hadn't heard of it.

'I don't like to brag,' Seamus bragged, 'but I practically ran the shop. It was a damn shame when they closed us down, so it was.'

'Why was that then? Too much competition from the Journal?'

'Not at all, we ran out of decent news.'

'That would do it,' Ebee tried not to laugh, 'You've done a great job here though, Seamus, the paper's loss is our gain.'

'I can have a word with that journalist,' Seamus says, 'add my input and get the best coverage for our babies.'

'Good man,' Ebee said, 'I'll leave you to it, I've people to see and things to do.'

'Righto, I'll finish up here and see you tomorrow.'

Ebee knocked on the door to the cottage and Jack opened the door with chocolate smeared around his mouth. 'We're making cakes,' he explained, 'come in and try some.'

Louise was in the kitchen, it looked as though a tornado had blasted through it, and flour was in her blonde hair and down her blue shirt.

'I don't know why I agreed to this,' she laughed, 'Jack wanted to make some cakes for when his friends come around later.

'You could have cheated and gone up to the hotel.'

'Yes, but he wanted to help me make them, besides, it's been fun, if messy.'

'And you get to lick the bowl,' he said thoughtfully, remembering when he was a child and his mum let him scape his small finger around the large mixing bowl.

'I never thought of that, maybe Jack won't like it,' she winked at Ebee.

'I think he's been trying it by the amount of mixture on his face,' Ebee grinned.

'In that case, you can have the honours.'

'The yurts and cabins are looking good, Seamus has done a good job.'

'Brilliant, I'll take a walk over later with Margaret, I didn't want to go before they were ready.'

'He asked about the hot tubs, what do you think?'

'They will add pulling power,' Louise said thoughtfully, knowing that that side of the road was Ebee's baby.

'Pulling power?' Ebee spluttered on a bit of cake.

'You know what I mean,' she said crossly, 'it will draw people in. Not only will they have the view of the sea, but also somewhere to relax in the evening. It will be magical.'

'So that's a yes then?'

'I'll think about it,' she teased. 'What time did the press say they were coming out?' she was quite sick of them if she was honest, they had snapped photos and they had given numerous interviews, and yet nothing had yet been published.

'Around two, they apologised about their tardiness, but the murder had taken precedence.'

'Bloody Denton,' Louise hissed, 'He's causing trouble even in death.'

Chapter 17

Margaret packed her case with a smile on her face and her thoughts miles away. Finn had told her how much he loved her the night before, despite the fact that they hardly had any time together, they had grown very close and Margaret knew she felt the same about him. The next step was to make quality time for Finn and Brian to spend together, but that would have to wait until they got back from Canada. She sighed, things had moved like lightening, one minute they were thinking of the idea of the trip and the next it was booked and they were leaving tomorrow.

She still had to pinch herself, this past year had been a dream, having Lou working by her side as they created their dream had been amazing. But it was also very crazy. In a few short months they had seen the erection of their hotel spa, restaurant and now the cabins and yurts were nearly ready. Karen had proved to be a godsend and Ebee was in his element, the perfect person to leave in charge, although she did wonder what surprise he had up his sleeve for them next. The crazy golf was constantly booked and the café was a gold mine, so he had certainly got everything right so far.

The episode with the Duffy sisters and Doctor Swain could have gotten them into big trouble but it backfired in a weird kind of way. Doctor Swain was told that he would have to give an in house interview, practising on two patients, while Aggie and Ellen were told that Doctor Swain would examine them in order to assess if they were fit enough for treatments. Ellen had gone in first, and before the door was closed, Olga heard the good doctor ask Ellen to remove her clothes and lie on the examining bed. She heard no more, but when Ellen came out of the treatment room, she had a wide smile on her face and a skip in her walk. Aggie went in next, and despite the heavy door, loud noises were heard coming from the room, grunts, and groans and moaning. She too had come out of the room with a big smile on her usual dour face.

'We've decided not to bother with treatments here,' she had told the receptionist slyly.

'I won't be practicing here either,' Doctor Swain said, as if he was letting them down, 'I've had an offer I can't refuse.' The look that passed between the doctor and the sisters was enough to curdle milk, but whatever floats their boat, Margaret had thought.

The gossiper's were agog with the rumours of strange things going on in the small house in the middle of the field by the back beach. One woman said it was like that old couple on Benidorm, the ones that liked kinky sex, she had stated, Margaret didn't want to think about what the weirdo's were up to, as long as they stayed out of their way, she would be quite happy.

'Are you in there Marg,' Louise tapped on the door, 'We've been summoned to the golf course.'

'Won't be a minute,' Margaret folded the last item of clothing and closed the case, she was going to travel light and bring some new stuff back.

'Deja vous,' Louise sighed.

'I hope it goes to press this time,' Margaret said, 'it's a good job we weren't relying on them to get bookings.'

Jack was asked to pose with a golf club, 'We want to let people it was partly his design,' one of the photographers, a girl called Cindy who hadn't been out before, told them, snapping away, asking Jack to pose first with a golf club in full swing, and then by the final hole with a cheeky grin, as though he had just putt the ball.

'He's so adorable,' Cindy cooed.

'Can I have a couple of the photographs to send to my parents?' Louise asked, Adele would love them.

'Sure, I'll put some in the post for you. We intend to go to press at the end of the week, I can't apologise enough for the delay. I know it's been ages since you had the opening and everything.'

'Seems like years ago,' Margaret said.

'It's that murder,' Cindy whispered. 'The guards still don't know who done it.'

'If we wait for them to solve the case,' stated Louise angrily, 'we will never get in the paper.'

'I take it you have no sympathy with the victim,' Cindy had her pen poised.

'No comment,' said the girls in unison. 'Are you ready to look at the log cabins and yurts? Ebee is waiting for you,' Margaret led the way across the wooden pathway that cut across the grassy bent, leaving Cindy no choice but to follow. Perhaps it was a good thing that they were going away for a couple of weeks, it would be nice to escape for a while.

Chapter 18

Ebee was as proud as a peacock with its feather puffed out now that he was now in charge while the girls had gone away. It warmed his heart that they trusted him and he would repay that trust 100 percent. He would take no funny business from anyone.

He had come a long way since working as just a number in a big company, where the manager didn't even know his name. Crunching numbers and filing invoices day after day, week after week until one day he decided to re train and went to classes. He proved what a great camera man he was and had an eye for cinematography. At first he was awe struck by the top stars, catching their every move on film and was even nominated for an academy award, but even the job of his dreams became repetitive, the sets were different the cast changed with each new production, but there was no thrill in the job, he still took pride in each film of course, but he was sick and tired of living out of a suitcase. He had left his long-time girlfriend in Nuneaton while he toured around locations all over the world, until she got lonely and went off with his best friend. He couldn't blame her, Layla was a stunner and deserved more than he could offer, but the betrayal still hurt like hell. It would be a long time before he trusted a woman again. Especially after the episode with Shirl the girl with the pearl. He tore his mind away from that disastrous incident, it was better not to dwell on what could have been and what nearly did happen.

Ebee took a walk across the road to check on the log cabins and yurts, they would soon be ready to let out for the summer. The only thing they needed now was a club house and they had plans in for approval, because of the size of the building they wanted, it was going to take some time. They also had to check that the neighbours approved, it was a good job Denton wasn't around to object, he thought, darkly. The site was taking shape, he was extremely proud of it, and young Jack who had given his opinion. It was his idea that they have a club where children could play pool and have a disco. He also suggested a youth club all year round. Things could be happening a bit too fast, the girls had paid out millions and it would take a long time before they would break even, a fact that always played on his mind.

The press releases were due out tomorrow and it was a shame that the girls would not be here to see them, he thought, although he promised to fax them to their hotel. It occurred to him as he walked along the edge of the site, overlooking the wide expanse of beach, the tide was out, that it would be nice to have a dog. He would broach the subject when they got back.

Karen was just finishing her shift when he went up to the hotel, she smiled as he walked up to her.

'Is everything in order?' she asked.

'Yes, it's looking good, how are things up here?'

'Quiet, we need more publicity to get the rooms full, hopefully the press release will put us on the map,' Karen sighed.

'Maybe we should ask the radio to promote the spa, we need some gimmicks'.'

'Good idea, we should get together for a brain storming session.'

'How about now?' Ebee suggested, 'Have you eaten?'

'No, but I've got a chicken casserole simmering in the oven, would you like to join me?'

'If you're sure, I was going to grab a snack from the café.'

'I've prepared too much for one, and I'd be glad of the company.'

'That was delicious,' Ebee wiped his mouth on a paper serviette, 'you're a good cook, Karen.'

'Thank you, but It's not difficult to throw it all in a pot and leave all day,' she laughed.

'I'd burn it,' he grinned.

'Shall we have coffee in the lounge?' The dining room was small but adequate for 2 people, the table was a collapsible with four chairs around it. Ebee followed Karen into the lounge, it too was small, but cosy, a green leather two seater sat under the window with a matching armchair on either side, the view from the window looked out over the bay.

Ebee sat in one of the chairs, 'it's a far cry from Nuneaton isn't it?'

'It sure is,' Karen giggled. 'I still can't believe that we both ended up here. What happened to Shirley?' the last she had heard, they were a couple on the verge of living together.

'I haven't got the foggiest,' Ebee told her. 'We lost touch years ago.'

'That's a shame, I thought you would have got married and had a couple of kids.'

'Maybe in another lifetime, anyway what about you? Weren't you dating Graham?'

'Greg,' Karen corrected. 'It turned out that he preferred men, he left me for a bloke at work.'

'I did wonder,' Ebee smiled, 'remember that Christmas do, the last one we went to at Antonio's? I'm sure he was giving me the eye.'

'He probably was,' she agreed, 'fickle as well as gay,' they both laughed.

'I'll make us a coffee then grab a pen and paper, time for some brainstorming before it gets too late'

Chapter 19

It was gone eleven when Ebee left Karen to walk up the hill to the hotel, it had been an interesting night and they had come up with some great ideas, subject to approval from the girls. They had both agreed that although the bookings for the spa had been wonderful when they had first opened, the impetus had dropped along with interest. The press should help for a while, but they needed something to bring in customers during the week, not just for their restaurant. His head was buzzing with all the ideas that had been scribbled in Karen's notepad, so the blow to the back of his head took him completely by surprise. He went down with a heavy thud, catching his head on a jutting rock that was built into the hard packed earth that formed a ditch.

A rough tongue slid over Ebee's face, prompting him to open his eyes. He slowly got to sitting position and winced as a million tiny darts seemed to pierce the area around his eyes. The shape of a dog sat down beside him, it was eerily dark and saved from total blackness by the light of an almost full moon, street lights hadn't been erected in this area of Clodbury.

'Thank you,' Ebee stroked the silky head and the dog licked his hand in response, and then the dog ran off towards a house near the bend in the road, yapping loudly, Ebee could see a light on in one of the windows.

Ebee gently ran his hand over the back of his head, he could feel a gash and dried blood along with a lump that felt the size of a goose egg, he realised that he had been out for quite a while.

'Are you alright? Fred just came to get me.'

Ebee was still sitting at the side of the road and tried to get to his feet, the man who had come running towards him, held out his hand and helped to hoist him to his feet.

'Thanks, some bastard hit me over the head,' Ebee explained, 'who's Fred by the way?'

'Your dog in shining armour,' the man chuckled, 'Fred's my dog, and I'm Paul.'

'You have him well trained, Paul, he woke me up, god alone knows how long I'd have been out for.'

'Come up to my cottage, I'll get you a hot drink.'

Ebee walked along side Paul, Fred at their heels, it was only a short walk from where he had been attacked.

'It must be late,' Ebee stated, knowing time was getting on when he had left Karen.

'Just after twelve, I was getting ready to go out fishing with my brother, Kevin.'

'I never thought to bring a torch out with me,' Ebee admitted, 'I don't normally walk far at this time of night.'

'Have you any idea who would attack you?' Paul was opening the door of his neat cottage, the heat inside hugged Ebee like a blanket.

'Not a clue, mate, I don't know that many people yet, I've been too busy getting the summer camp ready.'

'It's looking good,' Paul poured boiling water into a big brown teapot, 'my wife, Mary, said she must try out the spa facilities. She's away in England at the minute visiting her sister.'

Fred sat at Ebee's feet, watching him with warm brown eyes, 'checking up on me, fella?' he stroked the golden Labradors head.

'It's a shame he can't talk,' said Paul ruefully, 'he might have recognised your attacker.'

'What I don't get is, how would they know that I was down this part of the road?'

'Opportunist,' said Paul, 'although it's usually pretty safe around these parts.' He poured tea into mugs and handed one to Ebee, 'I've put 2 sugars in for shock.'

'Thanks, I'm going to have one hell of a headache tomorrow,' he jumped when there was a knock at the door.

'That'll be Kevin,' there was another knock on the kitchen door and a man, a younger version of Paul entered.

'Ebee here has just been attacked,' explained Paul. 'Do you want tea?'

'No, thanks, had one before left, I saw Swain up on the hill, he looked furtive, but then he always does.'

'The doctor?' asked Ebee.

'He used to be until he got struck off,' said Paul, shaking his head.

'I've never met him,' Ebee stated, getting to his feet, 'I'll head up the road now, thanks for the tea and hospitality.'

'No problem,' Paul walked with him to the door, 'I'll ask around and see if the locals know who it could have been.'

'Thanks, good luck with your fishing.'

'Thanks, I'll take that two ways,' he chuckled. 'Are you okay to walk up the road or do you want a lift?'

'The cool air will clear my head,' sighed Ebee, hoping that the dull ache behind his eyes would ease off, and the back of his head hurt like hell.

Against the black sky, Ebee could see all the major star formations, The Plough was particularly bright as was the North Star. It could've been a magical night instead of a nightmare one. He wondered if he made a wish it would come true. He also wondered if the knock on his head had caused him to lose his mind. Maybe he should write a book while it was full of fantasy.

He passed Sara Harkin's house, it was in darkness, so she was either in bed or away in Strabane at her nursing job. Besides, anyone in their right mind would be in bed at this time of night, or very early morning. He felt very weary and just for that moment, home sick for Nuneaton. What would his friends be up to? He wondered. He had left years ago to chase a dream, he was still chasing, and maybe he should wait and let it find him. He walked past Arthur's cottage, again in darkness, he missed the girls and Jack dreadfully and they still had another week in Canada. As he closed the door of his apartment behind him, he knew that if he was a woman, he would sit on the bed and weep. Instead, he took a hot shower and as he looked in the mirror, grimaced at the state of his face. He had a vivid cut at the side of his left eye brow and a circle of black and blue was forming. He was a role model for the pirate Jack mistook him for all those months ago. He filled a tumbler with water and swallowed two painkillers, he had an early start later that day and the press releases were due out. The girls would be waiting impatiently for him to send them. As soon as his poor head hit the pillow, he closed his eyes and slept solidly until the alarm went off at 7.

'Oh my God,' screamed Karen when she saw the state of Ebee, they were in the café having breakfast.

'Have you got a jealous lover?' Ebee quipped, 'I was attacked just past your house.'

'Not that I know of,' Karen said seriously. 'Didn't you get a look at who done this to you?'

'No, the bastard got me from behind, besides, it was pretty dark. Fred rescued me.'

'He's lovely isn't he?' Karen knew Fred, he often accompanied her along the beach on one of her walks.

'Yes, and very clever.'

'Have you told the guards?'

'There's no point is there? That stupid Riordan would come out and say it was my own fault.'

'He is pretty useless,' Karen agreed.

'Do you know of a Doctor Swain? Paul's brother Kevin said he was a shifty character.'

'I've heard the rumours, but I haven't met him, do you think it was him?'

'Why would a random stranger knock me out?'

'It can't be Denton,' said Karen. 'Because he's dead,' they said in unison.

They had a light breakfast of croissants, jam and butter and shared a pot of tea. Ebee's head still hurt and he had taken more painkillers, he just hoped that the guests wouldn't be scared off by his appearance.

'I'm going into the village to get the papers,' Karen called in to see him at the office he was using in the hotel. The girls had insisted that he had his own space to design and plan the holiday park. He was glad of that space now.

'Okay, has Josephine taken over reception?'

'Yes, everything is in order, sir,' she grinned.

'I just don't feel like facing anyone,' Ebee sighed.

Karen was concerned, Ebee was usually so upbeat, he really had taken a knock last night and not just to his head. She was determined to find out who was behind the attack.

A crowd had formed around the counter at Centra, and Karen realised that they were looking at the pictures that had been taken at the hotel and holiday park.

'Are they good?' she asked.

'Really good,' Mairead was skimming the centre page, 'the press have done a grand job.'

'I'd better buy a few copies,' Karen collected several copies of not only the local paper, but also the Journal and the Irish Press.

'I'm in one of them,' Mairead told her with a smile, 'it was a wonderful night.'

'I wasn't working there then,' Karen said, 'perhaps we can organise another one, like a dinner dance.'

'Great, and if you need any help let me know.'

'Okay, why don't you come up to the hotel later, we can share ideas.'

Karen bought a few goodies to cheer Ebee up, not that a bit of cake and chocolate would help that much, but it was a start.

With a wave to Mairead and the group of people that were admiring the press release, she set off to put a smile on Ebee's face, there were some good shots of him by the golf course, and Jack looked so cute with rosy cheeks, bright blue eyes and jet black hair. He could be a little male model, she thought as she manoeuvred her bright yellow Volkswagen beetle through the village and out to the place she now thought of as home.

She finally felt as though she belonged in Clodbury, even though she had lived here for just over a year. Her job in Letterkenny was not the career she had hoped for when she had accepted it from the comfort of her home in Nuneaton. She had imagined having her own office and the freedom to purchase items from the St Donald's clothing chain in the whole of County Donegal. She knew that fashion was her passion, her own quirky dress sense was proof that she had style and elegance, but the company had mislead her. It wasn't floaty dresses and gorgeous tops that they wanted her to select, it was thick tights and chunky cardigans. Donegal Tweed was to replace Chantilly lace in her imagination and her dreams had crashed and burned. She had been miserable for the past few months and had even toyed with the idea of going back home and her old job, the one she hated even more than the St Donald one. Ebee had rescued her in a way he couldn't imagine, and now she would rescue him.

'Will the girls be impressed?' Ebee was sitting at the computer, preparing an email to ping to Canada.

'I think they will be ecstatic,' she opened up the papers on the floor, spreading them out. There was an exquisite one of Louise and Jack in colour standing by a log cabin, her parents would love that one. There was a saucy one of Ebee in swimming shorts standing by the pool, it was hilarious but he wasn't impressed with it.

'When did the bastards take that?' he demanded.

'I wasn't here then, remember,' giggled Karen, wishing that she had of been.

'It seems as though you've been here for ages,' Ebee flicked through the pages and began to scan them onto the system, 'I'm not sending this,' he ripped the page with the picture of him by the pool out of the paper and folded it in half.

'It would make them laugh,' Karen chuckled. 'I'll keep a copy for when they get home.'

'It's been quiet without them,' Ebee sighed.

'Not so quiet that the villains knocked you out,' stated Karen.

'True, I won't be going out alone after dark,' he grinned, but half meant it, the attack had put a huge dent in his confidence.

'I'll come back later, we can finish what we started, but I'm going to drive though.'

Satisfied that he had scanned on the best photo's Ebee attached them to the email and sent it to the girls. He had already warned them to expect the post and could imagine the impatience and excitement across the water. He hoped that the advertising would give them a new lease of life after the drop in bookings.

Five minutes after the email had been sent, a reply pinged into the in box.

'They like them,' said Ebee, 'now let's go and get some lunch.'

'Like?'

'Okay, they loved them, especially the one of Lou and Jack.'

They went up to the restaurant, deciding to try out the new menu, the chef was pulling out all stops in readiness for the surge in bookings. One of the waiter's was studying IT and web design and had promised to build them a web site in exchange for meals and lodgings, it was a deal that suited all of them, although he had been told that once the season started he might have to share a room with another member of staff. He greeted them both and showed them to a table, they were all vacant, they had decided to only open at weekends until the season was under way, or if bookings warranted them to open.

'Where would you like to sit?' the eager waiter asked.

Ebee looked at Karen and she replied, 'the far corner overlooking the sea, 'she smiled, and they both followed to the table for two. Because of all the glass, the views from all windows were stunning, especially today where the sky was clear and sun was bright. The sea was calm and in the distance they call see a small boat, Ebee guessed that it was Paul or Kevin, and that reminded him that he should get Fred a big juicy bone from William the butcher.

Karen picked up the drinks menu and studied the selection, it was the first time she had dined in the restaurant, usually grabbing a snack in the café or cooking in her kitchen at home. The selection was good, but she opened her handbag and after a bit of fishing around, took out a notebook and pen.

'I've got a few ideas, is that okay?'

'Go for it,' grinned Ebee, 'the girls will have the overall say but they are open to new ideas.'

'I'm thinking cocktails,' she mused, jotting down a few concoctions that she had tried and liked in the past, especially during her holidays in Spain. 'I mean, things like 'sex on the beach.'

'Bit nippy yet,' said Ebee cheekily.

'How about, 'raging orgasm?'

'Same,' grinned Ebee, 'unless it's in my room,' he gave her a wink and she giggled, they both knew that their friendship was purely platonic, but it was a close easy relationship and they both felt comfortable to be able to say anything to each other without causing offence.

'I think we should make our own cocktails,' speculated Karen, 'Arthurs fantasy, Bewitched, that kind of thing.'

'Have you ever mixed cocktails?'

'No, but I can learn, or we could find an expert, someone that can perform behind the bar.'

'They might get arrested,' laughed Ebee, 'especially if they were having sex and a raging orgasm.'

'You're terrible,' Karen hit his arm.

The waiter approached their table with menus, 'can I get you drinks?'

'Maybe you should have asked us when we were seated, 'suggested Ebee, 'we've been waiting for ten minutes.'

'I'm sorry,' explained the waiter, his face going beetroot, 'we had an emergency in the kitchen.'

'I don't think paying guests would understand that, 'sighed Ebee, 'what kind of emergency?'

'The chef had underestimated how much meat he would need, and the soup ingredients weren't up to scratch.'

'It looks as though we need someone to oversee the kitchen if chef can't cope.'

'He can usually, but he's had a bit of bad news,' the waiter stammered.

'Again, that is not the paying guest's problem,' said Ebee, losing patience with the excuses.

'What kind of bad news?' asked Karen, taking pity on the young waiter.

'His Aunty Linda was found dead this morning, the worse thing was, she had been alone for weeks.'

'How did they discover her now then?'

'Chef went over to borrow some money, she was ninety next week, and always had a soft spot for him.'

'Didn't get his money then?' said Karen.

'No and the body gave him a shock, so it did.'

'He should have phoned me,' said Ebee, 'he could have took some time off, Bernie would've covered his shift.'

'He didn't like to let you down, anyway, everything is under control now, I'll get your drinks and then you can give me your order.'

'No,' said Ebee, 'you can take our order now, we haven't got all day.'

They both ordered the special dish of the day, and waited with bated breath for it to be served, they both decided on a jug of tap water with slices of lemon, it was too early in the day for alcohol.

The meal was delicious and Ebee quickly forgave the chef for his cockup in the kitchen. He had baked the salmon to melt in your mouth perfection with a thick creamy sauce and prawns covering it, new potatoes, green beans and garden peas were the sides. It was a good choice for lunch, being light yet filling. They both declined dessert, even though the choices on the menu were superb.

'Compliments to the chef,' sighed Ebee as he dabbed at his mouth with a linen napkin.

'Add mine,' smiled Karen, 'that's one of the best meals I've had in a long time.'

They were walking back to the office, Karen was due to take over reception and Ebee was finalising the details for the holiday camp, soft furnishings were to be delivered the following day and then the finishing touches would be complete. Karen turned off to the left and Ebee walked straight on, surprised to see a man waiting outside his office.

'Can I help you?' Ebee asked, not used to people coming to his office in person, usually decisions were made by phone or email, unless it was the planner or safety people.

'Hi, yes, I'm looking for Lou Lavender.'

'I'm afraid she's away at the moment and is not due back for another week.'

'I've just read the local paper and saw the photos.'

'Great aren't they?' grinned Ebee, 'is that why you're here? To make a booking? I can do that for you.'

'No, I'm quite local. I knew Lou ages ago, I just wanted to congratulate her. Who is the young lad in the picture with her?'

'Any reason that you want to know?' stated Ebee, he wasn't about to discuss family business with this dark haired stranger.

'No, not at all, I was just curious. I'll come back when Lou gets back.'

'Sure, shall I tell her who you are?'

'No, it doesn't matter, I can surprise her,' the man smiled widely and left through the main door. Something about him unsettled Ebee and for an instant he felt a cold shiver travel up his spine, this man spelt trouble, he could feel it in his bones.

Chapter 20

The press release worked its magic, booking rang through in a continuous stream and the email in box was full, Karen juggled dates and schedules and cajoled the therapists to cover more shifts, the bribery on more money worked like a charm. It did Ebee's heart good to see the hotel pulsating with life, they had been approached to run classes in the studio, and the dinner dance idea appeared to be just what the village needed. All the tickets for their first event had been sold, and he just hoped that the girls wouldn't mind that they had gone ahead with the plans before gaining permission. Karen had assured him that he was at the helm in their absence and added that if the night was a disaster, at least they had tried and wouldn't lose anything.

As they were approaching May, they had decided on a spring ball, with garlands strewn around the restaurant to portray a May Pole. The studio would be decked out the day before as they had Pilates, Salsa and Zumba classes taking place. They had booked two local bands, deciding that they needed to promote home grown talent. The chefs and waiters that they had employed from the catering college were proof that it worked.

'I'm off now,' Karen stuck her head in Ebee's office, smoothing her skirt down to her knees. She always made an effort, full make-up, jewellery and she had an eye for fashion that drew the eye, it was often commented on, and he knew Karen appreciated the admiring looks that she attracted. Her shoulder length blonde hair always shined and was never neglected. They were lucky to have her on reception, he knew he would have been lost without her these past few weeks while the girls and Jack were away.

'Are you coming back later?' he asked, the duty roster was one thing that wasn't under his supervision.

'Nope, I've got a date,' she grinned.

He looked up from the computer and gave her his full attention, 'really? You kept that quiet, who are you meeting?'

'That cockney chap that works in the butchers, David. Nothing fancy, we're just going for a drink in Butterfinney.'

'He seems like a nice chap, you deserve a night out.'

'So do you,' Karen told him, 'you work so hard and never have any fun time.'

'I enjoy what I do here,' he smiled, 'and when the girls get back I'll take a few days off. I might catch up with the film crew.'

'You must,' Karen agreed. 'See you tomorrow.'

'Have a good time, I'd add don't do nothing I wouldn't do, but that would be pretty boring.'

Karen laughed, and with a waft of Chanelle, she went out into the early evening.

He did need a night out though, but truth be told, he was nervous about going out since the attack. Laughable really, when he was a big man, tall and wide, but he felt vulnerable, especially since he had been hit from behind, someone had been lurking in the shadows and he hadn't sensed their presence. The next person might not be so lucky, unless of course Denton had also been a victim of that same person. Ebee shivered, he would be staying in for a few more nights with the door locked.

He was about to lock up for the night and settle down in his suite, when someone came through the door, it was too late for guests, they hadn't got over-night bookings until the following week. He caught the reflection of someone tall and slim with long hair. He turned around to face them and to his shock discovered Ellen.

'What do you want?' he asked, 'We're closed until tomorrow.'

'Gammon,' she snarled.

'Go and see William, although I'm sure he is also closed.'

'Brin cry den see ban,' Ellen hissed.

'Get out,' Ebee grabbed her scrawny arm and led her to the door. He recoiled as she spat in his face and yanked free from his grip.

'If you come back here,' he grated the words out while wiping his face clean of the woman's saliva with a tissue, 'I'll call the police and get you arrested.'

'Bungen,' she screamed and slammed the glass door behind her.

Ebee locked the door behind her and it was only when he was in the comfort and safety of his own suite that he realised that his legs were trembling. There was something demonic about the woman, she was certainly strange, and he had no idea why she would appear on her own at the hotel.

He had a hot shower, squirting a generous amount of shower gel on his purple sponge, he felt defiled from the fluid contact with the woman and scrubbed his face until it was raw. After he had dried and changed into fleecy joggers and matching sweatshirt, he phoned Karen to tell her what had happened, he needed to share, but it was only after her phone rang out three times, that he remembered that she was out on a date.

The following morning, he felt silly that he had allowed a demented woman to scare him so badly. He looked in the full length mirror and studied his physique, he knew a work out wouldn't come amiss and had looked at taking classes at the gym, but he was in good shape, massive shoulders and arms that could send Ellen from one end of Donegal to the other should he be inclined, but he was not a violent man. He smiled at how the crew often referred to him as the gentle giant and his smile broadened when he remembered Jack mistaking him for a pirate. So why did he turn into a wobbly jelly last night? He sat on the edge of the bed and tried to analyse why he had let that woman affect him so badly. Her language, if that's what it could be called, was weird, she had a wild look in her unusual very pale green eyes, and her long hair was a mixture of white and grey. He would find out what she was doing in the hotel last night, and also, was she safe to be out on her own?

Karen picked up on Ebee's sombre mood as soon as she popped in for their usual early morning coffee. She hoped he didn't mind her going out on a date, but was sure that he understood that their relationship was purely platonic.

'What's up mate?' she asked gently.

'I had a visitor last night, that weird Ellen came a calling.'

'On her own?' Karen had never saw the strange woman out on her own.

'Yes, standing there shouting words, meaningless words as usual.'

'Have you told the guards?'

'No,' he sighed, 'what would be the point?'

'I suppose,' Karen took a sip of her coffee, black with no sugar. She then took a big bite out of her croissant, thickly buttered and covered in strawberry jam.

'I'm wondering if we need to employ a security guard,' Ebee wondered, 'what with the attack and then Ellen's entrance, what would've happened if she had spoken to a guest? They would never come back.'

'Maybe just code the door entrance, you know, after a certain time only guests with keys can gain access.'

'It's like midsummer bloody murders,' Ebee groaned.

'Not quiet,' Karen laughed, 'I'll go over and talk to old Aggie, warn her to keep her sister away.'

'I'll come with you as soon as Josephine comes to take over reception. I could do with getting out of here and to clear my head, she gave me a scare last night and I don't like feeling so vulnerable.'

It was gone eleven when they finally got time to go over to the back strand. The clouds hovered dark and menacing with a threat of heavy rain, the wind was already building up to large gusts that rattled anything that wasn't tied down. A soda can went skipping along the road, gathering speed as the wind shoved it along. They cut across the beach, waves were crashing onto the jagged rocks and sending salt spray into their faces. Karen shivered, the sooner they had a word with the Duffy sisters the sooner they could get back to the warmth of the hotel.

Old Aggie was gathering sticks where the sand met the grassy bent, a ship wreck last month had tossed its wood onto the beach and Aggie was in her element.

'Could we have a word,' Karen asked nicely.

'Just one?' Aggie cackled.

'Did you know that your sister was out on her own last night?'

'I'm not her keeper, Mrs England,' she snarled nastily.

'I didn't say you was,' said Karen, ignoring the jibe, 'but just to let you know, if she comes into the hotel again we will have no choice but to call the police.'

'Of course,' Aggie laughed hysterically, 'and a blind bit of good that would do. She's a law unto herself, I can't control her.'

'Where is she now?' Ebee asked, shivering. He wished he'd put on a warmer jacket than the thin sweatshirt he was wearing.

'I don't know,' spat Aggie, 'go and have a look in the house. My man's coming later, so don't be too long.'

'Your man?' asked Karen, looking at Ebee, who shrugged his large shoulders.

'The doctor,' Aggie rolled her small dark eyes.

Ellen was sitting in a rocking chair with a patchwork shawl around her scrawny shoulders. She was chanting weird words as she gazed into the flames in the open fire. It was a tiny room, with just enough space for two chairs and a small table. A minute scullery led off to the side and another room which they assumed was a bedroom shared by both women, led off the opposite side of the dwelling. It couldn't be classed as a house, Ebee's garage at his old house was bigger than this small brick building.

'Ellen?' Karen asked gently. Ebee was unnerved by this crazy being.

Ellen continued to chant, words they had never heard either English or any other European language.

'Stop chanting and pay attention,' Ebee shouted, exasperated by her. Karen shot him a look, warning him to tread carefully, but he wasn't in the mood, he was at breaking point.

Her head swung around and the pale green eyes swept over them like a laser scanning an item at the supermarket.

'Gumden,' she hissed.

'What?' said Ebee, scratching his smooth brown head.

'Gumden der canta,' she hissed getting to her feet.

'Does that mean get out of here?' wondered Karen.

'Fuck knows,' said Ebee, 'Gumden up your arse,' he said to Ellen loudly, at which point she began to wail, a high pitched noise that threatened to burst their ear drums.

'Let's get out of here,' said Karen, alarmed at this turn of events.

'Gumden up your arse, Gumden you stupid weird bitch,' Ebee was getting into his stride and enjoying every minute. He turned to Karen, 'google Gumden when we get back to the hotel.'

Ellen continued to wail and screech while Ebee reigned all his frustrations down on her head. He felt as though someone had stuck a needle in a boil, the pus was flowing freely and the relief was intense.

'Come on mate,' said Karen, 'I think she's got the point.'

'If you Gumden near Arthur's again, I won't be responsible for my action,' Ebee blasted, 'You are one seriously weird psycho.'

They walked slowly back, each recovering from the trauma of the encounter. The woman should be locked away, Ebee could feel it in his bones. She was not safe to be out and as he felt a cold shiver pass through his body, he knew that she would cause a lot more damage before anything could or would be done to get her out of harm's way.

Mairead had done a fantastic job organising their first dinner dance, or cabaret night she had suggested as a more up to date description. Two groups, a solo artist and a comedian had been booked followed by a disco. The meal was to be served at 7 sharp and the entertainment would begin through the coffee stage, the solo singer, a young man who went under the stage name of Joshua Tree, was going to sing a few ballads, followed by the comedy act and then the tables would be moved back and the room extended to include a dance floor. The group would sing covers of The Beatles, Oasis and Take That. They were amazing, the five members of The Poteen's, were all in their mid-twenties and could play any instrument, all had been classically trained and had met at a college in Dublin, they had travelled the country, using the meagre fee to pay off their student loans and were optimistic about making the big time. Mairead had suggested to them about putting together a demo and sending it to SyCo. She had pointed out that they should try and write their own material and Con, the leader of the band, had assured her that they had hundreds of songs and would be performing some at the event. She wondered if Ebee had any contacts that could come and watch them play.

The dress code was formal, no jeans, trainers or tee shirts. The tickets had been priced at EU50 which would include wine on the tables and 10 percent had been promised to fund the new lifeboat station that was soon to be erected at Gleeman Pier. It was badly needed, so many fisherman and tourists had drowned over the past few years. They had sold two hundred tickets and if the night was successful, they would fine tune it and cater for more the next time. The fact that money was going to a good cause as well as providing a night out, which was local to a lot of them, was a bonus and because they had been able to source local food and use local people to organise and run the event, they managed to not only raise their profile as a venue for functions, but also raise a tidy sum for the charity.

It was a stunning event, every course was superb and compliments were rained down on the chef, who took it all in his stride, proving he was the worthy winner of the selection just a few weeks ago. The wine was savoured yet the bar remained busy, adding to the funds, Ebee and Karen were delighted, as was Mairead who had done a remarkable job with organising the acts.

'It's a grand night,' said Betty Grant, grabbing Ebee's arm, 'I've not had so much fun in a long time, isn't that right Gerry?'

'Yes,' he grinned, draping his arm around Betty's shoulder, 'let's have a dance, I'm in the mood for dancing.'

Ebee rolled his eyes as the Nolans' famous song was being played by the band. He felt proud though, most of the villagers had offered support and those that were unable to come promised to do so the next time. He felt confident that word would spread and they could even get booked out for weddings, the scenery would be stunning for the photographs. He felt someone tap his back and he whirled around to find Karen chuckling.

'What was that for,' he frowned.

'I was giving you a pat on the back,' she smiled widely and took his arm, 'time for us to have a dance, wouldn't you say?'

The slow song had just finished and the lights were on full, people were saying their goodnights, kissing and hugging and reluctant for the night to end when a loud voice piped up,

'What's going on here then?'

Chapter 21

Ebee and Karen whirled around, they were just thanking Mairead for her help when they heard the familiar voice.

'Lou, when did you get back?' Karen gave her a hug, squeezing her tight.

'Just now, we saw the lights on in the hotel and wondered what the hell was happening,' she explained, 'Margaret is getting Jack something to eat.'

'I thought you were back tomorrow,' said Ebee sheepishly.

'Obviously,' said Louise, lifting a finely plucked eyebrow and casting her gaze around the restaurant, noting the garlands adorned to the walls and the band packing away their instruments.

'Please don't be angry,' said Mairead quietly, 'it was my idea, all my fault, the lot of it.'

'You can't take all the credit,' growled Ebee. 'It was a joint idea, Karen too was involved,' he nodded his head towards the person in question, then added, 'in fact, the seed of the idea came from Karen, and you could say that she was the mastermind behind the event.'

'Oh, was she indeed,' Louise spoke sternly, 'well, in that case, I will see you in my office tomorrow at nine sharp, Karen. On that note, it's late and it's been a long day. Good night,' she turned to face Mairead, 'thanks Mairead, I really appreciate your help.' She rubbed her eyes, turned on her heel and headed out the door.

'Well, that went well,' Karen had a slight tremor in her voice.

'Like Lou said, it is late, let's talk about it tomorrow,' sighed Ebee, he was worried, maybe they had over stepped the mark and should have waited for the girls to come back before going ahead with the event, but they wanted to prove it could work and have facts and figures to produce, instead they were caught in the act like naughty school kids.

Louise found Margaret in the kitchen making hot chocolate, 'Is everything okay?'

'I think so,' Louise sank down into the comfy chair by the range, 'while the mice were away,' she sighed.

'What do you mean?' Margaret passed a mug of chocolate to Louise and sat opposite curling her legs and snuggling down into the chair.

'They were wrapping up some sort of party,' Louise took a sip from the mug, 'a band was packing up. They certainly kept that quiet.'

'We'll find out tomorrow, we trusted them remember, anyway, Jack is in bed, I think he's out for the count,' she laughed.

'I think I'll turn in too,' Louise stood up, 'I just need some sleep, I hate turbulence.'

'Are you talking about the flight or the staff?'

'Both,' Louise sighed, she kissed Margaret's cheek and carried her mug into the bedroom, she really hoped their trust wasn't misplaced.

Margaret sipped her chocolate, deep in thought, she had missed Finn, but he hadn't sent an email or text since she had been away and her imagination feared the worst, a good looking fella like him wouldn't sit around and wait for her to come back. She had sent him a post card from Niagara Falls adding that they had planned a trip on the Maid of the mist the following day, but he would have received it weeks ago and hadn't responded.

Jack was accepting Adele and Frank as his grandparents and was not too tearful when they bid them farewell at the airport. Although Adele's promise that she was seriously thinking of taking them up on the offer of a house being built on their land helped. She knew it would be great for Lou to have her parents close at hand, and the built in babysitters would be a bonus, she smiled into her mug, they were on the brink of something big and that was the problem tonight, she knew. The hotel and spa was their baby and they wanted to nurture and send it into the stratosphere. It was like missing a baby's first step and it did hurt, stupidly. She rinsed her mug under the running hot tap and went to get ready for bed, tomorrow was another day, and it was up to them to lay down the ground rules, obviously they had not done so before their trip.

Chapter 22

Louise was at her desk when a timid knock sounded on her door, it was exactly nine sharp just as she had instructed Karen to be there.

'Come in,' she said firmly, Margaret was going to come along in ten minutes, it was agreed that they should handle the situation together. She could tell that Karen was nervous, her face was pale and she could see the wobble in her knees, 'sit down,' Louise smiled, trying to ease the situation. 'We just want to know what happened in our absence, I spoke to Ebee earlier and I've got things from his point of view, and now I just want to hear it from yours. Margaret will be joining us, so we will hold fire until she arrives, I've ordered coffee.

'Thanks,' said Karen with a tremor in her voice.

'You are not in any trouble,' Louise assured her, 'we just need to know why the event took place without us being here.'

'It was my idea,' Karen piped up, hoping that Ebee wouldn't lose his job.

'I gathered that,' Louise sighed, 'Ebee has also told us about the attack, it was terrible.'

'Yes, we still don't know who done it,' stated Karen with fire in her voice.

'It's hard to believe,' said Louise, 'I used to come here in the summer and all of us kids played safe, now there's been a murder and attack in the space of a couple of months.'

'That Ellen is weird, I went over to her house with Ebee, and she was uttering obscenities in her own language, whatever that is.'

'Mum used to warn us to keep away from her,' said Louise, 'something happened when she was younger but she wouldn't tell us.'

'That's worrying.'

'We will have to keep her away from the spa, she can't be allowed to frighten the guests.'

There was a sharp knock on the door and it opened, 'I thought I'd get us all a coffee and cake,' grinned Margaret, closing the door with her backside.

'Have you began proceedings,' she said solemnly placing the tray on the big desk.

'Not yet,' said Louise, glancing at Karen and taking pity on her. 'Drink your coffee and eat your cake, and stop looking so worried.'

Karen explained how the brainstorming had started, explaining that they wanted to showcase the restaurant and let the villagers know what they could offer. 'It was after one of our sessions that Ebee got attacked,' she finished and took a gulp of coffee, and then coughed as it went down the wrong way, causing her to splash some on her bright pink skirt.

'Why didn't you wait until we got back?' queried Margaret.

'I suppose we wanted you to be proud of us, and surprise you.'

'To be honest,' Louise got to her feet and wandered over to the window, noting how high the waves were, the weatherman had warned about a storm on the way from America, 'we did leave Ebee in control and gave him full reign. We have no right to be angry with you, and we are proud,' she looked at Margaret, who nodded her head.

'We were shattered last night, Lou was especially tired, and she didn't get a wink of sleep on the flight.'

'I understand that you were shocked though,' said Karen, 'wanting to go to bed and find the tail end of the function.'

'Tell us about it,' Louise sat down and pulled her chair around to face Karen.

'It was a sort of charity event,' began Karen, 'but we wanted to promote and make money for the hotel too. We made a tidy sum from the bar and a fair bit for the Life Boat station.'

'Did the press come?' asked Margaret.

'No, it didn't seem right without you both being here,' admitted Karen.

'Did many people get up to dance?' Louise asked, she had an idea, but needed some answers first.

'It was packed, but everyone enjoyed it,' Karen told her.

'How many tickets did you sell?'

'200, and that left us full to capacity.'

'What's your thinking, Lou?' Margaret knew her cousin so well, she could almost see the cogs spinning around in her mind.

Louise got up and looked out of the window, it was still windy, the waves continued to crash over the rocks, some were as high as six feet, 'grab your coats, I'll show you, oh, and grab Ebee too.'

'Events were in the pipeline,' Louise told them as they stood outside the restaurant, the wind blowing them almost off their feet, 'and you pre-empted us somewhat,'

'Sorry,' said Karen with a quiver in her voice.

'I'm guessing your thoughts,' laughed Margaret, gazing at the wild beauty that surrounded them, the sea surrounded them and the wind was full of salt and the aroma of sea weed.

Ebee and Karen looked puzzled, yes the view was out of this world, but they didn't get how this would help with future events.

Margaret ran up to Louise and swung her around, 'imagine the potential, weddings, and parties, whatever.'

'Yes,' Louise's eyes were shining but Margaret wasn't sure if it was from the wind or excitement, 'so you think we should do it?'

'Without a doubt, don't you agree?' she looked at Karen and Ebee who were still looking puzzled.

Arm in arm, Louise and Margaret approached them, wobbling a bit as a gust of wind hit them from behind, 'if we had a massive room built just here,' Margaret swept her arms wide, 'reinforced glass, can you imagine how spectacular it would be? We could hold a lot more people and if we had the acoustics right, we could have big names performing, and in the summer we could maybe hold festivals.'

'Like Glastonbury?' screamed Karen, catching their excitement.

'Exactly, and Ebee has some contacts, don't you?' Louise added, noticing that he had gone quiet. 'What's wrong?'

'I will tell you later, but I think it's a great idea and I would love to be part of it. Yes I have contacts, and I admire your vision.'

Louise felt a cold shiver go up her arms, and it wasn't the wind. Something was upsetting Ebee, 'You all get the idea, let's go inside and get a hot drink.'

Karen was on reception duty and Ebee was explaining to Louise and Margaret about his plans.

'I need some time out,' he told them. 'I love it here and it feels like home, but I have personal stuff to sort out back home. I've realised that when I took the job with the film crew, it was to escape, and it was only by being here for so long that I figured it out. The bang on the head also made me think.'

'We need you, Ebee,' said Louise, nearly in tears.

'Yes, we can't cope without you,' added Margaret.

'I will be back,' he said gently, 'but I can't promise when. I do need a holiday, somewhere warm, and when I've sorted my head out, I will join your new venture. The yurts and cabins are ready to be booked up.'

Louise could feel tears welling and sliding down her cheek, Ebee was their rock.

'When were you thinking of going?' Margaret asked over the lump in her throat.

'Next weekend, that will give me a chance to sort out travel arrangements.'

'Where are you thinking of going?' Louise blew her nose.

'I've always wanted to go to the Indian Ocean, so maybe Mauritius, or the Maldives.'

'Sounds brilliant,' Louise sniffed, knowing that they were being selfish, they wouldn't have done half of what they had accomplished with his help, and she intended that they give him a big bonus to help with his trip, it was the least they could do.

A week later Margaret and Louise were at Belfast International airport saying goodbye to Ebee. At first he had refused the big cheque the girls had given him, but after imploring everything that he had done, broadening their vision and giving them more food for thought in return, for example the new nightclub they had planned, work was going ahead after the summer season had finished, they didn't want the upheaval of building work going on when they were full to capacity, and they were fully booked into September not only at the hotel, but also the yurts and cabins.

'Promise to send a postcard,' Margaret smiled through her tears.

'Have you got our address?' quipped Louise, her eyes were streaming too.

'I'll be back before you can say, Ebee Hedron,' he grinned.

'If we need you, can we call you back?' asked Margaret seriously.

'You won't be able to contact me,' Ebee told her, 'I'm sorting my head out, so no phones or electronic devices of any description.'

'How will you cope?' Margaret knew he was addicted to his phone and iPad.

'I will find out,' he sighed, knowing that it wouldn't be easy. He wasn't finding the emotional good byes easy either, he thought a lot of his girls, as he had come to think of them. But if he didn't go now, he knew he never would. He was flying from Belfast to Birmingham, and after a quick catch up with friends and family in Nuneaton, he was then catching a flight from Gatwick to Sir Seewoosagur Ramgoolam International airport. With the hefty cheque safely banked in his account, he was able to book a five star hotel and intended to clear his mind for a week of everything, all the clutter and past regrets, and with a clear outlook, he would know which step to take next.

Chapter 23

It took weeks of interviews and eliminations before they found someone to take Ebee's place. Brodie Edmondson was an American tracing his Irish roots and had come to County Donegal to find the descendants of his great grandfather, Macaulay Edmondson. He had reddish brown hair, twinkly green eyes and an infectious laugh. To the girls, it was obvious that Karen was smitten with him and teased her relentlessly.

'I've got a boyfriend,' she protested, much too profusely for them to believe her. Yes, she was seeing someone but it wasn't serious, she only saw him once a week and that was a conservative dinner date in Butterfinney. They agreed as they sipped the hot chocolate of an evening, that they would be perfect together.

Brodie had an easy way with people, staff readily completed any task he set them and he took charge of any problems that the guests might have. Nothing was too much trouble and he was soon a firm favourite with the guests and staff. He had moved into Ebee's apartment and used the gym and pool every day.

'He's got some abs on him,' Louise remarked to Margaret. Brodie was chatting to the workmen on the new development site, the sun was at its zenith and he was taking advantage of the rays, discarding his tee-shirt and baring his toned body. The plans had been submitted, Finn had spent hours going over them with the girls. Margaret was upset that he was keeping his distance, being friendly but civil, and not engaging in anything deeper than, how many toilets would you need?

'Yes, but he works at it,' Margaret sighed, knowing that she would love the time to work out.

'We should make time to do other stuff,' Louise said thoughtfully. 'All we do is work and go home, even Jack has more fun than us.'

'I don't mind,' sighed Margaret, 'Finn has moved on to someone else.'

'Where did you hear that?' Louise was shocked, she knew how close they had been before going away

'I didn't hear anything, but he is distant and cool, it's obvious.'

'Take a shot at Brodie then,' Louise giggled, 'Karen said she doesn't want him.'

'You take a bloody shot at him,' Margaret hit her arm.

'I'm off men,' Louise stated, 'I'd rather be celibate.'

'You're right about having a bit of fun though, its dull having too much work and no play.'

'Why don't we go into Letterkenny? We could stay over at that new hotel, steal some ideas. Your dad could look after Jack, or Mairead, she wouldn't mind.'

'That's a great idea,' Margaret had perked up, 'we could try that new nightclub, The Blue Lagoon in Doon.'

They summoned Karen to the office after a quick lunch of salad and chicken, they had decided to work on their bodies, starting with a good diet. They were both slim but their diet of wine and chocolate had sapped their energy.

'Is everything alright? Ebee's okay isn't he?' Karen came in, all of a fluster.

'Everything is fine, take a seat,' Louise smiled.

'We're planning a night out in Letterkenny and wondered could you take the helm.' Margaret asked, 'we need some time out, but if you can't we'll understand.'

'Are you sure you can trust me?'

'Of course, just don't go planning any events, well, not until we are all involved,' Louise winked.

'Yes no problem, and while I'm here could I book a couple of weeks off? I haven't been home for a while and I need a catch up with my mum.'

'It's a deal, and you're right, we have been selfish. When were you thinking?' said Louise.

'The end of September would be good, the summer rush will be almost over.'

'I can't believe how well we've done,' Margaret said, 'all the yurts and cabins are booked out, the hotel is full and all treatments are going strong, and its only our first year.'

'It's just as well,' Louise stated, 'its going to cost a bomb to build the nightclub.'

'It will be worth it though,' said Margaret cheerfully, 'I've already emailed Ed Sheeran and Harry Styles.'

'You haven't?' Karen gasped, gripping the table so tight that her knuckles turned white.

'Yes, I have, they haven't replied yet though,' she pouted.

'I'm not surprised,' laughed Louise, 'you need to go through their agents.'

'Ah, of course,' Margaret sighed, Louise and Karen laughed, but the idea wasn't so far- fetched, one day, they would be able to book superstars from all over the world.

They had booked a twin room in Rockhill House, two miles from the centre of Letterkenny. It was an impressive hotel with old world charm. It was also near to Glenveigh National Park and they planned to visit there before going home the next day. The grounds of the Rockhill were impressive with a gold fountain just outside the main entrance. Margaret had taken several photos with her new camera, bought from duty free at the airport in Canada.

'Just imagine if we copied some of these designs,' she sighed, we could have some benches and maybe a couple of those big swings over-looking the wild Atlantic.'

'Maybe next year,' Louise wondered if they were trying to do too much too soon. The nightclub, or venue or whatever they decided upon, was a massive project and would need a vast injection of cash, which they didn't have at the moment.

'I love this room,' Margaret was applying mascara and sipping red wine from an enormous glass that she had put in her case.

'It's very elegant,' agreed Louise, who was already dressed in a pair of tight fitting black jeans, ankle boots with a heel and a royal blue fitted shirt, emphasising her big blue eyes. She had spiked her blonde hair with gel and looked stunning.

Margaret had decided on a pair of white jeans and red silk shirt, setting off her glossy dark hair.

'You look fabulous, mate,' said Louise, taking a gulp of wine from her equally large glass.

'Thanks, cuz, so do you.'

They had ordered a taxi to take them to the Blue Lagoon at Doon, and they were waiting in reception when it arrived.

The doorman whistled as he opened the door to the night club, loud music blasted their eardrums as they made their way to the dance area. There was quite a queue at the bar, but the men ushered them forward, until they were quickly served, they ordered a bottle of red wine and two glasses and carried it to a table away from the big speakers.

'I think I'm too old for this,' Margaret filled her glass, 'the music is so loud I can't hear myself think.'

'The aim is not to think,' Louise gently pushed her arm, 'the aim is to get blathered and have a good time, drink up and we will boogie on the dance floor.'

'Bloody hell, what decade is that from?'

'Dunno, it's something my mum used to say.'

The music covered all genres over the last three decades, they danced every dance and only sat down when the tempo changed to a slow number.

'We should have got some water,' Louise complained, taking a big swig of wine.

'We can get some at the hotel, tap water,' Margaret chuckled.

Across the floor, out of sight, Gerard was watching the girls intently. Now he knew that they were back from their travels, he would make his move.

'Everyone's deserting us,' Margaret sighed as she lay on the luxurious bed in their room.

'Ebee will be back,' said Louise, hoping that was true, 'and Karen is only going away for a week or so.'

'What if Ebee doesn't come back,' Margaret was near to tears, too much wine and melancholy Louise thought.

'He will and if he decides to stay away too long, we will track him down.'

'Finn's giving me the brush off,' she gulped, 'he's hardly said two words since we've been back from Canada.'

'Have you asked him why?' asked Louise.

'No, but I hear that he's seeing someone in the village.'

'Silly gossip, just ignore it and get to the bottom of it.'

'I might,' Margaret sighed, 'I'm going to get ready for bed, sorry to be on a downer.'

'I know what you mean though,' Louise was feeling a bit down herself, 'everything is going according to plan, yet something is missing. I think we should go carefully with the planned venue, we should get to grips with what we have already accomplished.'

'I agree, and it's a headache getting the right staff, and no sooner do we find the perfect person when they up and leave.'

'It might be an idea to get some students in from Letterkenny, Josephine has been a godsend stepping in between her busy family life but we need more tangible help, and students would cover the holiday season. They can stay in the cabins during the winter, term time of course. The suite that Ebee used could be let out cheaply, like an apprenticeship.'

'I thought Brodie had claimed the suite, and we would need someone qualified to train them,' yawned Margaret sleepily.

'It's just ideas, we can look into it, good night, let's try and get to sleep.'

They both slept deeply awaking at nine thirty, Louise filled the kettle before Margaret had a shower, and after drinking her tea, Louise had one, while Margaret dried her hair.

They compared the hotel with their own, taking notes of what they could use, even at breakfast they took everything in, and had so many ideas that they could take on board better ways of doing things. But they also agreed that they would do things differently, adding their own personal stamp, they wanted to be quirky and unforgettable.

Driving up the Tulcan Road, they noticed Colm Sharkey outside his massive house on a ladder, 'back for a holiday?' Margaret wound down her window and shouted at him.

'Yeh, doing a few repairs before Wayne and his family come over for a few weeks.'

'Don't forget to tell them about our spa,' Margaret grinned, 'Amy and the girls would love our pool.'

'I've heard all about that posh place on the hill from Tamara and Sammantha,' he shouted down from his ladder, mindful not to fall like he did a few years ago when he was sorting out the aerial.

They waved goodbye and drove the short distance to their cottage. Jack was staying another day with Mairead so after a quick cup of tea, they went to check on Karen at the hotel. She was relieved to see them and appeared agitated.

'What's wrong?' asked Louise, 'has something happened to Ebee?'

'No, my dad has fallen down the stairs and is in hospital, mum wants me to go home as soon as possible, but I've told her I can't go until you come back, and even then, I can't leave you both in the lurch.'

'Calm down,' said Margaret gently, 'we will have to manage. Go and book a flight and we can get Mairead to cover for a few days until we can find someone more permanent.'

'I won't lose my job will I?' Karen was on the verge of tears, her dad had broken an arm, but was comfortable, and she could come back in a few weeks.

'Don't be daft, your part of the family now.'

'Thanks Louise, and I will get back as soon as possible. I'm going to drive over, it will be easier to drive to Larne and get a ferry.'

'If you're sure,' Louise told her, 'one of us could drive you to Belfast airport.'

'No, I'll drive, that way I will have my car over there.'

They could both see the sense in that, and while Margaret took over the reception, Louise helped Karen pack bags.

'I'll ring when I get to Nuneaton,' Karen promised.

'Make sure you do, and drive safely, there are speed cameras on the Glenshane pass.'

'I will,' they hugged and Karen locked the door of her little home.

Louise waved until the yellow beetle was out of sight.

She ran up the hill, realising that she needed to run more and had got out of the habit, but with the task of finding new staff, she knew she would have to get up at the crack of dawn to do so.

Chapter 24

Karen had tears in her eyes as she drove up the hill towards the ruins of the old church, across the road was a waterfall that she hadn't yet had a chance to visit. She noticed an elderly woman walking towards the village and slowed down,

'Would you like a lift?'

'Yes, please my dear, I would be most grateful,' the woman climbed into the passenger seat and Karen got a whiff of something unpleasant, wishing she had drove past her, but then feeling mean for thinking it.

'I'll drop you by William's' Karen smiled, knowing it wasn't too far. She turned to face the woman and recoiled in horror when she realised that she had she let Ellen get in her car. Ellen was also pointing a gun at Karen's chest.

'You can take me to the doc's house,' Ellen snarled, 'and be quick about it.'

'But I have to get a ferry home,' Karen felt as though a hand was squeezing her heart, 'my parents need me.'

'Well, that's too bad English woman,' she spat, spittle circled in the air like dust mites.

'I can take you to the doctor's house, and then get my ferry,' Karen said hopefully.

'No chance, you've seen the gun now, it's too late.'

'You pulled out the gun,' shouted Karen, anger consuming her, 'I didn't ask you to.'

'Whatever, keep driving.'

Karen manoeuvred the car up the Ballina road, accelerating over the craters that were classed as pot holes, causing Ellen to bounce off the seat. But she clung onto the gun and it didn't waver from Karen's chest. The doctor's house was a white washed two story building with a small front garden. The house needed a coat of paint and the weeds were choking the wispy flowers that were growing wild. Most of the houses along the row were holiday lets and all but one were empty.

Karen slammed on the brake, bringing the car to an abrupt halt, 'out you get,' she told the mad woman, 'you're home.'

'No, dearie, out you get,' she leant over and sounded the horn, letting the blast take several seconds until Aggie appeared at the gate.

'What's going on?'

'Brought you a present,' Ellen cackled. 'Get out,' she ordered Karen.

'I need to get home,' Karen spoke to Aggie, 'my dad's in hospital.'

'But you've seen the gun now,' Aggie sighed, 'it's too late.'

Doctor Swain arrived at the scene then, and made a decision, he opened the driver's side door and pulled at Karen, and when she didn't budge, he unclasped her seat belt, the smell of nicotine made her gag.

'Get off me,' she shouted, trying to push him away and close the door, but then Aggie joined in and with the gun still pointing at her chest and the other two dragging at her, Karen found herself on her knees on the damp grass. Aggie jumped in the small car and drove it around the back of the house, ensuring that it was out of view.

'I need to go home,' Karen sobbed, 'I haven't done anything to you, why are you doing this to me?'

'Ellen has taken a fancy to you, just humour her for a while and we can let you go,' Swain yanked Karen to her feet and pulled her towards the house.

'And why is Ellen talking English all of a sudden? It doesn't make sense.'

'Just don't upset her,' Swain warned, there's no telling what the lass will do.'

'Lass?' Karen hissed, feeling hysteria build in her chest, 'she's not a lass, she's a crone.'

'Gurden,' Ellen hissed, and then slapped Karen hard across the face.

Karen felt tears smart her eyes, her cheek was throbbing and fury was building in her stomach, she was normally easy going and placid.

'You're a psycho,' Karen yanked away and kicked Ellen in the shin, enjoying the contact with her bony shin. Ellen screamed in pain and let go of the gun. Karen picked it up and held it towards Swain and Ellen.

'Get me my car,' she ordered, her hand was shaking but she held the gun tight with her finger covering the trigger.

'Okay, okay,' spluttered Swain, holding up his hands, 'I'll go get Aggie to bring it round.'

'Any funny business and the witch gets it,' Karen warned grimly. She kept the gun trained on Ellen's chest while Swain hurried off to retrieve the car.

Karen could hear it approach but it didn't slow down, and as it clipped Karen's legs, her finger squeezed the trigger. Karen heard the scream just before she lost conscious.

Chapter 25

'Karen has only been gone a day and I miss her,' sighed Louise.

'Well, she doesn't miss us,' Margaret said sulkily, 'she hasn't even sent a text to say she got there.'

'We don't know what's going on over there,' reasoned Louise, 'her dad might have taken a turn for the worse and she hasn't had time.'

'No, I've got a bad feeling, I don't think she'll be back.'

'For god's sake, Margaret, what's wrong with you today?'

'I spoke to Finn, he said there's no future for us, and so that's that.'

'Did he say why?'

'Apparently, we are not compatible, there's plenty more fish in the sea,' she said unconvincingly.

Louise didn't get it, Finn was or at least had been, besotted with Margaret, but she realised that since they had returned from Canada, he had kept his distance.

'He'll come around when he's ready,' she put her arm around Margaret's shoulder, 'We're going to be busy for the next few weeks,' she smiled, 'no time for romance and stuff.'

Margaret sniffed, 'I know, we need to get more staff, bookings are up for the yurts and the cleaners are working flat out. Karen was so organised.'

'Brodie is doing an amazing job though, he knows how to organise the staff, and he's stepped into Ebee's shoes, even if they are a bit loose.'

Margaret managed a small laugh, 'Oh, I forgot to tell you, Marjory Hollis sent an email, you know that keep fit instructor in Letterkenny. She wants to know if we're interested in running classes up here, she's got some people, her words, that would like classes in our area.'

'That could be good,' Louise said thoughtfully, 'we did talk about using the studio for classes, Zumba would be a great class, and I'd do it.'

'I wouldn't mind a bit of Pilates,' Margaret searched the emails, 'shall I tell her to come in for a chat?'

'Yeh, why not, make it Friday afternoon around three, we need to start interviewing ASAP.'

'The quicker we get a new receptionist the better,' she sighed, 'Mairead does her bit, but she can't do every day.'

'Di and Julie from the upper hotel said they could share shifts,' Louise said, knowing that they would be poaching staff from their competition, 'they're saving for a cruise around the med.'

'That could work, at least they are experienced.'

They both looked up when there was a knock on the door and Brodie entered, his face was flushed and his blond hair was ruffled.

'Any news of Karen?' he asked, 'Only she said she would let me know when she arrived.'

'Not a dickie bird,' said Margaret, 'she was going to let us know too.'

'I'm sure that there is a good reason why she hasn't been in touch,' Louise was beginning to worry, it wasn't like Karen. 'Have you tried her mobile?'

'Yes, but it went to voice mail,' said Brodie, I wondered if you had a landline number for her.'

'No, I've sent her emails but if she's at the hospital she won't have got them.'

Margaret watched the exchange with a frown, 'Phone the ferry company.'

'What? What the hell for?' said Louise.

'Somethings not right.'

'Who did she travel with?'

'I don't know, Stena? P and O? Or was she going to Holyhead?' Margaret could feel her voice getting higher, why hadn't they asked her which route she was going to take?

'Calm down, if she had been in an accident we would've heard something.' Louise touched Margaret's arm, the panic in her cousin's voice was making her heart race.

'Not if it had happened on the M6 or one of those twisty roads in Wales.'

'Next thing you'll have her dead in a ditch, or unconscious out of sight of passing motorists.'

'Very funny, Lou, you explain why Karen hasn't been in contact then.'

'It's only been twenty four hours since she left, give it another day before our imagination runs wild.'

'Surely her Mom has a number you can contact,' they had forgotten Brodie, he had witnessed their raving.

'But we don't know what it is,' said Margaret slowly, 'if we did, we would have phoned her.'

'But don't you have directory enquiries?' he asked reasonably.

'Ex-directory,' Louise explained, 'I tried earlier.'

'So you are worried,' Margaret was triumphant.'

'Yes, of course I am, but I'm trying to stay calm and logical.'

'Best way, I'm thinking,' said Brodie, 'If Karen is at the hospital, worried about her dad, well, phoning or texting any of us would be the last thing on her mind.'

'Put like that,' grinned Louise with a relieved sigh.

'Anyway,' Brodie flashed them a huge smile, 'I called in to say a big party have just booked three of the cabins, from your neck of the woods too, I believe.'

Louise leaned forward with interest, 'really? Are they from Oxford?'

'Yes, near Summertown, they are coming as a team building experience.'

'I used to live in Summertown, I worked in an office near the university, what name is the booking under? It would be funny if I knew them, it's a big place. '

'Kim Carson, she sounds fun.'

'Oh My God,' Lou squealed, she was as excited a child at Christmas, 'I worked with Kim, she's great.'

'It would be a perfect opportunity to start those classes, and I have a few other ideas to run past you, oh, the booking is for twelve with the prospect of another four joining later.'

'How are we going to cope?' Margaret got to her feet, 'we are two major staff down and have nowhere near the cover we need.'

'I'm willing to do extra shifts, till Ebee gets back,' Brodie was so easy going, Louise could see why Karen liked him.

'Wonderful, that will help, and we have back to back interviews over the next few days, we're still sticking with the training on the job, using local talent, it's cheaper and the successful applicants gain experience.'

'It's a great idea, would you both like to come out for a drink tonight? I'm getting sick of my own company,' Brodie looked expectantly from one to the other.

'You go ahead, Marg,' said Louise, 'I'm taking Jack to see that new Star Wars film,' she laughed, 'the one Ebee was involved with at Malin.'

'Seems ages ago,' Margaret sighed, 'so much has happened since then.'

'You miss the big guy?' asked Brodie

'Yes, we both do,' said Louise, 'He'll be back when he's ready.'

'So, Margaret, would you like to go out tonight? Maybe a meal and a drink?'

'Do you know what,' smiled Margaret, 'I'd love to, I haven't been out for a while, well not without Lou, so yes, let's hit the town.'

'I'll pick you up at six,' Brodie ran his fingers through his hair, 'I'd better go and make myself presentable.'

'See you later, smooth operator,' Margaret grinned.

'I told you there were more fish in the sea,' she said to Louise after the door closed behind him.

'Not that one,' Louise warned, 'Karen likes him.'

'I thought she was seeing that guy from the village.'

'Oh, that was just a couple of drinks and a game of darts in the Swinging Diddies, I think she's quite smitten with Brodie.'

'I was joking, I don't fancy him, but it will be nice to go out with anyone that isn't you,' Margaret laughed, showing she didn't mean it.

'I know what you mean, we've been joined at the hip for what seems forever.'

Chapter 26

Karen opened her eyes and winced when a searing pain shot through her head. She was lying in a narrow bed with bars at the sides at the top end, and she realised it was the type that might be used in a hospital. Across the room was a similar bed where a woman with a bandage on her face occupied. It was a large room, but clinical, and Karen remembered with horror that she was at Doctor Swain's surgery, or what was once his surgery since he had retired years ago.

'Ah, you're awake, Karen. How are you feeling?' Swain asked, with concern.

'How do you think I feel,' she spat, 'I should be in England, my father needs me, not trussed up here with a blinding headache and my leg in a caste.'

'Calm down, dear, we will look after you.'

'I don't want to bloody calm down, just get me out of here, let me phone Lou or Marg, they will get me.'

'No can do, I'm afraid. Ellen has tipped over the edge, and thanks to your erratic shooting, her face is badly damaged.'

'It won't make any difference,' Karen said scathingly, 'the woman is as ugly as sin, and whatever damage I might have done will be an improvement.'

'There's no need to be so mean,' Swain's voice was sickingly sweet, 'I'll get you some nice broth and homemade bread.'

Karen lay back and put her head on the pillow, she was at their mercy, at least until her leg had healed and that could take weeks. Ellen groaned a guttural sound that sounded more animal than human.

'It's all your fault, you stupid woman,' Karen shouted in the direction of the bed Ellen was trussed up in.

'Eeek, Eeek,' Ellen screamed, the decibels so high that Karen though her eardrums might bleed with the pain, the sound was like a seal in the sanctuary at Gweek in Cornwall.

'Shut up,' Karen begged.

Ellen stopped the screeching but the noise was replaced with harsh sobs, Karen couldn't decide which was worse, the woman was so screwed up, she had severe mental issues. Yet, she was speaking English, before Karen let her get in the car. None of it made sense.

'Here you are my dear,' Swain was carrying a tray with a bowl of weak broth and a wedge of weird looking bread. 'My dear Aggie made it,' he smiled showing his nicotine stained teeth.

'I'm not hungry,' Karen told him, 'and can you shut that old crone up, she's giving me a headache.'

Swain placed the tray on a cabinet and strolled over to a medicine cabinet above a stainless steel sink, he rummaged around until he found what he was looking for. Karen saw the syringe in his hand and flinched, she wished she had kept quiet about the godam soup. She saw a thin stream of liquid emitted into the air, and then he walked towards Ellen and she saw him plunge the needle into her.

'That will keep her quiet for a few hours, have your soup, it will give you strength.'

'If I do, will you let me phone home?'

'I'll think about it,' Swain grinned, 'drink it up, there's a good girl.'

Karen had no choice, Swain stood over her while she finished every last drop of the vile liquid and disgusting rough bread.

'Good girl,' Swain said patronisingly, 'now have a little sleep.'

Karen could feel her eye lids close and realised that the bastard had put something in the foul crap he had forced her to eat.

Chapter 27

'Did you enjoy the film?' Louise and Jack were having pizza in Butterfinney, a shiny new place that had only opened the week before.

'Yeh, it was great, but I really miss Ebee,' he sighed.

'He'll be back, he just needed a break, look how hard he's worked over the past few months.'

'I guess,' Jack finished the cola and wiped his mouth on a serviette, 'and we've had a holiday, so it's only fair.'

'Exactly,' Louise smiled at her son, he had grown up so much since moving to Ireland.

'Can I get you anything else?' a young lad was asking, he had bright blue eyes and blonde hair.

'I'd like a strawberry sundae, what about you Jack?'

'Chocolate, please,' he grinned at the waiter.

'Are the drinks refillable?' Louise asked.

'Yes, would you like me to get them for you?'

'That's lovely of you,' Louise read his name tag, 'Josh, but Jack here can manage.'

'Can I?' Jack asked cheekily as Josh the waiter hurried away to get their ice creams.

'Yes, I'll have an orange juice, please.'

'Can I ask you something?' Louise asked as Josh put the sundaes on the table.

'Okay,' replied the boy, feeling puzzled, he hadn't worked here very long; he was saving for his college fees and driving lessons.

'Do they pay you well?'

'The tips make up for the salary,' said Josh diplomatically.

'Where do you live?'

'Mum, what are you doing? Leave Josh alone,' Jack was embarrassed by his mother.

'Just off the Clodbury road,' Josh told her, 'I travel here on my bike.'

'Do you know the new spa hotel, Cheyanne?'

'Of course, everyone knows it.'

'How would you like to work there? We are looking for new staff, you would be perfect. Come and see us tomorrow and we can talk business.'

Josh blushed, it was a lot nearer to travel to the spa than the pizza place, 'thanks, I'll come around two if that's okay.'

'Perfect,' she said and grinned at Jack. 'Always look out for an opportunity,' she told him, sagely.

When Josh brought over the bill, Louise gave him a twenty euro note as a tip, the lad was delighted, but not as much as Louise with her find, she had plans for the good-looking Josh.

Margaret and Brodie were sitting around the bar at The Pink Turnip in the village. A three piece band were playing songs by request from all popular genres. They all looked to be around eighteen to twenty.

'They're very good,' Margaret commented to the barman as he served them drinks. She was drinking a local cider, Stag, while Brodie sampled the Guinness.

'Aye, they are that,' said Bernard the barman, 'they come in every Friday.'

'Would they be tempted to play on a Saturday at the spa?'

'I don't know,' he grunted, 'I'm not their bloody agent.'

'Do you want me to ask them,' Brodie could see the excitement in Margaret's eyes and guessed these young musicians would be an asset on the planned dances they had in the pipeline.

'Would you?' Margaret asked gratefully, 'the boys are great, and the teenagers would love them.'

The band, who were yet to choose a name, loved the idea of performing live to a room full of teenagers, Margaret was ecstatic, their vision of a place where youngsters could go and have fun, was coming together.

'We will have to find a name for you,' she grinned.

'What about, The Brodie Bunch?' laughed Brodie.

'Can we think about it and let you know?' asked the leader of the band, Mitch, a tall thin lad with a mop of dark curly hair, and a cheeky grin.

'Of course, there's no rush,' Margaret told him, 'come out and see us tomorrow, we can have a chat about it all then.'

She linked her arm through Brodie's as they walked back along the Crostoneel road, it was pitch black, with just the lights from the few houses dotted about, to give them light. The moon was a sliver of amber in a velvet dark sky, dotted with millions of stars. It was a night for romance and as she held on to Brodie's arm, a tear slid down her cheek. Finn was the only man for her, and she knew Brodie would much rather be with Karen, the missing Karen and Margaret had a feeling of foreboding, something wasn't right, she would have phoned or sent a message by now, even if it only to let them know how her father was doing.

At breakfast the following morning, the girls competed to tell their exciting news, both had found talent and wanted to discuss it.

'You should see him,' Louise said, 'cute as hell, the girls will love him.'

'The band are amazing, they're coming up later, you can hear them,' Margaret was bouncing around, 'they cover any tracks, just wait till you hear them.'

'Josh is coming at two, let's call a meeting with Brodie and run a few ideas past him, should we give Mairead a ring too?'

'I think we should, this is the start of another phase,' grinned Margaret.

The phone on the wall rang and Louise, being the nearest, picked up the receiver. Margaret watched Louise's expression and felt that dread from last night.

'She left here two days ago,' she was saying, 'we wondered why we hadn't heard anything, but her mobile is switched off and we didn't have a contact number for her home.' Margaret passed Louise a pen and pad and she scribbled numbers down, 'I'll call you as soon as we find out what's happened.'

How is your husband? Oh, that is good news, we will tell Karen as soon as we find out where she is, or if she turns up, please let us know,' she placed the receiver back in its cradle.

'That was Karen's mum, Karen hasn't turned up,' Louise looked stricken.

'Time to do a bit of investigation,' sighed Margaret, 'we need to retrace her steps.'

Ebee had returned to his home town of Nuneaton to discover grey skies and dreary buildings, even the people had an air of misery about them, but to be fair, it was through his eyes only. The beach holiday had been just what the doctor had ordered but after the third week of lying around watching films on his iPhone, Ebee was bored and needed to get back into the action of his life. He had been back home for a week and had decided to re-join his mates on the film set in California, they were doing a remake of Gone with the wind, and his crew mate, Bartie, had asked him to go out there, all expenses paid, he said that they all missed him.

It had been good for him to catch up with his family, they were used to his wanderlust and not surprised that he was looking at flights to Los Angeles and with the beauty of Skype and Facetime, Ebee was constantly in touch, although he did manage to make his brother green with envy from his pictures of the pristine beaches in the Maldives.

'I'm going into Bedworth for a few things,' he told them, the neighbouring town was a bit of an escape and something was tugging at him to go there.

'See you later, then,' said Mrs Hedron, 'I'll cook your favourite meal later.'

'Thanks,' Ebee closed the door behind him, he didn't even realise that he had a favourite meal anymore. He was quite looking forward to discovering what his mother would create for him.

His car had been kept in the garage since he had set off from home a few years ago and he decided he would take it out for a run, unless it had ceased up. He turned the key in the ignition and grinned with satisfaction as it purred into life. His dad had told him to sell it when he had outlined his plans, but Ebee was adamant, it was his baby, he had bought the Jaguar XR2 from new and it still gleamed like a shiny boy's toy.

He wound the roof down and set off down the triple four bypass towards Bedworth, the wind was cold against his skin but he relished it, he felt invigorated and alive and something was stirring deep inside his gut, but it was elusive, he couldn't quite catch what it all meant, but he did know that somehow, Bedworth held the key.

He parked his precious car at the top of the multi storey car park, well away from any other car, and got the lift down to the town exit. He made his way up the main street, letting instinct be his guide. The aroma of freshly ground coffee lured him into a small café where the chocolate cakes on display tempted Ebee into ordering a large slice of a creamy mousse concoction and a frothy cappuccino. There was an empty table near the back and he carefully carried his tray over to it, bumping into the back of a chair holding a lady on the way.

'I am so sorry,' he said, 'there's not much space between the tables,' he explained, not mentioning his size.

'Don't worry,' the woman had a gentle smile but she looked rather pale, he thought.

Ebee went to move away when she reached out and touched his arm, 'would you like to join us?'

'Are you sure?' he glanced at the lady's husband who had a bemused expression on his face, and the table was rather small for three.

'Please,' she insisted, 'we've finished our cake,' she moved their cups to one side.

Ebee reluctantly sat down at the table that was meant for two and tried to eat his cake without hitting them with his elbows.

'Can I ask you something?' the lady was looking intently at him and he could feel his cheeks burn, he had never felt so uncomfortable in all his life.

'Of course,' Ebee said after swallowing a mouthful of cake.

'It may sound odd, but do you know Karen?'

'I do know a Karen,' he smiled, 'but it might not be the same one.'

'Is your name Ebee Hedron?' she asked slowly.

'Yes,' he was surprised, 'I don't think we've met before.'

'No,' she told him, 'we haven't met, but we've heard all about you from Karen. She raved about how she had bumped into an old friend and how they were working together at some fancy spa in County Donegal.'

'I'm delighted to meet you,' Ebee beamed, putting his fork on the table. 'How is she? I've been away for a few weeks.'

'I don't know,' she cried, 'Karen has gone missing. We don't know where she is.' Ebee watched in horror as the poor woman sobbed into a tissue.

'Yes lad,' Karen's dad explained, 'she was on her way over to see me but didn't turn up.'

Ebee finished his cake and coffee while they explained what had happened, the fall and the broken arm and the expected visit from their beloved daughter that didn't happen.

Ebee got to his feet, 'It was very nice to meet you both, I will go to Ireland tomorrow and will not rest until I find out what has happened to her.'

Chapter 28

Louise was in the office, the group from Oxford were due to arrive at the weekend and she had made sure that there was plenty to entertain them, the young lads were booked to play along with an up and coming young dee jay who went by the name of Cody Ray. Vikki Hughes had agreed to run Pilates classes and would do so on a regular basis if the demand was there. The only thing to mar the excitement was Karen, despite asking everyone in the village, they had drawn a complete blank. She was in the process of sending an email to the Derry Journal, when the door opened, expecting Margaret, Louise sighed and said, 'about time, I'm dying for a cuppa.'

'Is that right?' said a familiar voice, 'I'll go and get one from the café I saw on the way in.'

Louise shot around in her chair and saw a fleeting glimpse of dark hair, 'what the hell are you doing here?' she raged, getting to her feet and running towards the door.

'Who are you talking to?' Margaret was carrying two mugs and had a box tucked under one arm, 'sorry I'm late, you must be gasping.'

'I wasn't talking to anyone,' Louise grabbed a mug from Margaret, 'did you see Gerard?'

'No of course not, why would I?'

'Because he was here in the office,' Louise took a gulp of coffee, 'shit, it's hot.'

'I've just made it,' Margaret responded, dryly. 'Why would he be in the office? You must be doing too much.'

Louise went back into the office and sat back on the chair, 'he was here,' she sighed, 'he's gone to get a drink.'

'I've made you a tuna salad sandwich,' Margaret passed her the box, 'there's crisps in there, I had a snack in the village. I was talking to Patrick, he's been talking to a few mates working on the ferries, no- one of Karen's description boarded at Larne or Belfast. Unless she travelled from Dublin, which wouldn't make sense.'

'Who's Karen?'

'Bloody hell, you were right, what are you doing here Gerard?'

'I went to get Lou a drink, but I can see she already has one.'

'Funny haha, why are you here?'

'I wanted a chat with Lou, I read the article in the paper a few weeks ago, and then I saw you both at the dance in Letterkenny.'

'So?' Louise found her voice, 'that still doesn't explain why you are here.'

Gerard put the cups he had been carrying on the desk, 'I don't want to fight; I just want answers.'

'So we're doing a quiz now,' Louise sighed, 'well, I'm not in the mood for them or do we have the time. This is a business, not a meeting place for long lost friends,' she put a finger to her head, 'oh, I forgot, we are not friends, lost or otherwise, so clear off.'

'Why did you run out on me,' he sat down in one of the chairs away from the desk.

Margaret pulled out another one and sat down, 'You should know why.'

'Maybe I've forgotten then,' he said, 'humour me.'

'I'm not doing this,' Louise got to her feet, 'You cheated on me with that tramp from Doon and then taunted me with it, I refuse to go over it again.' She marched out of the office and slammed the door behind her, let Margaret deal with him.

She staggered her way down to the beach and sat on one of the rocks, it was deserted, as she had guessed it would be, giving her a chance to clear her head. Gerard still had the power to reach right into her very soul and she despised him and even herself for it. The reason she hadn't wanted to return was standing in her office, and she realised that the only way to deal with the problem was to face it head on. She had run away from her problems at sixteen, she couldn't keep running. She took a few deep breaths and made her way back to her office. He might have left, but she didn't think so.

She was right, he was still sitting in the chair, drinking out of the cup he had got from the café.

'Okay,' Louise sighed, 'start your quiz so that you can get your sorry arse out of my office.'

'Do you want me to stay or go?' asked Margaret.

'I'll be fine,' said Louise, 'We need to check on that list,' she reached over and picked up the sheet of paper she had printed off earlier, 'before the weekend.'

Margaret got to her feet, 'I'll have my phone with me,' she took the list and glared at Gerard, 'you hurt Lou again, and you will be very sorry.' She slammed the door behind her to emphasise her point.

'I assume that your big mate didn't tell you I was here the other week?' Gerard spoke into the silence, Louise didn't have a clue where this was going to go, but the sooner he left, the better.

'If you mean Ebee, I guess it slipped his mind, he had a lot on it. Start your quiz, then we are done.'

'Why did you walk out on me all those years ago?'

'I don't believe this,' Louise said angrily, 'you slept with the tart of the village, shoved it in my face and then ask why did I leave? You're incredible.'

'I didn't sleep with anyone, why would I cheat on you? The most gorgeous girl in my world.'

'Stop lying, I heard you, she was half dressed, I saw her saggy boobs,' the images of what she had witnessed still had the power to hurt. 'I can't deal with this, just go.'

'I was looking for you,' he explained, 'Veronica was on the grass, leering up at me, her brother Eamon was leaning against a tree, smirking, and then, she tugged her shirt over her head and took off her bra, I was gobsmacked.'

'I bet you were,' Louise spat, 'drooling over the tramp. I had something important to tell you that night, but instead, you broke my heart.'

'I didn't do anything wrong, Eamon had crept up behind me, and he gave me a hard shove in the back, I landed on Veronica, just as you appeared, they must have planned it.'

'Sure, of course, why was I so stupid to spend years crying over you, when it was all a little plot,' tears slid down her cheeks, the last thing she intended doing was cry in front of him.

'Lou, I'm telling you the truth.'

'I don't believe you, and anyway,' she sniffed and grabbed a tissue out of the box on the desk, 'if that was the case, why did you take off for America? You knew that I had something important to tell you so you did a runner.'

'Eamon Kelly told me that you had dumped me and had gone back to England, so what was I supposed to do, and no, I didn't know that you had something to tell me that night.'

'You hated Kelly, why would you listen to his lies? Especially after he had pulled the supposed stunt. End of quiz, just go please Gerard, I don't want to go over this again, nothing has changed, no grand enlightenment.'

'How can I convince you?' he begged.

'You can't.'

The door opened and they both looked up to see Jack, he was wearing his shorts and tee shirt and his hair was all sweaty and tousled, 'I've been looking everywhere for you,' he said, 'can I go to the café and get a snack before dinner?'

'Of course, I won't be much longer,' she took some money out of her purse, 'don't get rubbish though, something healthy.'

'I won't,' he sighed, 'I'll go and see Brodie for a while after.'

'Okay,' Louise smiled, 'just stay out of trouble.'

Jack left the door slightly open when he left the office and Louise was glad, the room was full of emotions that she couldn't handle, 'Please go Gerard,' her voice was quiet, but full of resignation. Whatever they had once had was now gone, it could not be resurrected, especially after all his lies.

'Who's the boy?' Gerard asked, staring at the door, 'I saw him in the paper, that's why I came over that time, the big man said you were away.'

'I was away, Ebee wasn't lying,' Louise spat, avoiding the question.

'Who is he, Lou?'

'My brother, Jack,' she lied.

'He looks familiar,' he took a wallet from his jacket pocket and took out a snapshot and the paper cutting, 'this is me when I was a kid, see the resemblance?' he passed both to Louise, yet she didn't need to compare the similarities, she had grown up with Jack being the image of his father.

'Uncanny,' she agreed, passing them back.

'What important thing was you going to tell me on that fateful night?'

'I forget now, it was so long ago,' Louise smiled at him.

Gerard got to his feet, 'Okay, I'll leave for now, but just try and believe me Lou, I did not cheat on you, and I only went away because I thought that you didn't want me anymore.'

'Good bye, Gerard, and please close the door behind you,' she dismissed him and turned to face the computer screen, she wished she could believe him, but she couldn't and never would. The phone on her desk began to ring, Louise took a few deep breaths before picking it up, 'Hello, Cheyanne's Spa, oh it's you,' she laughed, relieved, 'yes, he's gone now, be a love and grab us a coffee.'

Margaret had been in the café when she had called, so it only took minutes to get the coffee and bring them to their office.

'Are you okay?' she passed Louise a cup.

'No, not really, it was terrible, and the bastard had the audacity to say he was innocent, can you believe it?'

'What if he is telling the truth?' Margaret had known Gerard for a long time, he wasn't the kind to lie and cheat, but she also believed her cousin.

'How can you say that?' Louise was angry, 'you can't begin to understand what I went through.'

'I understand all of that, Lou, but I also know the Kelly's and they do lie and cheat. Veronica was always jealous of you, and Eamon is simple minded, he would do anything for her.'

'Let's move on,' Louise sighed, she was feeling utterly weary and intended to get an early night, she needed a good night's sleep.

'It's your call.'

'Did you see Jack in the café? He came into the office when Gerard was here, what a nightmare.'

'Yes, he was talking to Brodie, they get on really well.'

'They do, but he still keeps asking for Ebee.'

They spent the next hour going over the itinerary for the party that was due to arrive in just a few days, Louise wanted it to be an experience that they would never forget, that way they could pass on the word to their colleagues and also, she wanted her previous workmates to see how well she had done. No pressure, she thought.

'Let's leave the rest until tomorrow,' Margaret got up and stretched, 'there's not a lot else to do now, except check the yurts and cabins.'

'I'll go and get Jack, we can have the lasagne you made for dinner; do you mind putting it in the oven while I find him?'

'I'll put some garlic bread in too, see you in a bit,' Margaret set off for the cottage while Louise went to the café, poor Jack had been there for ages.

The café was quiet when she swung the glass door open, and as she scanned the tables, was surprised to see that Jack wasn't there, although she had taken far longer than she should have done.

'Have you seen Jack?' Louise asked the young girl behind the counter, Polly had started a few weeks ago. Everyone knew Jack.

'He was here for a while with Brodie, I think they went down to the yurts, Brodie wanted to check on something and Jack was bored.'

'Thanks, I'll go and find him.'

Louise strolled down towards their campsite, she took deep breaths of the salty sea air, glad to be outside for a while after hours in the office. Brodie was just exiting one of the cabins, so she quickened her pace.

'Hey,' she shouted. Brodie looked up and smiled when he saw it was Louise.

'Have you seen jack? The girl in the café said he was with you.'

'He was, but another guy said he was related to him and wanted a catch up.'

Louise could feel blood turn to ice in her veins, 'what did this guy look like?'

'Dark hair, a bit taller than me, good looking guy, said his name was Gerard.'

Chapter 29

Karen opened her eyes, the constant headache hovered behind her eyes and she had an inkling that Swain was putting stuff in her food. She heard the rustle of chains from the bed in the opposite corner of the room, and guessed that Ellen was still there, although she had been kept under sedation since her latest ramblings. If she had been of sound mind, Karen would have called out to her, but Ellen was far from sound. She had lost track of how many days and nights she had been locked up in this room. Her hair felt as though a bird had built a massive nest on her head, it itched like crazy and her skin felt grubby and greasy, she needed a shower, badly.

'Ah, you're awake,' Swain had entered the room with a tray containing toast, boiled eggs and a mug of weak tea. He put it down on the small chest of drawers at the side of the bed and put the ear pieces of the stethoscope in and leant towards Karen, she recoiled, his teeth were stained and his breath was rank.

'Let me listen to your chest,' he smirked, holding the flat silver metal towards her.

'I'll pass, thanks,' she retorted, 'go and work your medicine on Ellen.'

'I intend to my dear, don't you worry. It might be a good idea to keep your ears closed though.'

Karen shivered, he was a repulsive excuse for a human being, she knew the three of them belonged together, Aggie the spiteful witch, Ellen the demented hag and Swain the mad doctor, JK would have a field day with these characters, she smiled at the thought, they would give Harry Potter a run for his money. She watched the back of him as he slithered across to the bed Ellen was chained to, his grey hair was so thin she could see his pink scaly scalp. She turned her head towards the tray, there was no way she could eat that food or touch the tea; she had to stay alert, ready for the chance of escape.

Karen heard him whisper to Ellen, and then the rattle of chains, his raspy breathing quickened and Ellen screamed out and then groaned, it went on for so long that she had to bury her head in the pillow. After an age, she heard his footsteps nearing her bed, 'eat up my dear, we want you to get better.'

'What did you do to Ellen?' she said, but not sure if she wanted the answer.

'Something she enjoys,' he sighed, 'and maybe, if you behave, I'll do the same to you,' he laughed, the sound verging on hysteria, and as he slammed the door behind him, Karen lay cringing in the bed, her tears of terror flowing onto the sheets.

Chapter 30

Louise raced across the grass towards the beach, the long spikes of bent weed catching the bare skin of her shins, her cut-off jeans weren't the ideal attire for this terrain. She was fuming, in fact, that was an understatement, she wouldn't be surprised if smoke wasn't puffing out of her ears. She scrambled up the sandy hill and over the fence that was a temporary fixture until the designer had submitted his ideas, and then down the wooden steps that led down to the large expanse of sand. On the third step she saw them, identical dark curly hair, they were sitting side by side on one of the flat rocks near the sea. Gerard was leaning towards her son, and she could see that Jack felt comfortable in his presence.

'Jack,' Louise was breathless, 'how many times have you been told not to talk to strangers, let alone go to the beach with one?'

'I'm not a stranger,' Gerard said, and she heard the anguish in his voice, 'how could you do this to me Lou? All these years and you didn't tell me.'

Louise could feel rage build up again, choosing to ignore the naked pain in his eyes, eyes that matched her son's exactly.

'Jack, run up to the cottage, Margaret is getting the tea ready.'

'Can Gerard come too?'

'No, he is going home,' Louise told him, 'I'll be up in a moment, I just want a word.'

'It's not fair,' Jack stormed, 'you've left me on my own for hours and when I find someone I like and want to talk to, you go mental.'

'I'll speak to you later,' she warned, 'now go and get your tea.'

Jack went sulkily towards the steps, but stopped when he was almost there, 'will you come and see me again?' he asked, looking at Gerard.

'Yes, I promise,' he smiled sadly at the boy.

When he had climbed the steps, Louise turned on Gerard, 'How dare you criticise me for keeping quiet about Jack. I guess he told you that I'm his mother, but my parents raised him until last year, after all,' she paused to regain her composure, 'you had shown your true colours. I was a kid, Gerard, pregnant and scared and you sleep with that tart Veronica and take off to America, and now,' she wiped the tears of anger from her eyes, 'you ask why I didn't fucking tell you.'

'We were both wrong,' he said, 'you for not giving me the chance to tell you I'd been set up, and me for not proving that I hadn't done anything wrong. You broke my heart Lou, and you are still doing it.'

Louise looked at him and for the first time an element of doubt crept in, what if he had been set up by the Kellys? If that was the case, they had both wasted over eleven years of their lives being apart, and poor Jack, never knowing who is father was. She made a decision and hoped she wouldn't regret it.

'Come up to the cottage for dinner,' she told him, 'it's time you got to know your son.'

Jack was sitting at the table in the kitchen when they walked in, staring moodily at a comic, Margaret was getting the washing in from the line; she had been worried that the strong wind that had been forecast would toss all their clothes into the sea.

'Jack, come and sit on the settee, we need to tell you something,' said Louise, holding her son's arm and leading him into the lounge.

'Gerard,' he exclaimed, his eyes shining with delight, 'are you staying for dinner?'

'If there's enough,' grinned Gerard.

'There will be,' said Jack with conviction, 'Margaret always makes too much and we end up eating it for days.'

'Stop exaggerating,' Louise chuckled.

'Sit down both of you, I'll nip out and tell Margaret,' she gave Gerard a warning look, he got the message and knew to keep quiet until she returned.

Margaret had just taken one of her bras of the line when Louise put her arm on her shoulder,

'Bloody hell, Lou, you made me jump.'

'Gerard's here, we're going to tell Jack the truth, now.'

'Oh, that's a surprise, but I've said all along that he needs to know.'

'Yes, I know,' Louise sighed, 'I just hope I'm doing the right thing, but good or bad Gerard is or isn't, he is still my son's father.'

'Hurrah, the lady sees the light,' Margaret gave her cousin a fierce hug, 'I'll sort the dinner out while you tell Jack, and it can go either way.'

'Look at the way he treated me when he found out the truth,' Louise agreed, 'but it's weird, he has really taken to Gerard, and they look so alike.'

'Stop procrastinating,' Margaret gave her a gentle shove towards the door, 'get it over with.'

Jack was explaining to Gerard the merits of playing for the local hurling team when Louise walked in, she took her seat by the range, she always felt warm and cosy sitting in the old and worn chair, and locked eyes with Gerard.

'Jack,' she began, nervously, 'explain why you feel so close to Gerard, when you have only just met him.'

'I don't know mum, but we like the same things, we even look alike.'

'No need for a DNA test,' Gerard laughed, but Louise shot him an angry look, 'Stop it Gerard,'

Jack looked at her in alarm, 'what's going on?'

'I don't want you to get upset,' she reached over and grabbed his hand, 'but I think that you are old enough now to handle the truth.'

'What truth? I don't get it, you've already told me that my mum and dad are really my grandparents.'

'Yes, Jack, but now I want to tell you who your father is.'

'Is it Ebee?' he grinned, 'is he coming back?' and then he laughed, 'I'm not stupid mum, I know who my dad is.'

'You do?' asked Louise and Gerard together.

'When did you find out?' asked Louise, this wasn't going the way she thought it would.

'I heard Brodie talking to Gerard, he asked why he wanted to see me, and then Gerard said he was my dad, and I knew that he was telling the truth.'

'Oh, and you didn't say anything?'

'I was waiting for you to tell me,' he grinned.

'So I've been stressing about telling you for nothing!'

'How do you feel about it?' Gerard asked gently.

'Okay, I guess,' he pondered, 'do I get two lots of presents now?'

'Cheeky,' Louise told him, 'go and wash your hands, dinner must be ready.'

Jack sauntered into the bathroom leaving Louise stunned, 'the little monkey, I'll never work that kid out.'

'It says a lot though,' said Gerard, 'he obviously feels secure here, enough not to let a little trifle like me being his father rattle him.'

'Crazy though, she sighed, 'I was expecting tears and tantrums.'

They were sitting around the table, just about to eat, when there was a knock on the door.

'I'll go,' said Margaret.

She returned a minute later with Brodie in tow, 'Sit down,' she told him, 'there's more than enough.'

'I wanted to check on Jack,' he smiled at the boy and sat down, 'I was concerned that you went off with a stranger.'

'Oh, he's not a stranger,' said Jack seriously, 'he's my dad.'

There was a beat of silence and then they all laughed.

'You're a great cook,' sighed Brodie, tucking into the lasagne.

'Thanks, I've had enough practice.'

Another knock on the door made them all jump, I'll go this time,' Louise sighed, wondering who it could be, the dinner would be cold before they managed to eat it.

Finn was standing on the door step, his face flushed from the wind, 'Hi Lou, have you got a minute to discuss the design for the fence?'

'Well,' she hesitated, they needed the fence erected as soon as possible, 'We were just about to have dinner, would you like to join us?' There was one piece of lasagne and two slices of garlic bread left, even if Brodie had his eyes on them.

'I've eaten thanks, but could I come in and wait?'

'Of course,' she opened the door wider, 'sit by the range, I'll get you a cuppa in a bit.'

'Thanks, have your dinner first.'

'Finn wants to go over the design,' Louise looked at Margaret, 'he's going to wait until we've finished.'

It was an awkward meal after that, both women conscious of Finn waiting in the other room and Brodie unsure of what to make of this bloke, Gerard. Jack was oblivious and had kept up a lively chatter throughout the meal.

Finn was surprised to see four adults spill from the kitchen and looked moodily at Brodie, he had noticed him out with Margaret a few times and wasn't happy about it.

'I can come back if it's inconvenient,' he said moodily.

'Don't be silly, Jack, go and show Gerard your game console,' said Louise, the sitting room was too small for five adults and an eleven year old boy. 'Brodie, it will be good to get your input.'

'Sure, I've got a few ideas,' he said, looking at Margaret and smiling.

'I bet you do,' snarled Finn.

'Shall I get us a drink?' Margaret wanted to escape, she didn't want to be in the small confines of their sitting room with Finn of all people. 'I'm going to have a glass of wine.'

'Same here,' said Louise, picking up the vibes from her cousin.

'Have you any beer?' asked Brodie, oblivious to the tension.

'Yes, Finn, do you want one?' asked Margaret.

'I'll have a wine too, please,' he said.

'Fine, red or white?'

'Whatever you're having,' he replied.

Louise followed her out into the kitchen, 'I'll ask Gerard what he wants, Jack can have hot chocolate.'

Margaret reached for the glasses from the top cupboard, her hands were shaking, she hadn't seen or spoken to Finn for months, surely he could have gone to the office with his blasted plans.

'Are you okay?' Louise asked, 'It's totally bazar, Gerard and Finn in our humble abode, he wants a beer by the way.'

'Throw Brodie into the mix,' laughed Margaret, 'I don't know if I can sit in the same room with him.'

'Who? Brodie?'

'Don't be daft, Brodie's a mate, what is Finn doing here?'

'He must care about you, have you noticed the daggers he keeps shooting at Brodie?'

'No,' Margaret sighed, 'come, on, let's get it over with.'

Louise made the chocolate and poured the beers, taking one in to Brodie before taking the other drinks into Jack's room. They each had a gaming control in their hand and were playing some racing game on the screen, it was good to see father and son bonding, but unsettling too.

'What time do you need to head home?' she asked.

'Are there any rooms free at the hotel?'

'He can share my room,' said Jack.

'No,' said Louise, 'Gerard can stay up at the hotel, I'm sure there's a free room up there.'

'I don't want a free room,' he grinned, making her stomach clench.

'You know what I mean,' she bit out, 'I'll give Mairead a ring and get housekeeping to sort you one out.' She left the room, her legs shaking, this was ridiculous, and she would not let him have this effect on her. In the kitchen she called reception and arranged for a room to be ready for their guest, it did have advantages when you owned the hotel, she thought, a bit smugly. She stuck her head around the door, 'room will be ready when you are,' she told him pointedly.

Back in the sitting room there was an ominous silence, boy, this is going to be a long night, Louise thought, it had already been a hell of a long day.

'Okay,' she said taking a big swig of wine, her favourite red that they'd picked up from Letterkenny, 'let's get the plans started.'

Finn had brought a sketch pad and proudly showed the designs of the fence he had in mind, planning permission had already been granted, they wanted the fence to be high enough for trespassers to keep out, but low enough so the view would not be obscured.

'Good job, mate,' said Brodie, approvingly. 'I love the gates, and you designed the spa hotel too?'

'Yes,' Finn relaxed, Brodie couldn't be that bad if he approved of his work, and he couldn't blame Margaret for going out with him, he had dismissed her and lost her, it was his own fault.

'We want our holiday park to be secure,' said Louise, 'but we also need easy access to the beach.'

'Exactly,' added Margaret, 'and you've accomplished all that, Finn, when can we get started on the erection?'

Brodie spluttered, spraying beer everywhere, and Margaret, realising what she had said, turned a bright red.

'The fence, obviously,' said Louise dryly.

There was a loud knock on the door, a hammering to be more exact, 'what is this about tonight?' sighed Louise, 'knock three times?'

'I'll go,' said Finn, 'you never know who comes knocking at this time of night.'

'You've watched too many films,' Margaret told him.

'Nothing else to do,' he grinned, getting to his feet. He appeared moments later with Ebee, and the girls' screams of delight, brought Jack and Gerard running into the room to investigate. Jack threw himself into Ebee's waiting arms. 'I've missed you.'

'I've missed you too, little chap,' he turned to look at the girls, 'so, where is Karen?'

Chapter 30

Karen woke up feeling more alert than she had in ages, she had emptied the tea behind the headboard and stuffed the food under the mattress, and it could always be tested later when she escaped. Swain had paid a visit to Ellen during the night, she could hear the scream, moans and whimpers from her bed, and much as she detested the twisted crone, she also felt sorry for her. The good doctor was abusing a mentally unstable woman and her blood boiled at the atrocity he was committing. He reminded her of the sicko Saville, the way he prowled around the ward thinking his patients were asleep. She had lay still when he approached her bed, feigning sleep and tense to his closeness, but as yet, he had not touched her but she knew it was just a matter of time.

Daylight was spilling into the room through the thin curtain, Karen didn't know what time of day it was, she had lost track, but she knew that soon, someone would come and rescue her. She heard a whimper from across the room and called out, 'Ellen, are you awake?'

'Gumden.'

'Speak English,' Karen shouted, 'I know you can, you spoke it when you got in my car.'

'Help me,' she replied, 'I can't help it.'

'Can't help what?' asked Karen, she was amazed that this strange woman was actually talking to her.

'Being mad and bad, that's why he does it.'

'Does what?'

'Does things to me, I like it but I don't like it. He has always done it, since I was a teenager, Aggie likes it though.'

Karen could only guess what she was talking about. 'He's sick,' Karen told her.

'I'm sick, he told me.'

'He is mentally and physically abusive,' Karen was angry, she had no doubt now that this man had caused the problems that Ellen had.

'I'm bad, he told me to get you.'

'Why?'

'He likes you, your blonde hair and curves, he told me.'

Karen felt uncomfortable, she had to get out of here. She limped over to the sink; It was across the room under a small window where a dingy yellow net curtain hung shabbily from a thin wire. She turned on the cold tap, and using her hands she cupped them under the running stream and gulped fresh water steadily until she felt sated. She might not be able to trust the food, but if she could keep up her fluid intake, she would regain enough strength to somehow escape. She limped back and had just climbed under the bedclothes when the door opened and Swain walked in.

'She's been out the bed,' Ellen told him slyly.

Karen cringed and held on to the blanket, 'I just needed a drink.'

'That's fine my dear, don't fret. I'll get you a drink if you want one, we don't want you putting pressure on that poorly leg do we now?'

'I'm good now thanks,' Karen told him, 'I'll just have a little snooze.'

'You do that,' Swain grinned, he walked over to the cabinet where he kept his drugs, 'and this will help you sleep more easily,' he jabbed a needle in her arm and before she could fully acknowledge the pain, Karen's eyes fluttered and she slipped into oblivion.

It was dark when her eyes fluttered open, pitch black dark with not a shadow in sight. Karen's mouth felt as dry as sandpaper, but she couldn't risk drinking whatever Swain had left on the small table by the bed, and the sink was way over the other side of the room, she wouldn't be able to get her bearings and the thought of going near Ellen was enough to make her stomach rumble and roll with revulsion. Tears slid silently down her cheeks, she was a prisoner in this hell hole, and she knew that they would never let her go. She couldn't imagine what her parents were going through, they would worry themselves sick when she didn't arrive at George Elliot hospital, and while Lou and Margaret would think she had gone back to Bedworth and was not going to return to Clodbury.

From across the room, the high pitched chanting from Ellen the demented, drifted over to Karen, the alien language that made no sense.

'Shut up you evil crone,' Karen shouted, not caring about the consequences, although a flicker of fear swept over her as she remembered the warning Ellen had spoken the day before. If Swain dared to touch her with his grubby hands, she would kill him.

'Gumden,' Ellen screeched, 'you will never escape his clutches,' she cackled hysterically.

'You're insane,' Karen retaliated, 'just like your evil sister and the warped doctor.'

'It's you Miss Fancy Pants that's the evil one,' Ellen spat, her tone vicious and toxic.

Karen knew it was a waste of time batting venom back and forth with the spiteful witch, so she put her head under the pillow and imagined Brodie coming to her rescue and then she slipped into a fitful sleep.

Chapter 31

Adele gripped her husband's hand tight as they came into land at Dublin airport, 'We are doing the right thing?' she had asked the same question since deciding that they had spent enough time away from their daughter and grandson.

'Yes, and the offer to build a house is too tempting to turn down, Jack can spend time with us, he has adjusted well to his true parentage,' Frank gave her a gentle squeeze.

'Maybe we should have warned them we were coming,' Adele had a horrible feeling that they wouldn't be pleased to see them, or they might have gone away with Jack.

'Stop being silly,' he told her, 'they will be ecstatic that we are going to live nearby, although finding somewhere to stay while the house is being built could be a problem,' Frank sighed.

'It's going to take some time to sort out the sale of the house in Oxford, we can submit the plans for the build and go home to organise that end.'

The plane taxed towards the hangar and as soon as it had come to a stop, Frank stretched up to retrieve their bags from the overhead lockers. The plan was to spend a couple of days' sight- seeing in Dublin and then get the bus to Clodbury. It had been a spur of the moment decision, they had both agreed that they had spent too much time away and they wanted to go home.

'It might be an idea to buy a car,' Frank wondered. 'It will come in handy when we move over here for good.' They were exiting on to the street, most of their luggage was going to be sent on, which made it much easier, one case between them plus their two holdalls were easier to manage than lugging all the clothes they had accumulated over the past year and a half.

'One step at a time,' Adele laughed, it felt exhilarating to be so near her beloved daughter and grandson, 'we can get the plans mapped out with Finn and then go to Oxford and work out what to do with the house and everything,' she paused, the enormity of their decision suddenly dawning, 'and your job, Frank, what will happen about that?'

'Two choices,' he told her, 'I continue to travel to work alone, or give notice, I bet there will be a job at the hotel.'

Adele wondered if Frank could settle for a job that was out of his comfort zone, but she would cross that bridge when she came to it. As they crossed the bridge over the river Liffey, she clutched Frank's arm, 'we need to go to Clodbury now.'

'Where did that come from?'

'I don't know, but I've got a gut feeling that something is wrong, we can sight see another time.'

Chapter 32

Gerard agreed to take Jack up to the hotel and share a room with him to enable Ebee to have the lad's room. Finn wondered if he should leave, but he wanted to be near Margaret, he shouldn't have given her a wide berth, it wasn't her fault she was wealthy. Brodie didn't have any qualms about her money, he thought, bitterly. Ebee was obviously fond of Karen, he was distraught at her disappearance, although Brodie appeared concerned too.

'So,' said Ebee, taking a pen and writing pad out of his jacket pocket, 'her bright yellow car hasn't been spotted in the village?'

'No,' sighed Margaret, 'don't you think we haven't asked?'

'I'm not accusing you,' he soothed, 'but we need to follow her last steps. Obviously she didn't board the ferry, so between here and Belfast she has gone missing.'

'How do you know she went from Belfast?' asked Louise, 'we didn't know which route she had taken.'

'She once told me that that was the only way she would ever go, unless she went by air,' Ebee explained, 'I contacted Stena and they confirmed the booking and a no show.'

'How could she just disappear?' Margaret asked, 'and don't say she's been taken off in a spaceship.'

'I wasn't going to,' stated Ebee, he was not amused, he had hoped there would be some answers waiting for him, but the mystery deepened. 'I told Mr and Mrs Brown that I would update them as soon as possible.'

Finn was sitting by the range, listening but making no comments, he did remember a yellow car passing him on the beach road a few weeks ago, but was it Karen, he wondered? It had stuck in his mind because he was working on plans for Colm, he had been persuaded by his family to put a pool in at the side of his enormous house. Indoor of course, he had suggested. He recalled that they had both commented on the small car and had declared that they wouldn't drive a Beetle on these roads. Colm had remarked that it was a woman's car, and easy to park. Finn had laughed, they were both joking and not meaning it.

'I'm sure I saw a yellow car go past on the day in question,' he stated.

Margaret glared at him, 'why didn't you say so before?'

'How the hell was I supposed to know that she was missing?'

'I'm sorry, of course you wouldn't have known,' she apologised, 'is there anything else that you can add?'

Ebee had his pen poised waiting.

'Me and Colm watched it until the car was out of sight, that's all I know.'

'Right,' said Ebee getting to his feet, 'we will start by asking people from the bottom of the Church Bray to the Cross.'

'Good idea,' said Louise, 'but we had better wait until tomorrow, its 2am and most people will be in bed.'

'Bloody hell,' said Brodie, 'is it that late? I'd better get myself off to bed, tomorrow I'm going to find my love.'

Margaret spluttered, 'did you really just say that?'

'I'm tired,' said Brodie sheepishly.

Finn looked at Brodie with interest, 'Karen is your love interest?'

'I'm hoping she feels the same,' Brodie confessed, 'but we have only known each other a matter of weeks.'

'I thought you and Margaret were an item,' he grinned, relieved.

'No mate, she's all yours.'

'I am here,' Margaret said angrily, 'I'm nobody's and I'm going to bed,' she stomped off angrily without saying goodnight to anyone.

'You've well and truly pissed her off,' laughed Louise, 'she thought you cared for her, Brodie.'

'I've never given her a cause to think that,' he spluttered.

'Oh dear,' she smiled, 'you'd better apologise tomorrow, goodnight, Ebee you know where Jack's room is, see yourselves out Finn and Brodie.'

Louise was washed and dressed for bed and lay awake thinking of the day's events, she couldn't help teasing Brodie and it would do Finn good to know that Margaret hadn't hung around waiting for him, even if she did pine for him. Brodie's face had been a picture. But then her mind travelled to Gerard, she tried to analyse how she felt about him turning up and taking a place in Jack's life. She had to admit it was good to see father and son getting to know each other, but her own feelings were numb, too many years had passed, their boat had well and truly sailed. Anyway, she told herself, he probably had a significant other in his life, it was only Jack he was interested in.

She was up first for a change, usually Margaret was dressed and cooking breakfast at 7, but today, Louise was the first to stir, at 6, she couldn't sleep, too many things were chasing around in her head, added to the fact that they needed to make an early start, so after a run along the beach she had showered and changed into jeans and a black tee shirt. She groaned inwardly at the knowledge that the group from Oxford would be arriving tomorrow for their team building experience. Luckily the rooms were ready and the classes in place. Karnjit would expect a good work out, and Ana, a young Spanish girl full of enthusiasm, who had started working for them a month ago, had a full day of events planned for them, including a light hearted Spanish class. She felt torn in two, she needed to be at the hotel to oversee everything with Margaret, but she also felt hopeless in the quest to find Karen.

Louise had just put the big tea pot on the range to keep warm, when Ebee appeared, rubbing his eyes.

'Top of the morning to ye,' she quipped.

'Same,' he grinned, 'what's for breakfast?'

'What do you fancy?' she asked.

'Eggs Benedict.'

'How about poached egg on toast?'

'Done,' he laughed.

Margaret appeared just as she put the plate of toast and two poached eggs in front of Ebee, 'Can I have the same please?'

'Sure,' Louise passed her a mug of tea, 'I was just going to bring this in to you.'

A loud knock at the door made them all start, Louise looked at her watch, 'who the hell is that at this ungodly hour?' She stomped off to answer the door, it was too early for Jack, he wouldn't need to get ready for school for another hour. The last people she expected to see on her doorstep was her parents.

'Mum, Dad, what are you doing here?' She opened the door wide so that they could come in.

'Your Mum had a weird feeling that you needed her,' said Frank Lavender.

'Oh,' Louise said, bemused.

'Something has been going on,' said Adele, 'and strange as it may seem, I feel as though I can help in some way.'

'I'm just doing breakfast,' Louise led the way into the kitchen, not knowing how her mother could help with any of the pressing problems that they had.

Margaret was delighted to see her Aunt and Uncle and as they discussed the disappearance of Karen, Louise waited for her mother's input.

'I'm confused,' Adele said, 'I have a gut feeling that I have a missing piece but I haven't a clue what it is,' she took a sip from her mug.

'That's the trouble with jigsaws,' said Margaret, 'once you lose a piece it's useless.'

'Not helping,' said Louise, sounding like Judge Rinder.

'Has she had any arguments or is there bad feeling with anyone?'

'Karen is lovely, kind and gentle,' said Louise.

'The only trouble we've had is with that weird trio,' said Ebee, stroking his chin, 'Aggie and Ellen are as crazy as hell and that Doctor in the mix is toxic.'

'Tell me about them,' said Adele.

So Ebee related the tale of the trio, from the treatments at the spa to the confrontation at the little cottage after Ebee had been attacked.

'Ellen attacked me once,' said Adele, 'quite viciously. I was down the beach with Brian, he'd gone in for a swim and she came up behind me as I was folding a towel. Her claw like hands were around my neck, I'd tried to pull them off but they got tighter, I was on the verge of passing out when Brian saw what was happening. He had to hit her over the head with a rock,' she looked quickly at Frank, 'he had no choice, she had a demented look on her face, or so he said, she had no intention of letting me go. Brian hit her a couple of times until she fell to the ground, I was coughing and spluttering, my throat hurt for days. Ellen was put away in the psychiatric ward, apparently she had done it before,' Adele quivered and took a sip of tea, 'a five year old girl had also been attacked and suffered major brain damage, but her parents couldn't prove it was her.'

'Bloody hell,' Ebee involuntarily rubbed the back of his head, 'I wonder if it was Ellen that attacked me.'

'It sounds very likely,' said Frank, 'I think you should call the police.'

'Ha,' Margaret scorned, 'fat lot of good they would do, Denton got away with fraud and bullying for years, and they didn't give a damn.'

'She's right dad,' said Louise, 'they are as much use as chocolate poker.'

'What can we do then,' asked Frank, 'and why did they let Ellen out?'

'Your guess is as good as mine,' Adele sighed, 'I thought she would be in there forever. So many people came forward to tell their stories about her.'

'I'm going to phone the hospital,' said Louise, she picked up her phone and googled the number of Letterkenny Psychiatric hospital, when it began to ring, she took the call in her bedroom.

'I'm going over to that cottage,' said Ebee, 'they could be holding Karen there.'

'I'll come with you,' said Frank.

'I don't believe it,' Louise went into the kitchen and filled the kettle, 'the doctor said he couldn't discuss her case with me, and when I told him that Ellen was a possible murderer, he said I needed to go down the proper channels, stupid jobs worth.'

'I suppose its patient confidentiality,' said Adele.

'Where's the support for victims?' Louise cried angrily, 'What are we supposed to do here? Start our own vigilante group?'

'Possibly,' smiled Margaret, 'Your dad and Ebee have gone to Aggie's cottage.'

Ten minutes later the door flew open and Jack ran into the kitchen, and seeing Adele perched on a stool, he ran towards her and nearly knocked her off, 'I didn't know you were coming,' he cried.

'It was meant to be a surprise, darling,' Adele hugged her grandson and held him close, she had missed him so much.

'Hello Adele,' Gerard had been standing in the doorway watching grandmother and his son.

'It's been a long time,' smiled Adele, noting that the good looks of his youth had matured into a very handsome man.

'Too long,' he said pointedly, gazing at Jack. 'Where's Frank?'

They heard the door open, 'The cottage is empty,' said Ebee, 'the fire hasn't been lit for ages, and the place smells damp.'

'Is there a cuppa going?' asked Frank, 'I'm gasping.'

'I've made a pot dad, come and get one.'

There was a knock on the door and when Ebee went to open it he found Brodie on the doorstep.

'I'm going to look for Karen,' he stated, 'are you going to join me?'

'Of course,' he gave him a look, 'why the hell do you think I came back. We've been to Aggie's, so that trail is cold.'

'Its times like this,' sighed Margaret, 'that we need a bigger cottage. Has anyone heard from Finn?'

'Nope, but he mentioned he had a lot on,' said Louise.

'Right,' said Ebee, 'who's going to join us in finding Karen?' He looked around the small room.

'Me, of course,' said Brodie.

'I'll help,' joined Gerard.

'I'd help,' sighed Frank, 'but I'm exhausted after all that travelling.'

Louise's phone rang, she picked it up and passed it to Margaret, 'it's Finn.'

He wanted to help find Karen too and was on his way over.

They started knocking on doors, making their way towards the village, they were at the Glen House, it was an imposing hotel perched on the top of the hill, when they got the first clue. A young girl said she remembers a bright yellow car stopping just after the ruins of the old church, an old woman was looking for a lift and had got in the car.

'Why would Karen give Aggie or Ellen a lift?' asked Ebee, 'she knew they were strange.'

'It's worrying,' Brodie bit his lip, 'we need to find her fast.'

'Does anyone know where Swain's old surgery is?' said Ebee.

'Yes, it's down Binning Road,' said Finn, 'let's go.'

Chapter 33

'Wonder how they're doing?' Margaret sighed, 'Karen's been gone weeks, what state is she going to be in when they find her?'

'I think we should focus on the group arriving tomorrow,' Louise told her, 'a lot is riding on this booking and we need them to put a good word in for us when they get back,' Margaret scowled at her, 'we need to keep busy,' Louise exclaimed, 'what's the point of sitting around worrying when we can keep occupied and let the lads find Karen.'

'I suppose so, but Ellen sounds dangerous. I wonder if it was her that coshed Ebee over the head.'

'Possibly, she might even have murdered Denton.'

'Oh my god,' Margaret flopped down on the chair in front of her computer, 'I'd forgotten about that.'

'I'm sure Ebee hasn't,' Louise said dryly. 'Come on, let's go and check everything is in place.'

Together they went over the rooms, ensuring that everything was as it should be, twin beds were being used and were made up, they had requested them to cut down on the cost of having a room each, towels were laid out and the rooms were spotless, Louise made a note to thank housekeeping for a good job. They made their way down to the basement and again were impressed with the cleanliness, which is how it should be, but it meant they could rely on the staff that they had employed. Louise cast her eyes around the pool and surroundings, 'Those potted palm trees were a great idea of Finn's,' she sighed. 'In fact, if we didn't live here, I'd come for a swim, spa treatment and maybe even stay the night.'

'That's a thought,' Margaret sat on a lounger and lay back, closing her eyes, 'when was the last time we had a massage or manicure?'

'We haven't got time,' Louise sat down on the lounger next to Margaret.

'It's lovely here isn't it?' Margaret giggled, 'wish I'd brought my cossie.'

'Yes, it's wonderful,' came a chorus of voices from behind them.

Louise shot up, 'I thought you were coming tomorrow,' she hugged Karnjit who was standing in front of the team from Oxford.

'We were, but I sent you an email yesterday, saying was it okay for us to come today, we managed to get approval for an extra day.'

'Oh, sorry, a lots been going on, but your rooms are ready, we'll show you to them. How did you know where to find us,' she laughed.

'Your receptionist said you were checking everything and your last port of call was the pool, must be a tiring business,' sniffed Nancy Dunn, a tall woman with brassy blonde hair and a Birmingham accent.

'We had only just sat down,' Margaret said defensively.

'It's your hotel, you can do what you like,' grinned Karnjit shooting Nancy a look. It was obvious that there was no love lost between them.

'Well, I hope I can get a manicure, I chipped a nail at work yesterday, look at the state of them.'

Louise looked at the bright pink talons, 'Don't you find it hard to type with those long nails?' she asked Nancy, 'where is Kim?' Louise looked at Karnjit, she was looking forward to catching up with her friend.

'She left in a hurry,' Karnjit sighed and shot Nancy a look to indicate that there stood the reason why.

'I don't do much typing these days,' Nancy was oblivious to the exchange, 'I usually get Brenda to run off emails for me, she's a darling,' she turned to pat the arm of the woman standing next to her, she had short blonde hair and a big bum.

'I don't mind, Nancy, I like doing things for you.'

Margaret motioned sticking her finger down her throat behind their back, but Karnjit saw her and burst out laughing, 'I think I'm going to enjoy it here.'

Nancy insisted that she would be sharing a room with her friend, Brenda, 'I want the best room you have,' demanded Nancy, 'I'm the team leader.'

'Kim was the last I heard,' stated Louise, her time at the bank seemed a lifetime ago, 'all our rooms are magnificent.'

Lynne, a small girl with auburn hair spoke up, 'I'll share with Dianne, and Karnjit plans to share with Zara. Another two will join us tomorrow, they couldn't get away on time,' she looked pointedly at Nancy.

'Well,' Nancy snipped, 'it is the busy ISA period; they should have finished their work load on time.

'Margaret, if you take Nancy and Brenda to their rooms, I'll take the others,' Louise interrupted, the last thing she wanted to hear was what kind of pressure they were under at the bank.

'Aye, aye captain,' saluted Margaret.

'Sorry,' Louise sighed, 'I didn't mean to sound so bossy,' she couldn't say that her old life had come back to bite her, she took a deep breath, 'If you would like to escort two couples to their rooms and I'll take the others.'

Margaret had noticed that the colour had drained from her cousin's face, 'Follow me,' she said, looking at Nancy and then walking out of the pool area and up the stairs towards reception,

'Can I have the keys to Emerald and Sapphire, please,' she smiled at Mairead, who quickly prepared the keys and handed them to her. She gave one set to Nancy and the other to Lynne, 'I'll show you to your rooms,' Margaret walked alongside Lynne and Dianne. 'We're pretty flexible about breakfast, although I do recommend an early start as we have a full schedule of events planned for your stay.'

'Sounds great,' smiled Dianne, 'I can't wait to have a walk on the beach when we've dumped our cases.'

'Followed by a gorgeous meal in the restaurant,' sighed Lynne.

'We do snacks in the café,' Margaret told her as they reached the first room, 'this one is yours,' she said to Nancy and Brenda.

'Is it the best one?' Nancy asked, as she opened the door, flinging it wide.

Brenda walked in behind her, 'wow, its stunning.'

'It will do,' sniffed Nancy, 'can I order room service?'

'No,' said Margaret, 'you can't, there are tea and coffee making facilities in your room and a café down the corridor if you need refreshments.'

'I suppose that will have to do,' Nancy huffed, and then closed the door behind her.

'Is she always like that?' Margaret asked as they reached the room along the corridor, 'sorry you'll be so near to her.'

'She can be quite nice sometimes,' said Lynne, opening the door to her room, 'she likes to play the lady if she can get away with it.'

'Well,' grinned Margaret, 'she won't here.'

'I thought they were all coming tomorrow,' sighed Louise, she was sitting at her computer trawling her emails when Margaret caught up with her.

'They're here now,' Margaret sat down in her favourite swivel chair, 'and I'm dying for a coffee. How the hell did you put up with that Nancy? She seems a right bitch.'

'I didn't work with her much,' sighed Louise, 'Kim was my team leader, but she's not the only one like that, the place was full of them.'

'And now you're the boss, well, half a boss,' Margaret laughed.

'Yes, I'm sorry for talking to you like that earlier, as if you were a maid.'

'That's okay, you're the bossy one and I forgive you,' she picked up the phone, 'coffee for two, please,' she spoke into the receiver and replaced it on the cradle, 'Nancy might not have room service, but we do,' she giggled.

Chapter 34

'It's down here,' said Finn, 'although the old bastard hasn't practiced for years.' He parked the car in front of William the butcher's.

'Should we tell the guards?' asked Brodie looking across to the Guarda station, conveniently situated between a pub and a pharmacy. '

'Why?' asked Ebee, 'are they going to arm themselves and call for back up? Just think, we can be on news at ten tomorrow.'

'It was just an idea,' Brodie was hurt, they needed help from someone with experience, not like the bunch of cowboys they were.

'We called them out before,' sighed Ebee, 'fat lot of good it did us, and then they accused the girls of murder, no, we are better off going it alone. If you want to opt out mate, feel free, wait in the pub while we rescue Karen.'

'No, I'm with you guys.'

'We are the older version of the Goonies,' Ebee said seriously.

Gerard and Finn had watched the exchange and chuckled, 'Swain is nearly eighty, I think we can overcome the doddering old fool,' said Finn.

'It's alright for you, Karen is special to me,' Brodie was angry, she was in danger and they thought it would be easy to rescue her. 'And what if she's not here? He could be holding her somewhere else.' He shuddered, if they confronted him, he might even kill her.

'Or he might not even be involved,' said Finn. He had known Dr Swain for most of his life, he had even heard the rumours that he was a dirty pervert, but as for kidnap? To him that seemed extreme.

'Okay, maybe we should hatch a plan,' said Ebee, he realised that they couldn't go in half-cocked and they had a good chance of putting Karen's life in danger, unless they were already too late, but he wouldn't allow himself to think that.

'There's a café further up the street,' said Brodie, he needed a strong coffee to focus on their mission.

'Lead the way,' said Ebee, who only ever used the café in the spa.

They were dismayed to discover that most of the tables were taken with the villagers, it was pension day and it was a chance for friends to meet up and have a gossip after collecting their money from the post office.

'Shit,' swore Brodie, 'Now what?'

'We sit over there,' Ebee pointed to a large table at the back, 'it would look suspicious if we left now.'

'Do we order at the counter?' Brodie wondered.

'Let's sit down first,' Ebee was getting pissed off, he should have just come on his own.

Gerard followed them to the table, wondering what the hell he was doing here. He didn't even know this Karen, he should be back at the hotel getting to know his son and talking to Lou, She was back in his life and he intended to win her back. He picked up the menu, and passed it to Ebee, he was a bit in awe of the big guy, he knew Ebee was on a mission and would not let anything get in his way.

'Can I take your order?' A young girl with red hair asked, she held a notebook and pen in her hand.

'Coffee, please,' Ebee looked around the table, a warning in his big brown eyes, they didn't have time to eat a full Irish or any other food items on the menu.

'Same,' said Finn, smiling.

'I'd like a bacon .....,' Ebee shot Gerard a look, 'sorry, just a coffee please.'

'That's four coffees then please,' Ebee flashed the waitress a smile.

'Okay, if that's all, I'll be right back.'

'It looks as if they are trying to create an American diner,' Brodie looked around, 'it's nice but they are better off keeping it to a village café.'

'Okay,' Ebee looked around the table, he didn't think he could rely on any one of them to cover his back if needed, 'has anyone got any ideas?'

'No,' Finn grinned, 'not one, have you?'

'For f's sake,' Ebee yelled, causing everyone in the café to turn and look at them, 'stop messing around.'

'Sorry,' Finn felt ashamed, 'I was just trying to lighten the mood.'

Gerard, who still wondered what he was doing here, piped up, 'why don't you pretend to need his assistance and gain access to his surgery?'

'That's not a bad idea,' said Brodie, 'I could say my stomach hurts.'

'Or I could stab you in the hand with a fork and you could ask for a bandage,' snarled Ebee.

'What the hell is your problem?' Brodie snapped.

'It needs to be dramatic,' Ebee sighed, 'if you had a stomach ache you would go to the chemist.'

'Good point,' Brodie murmured, knowing that the big man was right, 'so what are you thinking?'

'It needs to be realistic, something that would require urgent treatment, but if it was a stranger, he wouldn't know who the real doctor was.'

'I've got ya, if you were a local, you would go to the practicing doctor in the square,' said Finn.

'You're catching on,' sighed Ebee, rubbing his head.

The girl returned with a tray of mugs of coffee, milk, cream and sugar, 'can I get you guys anything else?'

'No, thanks, we're good,' smiled Brodie.

The girl hesitated and smiled back, 'You're American?'

'Sure am,' he grinned, 'although my ancestors are Irish.'

'Thought so, your hair and eyes are a dead giveaway.'

'Thanks,' Ebee looked at the girl, 'but could we have a bit of privacy now?'

'Ok,' she gave Brodie a penetrating look, 'maybe I'll see you later.' She walked away wriggling her backside suggestively.

'Forgotten Karen already?'

'Of course I haven't, Ebee, I was just being polite.'

'This is crazy,' said Finn, 'we came in here to make plans, not rattle cages, either get planning or I'm going back to work.'

'Right, look sorry,' said Ebee, 'I'm just worried about Karen. She's been gone for weeks and I promised her parents that I'd find her.'

'We're in this together,' said Brodie, 'I want to find her too.'

'My idea is, we get hold of some make-up. I know how to make wounds look real after my time with the film crew.'

'What about that joke shop in Butterfinney?' said Gerard.

'Would they have stuff like that?' asked Ebee.

'Worth a try.'

They drank their coffee and went back to the car.

'It's sensible waiting a few more minutes if we can get a legit reason for gaining entry,' said Finn, starting the engine.

'Rather than going in all guns blazing, you mean?' asked Brodie.

Ebee couldn't imagine any one of them storming in, but it was better to take a more cautious approach, he admitted, 'Let's get that stuff, and who is going to volunteer a bit of acting?'

Chapter 35

Louise had finished typing up the check in and had emailed Ana to let her know that the group would be in her hands after breakfast in the morning, she felt restless and helpless, wishing she was out there with the boys in their rescue mission. Margaret had gone into the village to get meat from the butcher, the chef had been advised to prepare a top quality meal for their guests from Oxford. She never forgot that Mike had been an apprentice at the catering college when he was hired by them, he had grown not only in experience but also his experimentation was exquisite and the restaurant alone drew diners from all over Inishowen. Tonight, as always, he would be given free reign with the menu, and always had a tasty vegetarian dish if required.

Louise decided to pop down to the kitchen and have a quick word with him and his team, just for something to keep busy rather than the need to check up on him. As she was passing the café, she noticed Lynn sitting on her own nursing a mug of hot chocolate.

'Are you okay Lynn?'

'Hello, Lou, it's great to see you, yes I'm fine thanks, I've just been along the back beach for a stroll, it's a bit chilly,' she laughed.

'It can be,' Louise agreed, 'but you can't beat the fresh air.'

'Are you glad you came to live here?' Lynn asked, 'it so different from Oxford.'

'I'm in control of my life here,' she replied with a smile, 'and I'ts good for Jack.'

'Your young brother?'

'Well,' Louise paused, 'Jack is my son, but the story is a private one.'

'Of course, wow, you must have given birth very young.'

'Sixteen,' Louise told her, 'but I wasn't ready for parenthood, my mum and dad have been great.'

'How are they?'

'Great, actually they are staying here for a while, you will see them later; they're having a lazy day after all their globetrotting.'

'Maybe your mum could join us in some of the activities,' Lynne chuckled.

'She would, but isn't this a team building experience?'

'Yes,' Lynne sighed, 'Karnjit suggested it when she knew you were here.'

'We will make sure you have a great time,' she touched Lynne's shoulder, 'I'm just going to have a chat to our chef.'

The kitchen was a hive of activity, Mike was giving instructions to his team of young chefs, so Louise didn't hold him up, and instead, she went through the restaurant and across the fields to the yurts. Jasmine, one of the girls from the village, was airing them out in readiness for the weekend. They were all booked out, even the chalets were full.

'They are looking good, Jasmine.'

'Thanks, I gave them all a good clean earlier, not that they were dirty before,' she laughed.

'Are you coming to the dance tomorrow night? Most of the tickets have been sold.'

'Yes, wouldn't miss it,' Jasmine closed the door of the yurt, 'are you still planning to hold weddings up here?'

'Eventually, why?'

'I was just thinking it would be a perfect setting for my wedding,' she laughed.

'I didn't know you were engaged,' Louise was confused.

'I'm not, I haven't met Mr Right yet,' Jasmine laughed.

'By the time you do, maybe we could hold your wedding here,' Louise quipped, although she hoped it wouldn't be too long into the future when they could hold not only the ceremony but the reception too. Although a lot of the girls wanted to get married in the village church, there were some that wanted to break away from tradition.

She walked along the perimeter of the field overlooking the beach, waves were crashing on the rocks below, and she stood still for a while, watching the spray of sea mingle with the wind that was building up to a gale. It tore savagely at her short blonde hair and the salt stung her eyes, with a sigh, she made her way to the cottage, it was time to catch up with her parents. She hadn't seen them since breakfast, and maybe Karen would be there too, safe and surrounded by the people who loved her. With that thought, she had an idea and quickened her step, time to make some last minute plans and she didn't have a moment to lose.

Frank and Adele were drinking tea at the table in the kitchen, half a scone sat on a plate in the middle and a thick slice on each of their plates.

'Make yourselves at home why don't you,' Louise laughed.

'Have you got time for a cup?' Adele asked.

'I'll make time,' she took a mug from the dresser and poured tea and milk into it, I'll give the scone a miss though, thanks.' She joined them at the table, 'how was your day?'

'Good,' smiled Adele, 'we had a walk and then a rest. Will you have time for a proper chat later?'

'Not till late,' Louise took a sip of tea, 'the group from Oxford have arrived a day early.'

'Haven't you got a manager?' asked Frank.

'Yes, of course, but he is looking for Karen, we haven't heard anything yet,' she was worried, the boys hadn't made contact since they had left this morning.

'I'm sure she's fine,' Frank tapped her hand.

'I'm glad you think so, dad, but after what mum said, I think we have a cause for concern.'

'Ellen is crazy,' said Adele, 'and Aggie is a witch, if they have took Karen, there is every reason to be worried.'

'Margaret has been gone ages too,' Louise looked at her watch, she hadn't realised that it was over an hour since her cousin had gone to get meat.'

'She's probably gossiping in the village,' Frank buttered the scone on his plate, 'you know what women are like,' he popped a chunk in his mouth while Louise and Adele looked worriedly at each other.

Chapter 36

'You've done a grand job,' Ebee was examining the art work on Gerard's hand, Finn had shown artistic talent with the fake blood and gore that they had managed to get from the joke shop, it was so realistic that Brodie had gagged a few times until Finn had hit him.

'Now what?' asked Finn, 'are you ready to strike?'

'Yes, Brodie is new to the village so he can go with Gerard,' said Ebee, 'I'll go with Finn and search around the back; we will keep out of sight.' Their original plan was for Ebee to have the injury, but then he remembered the confrontation in the witch's cottage and realised someone else had to do it, Gerard wasn't local so was the next best man to do the job.

They parked near the butcher shop, 'shit, is that Margaret's car?' asked Finn.

'It looks like it, what the hell is she doing here?' Ebee growled.

At that moment, the lady in question came out of the shop with a heavy bag, which she put in the boot, and as she looked up, she noticed the lads.

'Have you found her?' she asked, walking towards their car.

'No, just get in your car and go home,' said Finn.

'Don't bloody talk to me like that,' she spat.

'Please, Margaret, get in your car and drive back to the hotel,' said Ebee with a straight face.

'No, not yet, I need to get some bits from Centro.'

'Okay, but don't hang around any longer than you need to.'

'Okay, Ebee, just find her, please,' she kissed his cheek and got in her car, started the ignition and drove up the street towards the village shop.

'What's she like?' Finn smiled, gazing after her car.

'Right, let's split into pairs, you two, Ebee nodded towards Brodie and Gerard, 'go first, we will find a way into the back of Swain's surgery.'

The surgery was a long white building on the corner of Billing Road. The white washed paint was badly chipped and the wood around the windows had the start of dry rot. The front garden was overgrown with nettles and dandelions and paper was blowing around in the strong gusts of wind that were intensifying. Ebee shivered, there was a bad feeling about the place, not only with the air of neglect, the grey curtains hanging at the grubby windows gave proof to that, but the place felt wrong. He shrugged his shoulders, maybe it was all the years working on film sets that had fed his imagination.

'There's a road at the back,' he motioned to Finn, 'we can gain access from there.'

'Okay,' Finn followed along the dirt path and they were both pleased to see that high bushes concealed the road from the house, giving them cover from whoever was inside.

Gerard clutched his wrist, blood dripped in thick clumps from the gaping wound, and he quickly topped it up from a plastic wallet in his pocket, he thumped loudly on the door, Brodie went to his side and joined in the banging until the door was slowly opened.

'Help, please help, he has badly injured his hand,' Brodie beseeched the elderly man in a white coat.

'I don't practice anymore,' Swain had partially opened the door.

'We didn't know where else to go,' Gerard whimpered, clasping his hand, 'please help me, I'm losing too much blood, I need some stitches.'

'Come in then,' he sighed, 'let me take a look.'

Brodie helped Gerard into the surgery and cast his eyes around for clues, he was jerked back into the room when Swain asked how Gerard had obtained the injury.

'We were fixing a fence along the sea front, by the caravan site,' Brodie quickly added, 'Gerard drove a stake through his hand instead of the sand.'

'It's a mess,' sighed Swain, 'I think you should go to Letterkenny.'

'Come on,' said Gerard with as much pain as he could muster in his voice, 'it's too far.'

'Wait here,' Swain told them, and opened a door at the back of the small surgery.

'Now what?' hissed Brodie.

'Use your initiative,' Gerard got to his feet and took a gauze bandage from the cluttered table, 'bind this up, mate, I'm losing too much blood.'

'Have you got any left to top it up with?'

'There's a bit, but I don't want to use it all,' he held out his wrist and Brodie took the wrapping from the bandage and he covered the wound, securing it with a knot.

'I learned that at first aid class,' Brodie grinned.

'It didn't stop you gagging at the sight of the wound though,' Gerard raised an eyebrow.

'Right, let's make a move,' Gerard led the way, opening the door and stepping out into a narrow corridor. They noticed several closed doors as they followed a corridor to the end, guessing that this would be away from the main entrance and private for Swain to keep prisoners.

They heard muttered voices and a door was slightly ajar, Brodie and Gerard stood outside listening, 'after three,' said Gerard, and after the count they both barged into the room and stopped in their tracks. Swain was about to inject Karen with a syringe. Brodie realised that he would have to take control of the situation, while Gerard held out his hand to show he needed help, he picked up a metal chair and hit Swain over the head, feeling immense satisfaction as the silver haired ex medic fell to the ground.

'What has he done to you?' Brodie was at Karen's side, pulling the bedclothes back and he gasped when he saw her broken arm.

'Please get me out of here,' Karen begged, sobbing in relief that Brodie had come to rescue her.

Gerard opened the back door and shouted, 'we've found her,' and Karen sobbed louder as Finn and Ebee came into the surgery.

'God,' said Ebee, holding his nose, 'it stinks in here.'

'Gumden,' came a snarling voice from a bed under a window, followed by high pitched screeches.

'What the f,' Ebee walked over to the bed and saw Ellen, her face destroyed by the gunshot wound, she reminded him of one of the batman films where a character had his face half burned.

'This is like a bloody film set,' Ebee gasped, 'we need to get Karen out of here, pronto.' He picked Karen up and held her against his chest, 'you're safe now,' he murmured.

Finn had discovered Karen's car covered under tarpaulin outside the good doctor's house, and were waiting for word to enter. He was shocked at the state Karen was in, her blond hair was dark with grease and her skin was yellow and blotchy.

'We need to get her to hospital,' he said urgently, 'she could lose that arm.'

Ebee was carefully putting Karen on the back seat of the car when an ungodly scream caused them to turn around, Aggie was running towards them, screaming obscenities, she was just about to reach out and grab Finn, when a car came speeding towards them, they managed to get out of the way, but Aggie was too slow and was tossed into the air like a bag of clothes and then landed with a thud on the tarmac, they could hear the crack as her head made contact with concrete. Bemused, they slowly turned to face the driver of the car.

'Oops, I didn't mean to do that,' Margaret pulled a face, 'I thought I'd have a drive down here to see how it was going with the rescue mission, when I saw that old crone chasing you.'

'I'd say it was perfect timing,' said Ebee, closing the car door, 'I'll take Karen into Derry and get her checked out, would you be able to give the merry men a lift home?'

'Of course, Lou will be pacing the floor, do you mind Ebee taking your car, Finn?'

'Not at all, my stuff is down with Colin anyway,' he turned to look at the heap that was Aggie Duffy lying motionless on the road, 'what are we gonna do about her?'

'We haven't got time to hang around worrying,' said Ebee, as he climbed into the car, he wound down the window, 'get the hell out of here, I'll see you at the cottage later.'

'Have we done the right thing?' asked Margaret, as she turned her car around, 'shouldn't we call the guards?'

'Didn't you tell me that they accused you of killing Denton?' said Finn.

'Yes, and they weren't interested when we told them he was threatening us,' Margaret remembered, memories of the witch telling Jack that Lou wasn't his sister made her realise that they had no choice but to leave Aggie in the road. She just hoped that she hadn't done too much damage to the car. They would also have to retrieve Karen's car at a later date.

She drove carefully through the village and put her foot down on the accelerator as they approached the hill that took them near the waterfall. Her legs were beginning to tremble, and she knew that it was a reaction to what had just happened. Aggie might be dead, but what they had done to Karen was unforgivable. She pulled up in front of the cottage and as Louise came out to greet them, she threw herself into her arms and sobbed against her shoulder.

'What's happened?' Louise looked at Gerard, Finn and Brodie and held Margaret tight, whatever it was and she knew it must be serious.

'Put the kettle on,' sighed Finn, 'and we will tell you all about it.'

Adele and Frank had taken Jack for a walk along the beach, and as they all sat around the big table in the kitchen, Brodie began the story while Finn and Gerard filled in what they knew. Louise was horrified to hear that Karen had been kept a prisoner by the demented trio, and took some satisfaction that Margaret had ran the madwoman down.

'We need to examine the car,' exclaimed Brodie, jumping to his feet, and the others hurried after him. There was a large dent on the front and a piece of black material had snagged on the fender.

'I can sort that out,' said Finn, 'drive it around the back,' he said to Brodie, 'I'll get on it now, in case the bloody guards come snooping around.'

'I'd better be heading back,' Gerard rubbed a hand across his face, 'it seems like I've been here for months.'

'Thanks for your help, mate,' Finn shook his hand.

'Yeah, you were great,' agreed Brodie.

'I'll tell Jack that you said goodbye,' Louise said before going indoors. It had been a long day and it was far from finished. They had to oversee the meal later and check that the team from Oxford were having a good time and meanwhile, they were worried sick about Karen until Ebee could give them some news. She wasn't in the right frame of mind to give Gerard any head space.

'Is it okay if I come again?' he asked before Louise closed the door, 'I'd like to get to know him.'

'Of course, Jack would like that, sorry you got caught up in all the drama.'

'I didn't mind, I was glad to be of help.'

'Well, anyway,' Louise paused, 'I have to go,' she closed the door firmly behind her and leant against it, hating the way her body trembled. She had to admit, he had been a rock today, and maybe he wasn't as black as she once thought he was.

Chapter 37

Lynne skimmed a stone across the water and counted the jumps, five was the maximum she had ever done, but she could only reach three this time.

'Hi, are you alright?'

Lynne, turned around to see Karnjit bending down to pick up a massive stone, and as she threw it into the river, it landed with a splash, 'that won't skim,' she stated seriously.

'Apparently not,' Karnjit laughed, 'why are you here alone?'

'I could say the same,' Lynne replied, 'seeing as there's no one with you.'

'I followed you,' Karnjit threw another stone in the river, a flat stone that made four jumps.'

'Why?'

'You seemed a bit distant, I wondered if you wanted to have a chat.'

'Do I? I'm sorry,' Lynne sighed, 'I was just wondering what the hell I'm doing here, I want a change of direction, not the same old, and Nancy and that fawning idiot Brenda are doing my head in.'

'I feel the same,' Karnjit turned her back on the river and walked up the nearest sand dune and sat down, raising her face to the sun.

'What would you like to do?' Lynne sat beside her.

'Now? Or when we get back?'

'Both, I fancy a paddle in the sea, and a swim in the pool, but as for when we get back, I'm going to look for another job.'

'I want to write a novel,' Karnjit gazed out across the bay, 'this would be a perfect place to get started.'

'Have you got any ideas for your book?'

'Plenty, I've made notes and drew up the characters, mythical dragons and unicorns and the suchlike.'

'I'd buy it.'

'Thanks, so, what is it you would rather do than work at the bank?'

'I'd love to open a coffee shop, the one they have here is amazing, it's really given me food for thought,' Lynne chuckled, 'pardon the pun.'

'It's nice to have dreams,' Karnjit sighed.

'What's stopping you from writing a novel?'

'Lack of motivation, mainly, I get so easily distracted, she picked up a small stone and threw it towards the river, although it was some distance away she managed to get it on the shore line. 'Why don't you open a coffee shop?'

Lynne laughed, 'money of course and finding the right location, it has to have the right footfall.'

'You should have a chat with Lou and Margaret, they must have some ideas for you,' Karnjit looked at her watch, 'shit, we're going to be late for that Pilates class.'

They got to their feet and jogged along the beach towards the hotel, they managed to reach the studio with minutes to spare, hot sweaty and laughing.

'Phew, that was close,' sighed Lynne as she dragged a mat into the centre of the room.

'Fun though,' Karnjit flopped down beside her, she noticed that Nancy gave them both a look that could kill.

'Hello, my name is Ana,' a young Spanish girl stood at the front, 'we will start with some breathing first, so if you would all lay down on your mat, we will begin.'

Two hours later, Lynne and Karnjit were sprawled out on loungers, when Louise joined them, 'are you having fun?' she asked.

'Yes, it's great, we've just had a swim, the pool is amazing,' Lynne told her.

'We aim to please,' Louise perched on the end of a lounger, 'I heard you were late arriving at the Pilates class.'

'Bloody hell,' said Karnjit, 'who told you?'

'Guess! But the aim of our spa is for you to have fun and enjoy, it's not a prison and the classes are not a punishment.'

'We did enjoy the Pilates, Ana was a great instructor, we just got a bit distracted and lost track of the time,' explained Lynne.

'You don't have to explain,' Louise laughed, 'I just wanted to say sorry that I haven't had a chance to catch up with you, we have had a bit of a crisis.'

Karen was in Altnagalvin hospital, recovering nicely, her arm had been broken and reset and put in plaster, she would be ready to be sent home after the doctor's rounds. They had arranged for her parents to be met at Belfast international later that day.

'I was hoping for a chat, Lou when you have a minute,' said Lynne, remembering her chat with Karnjit earlier on the beach.

'Sure, I've got a few minutes to spare now, shall we go and get a coffee?'

Lynne pulled on a towelling robe and slipped on the complimentary mules they had been given, 'are you going to join us?' she asked Karnjit.

'No, thanks, I'll swim a few more lengths and get back to my book, Dianne and Julie will be down in a few minutes,' she had just read a text from Julie saying that they wanted to escape the others for a bit. So much for the intended team building, she thought ruefully.

'Grab a table, Lynne and I'll get the drinks, tea or coffee, or something else?'

'Cappuccino, please,' Lynne loved the way the café was laid out, red leather chairs and silver tables, with a mix of booths set around the edge, and four and two seater tables in the middle, it had a touch of an American diner. Lynne chose one of the booths by the window, overlooking the bay, deciding that she didn't want to broadcast her plans to other diners.

'Have you got plans to put in a juke box?' she asked Louise as she put the drinks on the table.

'The jury is out on that one,' Louise chuckled, 'Margaret wants one, but they are so expensive. She said it would pay for itself, maybe she's right, what do you think?'

'Well,' Lynne thought for a moment, 'it could be either a cliché, or authentic.'

'True, although we have the statue of Arthur on the horse, and the spa is called Cheyenne, so it wouldn't be too out of place.'

'Maybe you could set up a shooting gallery and call it the Wild West,' Lynne wondered.

'Sounds great,' agreed Louise, 'but we have so many ideas in the pipeline, we need to focus on what we have and build slowly.' She took a sip of her drink, 'is that what you wanted to talk about?'

'No,' Lynne lifted her cup, 'that was just an idea on the American theme, the reason I wanted to have a chat is for advice, Karnjit said you might be able to help.' She outlined how her dream was to open a coffee shop and sell cakes that she had made, her vision was to open an old world café, serving real tea in china cups.

'How can I help? I mean, I'd love to if I can, but we are sort of making it up as we're going along.'

'Whatever you're doing is working,' Lynne was impressed, 'I just wanted to pick your brains on location and staff, really.'

'We used the catering college to begin with, it was a win win, they have a job, and also had ongoing experience.'

'That's a brilliant idea,' Lynne was wondering what catering college she could go to, although she wanted to make most of the cakes herself and said as much to Louise.

'Oh my god, you're wonderful,' Louise exclaimed, while Lynne was confused. 'We could hold cookery classes here, the villagers could learn how to cook special meals and fancy cakes.'

Lynne wondered how the conversation had led to the birth of that idea, but she got carried along with Lou's excitement, it was an amazing idea.

'We could have a Spanish night, Ana can give some tips on what meals to cook, and we can even have an American night, Brodie can help with that one.'

'Burgers and fries?' Lynne quipped.

'I've heard about clam chowder and meat loaf,' Lou was serious.

'Bat out of hell?'

'I haven't heard of that one,' Lou laughed and Lynne joined in.

'Don't you ever stop?'

'Just when I decide to, I get another idea, although I'll need to run it past Margaret, on that note, I'd better take her a coffee, she's been stuck in the office all morning.'

'Thanks for the advice Lou, I'll do a bit of market research when I get home.'

'You can always come and work for us, I mean it, Lynne. We're booked out all summer.'

'Howard would love that, and the boys, it was bad enough I came for a few days, all the moaning they did about deserting them.'

'House prices are quite low here compared to Oxford, you would get a big house with the money you'd make on the sale of your house.'

'I'm a home bird,' sighed Lynne.

'Give it some thought, the offer is on the table,' Louise took her empty cup to the counter, they really would need more staff over the coming weeks, especially to cover holidays. She asked for a coffee carried it through to the office.

Chapter 38

Karen was packing her clothes and toiletries when Ebee arrived to take her home. Her arm throbbed, but she could cope with that, it was the memories of being kept a prisoner that would be harder to come to terms with. They had made statements to the police in the village, but the response from them was not good. Swain had stated that Karen had shot Ellen in the face before she was hit by the car, Aggie had multiple injuries but was recovering in Letterkenny hospital, and the up-shot of it all was that if Karen let it go, they would turn a blind eye to their misdeeds. Ellen was in no fit state to make a statement and was being held at a psychiatric ward in the Glenties.

'I don't know if I want to stay in Clodbury anymore, Ebee,' she sighed as she followed him out to the car park.

'Don't make any rash decisions, yet,' he put her bag in the boot, 'the girls are looking forward to spoiling you.'

'It seems like I've been gone for months instead of weeks,' she buckled up and Ebee drove up to the roundabout and turned back onto the dual carriageway

'Do you want to stop at Tesco?' he asked.

'No, I'm good thanks, I just want to get back,' Karen was silent for the rest of the journey, taking in the views as they crossed the Foyle Bridge and then through Bridgend, Fawn and Lisfannon. The view was spectacular, especially after being in hospital, but she could take no joy in it.

As Ebee pulled up outside the cottage, Karen gasped as a familiar couple stood in the porch waiting for them.

'Mum, Dad, oh my god, what are you doing here?' she burst into tears as she hugged them both.

'We've been worried sick,' her father told her emotionally.

'We needed to see you for ourselves,' her mother held her daughter tight against her.

Supported on either side by her parents, Karen was overwhelmed to see that there was quite a welcome committee waiting for her. Banners had been put along a wall, and the table was laden with cakes, scones and sandwiches. Brodie stood by the range, looking bashful but pleased to see her.

'We've got a rota made out,' he told her proudly, 'and a bell for you to ring if you need anything.'

'I'm not an invalid,' she smiled at him, she had dreamt of him coming to her rescue and he had, along with the others of course.

'You need looking after,' he told her gruffly.

'That's why we are here,' Mrs Brown stated seriously, she needed to look after her daughter, after all the weeks of not knowing where she was and fearing the worst, it was the least she could do.

'We've prepared one of the log cabins,' Margaret explained, in case they were worrying where they would stay.

'They are very cosy,' Louise assured them, 'they have two bedrooms and all the mod cons you should need.'

'We must pay for our stay,' said Mr Brown, 'We can't have you being out of pocket.'

'The tea is getting cold,' said Margaret, 'come and sit at the table, the girls at the coffee shop have prepared this feast for us all.'

'I'll be off then,' said Brodie, 'I just wanted to check that Karen was okay.'

'Don't be daft,' Louise pulled out a chair at the big square table, 'sit there and help yourself, and you Ebee, tuck in. We will have a sandwich and a cuppa and then leave you to it.'

'Yes,' sighed Margaret, 'the crowd from Oxford need to be organised, we've got the band and a disco tonight, and the young group are playing.'

'I wish I could go,' Karen said sadly.

'Why can't you?' Brodie was surprised. 'I'll take you and escort you back to the cabin, and your mum and dad, if they want to go,' he was eager to please.

'No, lad, we will be in bed by ten,' chuckled Mr Brown.

'You young ones go and have a bit of fun,' said Mrs Brown.

'I don't feel up to dancing, Mum, but I would love to go and listen to the music.'

'It's a date then,' grinned Brodie, 'I'll pick you up at seven.' He finished his mug of tea and plate of sandwiches, and then went back to work.

'Do you think she'll be alright?' Louise asked as she walked with Margaret up to the hotel.

'Eventually, but it will take time, she knows that we will be there for her.'

'Maybe she should go home with her parents for a while, a change of scenery, and all that.'

'It's Karen's decision,' Margaret wondered if that would be the right thing to do, 'she might go home and not come back.'

'Ah, but Brodie is here,' Louise added.

'So she will be back, if she decides to go at all.'

They came across Dianne and Julie sipping prosecco on a bench, they were giggling and it was obvious that they had drunk most of the bottle.

'It looks as though you're having fun,' Margaret observed.

'I love it here,' said Julie, 'it's so peaceful and the views are breath taking.'

'Yes, but it can get a bit wild in the winter,' Louise wondered why they weren't at the Zumba class she had arranged, in fact, the group had not gelled as expected. 'Where are Nancy and Brenda?'

'Oh, they went into Letterkenny to do some clothes shopping, one of the workmen were going for supplies, so they begged a lift,' Dianne hiccupped, 'sorry, I don't usually drink, but Julie begged me to share the bottle with her.'

'I thought you were here to do some team building,' Margaret sighed, 'we have gone to a lot of trouble to fix classes and fun things for you all to do. You might as well have just booked some bloody chalets and got on with it.'

Louise stepped in, Julie and Dianne were looking rather sheepish and it wasn't their fault, 'We've had an emergency,' she explained, 'but Margaret is right, a lot of people have gone all out to make this trip a success for you all.'

'I'll make sure Nancy knows,' said Julie, who was feeling guilty, it was true, they had been given a sheet each of activities and between them, most had been poorly attended.

'Tomorrow morning we have organised horse riding along the beach, it's all paid for by your boss, and it doesn't come cheap.'

'I'll tell the others,' said Dianne, 'We will make sure to be at all future activities.'

'Okay,' smiled Louise, 'I'm not a nagging school teacher, but it's all paid for, you might as well enjoy everything while you're here.'

Margaret and Louise walked into the hotel and headed to the office, 'sometimes it makes you wonder if it's worth it.'

'Margaret, what's up? It's not like you to be so negative.'

She sat on the soft leather chair in the office, Its Finn, he's hardly said a word since Karen was rescued, I'm sure he's avoiding me.'

'He has been busy,' Louise rationalised. 'You need to have it out with him and see where you stand.'

'It's not up to me to sort it out,' Margaret said huffily.

'No, I don't suppose it is,' sighed Louise, getting fed up with her whinging, 'let's agree not to talk about him, at least until the Oxford mob have gone home. Some team building, it's a wonder they even agreed to come here.'

'I know,' Margaret agreed, 'sorry to have been in a mood, but I really thought we'd made a break through. Okay, no more Finn. What can we do to bring the team together? Any ideas?'

'How about some country music and line dancing? I could get Maggie from the village to walk them through the steps and the band could play some Garth Brooks or Hal Ketchum.'

'That would be great,' Margaret got to her feet, 'I wouldn't mind having a go; it looks brilliant when they are all in step.'

'When they are all in step,' Louise laughed, 'but it would be a good way for them to do some bonding. I wonder if Nancy is back from her shopping spree.'

'She's a case,' Margaret grinned, going over to look out of the window, 'Nancy is more interested in having a good time than sorting out her dysfunctional team.'

Louise picked up the phone on her desk, had a quick chat with Maggie who was willing to come out for a few hours and then the boys, who jumped at the chance of doing something different.

'I'll ask Brodie to clear out the function room, if he's free,' Margaret left the office leaving Louise to email Nancy and advise her of the evening schedule, stressing the importance of all the party being present. She also roped in a few friends to make up the numbers and then, as an afterthought, asked Brodie, Finn and Ebee along so that there would be some males present, maybe her dad and uncle might fancy giving it a go, she pondered. When the image of Gerard's dark, handsome face swam into her mind, she quickly banished it, Jack might be won over by him, but she certainly was not.

Chapter 39

It was perfect the way the evening fell together, Karen was eager to watch from the side-lines with her parents, although it took a lot of persuading to get Ebee to join in. Louise and Margaret were amazed at the interest the villagers had shown in the impromptu event and arrived in droves to join in. Maggie, not one to miss out on an opportunity, suggested that they start a beginner's class twice a week, and it was agreed that every Monday and Wednesday they would hold the classes, charging a reasonable fee to cover her tuition and the use of the function room. Money in the pot to reinvest in their hotel. Maggie had also suggested lessons of Irish dancing to youngsters, but that was under debate, Louise and Margaret wasn't sure how they stood with insurance for children.

Nancy was the biggest surprise of the night, she was a natural dancer and soon the team were following her lead. Soft drinks and water were on offer, line dancing and alcohol were a recipe for disaster. The band were a massive hit and a new outlet had opened up for them when an owner from a hotel in Letterkenny just happened to be staying the night and had took an interest in the dance, he had been impressed with the boys and had booked them for a regular weekend slot, offering to put them up for the night if required.

Louise noticed how Brodie and Karen sat closely together, with her parents at her side. Louise knew that being locked away by the weird trio had left her severely traumatised and wondered if the happy go lucky Karen that they knew and loved would ever return.

Margaret on the other hand, was throwing herself into the line-dancing with gusto and she had an inkling that she had consumed a couple of red wines beforehand. Louise was baffled by Finn's behaviour, she could tell that he liked Margaret a lot, more than that she suspected, but why was he keeping his distance? She sighed heavily, maybe they should hold a singles night and sort them all out, herself included, because one thing she was sure of, she was well and truly cured of Gerard.

The tempo of the music changed and Maggie was on the stage barking out directions to the sweaty dancers. Nancy was at the front showing off with her side kick Brenda. The dance was a complicated number with plenty of twists and turns and Brenda was watching Nancy closely, copying all the moves. As the pace of the dance increased, the turns were more frantic and Brenda, who was not so quick on her feet, tripped Nancy who fell hard onto the dance floor. It took a few minutes and a few kicks by the oblivious dancers before Brenda signalled to Maggie to stop the music. Nancy was unconscious due to a heavy foot to the head by Brenda who hadn't noticed that her adored leader was on the floor. She screamed as she saw a trickle of blood slide down Nancy's cheek,

'Oh my god, she's dead, I've killed her.'

Ebee, who had been walking past with a tray of drinks for Karen and her parents, placed it on a near table and then dropped to his knees at the side of Nancy's head. He placed a finger on the side of her neck and nodded his head at Louise,

'She's not dead,' he sighed with a grin.

'I'll go with her in the ambulance,' stated Brenda importantly.

'Sorry, but we're not in an episode of casualty,' said Ebee, 'the nearest hospital is in Derry, or failing that, Letterkenny, I'd say go with Derry as its part of the UK.'

'How can we get Nancy to hospital then?' Brenda wailed.

'I've asked Dennis to take you,' Louise said calmly. 'Go and get a coat for yourself, I'll find a blanket.' She sighed heavily as she made her way to the store cupboard, stupid bloody woman, she thought, and wondered if she meant herself or the injured woman. Nancy was a piece of work, there was no doubt about that, but what would it do to their reputation? She grabbed a thick tartan blanket from the top shelf and carried it back to where Nancy was still on the floor, being advised by Ebee that it would be best not to move her. Louise passed the blanket to Brenda who gently wrapped it around Nancy.

Dennis O'Donnell arrived a few minutes later and whisked the women off to Altnagalvin hospital.

'Hopefully they will go home from there,' Margaret sat down beside Louse, 'they are hard work. No wonder you wanted to escape from that office.'

'It was toxic,' Louise agreed, and she felt as though a weight was lifted from her shoulders. Her life is a world away from the drudgery and vindictiveness of the place she had once worked. How could she have forgotten how bad it was there? She gave Margaret a quick hug, thank you for reminding me of why I am here. Mum and Dad are back tomorrow with Jack, we can help them chose their site.'

I'm going to turn in for the night,' they both looked up to see Karen standing in front of them with her parents on either side.

'You must be tired,' Margaret told her, touching her arm.

'Exhausted,' she agreed.

'Have a lie in tomorrow,' Ebee told her, 'I'll go and bring the car around to take you all home.'

'Thank you,' Karen told him gratefully.

Maggie was the only one left and she was still on a high, 'thanks girls,' she beamed, 'I've got loads of bookings from tonight.'

'It was a great night, thanks Maggie, just a shame that Nancy and Brenda had the collision.'

'Oh, I've seen worse than that Lou,' she grinned, 'especially when the dancers have had a drink, as I suspect those to inebriates had.'

'Do you think so?' Margaret asked hopefully.

'Definitely,' Maggie laughed, 'they must have had at least two bottles of Prosecco. I noticed them both swigging from a large bottle.' She picked up her iPad and speaker and tossed her dark hair over her shoulders, 'see you Monday girls, it's about time the villagers had a venue like this. Have you thought about Zumba or salsa? I can do both,' she gyrated her hips and beamed at the cousins.

'Well,' laughed Margaret, 'she's a live wire, I'm worn out just watching her.'

'It's worth giving a thought to the other classes,' Lou stretched, it had been a long night and an eventful one. 'Let's go home.'

Chapter 40

The next day was a mixture of people arriving and some leaving. Ebee knocked the door at eight and Margaret answered it with a bleary smile.

'What's up, Mate?'

'Karen has decided to go home with her parents,' he sighed heavily as he walked into the kitchen, Louise was sitting at the big table with a mug of tea and a slice of thick buttered toast in her hand.

'I'm not surprised,' said Margaret, 'she needs to get away after everything she's gone through. Any idea how longs she's going for?'

'She isn't coming back,' Ebee sat on a chair and Louise poured out a mug of tea, leaving him to add sugar and milk.

'Never, ever?' the girls gasped in unison.

'Not for a while, she loves her aunt's cottage, but she's decided not to come back to work here.'

'That's a shame,' said Louise as she slowly stirred her tea, 'but Mairead has picked up most of her shifts and her daughters will work when we need them.'

'Karen was our friend,' sighed Ebee.

'She still is,' Margaret touched his arm, 'and can you blame her wanting to forget what happened to her? They are still out there, the evil threesome.'

'I don't blame her, I will miss her though.'

'You won't have time to miss her,' Louise laughed, 'We have lots of work for you, mate.'

Louise decided to take a cake she had just made down to Karen, and to say goodbye. Karen needed space and time to recover after her ordeal, being back at home away from any reminders could be the best thing for her. She jogged down the hill towards the small cottage by the sea, and with a smile on her lips, rounded the bend and just before she reached the gate, Louise noticed a familiar car on the drive. If hearts could really stop with a sudden shock, then her's surely had and it felt as though her blood had turned to ice in her veins. What the hell was Swain doing here?

She banged on the door, for the first time since Karen had begun working for her she felt uncomfortable about just walking in. Karen opened the door and smiled when she saw it was Louise, 'Hi Lou, come in, I was just telling the doctor to leave me alone.'

Louise followed her into the kitchen.

'What are you doing here?' she asked the man that had made their lives hell.

'Ah if it's not the lovely Louise,' he grinned, showing his yellow teeth. 'I've just come to tell Karen here that we won't be pressing charges against her, or anyone else,' he said pointedly.

'You held her captive for weeks, tortured her, drugged her, you are a sick bastard,' Louise shouted into his mottled face.

'I was treating her for a broken arm, my dear,' he patronised, 'she is getting better now.'

'Not mentally, you sick prick, and I've heard what you and Ellen get up to.'

'That's private,' he spluttered, 'I just wanted to make my peace with Karen before she left town.'

'I hope you are not going to kidnap her this time,' Louise was sarcastic.

'Mum and dad are picking me up in an hour,' Karen said softly, 'they've gone to get a few things from the village. Keep in touch Lou, thank you for everything.'

'Are you leaving?' Louise asked Swain.

'I'm on my way,' he grabbed his hat from the table, 'safe journey, Karen, it's been nice meeting you and if you decided to return, maybe we can get to know each other a bit better.' It was obvious from his innuendo exactly what he meant and Louise was livid.

'Get the fuck out of this house, and if I see you near the point again, I would like you to think about Denton.'

'So it was you,' he smirked.

'No it wasn't, but I know people that could be responsible,' she hinted.

He slammed out of the small house and it was only when his engine started that Louise realised that she had been holding her breath.

'He's dangerous,' Karen was worried for her friend, 'I only let him in because I thought mum and dad would be back sooner. Now you see why I can't stay.'

Louise gave Karen a hug, 'yes, you need to put some miles and time away from that evil trio, but one day, and hopefully soon,' Louise pulled back and shuddered, 'they will be brought to justice for what they did to you.'

'I'll miss you all,' Karen fought back tears, 'I've loved working up the road, but I've got the offer of a new admin job in Warwick university.'

'It sounds good, and if you ever need a spa break, you know where to find us.'

'I'll come up when we set off, to say goodbye to everyone.'

'What about Brodie?' Louise asked, knowing that the young American was important to her.

'He's coming over as soon as he gets his paperwork sorted out and worked his notice,' Karen smiled softly, 'he is the one good thing to come out of all of this.'

'I'll see you before you go then, Karen,' she gave her a quick hug and let herself out of the small house. It would be weird to see it empty.

As Louise was walking up the hill, her legs began to shake and a wave of nausea washed over her, she hurried over to a thick hedge and emptied the contents of her breakfast.

'Are you alright, Lou?'

Louise startled, quickly wiped her face on a tissue, it was not a great place to bump into Gerard after his weeks of absence.

'Yes, fine,' she blew her nose, 'just sent that evil doctor packing. I haven't seen you for a while, I thought you wanted to see more of Jack,' her words tumbled out of her mouth in a rush, she wasn't in the right frame of mind to see him of all people.

'Yes, of course I do, but I had to go to America on a family emergency.'

'Sure, I remember you had to do that before, what was it? About 12 years ago,' Louise's voice caught on a sob.

'Hey, what's wrong, Lou?' he pulled her to him and she noticed with a shock that he still wore the same aftershave that he wore years ago.

She buried her face in his shoulder, the soft wool of his sweater tickled her cheek, Gerard kissed the top of her head and she pulled back in horror, what the hell was she doing?

'I'm sorry,' she told him, 'it was a shock seeing the pervey doctor in Karen's house. I can't get my head around why she let him in.'

'She might be suffering from Munchausen syndrome,' he said seriously, leaving his arm draped around her shoulder.

Louise chuckled, 'Stockholm syndrome,' she corrected, she allowed his arm to stay there while they walked up the road, her legs were still like jelly and it was weirdly comforting.

'Did you know,' Louise pointed to a house further up the road, 'a paedophile used to live there. He was a teacher in the north apparently. They can't bring him to justice and he's now working in France with young boys, what the hell is wrong with this country?'

'It's a crazy world, alright,' agreed Gerard, 'but I believe in Karma, don't you?'

'Not always,' she sighed.

Margaret was in the kitchen making lunch and gave them a quizzical look as they came in together.

'I went down to see Karen,' Louise explained, 'The Evil Doctor was there.'

'What? Is she insane? It's a good job Karen is going back to England, out of his slimy clutches.'

'I agree, has Brodie given in his notice? Karen said he's due to follow in a few weeks,' Louise sat down at the table and Gerard sat next to her, keeping as close as he could.

'He mentioned something,' Margaret said, 'but he was going over plans with Ebee earlier, and they were talking about showing them to Finn.'

'Maybe he wants to get his paperwork in order, he should get a job easily though, he's a skilled carpenter. Is there any tea in the pot?'

'I'm just making fresh,' Margaret warmed the big brown tea pot and added 3 tea bags, 'Adele phoned earlier, they were in Derry getting a few bits, your dad wants to try Frank Longs for a change.'

'I don't blame him after that little madam had a go at him in Lisnagalvin,' Louise sighed, 'jobs worth.'

'What happened?' Gerard asked, 'Tell all.'

So in between giggling and indignation, Margaret and Louise told him how Adele had been treated badly at the Lisnagalvin branch of Tesco when she had forgotten to scan a packet of frozen peas.

'She was treated like a common criminal,' snarled Louise.

'Well,' said Margaret, 'I won't be going in there again.'

To add emphasis to her declaration, the door was threw open which such forced it bounced against the wall.

'Jack,' admonished Louise, 'be careful, you've made a hole in the wall.'

'Sorry, but Ebee said my dad was here,' he spotted Gerard at the table, 'where have you been? I've missed you.' He ran over to him and sat down, forcing Louise to stand up.

'I'm going up to see Mairead while you two catch up,' she grinned at them, 'I'll get a coffee up there.'

'I've poured your tea,' Margaret sighed.

'Give it to Jack, I won't be long.'

Louise was glad to escape for a while, she hadn't been prepared to see Gerard and it had knocked her off kilter. Feelings from the past had rushed back to her, reminding her of what they had once had and had since wasted. The one constant being Jack, and even he had suffered because of lies and deceit. Had too much happened for them to have another chance? Another thought came unbidden into her mind, what did she really know of how Gerard had spent the last eleven years, he might have more kids out there, wives, girlfriends, her mind was tortured as she entered the hotel.

'Lou,' Mairead shouted as she noticed her walking towards her with two mugs of coffee she had grabbed from the café on the way. 'I was just about to call you both.'

Louise walked quickly over to the reception desk and handed her friend a mug, 'don't tell me, there's more bad news.'

'Good and bad,' sighed Mairead, 'which do you want first?'

'The bad, so we can deal with it and get it out of the way.'

'Nancy developed sepsis and has had to have her leg amputated,' began Mairead.

'Bloody hell, she only fell over on the dance floor.'

'I know, but when they operated the wound became contaminated, she was going to sue us, but she has been advised that it's not our fault, an accident, even though it was caused by her barmy mate.'

'Is that the bad news?' Louise hated to sound callous but if they weren't liable it was a relief, 'I'm sorry for Nancy, of course, but I've got enough going on to lose sleep over her.'

'Yes, that's the bad news, the good news is that, well, do you know Tamara Trent?'

'Is she that singer that is storming the charts at the moment with, True Love?'

'Yes, well, she wants to book the hotel for her wedding next year. I told her we weren't quite ready, but she insisted that this is the venue she wants. She is coming next week after her gig in Dublin to talk it over with you and Margaret.'

'Oh my god, this is just the break we need. Oh, and a wedding planner,' she laughed.

'Karnjit would be good at organising the event and Natasha is brilliant at design,' said Mairead, proudly. Her daughter was an up and coming designer and very talented.

'Can you set up a meeting for tomorrow morning with them both? We will have to get Finn involved too, and Ebee, well, the team, you included.'

'I'll get on it,' Mairead took a sip of her coffee, 'it's so exciting, just think of the press coverage? The world's your oyster.'

'Isn't it lobster?' Louise laughed, 'I'll go and tell Margaret, Mum and Dad should be back soon and Karen is stopping off to say goodbye, I'll tell her to come up here as well if she has time. I forgot to mention that doctor had wheedled his way into her house, she needs to get away.'

'He has always been weird,' Mairead shuddered, 'and the strange sisters. They should be punished.'

'I agree, see you later.'

Chapter 41

Adele wanted to be involved with the team and Louise knew it would be good for her mother to have an interest once they had moved in to their new house. It was amazing how fast the builders had erected the four bedroom house and it was only the finishing touches that were needed before her parents could move in.

'It will be heaven when we can get our stuff from storage,' Adele confessed, 'but lovely of you girls to free up a suite in the hotel.'

'We haven't worked the bill out yet,' said Margaret with a straight face.

'No, we haven't,' added Louise, 'breakfast in bed, lunch, dinner, and the Jacuzzi,' she scratched her head.

'Well, whatever it is, we will pay it,' said Adele, letting them know that she was not expecting preferential treatment.

'Jack's working it out now,' Louise sniggered, she knew her mum would insist on paying so had worked out a plan with her son.

Gerard had gone back to his house promising to return the following weekend, he had left soon after she had told them the exciting news about the wedding booking. Ebee had grinned from ear to ear, he loved getting his teeth into new projects. He assured them that he would not be returning to Nuneaton and following Karen, but wanted time off to travel when possible. The girls agreed that everyone was entitled to a holiday and Margaret herself was long overdue a break.

'You girls could go off on an adventure,' Adele had told them, 'I'm here now to run things in your absence.'

'Don't tempt us,' Margaret had laughed, although it would be tempting to get away from Finn for a week or so, he was keeping his distance and she didn't know what was going on with him. In fact, she was sick of him blowing hot and cold.

'What do you think, Lou? Should we go off on a holly bob?'

'What about Jack? He's taking his exams at the end of the month to decide what class he will be in.'

'It's going to take that long to organise anything,' Margaret stated, and the half term break is coming up.'

'I can look after Jack,' Adele sighed, 'It would be nice to spend time with him.'

Louise realised that it would be good for her son and parents to spend quality time together, they had been separated for over a year to leave mother and son to bond, she should return the favour, and Margaret badly needed a break. Finn was keeping his distance yet not telling her why.

'Okay,' she agreed, 'we will plan a couple of weeks away, Gerard can spend time with Jack too without me hovering in the background.'

Margaret screamed and hugged her cousin, 'thanks Lou, you don't know how much this means to me.'

Louise could feel tears sting her eyes, 'I think I do, cuz, but I do need to run it by Jack first.'

Sitting in the cosy kitchen in the cottage, Louise on one side of Jack and her mother the other. Margaret at the table nursing a huge mug of tea, and had her fingers crossed. Frank and Brian had walked into the village for a pint or two, deciding they weren't needed. Adele knew that he didn't really need an excuse, but it was wonderful to see her brother and husband getting on so well after years of living far apart.

Louise took her son's hand, 'Jack, I'm going to ask you a question and I want you to be truthful, I need to know exactly how you feel.' She could feel him tense and the grip on her hand tightened.

'It's okay darling,' Adele soothed, noting that the colour had drained from Jack's face.

'Would you be okay staying with Nan and Granddad for a couple of weeks? I want to spend some time with Margaret away from the hotel. We will be in constant touch, but if you need me to stay, I won't go away.'

Jack chuckled, 'Mum you had me worried then, I thought you were gonna say we're moving back to Oxford. It will be great spending time with my other mum and dad, go and pack.'

Louise didn't know whether she should feel elated or hurt, but it proved that Jack needed some quality time with his grandparents. She would phone Gerard later and ask if he would like to spend time with his son, it would be easier all round if she wasn't here. Her feelings for him were totally mixed up. One minute she hated him, it was hard to get rid of the resentment of the last twelve years, but then she saw a softer side to him and wondered if he felt as confused as she was. One day they would have another conversation, but she wasn't ready yet.

Chapter 42

The girls had created a conference room out of one of the larger ones near the gym and swimming pool. It was also near the café so convenient for grabbing a hot drink before the meeting started. The table that took over the middle of the room was rich mahogany, specially made for them by a local man, the girls loved it. The room created order and professionalism and today they needed order and structure. Ebee sat at the head of the table with Finn at his left side,

Mairead sat to his right next to Natasha, Finn and Brody. Karnjit sat next to Finn with a pad and pen in front of her, this was her first meeting with the team and she was thrilled by it all.

'Glad you could join us,' Margaret said to him, from the other end of the table, 'how long have we got you for?'

Brodie blushed, 'well, it's a bit delicate,' he mumbled.

'Delicate?' Louise laughed, she was sitting at the side of her cousin, 'Why? We have agreed for you to leave whenever you need to, although we would prefer it if you could stay.'

'Have you ever been to Bedworth?' he asked everyone around the table.

'I have,' Ebee spoke, 'I used to live in Nuneaton and Bedworth is its neighbour.'

'Is it nice there? The reason I ask is, well, Clodbury is in my blood now, the open fields and the ocean, even the wind, but Bedworth is miles away from the nearest beach.'

'Yes it is,' agreed Louise, 'so was Oxford, everyone can't live near the seaside.'

'I lived near the beach back home,' sighed Brodie.

'Does that mean you would rather stay here than go to Bedworth and be with Karen?' Louise asked him.

'In a nutshell, yes. I received an email from her the other day and she is working as PA to that horrible woman that broke her leg. It got me to thinking that if she could be that fickle, could I leave this wonderful place to be with her and hate it there.'

'The way I see it,' said Finn, 'If you really loved Karen, you would be at her side no matter where she was.'

'My problem is, did I really know her to start with? Was I in love with the person I thought she was?'

'Why don't you go over for a long weekend,' said Ebee, take her out for a meal, have a chat about what she wants and what she expects from you.'

'I think Ebee should be the in house councillor,' Margaret chuckled.

'Don't you think I've enough to do around here?' he growled.

'Anyway,' Louise said with authority, 'let's get this meeting started. Next week, my cousin and I are going on a field trip and we will need some deputies to hold the fort while we are away.'

'What do you mean, Field Trip?' said Margaret in disgust. 'I thought we were going somewhere exotic, like the Maldives.'

'Mm, its nice there, sighed Ebee.

'Thanks Ebee, I would like to find out for myself.'

'Margaret, we will talk about this later, I've got a few things to run past you, but after this meeting.'

Margaret glared at her cousin, 'right after this meeting,' she said sharply.

'Okay, right,' Louise looked at her notepad, 'Mairead will be in charge of reception and housekeeping, Ebee will be head of maintenance along with Finn and Brody, and Karnjit will be in charge of all events with the help of Natasha. Anything I've missed?'

'We need a new life guard,' said Ebee, 'Jimbo is going to live in Queensland.'

'Great, okay, can you put an add out today, hopefully we will find one before we go away,' said Louise.

'I'll get straight on it,' said Mairead.

'That went well,' grinned Louise as the door closed behind the team leaving just herself and Margaret sitting at the big table.

'Did it? I'm too pissed off with you to take it seriously at the moment, Lou.'

'You haven't heard my plan yet,' said Louise indignantly.

'Okay, go ahead, the floor is all yours.'

'Hang on one sec, I just need to get leaflets from the office,' Louise ran out of the room and returned seconds later with a bundle of brightly coloured pamphlets, she put a few in front of Margaret.

'There's a massive hotel opened on a foreland in the south of Cork. They do everything that we do, except more. I've booked us in for a couple of nights and thought we could try out the classes and treatments, all inclusive. It will be a wonderful way of having a break while picking up some valuable tips, especially for when we go into the wedding planning side of things. On the way we will stop off at some of the other competition, the first stop is Bunndoran. '

'But what about the exotic holiday you promised me?' Margaret was not pacified.

'We can do that later in the year, also, if things go wrong here we can come straight back.'

'What can go wrong? Besides, we need a break from here, from thoughts of here, from people that are here.'

'You mean Finn?'

'Especially him.'

'Go and pack your bag,' Louise told her, 'we are leaving Friday morning. We can take my car and I'll drive.'

Jack was ecstatic about being left with his grandparents and as Louise had assured him that they were only going to be away for a short while that pacified him further,

'I'll be busy with school and football, anyway,' he told her, 'go and have some fun, you deserve it.'

'You sound like a little old man,' his mother laughed.

'When are you leaving?' he asked.

'In an hour, it should take us about two hours to get to Donegal town. I'll ring you tonight before bedtime,' she gave him a hug and kissed his cheek, 'be good boy for your grandparents.'

'I will,' he sighed, wiping his cheek.

She waved him off as he boarded the school bus and went to load up the car. Margaret was still in a bit of a mood but she had packed her bag. They were waved off by Adele, Frank and Brian. The staff were up at the hotel making sure that things ran smoothly in their absence. The girls had every faith in her team.

Chapter 43

'You can chose the music,' Louise told her cousin, 'some lively driving music.'

Margaret slid in a CD of power ballads and as they sang along to Bat out of hell, the mood in the car changed and they were laughing and enjoying the journey. It was a beautiful spring morning and Louise began to relax and feel revitalised.

She reversed into a space of a car park in the centre of Donegal town and they walked towards the high street.

'I'm starving,' said Margaret, 'I didn't have time for breakfast this morning.'

'Why? Oh, you had a bit of a lie in,' Louise laughed. 'We will grab some lunch here and have dinner at the hotel later,' she looked around at the quaint shops,' it reminds me a bit like Oxford.'

'I've never been,' sighed Margaret, 'why didn't you invite me?'

Louise stopped, 'I'm so sorry, I wasted ten years of not keeping in touch properly, all because of misunderstanding and well, you know why.'

'I know, and I should've made more of an effort. Maybe we could go there one day.'

'I'd like that,' Louise gave her cousin a hug and they linked arms as they walked towards an impressive restaurant.

Red and gold canopies hung above the small bow windows and a leather bound menu was set up on a wooden stand.

'This looks terribly posh,' said Louise with a giggle.

'It looks empty too, but we might as well go and see what's on offer.'

'Table for two is it?' the woman was dressed in a long grey dress and her hair was pulled back in a tight bun.

'Er,' Margaret looked behind her, pointedly, 'yes please.'

'Follow me,' she led them towards the back away from the windows.

'Can't we sit by the window?' Louise asked, 'it's not often we get such a lovely sunny day.'

'I'd rather you sit here, out of view,' the woman replied in a sniffy voice, 'to be honest, if I had my way, I wouldn't let you in at all, but with the change in the law I have no choice.'

'What the fuck are you on about?' Louise snarled, 'our money is as good as anyone's, just because I'm wearing my jeans, they are designer by the way.'

'It's not your attire,' she spat, 'it's your sexuality. I don't condone it, never have, it's against what the bible says.'

'You need locking up, you nutter,' Louise pushed the chair back, toppling it over and barged into the kitchen.

'You can't go in there,' the sour faced woman shouted.

'Watch me,' Louise slammed the door against the wall startling a small fat man in a chefs outfit. He was leaning against a stainless steel cooker reading the Irish Times.

'Who are you? Get out of my kitchen.'

Louise gave him a deadly stare, 'I'm just getting more evidence for my article, I'm a writer, and also I will be commenting on trip advisor.'

'You can't do that, you haven't had a meal,' he spluttered.

'Nothing is cooking in here except my temper,' Louise fumed. She stormed out, slamming the door again into the wall, bits of white paint fluttered to the floor.

Margaret was taking photos on her phone and writing notes down in the pad she carried in her bag.

'Are you ready to leave, darling?' Louise asked her, putting an arm around her shoulder.

'Yes, my sweetheart,' Margaret smiled, 'this is a terrible place, so homophobic.'

They kept a straight face until they reached the opposite side of the road, 'what a godawful woman,' Louise spat.

'Are you really going to write about her?'

'Too right I am, I'm fuming.'

'I wouldn't have guessed,' laughed Margaret, 'was it because she assumed we were a couple or her attitude?'

'Both to be honest,' Louise sighed, 'she is a nasty bigot. Let's try this pub, they might do bar snacks.'

The first thing they noticed was that the bar was full of men and the second the absence of food.

'Can I help you young ladies?' asked a friendly bar man with red cheeks and white hair.

'Do you serve food?' Margaret asked.

'No, sorry wee pet, try over the road.'

The both turned their heads in horror towards the grim restaurant. The barman laughed, 'No, not the Black Eagle, the café further up the street.'

'Thank you,' Louise smiled, 'We will never set foot in that place again.'

'Don't blame you,' said a young man sitting at a table with his arm draped over his boyfriend, 'she's a real dragon that one.'

The girls walked despondently down the high street, both hungry and then they saw the black and white building with red gingham curtains at the window.

'This looks more promising,' sighed Margaret.

The bell above the door tinkled as they made their way in to the cosy café. The atmosphere was warm and welcoming and the delicious aromas drifting from the kitchen made the girls salivate in anticipation. Most of the tables were full but they managed to squeeze into one along the side wall. Menus sat in the middle of the table with cutlery and condiments.

'I'm toying between the lasagne and the quiche,' said Louise.

'Me too,' laughed Margaret.

A woman came towards their table dressed in a black skirt and white blouse her dark hair was tied back in a shiny pony tail, she had a pad and pencil in her hand and as the girls looked up to give their order, Margaret screamed.

'I don't believe it, Elizabeth Kearney, what are you doing here?'

'I could ask you the same thing, Margaret Grant,' the woman laughed.

'Let me take your order into the kitchen and I'll pull up a chair.'

A big pot of tea in a silver pot was put on the table along with a jug of milk and bowl of sugar cubes.

'This is my cousin, Lou, from England,' Margaret grinned, 'she is also my business partner.'

'Very impressive,' Elizabeth shook Louise's hand. 'I met Margaret on a course a few years ago, we had a great laugh.'

'Yes we did,' Margaret agreed, 'I thought you were going to teach.'

'I was, but then I got the offer of this place, it's my aunts and she wanted me to run it for her while she travelled the world.'

'Where is she now?'

'Texas, she met an oil billionaire and has decided to stay there.'

'Nice, so has she signed over the café to you?'

'No,' Elizabeth sighed, 'she wants me to carry on running it until she decides what to do with it.'

'Tricky,' Margaret poured tea into three cups, 'sugar?'

'No thanks,' Elizabeth took a sip of the tea, 'so what are you girls doing here?'

'We're having a bit of a road trip,' Louise told her, stirring her tea, 'it's been an adventure finding somewhere to eat.'

Elizabeth raised an eyebrow, 'why?'

Margaret explained their experience in the horrible restaurant and the men's bar up the street.

'Nobody goes in the Black Eagle, I don't know how she manages to stay open. The pub is a gay bar.'

'Wow,' laughed Louise, 'and it's opposite her restaurant, talk about karma.'

'This lasagne is delicious,' Margaret popped a meaty chunk into her mouth.

'So is the quiche,' Louise slowly chewed the light pastry. 'Who does the cooking?'

'I do most of it, I have a young girl that helps with the fries, salad and garlic bread.'

'Well,' Louise swallowed the last morsel of quiche, 'if you ever need a job, get in touch.'

'What type of business to you run?'

'A hotel and spa retreat,' smiled Louise.

'That's amazing. We have been trying to find somewhere to stay up the North West for ages, for a girly weekend.'

'We run those,' Margaret told her, 'dances, spa retreat, disco, that sort of thing.'

'Is it expensive?'

'The log cabins and yurts are your best bet, they sleep four to six.'

'Do you run tribute nights or anything like that?'

Louise looked at Margaret, 'what a brilliant idea, why didn't we think of that?'

'The purpose of this road trip,' said Margaret huffily, 'is to get new ideas.'

Louise burst out laughing, 'see, you're getting it at last,' and then pushed her playfully on her arm.

Margaret pulled out her note book and added tribute night to the last page and then passed a business card to Elizabeth.

'If you have any more brilliant ideas or want to make a booking, give us a call.'

'I will, that's great, I will definitely be in touch.'

Louise paid the bill and added a Ten Euro tip, 'and don't forget,' she smiled, 'if you need a job...'

Elizabeth laughed, 'Thanks, but Aunt Peggy has been good to me. If she decides to sell, then I might just come back to Clodbury.'

Less than an hour later, Louise pulled up in the car park at the impressive hotel looking out over the sea.

'Look at that view,' exclaimed Margaret, 'it's stunning.'

'It reminds me of Newquay in Cornwall,' said Louise with a hint of longing in her voice.

Great rolling waves crashed onto the sandy shore, perfect for surfers and there were quite a few out on the ocean today.

'Let's go and check in,' Margaret opened the boot and took out her case, put it on the ground and removed Louise's.

'Yes,' Louise took a deep breath, 'and after we've had a cuppa I fancy a walk along the path down there,' she pointed down to a tarmac walkway that spanned the perimeter of the beach.

The girls had been allocated adjoining rooms which they loved especially as an inner door separated them, which they could leave open or closed, locked or unlocked.

'Perfect,' Margaret filled the kettle, 'we can be together but also have our own space.'

The rooms were identical, heavy brocade curtains hung at the massive window which looked over the stunning view. A window seat ran along the length, ideal to sit and gaze at the waves or to read a book in sunlight. The bed was queen size, the duvet cover matched the curtains but the sheets were pure white cotton. Two winged chairs were arranged at the bottom of the bed and a writing desk with a telephone sat against the wall. A flat screen television hung from a heavy bracket giving the choice to watch in bed or from one of the chairs. The deep shag pile wool carpet was a deep rose.

'I love it,' sighed Louise, sitting in one of the chairs, 'it's elegant without being over the top.'

'Different to our rooms,' Margaret passed a cup of tea to Louise.

'Our aim is to be unique,' Louise smiled.

They booked a table for dinner on their way out, both were wearing white trouser and red jumpers, a coincidence they both giggled about.

'I should've put on a blue scarf,' teased Louise.

'Why?'

'Red, white and blue of course.'

Margaret nudged her arm playfully, 'you are half Irish.'

'Yes, I know, but I was born in England.'

'Do you miss it?' Margaret hadn't asked the question before, assuming that Lou loved it in Clodbury as much as she did.

'I hadn't really thought about it until today,' she answered honestly, 'but I just had the urge to go to Cornwall again, crazy isn't it? I used to go with mum and dad between the times we used to visit Clodbury.'

'You can go, take Jack, it's not that impossible.'

'I know, ignore me.'

Margaret was unsettled, it was the first time Lou had shown any signs that she could be homesick.

They walked for an hour, their jumpers tied around their waists. As they made the way back, Margaret pointed out a crazy golf course, and on a whim they decided to have a game.

'That was fun,' Louise laughed as they headed towards their rooms.

'Only because I let you beat me,' grinned Margaret.

'I brought a bottle of wine, do you fancy a glass after we've showered and changed?'

'Would it shock you if I said no?' asked Margaret.

'Yes, it would.'

'Well, in that case, I would love a glass.'

They had both dressed carefully, Margaret in a deep blue fitted dress and Louise in classic black trousers and an off the shoulder white shirt that set of the beginnings of her tan. They had applied just enough make up, blusher, mascara and lipstick, they weren't out to impress. Despite that, heads turned their way as they were escorted to their table.

They both ordered duck in a rich orange sauce with an assortment of vegetables. The portions were enormous but they managed to leave clean plates apart from the bones.

'That fresh air,' Margaret sighed, 'is not good for my figure.'

'Shall we have a cocktail to finish? I don't think I could manage a pudding,' Louise rubbed her flat stomach.

'We could take them back to our room,' suggested Margaret.

They both ordered sex on the beach and it arrived in long goblets with lots of fruit and ice. It was delicious.

'We can order others to our room, should we want them,' grinned Louise.

To have a change of scenery, they chose Margaret's room to relax and chat over their drinks.

'What's the plan for tomorrow?' Margaret asked, she had left everything up to Louise, her plan had been postponed for the time being.

'Breakfast, a walk along the beach, a facial followed by a full body massage and then after a couple of hours chilling out we can have a swim. Then dinner.'

'Sounds good,' Margaret held her glass up, it was almost empty.

Louise reached over and picked up the phone, '2 sex on the beach for room 112,' she requested.

After the drinks had been delivered along with various nibbles in silver bowls, Louise studied her cousin for a moment before speaking.

'So, how a things with you and Finn?' she asked slowly.

'The same, why? He doesn't speak to me unless he has to, never comes into the office if it's only me in there.'

'I think I know what the problem is,' Louise took a long drink, 'he feels intimidated by your role in the company. I can tell he cares for you, well, more than that.'

'It's not my fault,' Margaret said crossly.

'Of course it isn't, but we can change that. Do you trust him?'

'Yes, he's been working for us for ages, Finn is well known for his honesty.'

'Then why don't we form a board of directors? I'm not sure how it works, but if Finn had a say in how we run our business, he might feel more of an equal.'

'We can run it past him,' Margaret agreed, 'what about Gerard?'

'That ship has well and truly sailed,' said Louise, 'pardon the cliché, we are different people now and the only thing we have in common is Jack.'

'The spark must still be there,' Margaret insisted.

'If you leave a candle burning for nearly twelve years, would it still be burning?'

'That's a silly comparison,' Margaret huffed.

'Maybe. Shall we watch a bit of the news before we turn in for the night?'

Margaret pointed the remote at the flat screen television and selected the local channel. The news had just started and a roundup of what was ahead was being explained by a glamorous news reader with blonde hair and a fake tan.

'There has been a shocking murder in the small village of Clodbury,' the woman began.

Margaret quickly turned up the volume, 'Oh my God,' she screeched, 'I hope it's not anyone we know.'

They both turned back to the screen as a picture of a familiar face stared back at them, 'Doctor Swain was a respected member of the community, much loved by all that knew him.'

'That's a bloody lie,' shouted Margaret, 'he was a pervert.'

'She can't hear you,' Louise smiled.

The newsreader continued, 'Two women have been held for questioning, Aggie and Ellen Duffy, both known associates of the doctor. Ellen Duffy is reported to have mental issues and has only just been released from hospital. We will update you when we have more information.'

Louise turned off the television, 'I hope they lock them up. Look what they put poor Karen through. I wonder if it was them that attacked Ebee.'

'Makes you wonder,' said Margaret, 'do you fancy a hot chocolate before we go to bed?'

'Not really,' Louise sighed, 'I'm going to phone mum, she might have some more information,' she went through to her suite and grabbed her phone from where it was charging. She had a weird feeling about this latest murder, it had unsettled her.

Louise re-joined her cousin who was sitting in bed watching a comedy on the wide screen television.

'You look comfortable,' Louise told her as she lay next to her above the bed clothes. She was wearing her pyjamas and dressing gown.

'I am,' Margaret yawned, 'did Adele know anything?'

'Not really, although it's got everyone in a tizzy. Jack is being kept a close eye on, they have said Sean, his friend from school, can stay overnight for a sleep over. I asked if we should go home but they said there really is no need.'

'What could we do?' Margaret yawned again, 'the perps are in custody.'

'Perps?' Louise laughed, 'You'll have to stop watching those American crime programs.'

'I love them, don't you?' Margaret turned the television off, 'sorry Lou, I'm going to sleep, I can't keep my eyes open.'

Louise rolled off the bed, 'Night love, see you in the morning, breakfast is at 8.'

The girls decided on a light breakfast, Margaret had a cheese omelette and Louise had eggs benedict, with fruit juice and coffee. After a brisk walk on the beach which took them over an hour, they had a swim in the pool.

'It's not as big as ours.' Margaret stated as she flopped onto the pool side lounger.

'No, but I do like the décor,' Louise spread her towel on the other lounger and lay down.

The tiles were a mixture of blue, gold and green, giving the area around the pool a tropical feel. Giant palm trees, very realistic but obviously fake, were strategically placed around the loungers and giant golden globes hung from the ceiling.

'Don't you think it's a bit OTT?' Margaret gazed around, squinting up at the lights.

'Maybe, but it's very effective.'

'I feel like I'm advertising a new swimwear range,' Margaret grinned.

'I'll buy five,' laughed Louise.

After a shower, they went into separate rooms for their treatments. Over an hour later they were relaxed and shining, after the full body massage, facial and Indian head massage.

'Shall we go up to our rooms and have a nap before dinner?' Margaret asked sleepily.

'That sounds very sensible,' agreed Louise.

In the end, they decided on room service and an early night. They were moving on to the next hotel, further south and a two hour drive away the next morning and they wanted an early start.

Chapter 44

The girls decided that after a long drive to County Cork and then down to County Claire, back up to Dublin and then homeward bound, that all the hotels had nothing special going for them. The views were spectacular, but so were they at Cheyanne. Margaret had been smug on the way home, not quite saying, 'I told you so,' but near enough with remarks like, 'I bet it is hot on the Indian Ocean,' or 'Barbados is nice this time of year.' Louise had made a promise that their next holiday would be something special, although she hoped that it wouldn't be too long before Finn got his act together.

Adele had put together a welcome home tea, with sandwiches, scones and various cakes she had baked using her favourite recipe book. Jack was delighted to see his mother home, but after a hug was soon back playing on his X Box.

'Any more on the murder?' Louise asked before biting into an egg and cress sandwich.

'The sisters have been allowed to go home, pending further enquires,' sighed Adele, 'I didn't tell you because you would have come back home.'

'We might have,' said Margaret, 'but we were enjoying ourselves too much.'

'Sarcasm,' groaned Louise.

'Am I missing something?' Adele looked from one to the other.

'No,' stated Louise, glaring at Margaret, 'the field trip was useful, we got some great ideas and also realised how brilliant our place is. I've promised Margaret she can have her exotic holiday soon.'

'Good, well, tuck in and I'll pour the tea,' Adele said bossily.

Louise excused herself after an hour of explaining to Adele the pros and cons of the hotels they had stayed in and while Margaret told her about the hotel in Bundoran, she took this as her queue to slip out.

'I'm just going up to the hotel,' she told them, 'I'll see you later.'

'Shall I come with you?' Margaret asked.

'No, tell mum about our trip, your view is different to mine,' she laughed.

Mairead looked up from the computer and her face lit up at the sight of Louise, 'Hello, it's great to see you back.'

'I was only gone a week,' she smiled, 'How have things been here? We heard Swain had been murdered.'

'Did you, I suppose it was on the news, terrible business.'

'Not that terrible, he was a horrible man. Have you seen Finn anywhere?'

'I think he went down to the Chalets, one of them had a problem with the door.'

'Thanks, I'll call back up when I've had a word with him,' Louise gave a quick wave to her friend and set off with purpose across the field below the road towards the chalets. Most were already booked out for the weekend and the yurts were always booked out, even during the quiet season.

'Hi ya Lou, you're back then,' Finn beamed as he saw her approaching.

'No, I thought we'd spend another few days in Dublin,' she grinned.

'Funny. Have you come to check on my handy work?'

'You could say that,' Louise replied, 'can we go inside?' she pointed at the chalet Finn had been working on.

'What's up?' He led the way into the chalet and took a seat in the living area.

Louise sat opposite in one of their trendy chairs, it was a wicker affair padded with sumptuous cushions.

'Can you be honest?' she asked him candidly.

'I've always been honest,' Finn was offended, 'I've worked with all the specks you have given me, designed not only the hotel, your cottage and now your parents.'

'Calm down,' Louise touched his hand, 'I don't mean professionally, I mean personally.'

'Why?'

'Are you dating anyone?'

'No, but is that any of your business? I'm sorry Lou, but I don't know where this s going.'

'Well, if you answer my bloody questions you will find out,' Louise was tired after the journey and over dose of carbs.

'No, I'm not dating and I'm not gay,' Finn sighed.

'Good start,' grinned Louise to let him know she was sorry for being abrupt. 'How do you feel about Margaret?'

'You know how I feel about your cousin, but what's the point?'

Louise gazed out of the window, noting that the view was pretty spectacular from here. The tide was in and big waves crashed fiercely against the rocks. Margaret would not be happy with her if she knew that she was interrogating her beloved in a chalet.

'I've got a proposition for you,' Louise turned her blue eyes back to Finn and batted her long eyelashes at him.

'Sorry Lou, you are a beautiful young woman, but I don't have feelings for you in that way.'

Louise glared at him and then bent over in mirth, 'I don't fancy you either, matey. As you have already stated, you have been a massive part in our dream, project, call it what you like, and I think you should have a bigger part.' She paused to let him take that in, 'how would you feel about being a director in our company? You would have a say in what we do, vote as one of the directors and be equal to the other board members.'

'How much will it cost?' Finn was being practical, he was a good grafter but didn't have millions of euros in the bank.

'Nothing, we don't need your money, we need you. I am going to ask Mum and Dad, Ebee and Jack when he is older, to be board members and then we can get it drawn up properly with Eustace.'

'Okay, and what is the catch?' Finn was watching Louise now for a flicker of humour, it was a sick joke if she wasn't being sincere.

'To take Margaret on holiday,' Louise said straight faced, 'if you say no to the holiday, you can still be a board member.'

'Is it an all-expenses paid holiday,' Finn quipped.

'Yeh, why not, she wants to go somewhere exotic, let her chose. Oh, and don't get married out there, we would never forgive you.'

'Deal, to both,' they stood up and Finn gave Louise a big hug. 'You know how I feel about Margaret, how could I compete with all this?'

'Well, now you don't have to,' Louise kissed his cheek. 'Go and take your girl for a walk.'

Chapter 45

Margaret was packing her case for a surprise holiday with Finn, still in a daze from his declaration of enduring love. It wasn't quite like that but he had told her how he felt about her in a round a bout kind of way, which she had found very cute. He had explained how she had seemed out of his league with all the money and the booming hotel business, but now he was to be a part of the business he felt different. He appeared different to Margaret too, more confident and with a spark that had been missing since the reading of Uncle Arthur's will. She couldn't believe how blind she had been and how insightful her cousin was.

'Are you nearly done?' Louise stood in the doorway with her hands on her slim hips.

'Yep, just need to throw in the toiletries and sun cream. My passport is packed but Finn won't let me see the tickets, he said it's a surprise, I just hope it's not another bloody road trip.'

'I hope you've packed your thermals just in case,' Louise quipped.

An hour later, Louise, Adel, Frank, Brian and Jack stood by the gate and waved the happy couple off. Ebee was giving them a lift to Belfast airport where they were flying to Manchester. Margaret didn't have a clue where they were going after that but Louise knew that they were booked into a hotel near the airport and then were flying out to Florida for a fly drive around the state.

'About time those two got together,' Brian said, wiping his eyes, 'sometimes I felt like knocking their heads together.'

'It's a good job it didn't come to that,' Adele gently punched his arm.

'Is it okay if I play on my X Box for an hour?' Jack looked hopefully at his mother.

'One hour,' Louise told him, 'I want a word with Mairead and check that everything is okay. Brodie is covering Ebee for a few hours.' She kissed her son's cheek, 'be good and make sure you've done your homework.'

'It's done,' Jack told her cheerfully before going into the cottage.

'I'll be back in a bit, are you okay to keep an eye on Jack?'

'Yes, we're not going out until eight,' Adele said.

Mairead was talking to Brodie when Louise walked towards the reception area, they were laughing and Louise saw an easiness in their relationship that she hadn't noticed before.

'Hello Lou,' Mairead smiled, 'you're going to love this,' she turned the computer screen towards her and Louise leant forward to see what was making them giggle. A national newspaper was on the screen with the headlines, 'British women arrested in Dubai.'

'Why is that funny?' Louise asked.

'Read the item,' Mairead urged.

With a sigh, Louise read about the two British women who had not only sunbathed topless on the beach, but had also drank cans of lager which they had kept in a bag of ice. Good thinking, but against the law in Dubai on both accounts.

'Silly cows,' laughed Louise, 'what will they get for being caught?'

'Didn't you read their names? Its Nancy and Brenda, remember the horrible women that came for the team building exercise.'

'I'll never forget,' Louise wouldn't either, they had caused a lot of trouble, but had brought Karnjit into their fold, so some good had come out of it. 'How did you find out about them?' it was too random that the article just appeared on the screen.

'Brodie phoned Karen last night to ask if she was busy, he was thinking of going over for a few days. She told him that she had to hold the fort at work until further notice. When Brodie asked her why and thought she was just the PR, Karen told them about the drama in Dubai, so he is staying here instead.'

'Well, it proves that you always need to phone ahead, just imagine if he had decided to surprise her?'

'I know, that's what he thought,' Mairead sighed. 'He said he was going to postpone his trip for a while.'

'That's okay with me, at least it saves me the worry of finding a replacement,' she rubbed her eyes, suddenly tired. 'If everything else is okay I'm going back to the cottage. If you need me, give me a shout.'

'Okay,' Mairead smiled, 'but we should be grand, go and have a rest and a cup of tea.'

'I might just do that,' Louise told her.

As she walked the path that led from the hotel to the cottage, Louise took in the raw beauty of the view that surrounded them. The wild Atlantic way was certainly an apt description. She took in a deep breath of salty air mingled with the rich smell of grass, a heady mix that cleared her head. The house that was being erected for her parents was almost complete and then they could make it their home. But what happened when Margaret and Finn came back from their holiday? She wondered. Where would that leave her?

For a while now she had been feeling out of sorts with how her life was going. She knew she was being silly, the hotel and spa were doing well and the holiday camp was a massive success, yet something was missing. She sighed and walked slowly towards the cottage that had now been home for her and Jack for a couple of years. It was a full tide that evening and she could see the waves were over six feet high, pounding on the rocks that were clustered around what was known locally as the Priests Hole. No one appeared to know why it was called that, maybe an old priest had once fallen in on his way back from doing mass at someone's house. Too much wine, she pondered with a smile. Or perhaps it was a murder. Louise shivered as her mind went down a dark track. Murders were rife at the moment, maybe Clodbury was like that village in Midsummer murders, or that one that Jessica Fletcher wrote about. The person who attacked Ebee was still out there and the motive was a mystery. She made her way home with an air of despondency.

As Louise opened the door that led into the kitchen, she could hear Gerard's voice along with her parents. She had the urge to turn around and flee, she wasn't in the mood for facing her son's father at the moment.

'Is everything okay?' Adele asked her daughter, noticing how pale she was.

'Brodie is staying, for a while anyway, so that helps. What are you doing here, Gerard? Sorry, that sounded rude.'

'I wanted to see Jack, it's been a while,' he explained.

'You saw him when I was away with Margaret.'

'How did that go?' he smiled, causing her heart to flip. She hated that he had that effect on her.

'Interesting. Is there any tea in the pot, mum?'

'I'll pour it,' offered Gerard, 'would you like a biscuit or some cake?'

'No, thanks, I'm cutting down on carbs.' He was certainly making himself at home, she thought. 'Where is Jack, by the way?'

'He's loading up the new game I got him for his X Box,' he passed her a mug of tea, 'I told him it's an early birthday present, I hope that's okay.'

'Yes, of course, thank you.'

'Hi mum,' Jack appeared in the kitchen, 'dad's going to help me play that new call of duty game, Sean said he is going to beat my score.'

'I hope its age appropriate,' Louise glared at Gerard.

'Mum,' Jack groaned, 'all the kids at school are playing it.'

'Well, in that case, you had both better go and practice,' Louise took a sip of tea, dismissing them both.

'Are you okay, Lou?' Adele asked as soon as father and son closed the bedroom door.

'I'm fine, I think I'll go for a walk, though. I heard Teresa is back from London, I want to ask her if she will make some hanging baskets for the hotel.'

'They would look lovely, by the way, I've asked Gerard to spend the night, and Jack has missed seeing him.'

'I'll see you later,' Louise finished her tea and grabbed a jacket from the back of a chair.

As she walked down the road towards Teresa's house, Louise again had that feeling of her life being out of control. Her mother seemed to be calling all the shots in the cottage now, it would have been nice to be consulted about Gerard staying. Even when she moved out and into her own house, Margaret would be back and even though she loved her cousin dearly, things would be different now.

Chapter 46

Teresa was in her yard as Louise approached, and ran to give her a hug, 'Lou, how lovely to see you. 'It's been ages since we had a chat.'

'Yes, it must be a few months,' Louise agreed, 'I thought I would use the opportunity of going out for a walk and coming to see you at the same time.'

'Would you like a tea or coffee? Or something a bit stronger?' Teresa asked.

'I've just had a cuppa, but thank you.'

'Come inside, Dave has just gone to Derry we can have a catch up.

She followed Teresa into the large family room and sat down on the comfortable sofa, Teresa sat next to her and turned to face Louise.

'How are things going up the road? I keep meaning to come up for a treatment, but never seem to find the time.'

'I'll book you one in,' Louise laughed, 'then you will have to go. The hotel is attracting a reputation for the spa facilities and restaurant for its amazing meals, thanks to the great staff we managed to find. The holiday village is fully booked most of the time and we are always looking for added extras. Ebee is sorting out the crazy golf, there isn't one around here, so it should be popular.'

'All systems go then, I've walked to the point a few times and had a look, I love the statue.'

'Thanks, you should've called in, I could have given you a guided tour,' Louise told her.

'To be honest, I've been rushed of my feet with the kids at university and going to England,' Teresa sighed.

'I forgot that you were away,' Louise smiled, 'we all get caught up in our own lives and the months just fly by.'

'Very true, and what with the murders, I asked Dave if we wouldn't be safer back in London.'

'You're kidding, right?' Louise laughed.

'Maybe,' Teresa said, 'but I asked Dave to put one of those CCTV thingies in a last year. It catches everything from outside our house to right across the field leading to the beach.'

'Wow, can I have a look? It might be worth getting one for the hotel and cottage.'

'Have a glass of wine first,' Teresa got to her feet and took two glasses out of the cupboard, 'red or white?'

'Red please,' Louise got to her feet and went to look out of the large window overlooking the road, she had a good view of where Karen once lived and felt a pang at the loss of her friend, Karen was caught up in her life in Bedworth now. Maybe one day she would come back for a visit.

'The camera catches all of that,' Teresa passed a large glass of wine to Louise, 'I haven't looked at it since we had it installed though, I haven't had the time.'

'What would it capture when it's dark?' It was pitch black in the evening with no street lights around.

'Let's go and take a look,' Louise followed her into a room leading off the kitchen that was used as an office.

'Before I forget,' Louise took a sip of her Merlot, 'could I order some hanging baskets for the hotel? You could put some tags on and take orders.'

'Thanks Lou, I'll draft some designs and prices and bring them up.'

'Ah, now you have an excuse,' Louise chuckled.

'Very true, maybe I'll bring my swimming costume.'

'Yes, do that, and I'll join you for a swim, I really must use the pool more.'

Teresa switched on the light and fired up a monitor, 'Dave is all for conserving energy and with the power cuts it's easier to keep the monitor turned off.'

'Does the power cuts effect the camera?' It would be of no use up at the point when a gale force wind was gusting so much it feels as though the roof is going to blow off, Louise thought.

'No, the fitters told us that it's not powered by electricity, although the system in the house is, it went over my head if I'm honest,' Teresa said ruefully. 'I'm pretty good at modern technology but this is far too complicated. I do know how to play it back though,' she smiled.

'Each icon is a date range,' explained Teresa, 'first it breaks down into months and then divides into weeks and then days,' she took a sip of wine, 'so, for example, if I click on this one,' she moved the cursor over the nearest icon and it subdivided into four icons, and then seven.

'Clever,' said Louise, 'let's have a look at that one,' she pointed at the day before. An image of the road filled the screen and became a hive of activity. Familiar cars went up or down the road, neighbours were taking their dogs for a walk, and then she saw Ebee drive off with Margaret and Finn to the airport. 'How far does it go back?'

'We had it fitted about eighteen months ago, so up until then. Why?'

'Ebee was attacked just over the road, it might show us who done it.'

'Interesting, I always fancied being a PI. What date are we looking at?' asked Teresa.

'It was when I was in Canada, so around October.'

For the next few minutes Teresa clicked and they watched each piece of film until Louise exclaimed, 'Bingo.'

The footage showed Ebee leaving Karen's around 10pm and a figure hiding near the entrance to the beach car park.

'Can it be zoomed in?' asked Louise.

'I'll try,' Teresa pressed a few keys and an enlargement of the screen showed Ellen with a metal bar in her hand. They watched horrified as she rained blows upon the unsuspecting Ebee.

'Oh my God,' exclaimed Teresa, 'she's a mad woman.'

'Literally,' said Louise, 'she gets away with murder. Can we show this to the police?'

'I'll give them a ring, the station should still be open.'

An officer came out fifteen minutes later followed by an agitated Gerard.

'What's wrong?' Louise asked him as Teresa ushered the police officer into the office to show him the film. Her heart was beating hard in her chest, 'is Jack okay?'

'Yes, he's fine, we were worried about you, you've been gone ages,' he touched her arm.

'What did you think had happened to me, Gerard?' she fumed.

'Lou, there is a murderer out there and it's getting dark. What is the Guarda here for?'

Louise could see how worried he was and felt guilty for being so sharp with him, 'sorry,' she meant it, 'we've just discovered who attacked Ebee. Come on through.'

Gerard followed her into the office where Teresa was showing Officer Riordan the footage.

'It's not really admissible evidence,' he explained. 'I'm sorry but we can't do anything without more proof.'

'Are you mad?' Louise shouted, 'it's as clear as that bloody nose on your face.'

'Lou, calm down,' Gerard gabbed her arm, Louise shook it off. 'Don't tell me to calm down,' she fumed, her cheeks bright red. 'Clear proof that the psycho bitch attacked Ebee who was badly hurt, and you can't do anything. You can't do anything when she murders people either. In fact, what do you bloody well do? I know, arrest people for double parking or jumping an amber light.'

'I can arrest you for wasting police time or abusing an officer,' Riordan told here severely.

'I rest my case,' she spat, 'or should I say, 'I arrest my case?'

'You're not funny young woman,' he patronised.

'But you are, you're hilarious, what are you going to do the next time she kills someone? Give her tea and cake? Sorry Teresa, I'm going to have to go before I say something I'll regret. Speak tomorrow,' she gave her friend a hug and stormed out of the house, Gerard close at her heels.

'You didn't help,' Louise accused him, 'the patronising bastard. How dare he speak to me like that?'

'Because he's a jumped up arsehole,' said Gerard, grabbing her hand. 'His dad was the chief a few years ago and was caught on the take. You will never win against them, Lou, and he can be a dangerous enemy.'

'Do you think he killed Denton and Swain then?'

'Who knows? I do know that your mum has been worried about you lately, that's why she sent me to find you.'

They had reached the gate to the cottage, 'thank you for the escort home, Sir Galahad,' she forced a smile, 'see you later.'

'Now where are you going?' he asked her.

'To check on the hotel, I won't be long,' she kissed his cheek and noticed the way his eyes lit up. Maybe it would be fun to wind him up a bit, she thought as she made her way to see Mairead and Ebee.

Chapter 47

Mairead was just finishing her shift and her daughter, Natasha was taking over when they saw Louise walking towards them.

'Is everything okay on the western front?' Louise teased.

'All quiet, Ebee is back and has done the rounds, did you want to see him?' asked Mairead.

'No, I just wanted to check in with you before you left. Have you got time for a drink?'

'Yes, it will have to be a soft drink though, I'm driving.' Said Mairead, slipping the strap of her bag over her shoulder.

'I was thinking hot chocolate at the café,' Louise grinned.

'Sounds good, with marshmallows and cream,' smiled Mairead.

There were a couple of people enjoying hot drinks and cakes but they easily found a table away from them.

'What's up then, Lou? I can tell something has rattled you.'

'The police in Clodbury are crap,' she burst out, 'I mean, look at all that trouble we had with Denton and they did nothing. And now we discovered who attacked Ebee and they still do nothing.'

Marie, a young girl who was working in the café during a break from university came over to take their order.

'Two hot chocolates with all the works,' Louise told her, 'and have one yourself, you look as though you need one.'

'Thanks, Lou,' Marie sighed, 'it's been busy this afternoon, I think there was a late seminar and they all came in at once.'

'Do you need help in here? Don't struggle on your own, we can get someone from the restaurant or café at the holiday camp.'

'Peggy came up to help for an hour, I rang down to the holiday village to ask them, I hope that was okay.'

'Using your initiative, I like that,' said Louise, 'I'll put a bonus in your pay-packet.'

'You're a good boss,' said Mairead when Marie went to get their drinks.

'Treat people how you would expect to be treated yourself, that's my motto,' Louise was serious. She had had a lifetime of jumped up managers who should never have been promoted in the first place.

'Okay, what's bugging you?' Mairead looked Louise in the eye.

'Teresa has got a fancy CCTV fitted, I'm going to order some,' Louise told her.

'And?'

'We discovered who attacked Ebee. It was that demented bitch, Ellen.'

'Are you really surprised?' Mairead wasn't. She had guessed it was either her, Aggie or Swain. Her hunches were usually correct.

'I suppose not, but it was still a shock to see her beating him around the head with a metal bar. She could've killed him. Why would she pick on Ebee of all people?'

'Probably because he is different and not from around here. She hates strangers.'

'That makes sense,' Louise agreed, knowing how much she hated her and must have disliked Karen too. 'The police won't doing anything, it frustrates the hell out of me.'

'They never do unless it suits them,' Mairead sighed, 'it's never going to change.'

'It's good to see you and Brodie getting along,' Louise said, needing to change the subject before she exploded.

'He's a lovely guy,' Mairead smiled.

'So when is he taking you out?' Louise teased.

'If he does,' Mairead said firmly, 'it will be as friends. We have a lot in common and no chemistry to get in the way. I don't want another man in my life after Jimmy, he was the love of my life.'

'I know, I was just messing,' Louise touched her hand, 'but it would be good for you to get out and about and with a male companion to pay the bill,' she laughed.

'Trust you, Lou,' Mairead giggled. 'I'd better head home, there's a stack of ironing waiting for me.'

'And I've got Gerard staying over,' Louise sighed, 'I could always help you with your ironing.'

'How long has Margaret and Finn gone away for?' Mairead asked as she got to her feet.

'Three weeks, everything is under control here.'

'It will be different when they get back,' Mairead said, 'where will they live if they get married?'

'In the cottage I guess,' Louise had been running this problem around in her head for days now and it wasn't getting any easier. 'See you tomorrow, I'd better go and show my face down the road.'

Mairead laughed and walked to her car, 'bye Lou.'

Brodie was walking towards the hotel and she met him half way up the road.

'I've just been down to the holiday camp,' he explained, 'there are no problems there, I'll go and check on the hotel and housekeeping before I head off for the day. Natasha and Karnjit are on duty tonight and I'll be on call if I'm needed, Ebee needs a break.'

'We're lucky to have you all,' Louise told him seriously.

'The feelings are mutual,' he laughed, 'see you tomorrow and don't worry about anything.'

'Are you a mind reader now?' she asked him.

'I could be,' he grinned cheekily. 'Fancy going for a drink later? I could do with some time out.'

'Do you know what?' Louise pondered, 'it sounds like a great idea.'

'I'll pick you up in an hour,' he didn't wait for her reply, but waved as he carried on the walk to the hotel.

Gerard was in Jack's bedroom when she entered the cottage and her parents were watching a drama on one of the Irish channels. She had a quick shower and changed into black trousers and a lacy white top. Louise carefully applied make-up, the mascara emphasising her big blue eyes. Her blonde hair curled gently around her face. She didn't know why she was making such an effort for Brodie, but a small voice in her head taunted her that it did.

He arrived exactly when he said he would and she ran out to his car after telling her mum she was going out for a drink.

'Where would you like to go? And by the way, you look absolutely stunning, Lou.'

'Thank you,' she blushed, 'shall we go into Donath? A new bar has just opened, we could try it out.'

Lou discovered that Brodie was an easy person to talk to and understood what Mairead meant about it being easier when there was no chemistry between them. It didn't matter, they were having a nice time getting to know each other and she learnt a lot about him over the couple of hours they had been chatting over soft drinks. Louise didn't want to drink in the week and Brodie was driving.

'Have you spoken to Karen?' she asked him.

'Yes, I called her this morning. We've decided to have some space for a while. It was too intense in too little time. She feels the same.'

'That makes sense and it allows you to stay with us for a bit longer,' she smiled.

'That was the other thing, I couldn't face going to live in Bedworth. I think I would suffocate.'

'You can't take the country out of the boy,' she quipped.

'I've got a feeling that you are still a city girl,' he was serious.

'I'm confused, Brodie. I love it in our little cottage but sometimes,' she paused, 'I long for the city. Or I feel as though something is missing in my life.'

'Shall I tell you what I think?' he asked.

'Please,' she waved her hand to go ahead.

'For two years your work schedule has been manic, you haven't had a minute to stop and taste the coffee, or smell the Roses, or whatever the saying is, and now, everything is running smoothly. There is a void. Your parents are here, you think you should be feeling content but you're not.'

'Wow,' Louise smiled, 'you're good. Would you like to be our resident psychoanalyst?'

'I'm not that good,' he laughed, 'but I can give you some advice, it's up to you whether you take it or not.'

'Go on.'

'When Margaret and Finn get back, go away for some alone time. Leave Jack here for now. Find yourself and what it is you want from life.'

'Should I go to India or Tibet?' she quipped.

'Do you want to go there?'

'Not really, but I thought you had to go to places like that to find yourself.'

'Not always, I found myself, my true self, here in County Donegal.'

'I'll get the map out when I get back and start planning a trip.'

'And when you get back, you will know if you belong here or not.'

'It sounds so easy,' Louise finished her orange juice and got to her feet, 'let's go home before mum sends Gerard out looking for me.'

Chapter 48

Gerard was pacing by the cottage door when Brodie dropped her home with a kiss on her cheek.

'Where have you been?' he demanded.

'Brodie took me to that new bar in Donath, The crooked Shamrock. It's really nice.'

'I would've took you,' he whispered.

'Thanks but you need to spend time with Jack. Isn't that why you've come here?'

'It would be nice to spend time with you as well. We could get to know each other better.'

'Why don't we take Jack out for the day tomorrow then? Spend time together like a family. We could go to the archery place near Letterkenny.'

'I'd love to,' he groaned, 'but I've got to get back to the farm.'

'Okay, no worries,' she turned her back on him and went into the kitchen, 'has the kettle boiled?' she asked Adele, who was sitting at the table doing a crossword.

'No, it's too late for tea,' she mumbled with a pen in her mouth.

'I'll have a glass of wine instead then, do you want one?'

'No, thanks Lou, it's too late,' she removed the pencil and frowned at her daughter and looked pointedly at the clock.

Louise took a large wine glass from the cupboard and poured a good measure of Merlot into it, 'cheers,' she said and took a large gulp, she really didn't want to drink alcohol but the devil on her shoulder had encouraged her, what could she do?

Gerard joined them and Adele rolled her eyes, 'Lou has decided to have a glass of wine, its gone ten.'

'Could I have one, too?' he looked at Louise, noticing the glint in her eyes and the high colour in her cheeks, she looked beautiful.

'Sure,' Louise filled a glass with wine and passed it to him. She sighed, it was so much easier with Brodie, and there was too much, way too much chemistry with Gerard. She sat in one of the chairs by the range and Gerard sat opposite.

'I really do need to go back for a few days,' he told her sadly. 'Dad can't cope on his own.'

'That's fine, don't worry about it.' She knew then that it could never work between them. He had to stay at the farm over fifty miles away so there was no chance they could be together. She cursed herself for imagining for a Nano second that it could work, even for Jack.

'I'm going to turn in,' Adele told them both, yawning. 'See you in the morning.'

'Good night, mum,' Louise raised her glass.

'Night, Adele,' Gerard told her softly.

'Are you okay?' he asked Louise.

She wanted to shout that no, she wasn't okay. She hadn't been okay since he had walked out on her when she was pregnant. She would never be okay again because of him. Instead she said, 'I'm fine, just a bit tired.' She finished the wine in her glass and topped it up, 'more?' she offered Gerard and not waiting for a reply she topped up his glass up as well.

'Would you let me take Jack to meet my parents?' Gerard asked, in a tone that suggested that she wouldn't let him.

'It would depend on how long for and when. He can't miss any school.'

'I could take him on the Friday after school and bring him back on the Sunday.'

'I will ask him first, you know what kids are like,' Louise took a long drink from her glass. 'Why now?'

'They're not getting any younger,' he told her, 'and dad's health hasn't been so good these past few months, that's why I need to head home sooner than I'd like.'

Louise softened towards him, 'so it wasn't to escape me?' she teased.

He looked her in the eyes and his expression was hard to read, 'you must know how I feel about you, Lou.'

She shivered. No she didn't know, she wasn't bloody psychic. 'How am I supposed to know? I've hardly seen you for months.'

He knelt on the floor beside her and placed a hand on either side of the chair she was sitting in, 'It's complicated, Lou.'

She was about to utter that it always was when he leant closer and placed his lips softly on hers. For a moment, she sat there in shock, but as his lips became more insistent, she responded, lost in emotions she hadn't felt for nearly twelve years. Even as she rationed that it was the wine, she shouldn't have drunk two large glasses, she took his hand and led him to her bedroom. As soon as the door closed firmly, giving them the privacy that they craved, they quickly undressed and fell onto the double bed arms and legs entwined. Louise was lost in every caress and kiss and returned each one hungrily. Eventually, both sated and exhausted, they fell asleep in each other's arms, not wanting to let go.

Louise awoke the next morning with a heavy head and a dry throat. Sounds from the kitchen were filtering through to the fog that was her brain and as she slowly remembered that Gerard had shared her bed, her eyes sprang open in horror. To her relief she discovered that she was alone in the bed, his clothes were gone and she realised that he must have got up while she was in a deep sleep. She groaned as she made her way into the bathroom and stood under the shower longer than was necessary. Quickly drying her body and wrapping a towel turban style around her head she hastily donned clean underwear, black jeans and a white jumper.

Adele was at the stove frying bacon and eggs, 'morning, love. Gerard left about ten minutes ago, he had to rush home, some family emergency he said.'

'I bet,' Louise muttered, 'I'll just have a coffee, please, I need to clear my head.'

'I told you not to drink that wine,' Adele said in a knowing voice.

'I'll be fine after a brisk walk,' Louise took a gulp of coffee, 'I want to talk to Ebee and Brodie, there's a few things I want to run past them.'

'As long as you keep Margaret in the loop,' Adele warned.

'It's got nothing to do with Margaret,' Louise fumed at her mother before slamming out of the cottage. It was a good job it was the weekend and Jack could have a sleep in, she thought.

Ebee was sitting at the desk in the office and looked up as she entered, 'Hi Lou,' he noticed her pink cheeks and sparkling eyes, Ebee knew her well enough by now to guess that something had upset her.

'Morning Ebbes, how's things here?'

'Everything is running like clockwork,' he quipped, 'but how are things down there' he nodded toward the cottage.

'You can tell that I'm angry?' she smiled.

'Yep, talk to Doctor Ebee.'

Louise pulled a chair towards the desk, it was funny being on the opposite side but Ebee was running the office today, giving her a bit of time off. 'My mum is driving me crazy,' she began, 'I remember now why I left home in the first place. She treats me like a child.'

'You are her child,' Ebee laughed, and then stopped when he saw the angry flecks spark in her eyes again. 'When will your parent's house be ready?'

'Not soon enough,' she replied. 'Dad is a sweetheart, he is happy spending time with Brian doing farm stuff, but mum...argh...I could strangle her.'

'It sounds as though she needs a hobby. Didn't you mention that she was going to be appointed to the board of directors? Why don't you get her up here to learn the ropes? Mairead could show her reception and housekeeping and Karnjit could give her a run down on events and planning.'

'Ebee, you are a superstar,' she kissed the top of his shiny head. 'I will go and tell her now over breakfast. When you see Brodie, can you mention that I need that house finished as soon as possible, for example, top priority.'

'Will do,' Ebee laughed. 'Go and have your breakfast, Natasha will be here in an hour then I can sort out the bookings for next month. We have a few team building sessions coming up.'

'Any news of the terrible twosome arrested in Dubai?' Louise asked as she was about to leave the office.

'Karen emailed to say that Brenda has been given a six year sentence and Nancy has been rushed to hospital, apparently her leg has flared up and they think gangrene might have set in.'

'Bloody hell, you couldn't write about it,' Louise chuckled.

'You don't feel sorry for them?' Ebee laughed.

'Nope, do you?'

'No, awful women,' he stated, 'see you later.'

Adele was sitting at the table drinking a mug of tea when Louise returned to the cottage. She turned to look at her daughter with a frown, 'are you in a better mood?'

'Compared to what?' Louise poured tea into her favourite mug, pleased to see that her mother hadn't claimed it this morning.

'You are a grumpy bugger Lou, did you get out of bed on the wrong side?'

'I think I must've done,' she muttered. 'Anyway, I've had a word with Ebee and he has come up with a brilliant suggestion for you.'

'For me?' Adele exclaimed, 'Why?'

'If you want to be on the board of directors you can earn it,' Louise told her. 'So, if you have no objection, it would be good if you learnt the ropes and become a part of the team.'

Really? I would love that Lou, I've been going stir crazy stuck in the cottage.'

'I'm sorry mum,' Louise realised that Ebee had got it spot on, Adele had been bored. 'I should've thought of it earlier, but I didn't want to impose on you. I've also asked Ebee to get Brodie to hurry things up, you need your own home, your own space.'

Adele laughed, 'yes I do, and we are driving each other nuts.'

'Bonkers,' Louise agreed. 'Gerard wants to take Jack to meet his parents, but I'm thinking I might drive him up there for a surprise visit.'

'It makes sense, but why now?' Adele asked.

'Jack has got to know his dad now and I thought the next step would be to meet his grandparents. I'm going to run it passed Jack first, he can make the decision.'

'Jack's a shrewd little boy, he will probably agree,' said Adele, getting up from the table. 'By the way, Teresa came up looking for you. She asked if it would be okay to use the pool later, I said you wouldn't mind. You don't do you?' she looked at Louise worriedly.

'No, I don't mind, I told her she could use it whenever, did she mention the baskets?'

'Yes, they are nearly finished, she is looking for the right colour scheme for you.'

'Great, I think I might go for a swim, would you like to join me? We could have a massage too, or a manicure. I can't remember the last time I did something for myself.'

'What about Jack?' asked Adele.

'He can help Mairead or Natasha, it won't hurt him. I think we will go to the restaurant for dinner too, let's push the boat out.'

'Sounds like a plan,' Adele grinned, glad that peace was back in play, 'we just need to rouse little sleepy head from his pit.'

Chapter 49

When Margaret and Finn arrived back from their holiday they discovered that Adele and Frank's house was almost finished, it just needed appliances and furnishings to be fitted, and then they could move in. Brodie and his team had worked nonstop to get it finished and had been promised a bonus and a holiday in return.

'It's good to be back,' Margaret hugged Louise, 'I've missed you.'

'I'm sure you have,' Louise said sarcastically and winked knowingly.

'I still missed you,' Margaret sighed, 'I wanted to phone you, but Finn said it was our time.'

'He was right.'

'I bet your mum's pleased that her house is nearly ready, two women in a kitchen never work and three is a disaster.'

'Yes, but she is a lot happier now I've asked her to be involved with the hotel, you don't mind do you?'

'No, of course not, it's a great idea,' Margaret filled the kettle, 'fancy a cuppa?'

'Fancy a bacon butty?' Louise chuckled.

'Have you seen much of Gerard?'

'He stayed over last week then dashed off, yet again,' Louise got the bacon out of the fridge and put strips under the grill, 'I realised that it will never work between us, even if I wanted it to. He wants to take Jack to meet his parents.'

'Oh. How do you feel about that?' Margaret stirred the tea and put the pot on the table.

'Okay, but then I had the idea to take him up there myself, it would give me a chance to see what they're like.'

'Good idea. Do you want me to come with you?'

'No, thanks anyway, it will be good to have a day out with Jack. Oh, I nearly forgot to tell you, I found out who knocked out Ebee, that psycho Ellen.'

'OMG, how did you forget to tell me that? Tell me all.'

Louise quickly explained how she had discovered the incident and explained why she hadn't yet told Ebee, 'he would get frustrated, I can't believe the police here, they are so corrupt.'

'Lou, the bacon needs turning,' Margaret ran to the grill and pulled the pan out and blew on the flames.

'Sorry,' Louise put a plate on the work top, 'it a good job you like it crispy.'

'Not cremated,' Margaret grinned.

'I'm going up to the hotel, fancy coming with me?' Margaret asked as she cleared the table, the bacon had been edible, just.

'No, I was up earlier, I'm going to sort out Jack's bedroom, he's had a growth spurt and I'll need to take him shopping at some point.'

'I'll be back in about an hour, then I'll go and see dad for a bit.'

After Margaret had left the cottage, Louise looked around the small sitting room where they had spent hours planning their future at the side of the range that had never let them down while they drank copious amounts of wine. They had turned their inheritance into a successful business and knew that Uncle Arthur would be proud of them both. She knew that it was only a matter of time before Margaret and Finn set a date for their wedding and then would need somewhere to live. It was time for her to move on, but before she did, she decided she would take Jack to meet his grandparents. After all, they had a right to know about him.

Chapter 50

'Where are we going?' Jack asked as they turned at the junction for Letterkenny.

'You need new clothes,' Louise told her son, 'and I thought we would visit Glenveigh national park and Doon well.'

'Why didn't Margaret come with us, or Nan and Pop?'

'Jack,' Louise chided, 'can't we spend some time together without other people?'

'I guess,' he sulked.

They drove in silence until Louise parked at the shopping centre and he noticed the MacDonald's sign and perked up.

'Can I have a big mac?' he asked.

'Maybe later,' Louise said, 'after we get you some shirts and trousers. Luckily your feet haven't grown in the last few weeks.'

'I still need new trainers,' he told her.

'Since when? The ones you've got are perfectly fine.'

'No they're not,' Jack stated.

'Okay, we will take a look in Primark shall we for some new ones?'

'They don't do the Nike ones I want.'

'You will just have to save your pocket money then, Jack,' Louise opened the car door and climbed out and waited for Jack to join her before locking it. Maybe it would do them both good to move away, Jack must be confused having not only her to look after him, but also her cousin and parents to offer their input. Was he acting up because of that, she wondered?

It was hard work getting the clothes he needed but eventually he was kitted out and because of his petulant behaviour, she refused to reward him with a fast food burger. Instead, she ordered fish and chips for them both in the restaurant, much to Jack's annoyance.

'Cheer up and I'll get you an ice cream,' she smiled.

'Chocolate?'

'Sure, after you've cleaned your plate.'

'Mum, I'm not a baby.'

'You've been acting like one all morning. I just wanted to have a nice day out with my son, is that so terrible?'

'Sorry,' Jack said meaning it, 'I didn't mean to be horrible to you.'

'I know, but I'm just wondering if it would be a good idea to move back to England for a bit.' She didn't mean to say anything, but the words left her lips before she could stop them.

'That's a terrible idea,' Jack said loudly, 'you brought me over here and now that I've made loads of friends, you want to take me away.'

'It's just an idea, Jack. I don't know what to do for the best.'

'What's wrong with the cottage? I thought you liked sharing with Margaret.'

'I do, but she won't want us there when she marries Finn.'

'Why?'

'I'll order the ice-cream and we'll go to the well,' she changed the subject, it was hard to explain to a twelve year old and she was too tired to even try.

They drove through Kilmacreen and followed a lane that led to Doon Well, a shrine where people captured holy water in their bottles or hung trinkets and mementoes to a tree near the well. She knew that the farm belonging to Gerard's family was a little further along the lane and she had the choice now to either go there, or turn around and go to Glenveigh. Her gut told her to do the latter, but her heart urged her towards the farm.

Louise was surprised how big the farm was, she was expecting a small house with a few chickens and sheep grazing in a field, not this impressive set up that resembled home farm in Emmerdale. She drove up the yard feeling her heart hammer wildly, she still had time to turn back, but she drove on until she parked outside the barn door. A dog barked inside the house and she had no choice but to knock on the door.

'Who lives here?' Jack asked.

'A friend,' she lied, just in case Gerard was not at home.

Louise knocked again and rehearsed what she was going to say to the person that answered. It took a few moments before the door opened and a small woman looked at her quizzically.

'Hi,' Louise smiled, 'I was passing by and thought I'd say hello to Gerard, is he in?'

'He's helping repair fencing in the lower paddock,' the woman told her, 'he should be up in a few minutes for a break, would you like to come in and wait?'

'Thank you, my son is in the car, I'll go and get him.'

The inside of the house showcased the wealth of the family, portraits of ancestors hung on the walls, and the likeness to Gerard was obvious. She wished that she hadn't come here, she should have let Gerard meet his family, the whole scene made her uneasy. Louise followed the woman into a room that could be described as a drawing room, lounge or sitting room, she wasn't sure how rich people labelled their rooms.

'Would you like a cup of tea or coffee?' the woman smiled.

'No, thank you, we've just had one,' Louise said, debating if she should sit on the chesterfield chair or wait to be invited.

'Please, sit down,' the woman said as if guessing her dilemma. Jack sat beside his mother and stared at the woman. Louise didn't even know if this was Gerard's mother or family friend or even a servant.

'How do you know my son?' she asked.

Bloody hell, Louise thought the woman is a mind reader. 'We were friends years ago, teenagers in fact.'

'You have an English accent,' Mrs Gallagher stated. God, she was good, Louise thought sarcastically.

'My mum is from Clodbury,' Louise explained, 'I was born in Oxford.'

'I see, Gerard used to go there in the school holidays.'

'Yes, that's how I met him.'

'And what is your name?' Mrs G asked Jack.

'Jack,' he looked at his mum with a question in his eyes and he could tell by her answering stare that he wasn't to say that Gerard was his father.

'You're very cute,' she smiled.

'Thank you,' said Jack with an angelic smile.

Louise gazed around the room, taking in the rich fabric of the curtains, matching to perfection the colours of the suite. Louise didn't really like Chesterfields, you couldn't curl up on one of their rigid chairs. The carpet was a shade darker, maroon rather than ruby. The coffee table was solid oak and the massive television hung from brackets on the wall. The kitchen and sitting room of the cottage could fit into this room and still have space for a bathroom. She made a snap decision.

'I think we should leave,' she looked at her watch and pulled jack up with her, 'please tell Gerard I said hello and am sorry to have missed him.'

'Are you sure? He should be back any minute.'

'Yes, we really need to go.'

Mrs G showed them out to Louise's car, 'I will tell Gerard you dropped in. Who shall I say called in?'

'Just an ex-girlfriend,' Louise smiled, 'I'm sure there have been plenty of us over the years.'

'No, not really,' Mrs G was puzzled. 'He has only loved one woman as far as I know, and she isn't an ex.'

Louise felt as though she had been punched in the stomach, why hadn't she listened to her gut? No wonder he had rushed off the other night, the two timing bastard.

Tears blinded her as she drove out of the farm, not seeing Gerard running towards her car and after wiping her eyes, she accelerated away in a cloud of dust. Jack sat silently beside her, knowing instinctively that now was not a good time to ask questions.

Chapter 51

When Louise and Jack returned to the cottage she knew that everything had changed, there was no going back she had to get away. She had worked out a plan in her head on the drive back, they had agreed to give Glenveigh a miss and instead stopped at McDonalds to get Jack a big mac with extra cheese for being such a good boy.

'You can't go yet,' Margaret begged with tears streaming down her cheeks, 'you and Jack can have the cottage, me and Finn will find somewhere else to live.'

'It's not just that,' Louise was nearly crying too, luckily Adele and Frank had gone out with Brian to the village hall to take part in a quiz. 'I can't face him again, I've been so stupid, Margaret. I let Gerard get close and now he's broke my heart again.'

'Let him explain,' Margaret said, 'there could be a simple explanation.'

'No. He didn't even tell me his family were rich for god's sake. I can't trust him.'

'So what are you going to do?'

'I'm going to leave Jack here until the end of term while I find a house and job, I only need a part time one.'

'That's ridiculous,' Margaret exclaimed, 'You own a business, you can't work for someone else.'

'It will be hard,' Louise agreed, 'but I need to get away.'

'You mean run away? You can't keep doing that Lou, it's not fair on you or Jack. Or your parents, they have given up their life in Oxford to come here and now you have decided to go back? You can't.'

'I don't have a choice,' Louise wished that there was another way out of this mess.

'Wait until the summer rush is out of the way, and then go away for a holiday,' Margaret pleaded.

Louise knew it made sense not to rush into anything, 'I will stay for three months and go away then. I need some space to work out the best thing for Jack.'

'You know that song, Run-around Sue? In your case its runaway Lou,' Margaret called over her shoulder as she walked out the door.

Louise knew this was probably true. She had been running from one disaster to another and the only time she had stood still was when they embarked upon their business. Maybe it was time to face things head on. At least she had three months to make her mind up, but she would keep Gerard at arm's length, no way was she going to let him get close again.

She rinsed her face in cold water and walked across the front beach, imagining the wind blowing away the doubts and fears she faced when Gerard came to visit their son. She broke out into a run and raced to the river, the tide was out so she splashed through the river and jogged up the path that led to the top of Binion. By the time she reached the summit she was out of breath but the endorphins released into her system gave her the high she needed. She shouted into the wind, 'I am in control of my life,' and even though the words were lost in the silence, she knew that they had been heard somewhere in a higher realm. It was validation and she couldn't go back on them now, no matter what was thrown at her. Louise sat on the mossy grass and watched the waves below crashing over the rocks and with each wave she felt calmer and a firm resolve took hold. Only Jack mattered and the business she had built up with Margaret was his birth right, she had no right to take him away from it and she had to stop running. Margaret was right.

After taking a few deep breaths, Louise made her way back down, slower this time but savouring each step as she headed home. Oxford was no longer her home. The thought of bumping in to Jonathon filled her with horror and was a possibility if she had gone back to her old life. She couldn't work for someone else either, she was used to delegating and organising, not taking orders. Louise imagined what it would be like if she worked for someone like Nancy Butcher, a tyrant and bully, or with workmates such as Brenda Armitage. She shuddered as a cold shiver swept through her. If anything could make her face what would happen should she go back to England that would certainly do it. But she would need to take some time out, and spending quality time with Jack was a must, he needed to know that Louise was his mother, not Adele. She didn't blame her mother for stepping back into the role, but she needed to set the boundaries.

The tide had crept in and Louise had to walk to the bridge to cross the river. She was aware of the dangers of the current that lurked beneath the swirling depth. Many a fisherman had lost their lives over the years underestimating the swell of the river meeting the mouth of the sea. To her dismay, the sky began to darken, black clouds had replaced the fluffy white ones that had floated in the sky just an hour ago. By the time she reached the car park the heavens had opened and the deluge had soaked Louise to the skin. Her mother was in the kitchen making dinner when Louise let herself into the cottage.

'You look like a drowned rat,' Adele exclaimed.

'I can imagine,' Louise said ruefully. 'I'll jump in the shower and then give you a hand.'

'It's all under control,' Adele smiled, 'but I'll have a glass of wine poured when you're ready.'

'Thanks Mum,' Louise kissed her cheek, 'I don't know what I'd do without you.'

It cheered Louise up to see her mother beam with pleasure and as she stood in the shower with hot water cascading over her, she realised that she meant every word. She wouldn't have coped without the support of her parents when Jack had been born and the way her mum was handling the work at the hotel filled her with pride.

Chapter 52

'So, can I take that trip with Brodie?' Ebee was in the office begging Louise and Margaret for an extended holiday. Not only would one member of staff be off for over a month, but the two of them would be gone, leaving a gap in the workforce.

'It's going to be difficult with you both away,' said Margaret, 'who will monitor the cabins and yurts?'

'What about Finn?' said Louise, knowing how much Ebee and Brodie needed this break.

'I can ask him,' Margaret agreed, 'it would make him feel part of the team.'

'I will still have my job when I get back?' said Ebee with a worrying thought.

'Of course you will,' Louise laughed, 'where are you thinking of going?'

'Australia,' Ebee grinned, 'stopping off at Singapore on the way for a few days.'

'We're obviously paying you too much,' said Margaret seriously.

'Really?' Ebee frowned.

'She's kidding,' laughed Louise, 'go and book your holiday. Just let us know the dates when you're ready.'

'I'd better leave mine until he gets back,' sighed Louise. 'I was going to take Jack away for the summer.'

'You can still go,' her cousin exclaimed, 'Adele is brilliant and even your dad can do his bit. '

'Yeh, he's enjoying doing the book work, he's even suggested a few things for the future, barn dancing, pop concerts,' Louise laughed, 'he gets a bit carried away sometimes.'

'We can think about them though,' Margaret smiled, 'we need to diversify. The restaurant has gained great reviews in trip advisor, especially since we poached that chef from The Cabin. He was trained in London by Gordon Ramsay.'

'Wasn't it Jamie Oliver?'

'Or maybe it was the other one, Erm, what was his name?'

'Gino?'

'No, not him,' Margaret giggled. 'Anyway, our chef is amazing.'

'Why don't we run classes to train up chefs?'

'No, I don't think so,' sighed Margaret, 'at least not yet. We need to concentrate on what we have. I was thinking of us running a retreat during the winter for writers and artists. It would fill the rooms up during the slow months.'

'That's a great idea, even a detox retreat where people can lose weight or get away from technology.'

Both looked up when Mairead knocked on the door, 'You'll never guess who's just made a booking,' her face was flushed and they could see anger glint in her blue eyes. This was out of character for the placid woman who was always kind to the staff and visitors.

'Chubby Brown?' laughed Louise, wondering if he would do a turn for them.

'No, anyway who's he? No, that woman from the team building, the chubby one with mousy hair.'

'Not that bloody Brenda?' Louise fumed.

'Yes, that's the one, spiteful, just like her crony Nancy. She's booked a room for a week.'

'I thought she'd been jailed,' Margaret said in confusion.

'They released her on appeal, I heard she hired a fancy lawyer. It's typical of people like her, slick and oily. I read about her release on the website,' said Mairead, 'but why would she come back here?'

'To cause trouble I'll bet,' stated Louise through gritted teeth. 'What about the other bitch?'

'She wasn't mentioned, maybe she can't travel with one leg.'

'Or did you tell her to hop it?' Margaret laughed, 'she could travel, what about the soldiers who get injured?'

'That's true,' Mairead agreed, 'should I have refused the booking?'

'No, I guess not, Louise sighed heavily. 'Maybe it's a good thing if I take Jack away for a while. I might do or say something I shouldn't.'

'What, you Lou?' Mairead chuckled, 'where are you thinking of going?'

'I'm driving to Belfast and catching the boat to Liverpool, then we are going on a road trip around the UK.'

Can I come?' Mairead teased.

'Of course, we will plan it together,' Louise said warmly. Mairead was a dear friend now and a trip together would do her good.

'I wish I could,' Mairead sighed, 'I've got a lot going on at home and I wouldn't want to leave you short staffed here.'

'Thanks, you're a star.'

'Maybe next time.'

'For sure, but I don't know when that will be. Ebee and Brodie are heading off for a few weeks and then the holiday rota will kick in for the summer. I'm lucky to get away with Jack for three weeks.'

'I promised Natasha I'd take her away for a bit, she fancies Lanzarote.'

'Book it,' Louise insisted, 'It supposed to be lovely later in the year.'

'Thanks, I will time it for when you get back.'

'Okay, I'll book the ferry and a couple of night's hotels and get the wheels in motion. To be honest, it's the quality time with Jack that I really need, he's a good kid, but it must be confusing having too many adults giving out orders.'

'I'm sure it is,' Mairead agreed, 'when are you thinking of setting off?'

'Friday night, so we will arrive in Liverpool Saturday morning, the plan is to head north and stop over at the lakes for a few days.'

'While you're doing that, I'll check out holidays to Lanzarote,' grinned Mairead.

Margaret was sitting at the table sharing a pot of tea with Adele, 'fancy a brew?' she asked, looking up at Louise.

'I'd love one,' she replied taking a seat at the big table, 'and a bit of cake if it's going.'

'I've just made a coffee and walnut,' said Adele with a smile.

'I've decided what to do,' Louise told them both.

'You're not leaving, are you Lou?' asked Margaret with a tremor in her voice.

'No, my days of running are over, but I am taking Jack away for a few weeks, but we will be back, I can't up root him again and besides, I belong here now with all of you.'

'I'm so relieved, you had me worried for a while,' said Adele.

'You seemed determined to go back to England,' Margaret had hoped that her cousin would change her mind about running away, 'did you really consider it?'

'Only fleetingly,' Louise told her, touching her hand as she placed a big piece of cake in front of her. 'But I do need to get away for a bit, that horrible woman Brenda's coming back and I don't want to be here when she arrives. I wouldn't be responsible for my actions.'

'I might not be either,' said Margaret.

'You're too loved up to be very angry,' Louise laughed, 'unlike me. Oh if the G should show himself while I'm away, tell him you don't know when I'm coming back.'

'What on earth has the lad done now?' Adele exclaimed.

'I don't really want to go into it, Mum,' Louise dismissed that part of the conversation with a shrug of her shoulders.

'Are you going to keep in touch while you're away?' Margaret asked.

'I hadn't really thought about it, but maybe I should have a complete break from the hotel and business. Just concentrate on Jack and send postcards to you both along the way.'

'What if we need you?'

'You won't, Brodie and Ebee are postponing their holiday till I get back, its winter in Australia so they are going to save a bit more and go when it's autumn over here.' Louise finished her tea and getting to her feet said, 'I'll go and book the ferry. It might be easier to book a single crossing to give me more options on our return.'

Chapter 53

Jack waved through the open window as they pulled out of the drive. He carried on waving until they had turned the bend in the road, 'how long will we be gone?' he asked.

'I'm not sure,' said Louise, grabbing his hand.

'She will be back?' Adele looked at Margaret for reassurance.

'Of course she will, you heard what she said, Jack needs some alone time with his mum.'

'You're right, I should've kept my nose out of it,' Adele was getting worked up that she could have sent her daughter away because of her actions.

'Louise knows what an amazing job you've done with Jack, now let's go and get some of that delicious lemon drizzle cake you made earlier.'

An hour later, Margaret walked slowly across the path that led up to the hotel. Finn had been working on a project in Letterkenny and she hadn't seen much of him since they had got back, although she knew he was trying to make as much money as possible to build a home for them both, he had shared the family home with his younger brother, Martin since their parents were killed in a car crash. Brian had already given them a plot of land near his own cottage which would make them completely independent of the business. She hadn't discussed it with Lou as the timing hadn't been great, what with Gerard being a complete bastard again. She was still seething as she walked into the reception area and practically collided with that horrible Brenda woman.

'Watch it,' the woman snarled.

'Sorry,' Margaret fought to control her temper, 'what brings you here? I thought this would be the last place you'd want to visit after the last time.'

'I'm not staying here,' the woman snapped, viciously, 'I've just come to warn you that you will be sorry for what happened to Nancy and to cancel the booking I made.'

'It was an accident,' Margaret sighed, 'pure and simple, in fact, wasn't it your fault for tripping her up during the line dancing?'

'That's beside the point,' the woman's face screwed up, spite glistened in her small blue eyes.

'Could I suggest you remove yourself from the hotel if you are not staying here, and I might add, you would not be welcome here if you did want to stay.'

'Where's that bitch of a partner of yours?'

'None of your business, and if you don't move your sorry ass out of the building, I will call security.'

'I'm going,' Brenda snarled, 'I just wanted to warn you that I'm joining forces with Aggie and Ellen. We will bring you high and mighty bitches down.'

'Mairead,' Margaret called across to her as she watched aghast from behind the front desk, 'can you call Ebee and Brodie please, I want this woman removed from the premises.'

'Of course,' Mairead lifted the receiver and punched numbers into the switchboard, 'Hi, Brodie, can you get Ebee and come to the hotel reception please, we have a problem.' She listened to his reply and hung up, 'He'll be here in five minutes,' she glared at Brenda.

'I'll wait then,' she grinned slyly, 'see what happens when I'm man handled.'

Margaret laughed, a big belly laugh and once started she couldn't stop, she was still laughing when Ebee and Brodie appeared.

'What's going on?' Ebee asked in amazement.

'This sorry excuse for a woman wants to be man handled by you,' she chuckled.

Ebee frowned and looked at Brodie, 'we're not into that, what we would say is, please leave the building otherwise we will call the guards and tell them you are disturbing the peace.'

'I'm going,' Brenda hissed, 'but you will all be sorry for what happened to Nancy.'

'Good bye,' waved Margaret, 'and don't come back.'

Brenda stormed out of reception and nearly knocked a woman over as she came through the glass doors, 'whatchit,' she snapped.

'You watch it, you rude woman, I hope you're not staying here.'

'No she is not,' Margaret smiled at the dark haired woman. 'She is just leaving.'

The new guest reeked of perfume and aftershave, it was quite over powering and Margaret could feel her eyes begin to sting, she quickly grabbed a tissue before she gave a loud sneeze.

'Bless you,' the woman smiled, 'I bet it's me that made you sneeze.'

'What makes you think that?' Margaret wondered why the woman would wear so much perfume if she knew it was too much.

'I had an accident on the boat,' the woman explained, 'my name's Jenny Nicol by the way. The sea was right choppy and I lost my balance in the shop. I caused a proper scene, it was a nightmare,' Jenny paused for breath, 'there were smashed bottles everywhere. It's their own fault, there was nothing to grab hold of.'

'Oh dear,' Margaret sympathised, 'did they make you pay for the damages?'

'No, thank goodness, it would've cost a small fortune. But I'm reeking of every perfume and aftershave in the shop. I couldn't wash it all off cos I was catching the coach up here. The taxi driver seemed overwhelmed by me.'

'Never mind. I'll get you checked in and you can have a good shower. If you leave your clothes outside in the bag provided in the wardrobe we will get them washed and pressed for you.'

'That is so kind, thank you,' Jenny smiled in gratitude.

'Are you travelling alone?' Margaret asked.

'No, my daughter Sharon will be here later, she is flying over, unfortunately my passport ran out last year.'

'You've had quite an eventful journey by all accounts,' Margaret checked her name on the computer and scanned the room key. 'Here you go, number 207. We will give your daughter another key when she arrives. I'll get one of the boys to give you a hand with your case.'

Ebee appeared as if by magic and escorted the woman to the lift, taking the largest case from her.

'She's a live wire,' grinned Mairead.

'Yes, but she seems lovely. Different to that woman, Brenda. It's a scary thought that she's joining forces with the devil's sisters.'

'It's a pity the guards didn't lock them up for good, they're both horrible, and they probably did murder Swain.'

'I'm glad the boys have postponed their holiday, I've got a feeling we are going to need them.'

'Should we let Lou know?' Mairead asked.

'Definitely not,' said Margaret, 'besides, we don't know where she's staying and there's nothing for her to come back for, we can cope, and you can go and take a break.' Margaret smiled, 'I can take over for a few hours and then Natasha will be here to cover the shift.'

Mairead picked up her bag, 'thanks Margaret. I've booked the trip to Lanzarote for two weeks next Friday, is that okay?'

'Yes of course, I bet you can't wait.'

'See you tomorrow,' Mairead went through the glass doors while Margaret checked the week's rota. A bunch of CV's were in the top drawer of the desk and she decided to go through them, the hotel was at last making a profit while the Yurts and cabins were breaking even. They had ploughed all the money made back into the business and decided against taking out a loan, but sometimes they both wondered if they should borrow against the hotel as their vision was still a way off from what they could afford. What they really needed was a wealthy investor and Lou had some ideas about that. Margaret was reluctant to share their business with strangers but she couldn't really rule it out.

Chapter 54

Louise and Jack had been gone a week when Gerard's car pulled up in front of the cottage. Adele was at the range stirring soup for lunch as despite it being July, there was a definite nip in the air. Margaret had gone into Donagh with Ebee and Frank had gone to help Brian with planning permission for the new build that would be Margaret and Finn's new home. The knock on the door took her by surprise as normally people would just walk in. She put the spoon she was using in the sink and went to see who was calling. Adele was surprised to see Gerard standing on the step with a woman she assumed to be around her own age. She was momentarily distracted by three women going up the road in the direction of the point, the trio were cackling like witches and when she realised it was the evil Duffy twins and their new side kick, Brenda Armitage, she quickly ushered Gerard and the woman into the kitchen.

'Is Lou about?' Gerard asked.

'No, Gerard, she has taken Jack away,' Adele told him in a tone that showed him that he was to blame.

'Taken him where?'

'I don't know, she doesn't want to be disturbed,' Adele noticed the woman gripping the straps of her hand bag, 'please sit down, I'll make a cup of tea.' Adele's hand shook as she poured boiling water into the tea pot, she wished Margaret was here to help her deal with the guests.

'Why do you need to see my daughter?' Adele asked as she sat by the range. She had planned to go over to their new home to write notes on where she wanted things to go, but she had promised Margaret to wait in the cottage in case Lou should phone, the irony wasn't lost on her.

'Mum's just told me about Lou's visit the other week, why did she run off like that?'

Anger shot through Adele like a bolt of electricity, 'She wanted to surprise you,' she fumed, 'it was her idea to take Jack out to see you. Instead she found out that you've been lying again.'

'I don't understand,' Gerard was bemused, 'I haven't lied about anything. I was trying to win back her trust and respect before taking Jack to the farm to meet my parents. Mum didn't know who she or who Jack was.'

'And that's supposed to exonerate you is it? I'm sorry you feel so ashamed of my daughter and grandson, and I really can't understand why you need to come here looking for her,' tears of rage rolled down her cheeks, 'I'll go and pour the tea.'

Adele fought to control her temper as she put cups, milk sugar and the tea pot on the tray. She carried it through to the kitchen and placed it on a sturdy coffee table, being the perfect hostess, Adele cut slices of her lemon drizzle cake and took it through with small plates.

'Jack is a handsome young man,' Mrs Gallagher found her voice. 'Gerard didn't want to tell me about him until he had got the go ahead from Louise. He didn't want us to have false hopes.'

Adele let the words sink in, 'but you are still Jack's grandparents, why would you think Lou would deny you seeing him?'

'Jack was almost eleven when I found out about his existence,' Gerard sighed, 'I didn't want to tell my parents until we had reached some kind of truce, I never know where I stand with her.'

'You look down on her,' Adele snapped, 'living in your swanky house, the lord of the manor,' Adele was aghast as the words spewed out of the mouth, this wasn't her. 'I'm sorry, I didn't mean that the way it sounded, but my daughter was very upset when she returned from your farm, in fact, she was even going to return to Oxford with Jack.'

'Oh God,' Gerard put his head in his hands, 'what a mess. I should've been honest with her.'

'Drink the tea,' Adele passed a cup and saucer to Mrs Gallagher, 'and then we will talk about it rationally.'

As he sipped the hot drink, Gerard explained the situation at the farm, 'The farm belongs to my Uncle, my dad's brother. He lives in America and now he wants to sell the farm. We have been trying to raise the cash to buy it from him, he doesn't want the going rate, he's being pretty good about it, but we still need to raise another £50 thousand.'

'For the past year, my husband, Gerard's dad, has been working all hours of the day and night, that's why Gerard hasn't been around much. It's all hands on deck.' Mrs Gallagher finished her tea and put the cup and saucer on the tray, no one had touched the cake.

'So the big swanky house belongs to your Uncle?' Adele digested the words.

'Yes,' Gerard rubbed his eyes, 'we've had guests, bed and breakfast, to raise some cash.'

'Can't the bank help?' asked Adele. She hoped they weren't looking for money from Louise.

'Yes, they will give us the balance when we need it. I wanted to explain to Lou why I haven't been around and my time with Jack has been limited to the odd weekend.'

'It's a bit late in the day,' Adele released the breath she had been holding, 'Louise was devastated when she got back here.'

'Just because she thought I lived in a posh house? Well I do, but why would that matter? Lou and Margaret own a big hotel and thriving business.'

'The fact that you hadn't told your parents about Jack made her feel worthless. There was something else but Lou wouldn't tell me what it was.'

They looked up as a car pulled up in front of the house, 'That's probably Margaret,' Adele told them as the car door slammed and the cottage door opened.

'What are you doing here?' Margaret demanded, 'haven't you done enough damage?'

'We're trying to get to the bottom of it,' Adele told her, 'the soup is ready for your lunch.'

'I'm okay for the moment thanks,' she glared at Gerard, 'Did you know that Lou was going to run again? After all that shit you put her through last time and then you do it again. I can't believe it and then to show your face here.'

'I only just found out that Lou came to the farm, and that was from a chance remark mum had made,' Gerard explained, he was beginning to feel like a pariah and needed to put things right.

'I didn't know who Louise was,' said Mrs G, 'I noticed the uncanny resemblance with Jack and Gerard. I wasn't horrible to her, she was waiting for Gerard to come back and then all of a sudden she shot up and left the house.'

'It must have been something you said,' fumed Margaret, 'and the resemblance isn't uncanny, Jack happens to look like his father.'

Adele half expected Margaret to say, 'Duh,' she was glad she had come back in time to give her support. Mrs G seemed a timid woman and Adele felt a stab of guilt for the way she had spoken to her.

'So your beloved son didn't tell you that when Louise was sixteen Gerard made her pregnant and ran off with another girl, a tart from the village?'

'That's not how it happened,' Gerard pleaded, 'I didn't know Lou was having a baby and I didn't run off with that girl, it was a set up to split us up.'

'It worked though didn't it, and now you're full of crap. You will not hurt Lou ever again.'

'I don't intend to hurt her, I wanted to explain why I haven't been around much.'

'Well, you're too late, Lou has gone away and we don't know when or if she is coming back,' Margaret snapped.

'You must have a contact number or something,' begged Gerard.

'No, she didn't want to keep in touch, it's a complete detox from YOU.'

'I think we'd better go, son,' Mrs G got to her feet.

'You haven't asked one question about your grandson,' Margaret turned on her. 'It's obvious that you don't give a damn about him.'

'That's not true,' tears streamed down her face, 'I wanted to meet him properly. I have told Gerard that I should have known about Jack when he discovered that he had a son.'

'It's too late now,' Margaret wouldn't budge, 'I'll tell Lou you came a calling if she comes back.'

'Tell her I'm sorry, for whatever she thinks I've done,' Gerard went to the door of the cottage and waited for his mother to catch up.

'I really want to get to know the boy,' Mrs G sobbed.

'I'll pass that on to Lou,' Margaret walked with her to the door.

'Do you think we were too hard on them?' Adele asked as their car reversed out of the yard and headed down the road.

'No,' Margaret was still fuming, 'Lou was in a terrible state when she came back from their place and until we get proper answers, they can stay away.'

'I agree, now have that soup before it goes cold, I took it off the main heat when our guests arrived.'

'Thanks, Adele, I'll have lunch then go and hold the fort at the hotel. We have a new girl training on reception and it hasn't gone that well so far,' Margaret sighed, 'I don't even know why she applied for the job.'

'I'll do a shift tomorrow, I got a bit waylaid today,' Adele pulled a face, 'oh and as Gerard and his mother arrived the evil sisters and their new side kick cackled their way up the point.'

'Oh god, I wonder what they're planning,' Margaret groaned, 'Armitage warned that she would cause trouble.'

'It's a good job you invested in the security camera,' Adele stated, 'at least if they try something you will catch them on film.'

'I'd rather not have the hassle, though. It beggars belief what harm they could do,' Margaret dipped a chunk of crusty bread into the tomato soup.

'Thank heavens that Ebee and Brodie are postponing their trip, would they be able to cover security on reception?'

'They don't get paid to do that,' Margaret told her, wiping her chin on a serviette, 'but it might be an idea to find a concierge, we could set up a desk near the door for him. It would be an added expense though.'

'Is money an issue?' Adele asked worriedly.

'Not yet, but we need an influx of cash at some point, an investor.'

'Why? I thought you were self-sufficient with all profits being ploughed back into the business.'

'We are doing well, but we got a bit carried away when we extended the holiday camp. It will be a gold mine eventually,' Margaret tried to reassure her aunt and wished that she hadn't said anything about the finances.

'We have the money in the bank for our house,' Adele offered, 'we didn't expect it for free.'

'I know, don't worry. We'll be fine' Margaret slipped on a jacket, 'thanks for lunch, I'll see you later.'

As Margaret walked across to the hotel, she wondered how long Lou would be away. She had only been gone a week and she missed her, especially to discuss the investor. She shouldn't have mentioned anything to Adele, a few hundred thousand was a drop in the ocean to what they needed. Lou would not be impressed that she had put pressure on her mum for money. She had a horrible thought that maybe Lou thought it too much stress to build up their business. Maybe she would rather sell the business and move on. Margaret walked through into reception and wished she could get hold of her cousin.

Chapter 55

Gerard turned right into the road that led to Letterkenny and after forty minutes of silence finally asked his mother, 'what did you say to Lou? Why would she be so upset with me?'

'I didn't say anything, love. I can't even remember what we were talking about, one minute she was sitting in the chair with her son next to her and then she jumped up and practically ran away. If you ask me, you're better off without her.'

Gerard slammed on the breaks, his hands were shaking so much he didn't trust himself to drive at the moment, 'Her son is my son too,' he said through gritted teeth, your grandson. Adele was correct, you didn't ask anything about him and that's why I didn't tell you or dad about them. You are both selfish, I've been at your beck and call since I left school. Well, I've got news for you, I'm thirty next month and I think it's about time I left home.'

'Gerard, I know you're upset but less of this silly talk. Drive us home your dad will want his dinner.'

Gerard cast a glance at his mother, for the first time he really looked at her, the weak mouth and watery blue eyes. This is how he was going to end up if he didn't escape. He re-started the engine and drove over the speed limit towards his uncles farm. Not his dad's, his uncles and took grim satisfaction that his mother clung on to the door handle as he screeched around sharp bends and corners. Gravel shot up from the forecourt as he pulled in front of the impressive homestead. No wonder Lou felt intimidated.

His father, Eamon, was in the hallway removing his work boots and as they entered the house he glared at them with his steely eyes, 'where the hell have you been? This is the third time I've been back for my dinner.'

'Sorry love,' stammered Mrs G, 'we went for a little trip out and lost track of the time.'

'Well you'd better get a move on before I die of hunger,' he stormed, 'and you me laddo, you haven't done a stroke of work all day, so you'd better get out there now while there's some daylight left.'

'I'm going to get a bite to eat first and change my clothes,' Gerard said as he walked past him.

His father, picking up on his son's mood, decided to let it pass, 'make sure you get out there before all daylight has gone,' he retorted.

Gerard had been working hard in the fields for four hours when he decided that he'd had enough for one day. He sat on a bale of hay and took a few deep breaths, and not for the first time wondered what it was all for. The sky was a purplish pink and another long day lay ahead of him. What he couldn't get his head around was why Uncle was selling the farm. He was a self-made multi-millionaire and certainly didn't need the money, or at least Gerard didn't think he did.

The time he had spent in America with him seemed eons ago. He had always had a close relationship with his uncle and when he wrote and poured his heart out about his relationship with Louise and then her disappearing from his life, he had urged him to get a passport and visa and fly out as soon as he possibly could. Eamon Gallagher had set against the idea with passion, 'how dare their only child leave them in the lurch on a fool's folly,' he had fumed. 'How was he to cope with the running of the farm with only his wife to help him?'

Gerard's only thought had been to escape the pain of a broken heart and the rumours that Lou had been carrying on with a lad in Clodbury. He had to face the fact that their relationship was over and the only way to get through it was to go overseas with as many miles between them as possible. Despite his mother weeping copious amounts of tears, begging and pleading for him to stay and forget this nonsense, Gerard had packed his bag, got a taxi to Belfast Airport and flew out to Dallas where his uncle had met him at the other end.

Gerard smiled now as he remembered him turning up in a white Cadillac the size of two cars to pick him up. He had an enormous Stetson perched on his head and a wide smile to greet his favourite, albeit only, nephew.

'Gerard, I didn't think you would come,' were the first words he had uttered.

'If dad had his way, I wouldn't be here,' Gerard had admitted.

Gerard had soon settled in at the ranch, even though he had never had experience with horses, he learnt to ride bareback and to take part in rodeos. The homestead was massive and Gerard had his own suite of rooms although he preferred to be out doors with the other lads that were hired by his uncle to break in the new arrivals of wild horses sent for them to break in. Gerard had found his niche, his love of horses helped to heal him. He developed muscles and a constant tan under the blazing Texas sun, but he shied away from the girls, even though they often flaunted their beauty at him. Lou was the only girl for him and deep inside his heart, he believed that one day they would be together.

After four years of living in America, his mother had phoned to let him know that Eamon had had a heart attack and he was needed home. His uncle was devastated to let him go, 'you're like a son to me,' he had literally sobbed.

'I'll come back one day,' Gerard had promised, but the time had never been right for him to go. Email made it easier to keep in touch and then skype, where Gerard noticed his beloved uncle slowly aging, his hair now snowy white instead of dark brown.

Gerard got to his feet and walked towards the place that had been home since he was a small boy. His father had been made redundant from his job at a car factory when Gerard was four and his mother's brother had offered the farmhouse to Eamon at a low rent to enable him to go and seek his fortune in America. 'Fortune favours the brave,' he had quipped. His uncle was brave and fearless and it had paid off, even though Eamon had poured scorn on his brother in laws dreams it didn't stop him taking over the running of the farm.

'Fortune favours the brave,' the words echoed in Gerard's memory. He needed to take a leaf out of his uncle's book and stop being the downtrodden wimp his father had made him. He ran swiftly up the stairs and into his room where he fired up his laptop. Modern technology had made life a lot easier to travel, his tickets and boarding pass were stored on his mobile and luckily he had kept his passport up to date.

The next morning after breakfast he told his parents that he was going away for a few weeks.

'It's impossible,' stormed Eamon, 'the hay isn't finished yet, I can't spare you.'

'That's your problem dad,' Gerard got to his feet and shoved the dining chair back across the polished floor. 'Hire a couple of lads from the village, I bet they'd be glad of the money.'

'Where are you going?' his mother sobbed, 'to see that wretched girl? She doesn't want to be found by you.'

'I don't blame her,' Gerard said bitterly, 'why should she? I haven't been there for her and Jack when I should've been. I don't know when I'll be back,' he made a phone call for a taxi and grabbed his case from the bedroom.

'Where are you going?' his mother shouted, repeating herself.

'Where fortune favours the brave,' he waved, picked up his case and walked down to the drive to wait for his cab.

Chapter 56

'Are you alright, mum?' Jack stood outside the bathroom door. Louise had been throwing up for the past three days and he was worried about her.

The toilet flushed, he could hear the tap running and the door opened, 'I'm fine, Jack,' she didn't feel fine. She was sure it was the fish she had eaten the other night while Jack had his usual chicken nuggets.

They had been in the cottage on the outskirts of Swansea for four days with the plan of sightseeing the Gower Peninsula. She filled the kettle and got dishes out of the cupboard and put them on a circular table in the kitchen. The cottage was ideal for them with two bedrooms and a bathroom upstairs and a kitchen, small living room and toilet downstairs. The views over a wide expanse of beach were stunning, if only she wasn't feeling sick. It was crazy the amount of sightseeing they had packed into the three weeks they had already been away and the week in the cottage was to be the last before heading back to Clodbury. Jack had made friends along the way with boys and girls near the lakes or on the beaches. In fact, he had proved that he could adapt anywhere.

'Will I see my dad again?' he asked suddenly out of the blue.

Louise wiped damp hair out of her eyes, 'is that what you want?'

'I suppose so, we were having fun when he did turn up.'

'That's the problem,' Louise sighed, 'he can't give you any quality time. But it's your choice, Jack, I won't stop you.'

'If he comes to visit I'll see him,' he said firmly.

'Okay, we will leave it like that. Now, what cereal do you fancy?'

She was feeling slightly better as they set out for a day on the beach. Louise had read up on the local attractions and noted that Oxwich Bay was worth a visit and then she planned to drive to Rhossili and take some photo's to send to her parents. They had once told her that it was an area of outstanding beauty and a picture with Jack in the background would be a wonderful gift idea if she could find an appropriate frame.

It was a steep climb down to the beach but it was worth it. With the stunning sandy beach surrounded by grassy mountains, she could feel herself unwind and let go of the turmoil she had left behind her in Clodbury. They kicked off their sandals' and walked towards the water's edge, the sea was cool and refreshing on their skin. Jack had developed a healthy glow during the weeks they had been away although being near the sea in Ireland would have worked the same magic. He was growing to look more like Gerard every day and it broke her heart. Why couldn't Jack have had her blonde hair?

They splashed around in the sea for a while and then collapsed giggling on the sand.

'Are you feeling better?' Jack asked with concern shining in his eyes.

'Much, but I'll give fish a miss for a while.'

'Can we go home soon?'

Louise noted the yearning tone in his voice, 'after our few days in the cottage, is that okay? I'll drive up to Holyhead and we'll cross over to Dublin.'

A smile split Jack's little face, 'cool. Why don't we keep it a secret and surprise everyone.'

They high fived, 'I like your thinking young man. I noticed a nice pub along the road, shall we have steak and chips?'

'Yeh,' he grinned.

Chapter 57

'We can't go on like this,' Margaret said in despair. Bookings had dropped by fifty percent and others had been cancelled.

'What's going on?' Mairead asked, she had just returned after her week in Lanzarote, 'business was booming when we left. Have you asked people why they have cancelled?'

'Yep, they said they found somewhere better. Luckily the regulars are still coming but it still means that we have empty rooms.'

'Have you looked on Trip Advisor?'

'No, why?'

'People leave reviews, there might be some about The Cheyenne,' Mairead clicked on google and put a search in for Trip Advisor, then she searched the hotel. 'Oh no,' she had gone pale despite her holiday tan, 'there's loads of negative comments.'

Margaret pulled a chair over and they scrolled through the comments, 'rats in the rubbish outside. Swimming pool dirty, sheets not changed, treatment staff not qualified. Where the hell is all this slander coming from?'

'I can guess,' said Mairead, 'Didn't you say Armitage was joining forces with the devil sisters?'

'They're not that clever,' said Margaret.

'They are that evil,' said Mairead darkly.

'Serves ya right,' sniggered Ellen, 'just been to ya bathroom, bit smelly in there,' she cackled.

'How the hell did you get in?' Margaret demanded.

'Through those doors there,' she waved a gnarled finger at the glass doors, 'Aggie's in there now doing a number two, she couldn't wait till we got home.'

'Get out,' shouted Margaret.

'I see your body guards have gone away, nothing gets past my eyes.'

'I notice you're not using that stupid language,' Margaret sneered.

'Nah, it was for mental effect, it works well.'

'Especially when you murder people.'

'I've not shed any blood, ya liar.'

'It must've been your sister then,' said Margaret, 'tell her to get out of the toilets before I call the guards.

'They won't come, ya know they won't.'

Margaret knew that was the truth, the guards in the village were useless. Mairead touched her hand, 'they're not worth it.'

'The guards or the devil's spawn?' Margaret raised an eyebrow.

'Both,' Mairead glared at Ellen, 'where's your new side kick? I bet you've got her well trained in casting spell and curses.'

'She's been training us, clever little bugger that one.'

'Toilets need a good clean,' Aggie sneered as she joined her sister's side.

'Can you both get out,' Mairead got up from the desk and steered them towards the exit, 'and don't come back.'

'There will be no hotel to come back to soon,' Aggie cackled, 'thought you were too good for the likes of us simples folk, well it's all backfired missy. Your empire will come a tumbling down.'

'So it was you!' Margaret sank down onto her chair.

'With a little help from Brenda baby. Pure genius.' The glass doors opened and the evil duo spilled outside leaving a pungent smell in their wake.

Mairead sat down and wrote several responses to the hateful reviews left by the demented trio.

'What are you doing?' Margaret asked her, shaking from the ordeal.

'Adding comments to say it's all lies and defamation, it might stem the flow of cancellations.'

'Thanks Mairead, I'll get on to the press and get them to run a piece for us, we need some good publicity, I'll give Adele a buzz and ask her to come up here.'

The door that separated the lifestyle area was thrown open with such force that it whacked against the wall, 'Now what?' Margaret got to her feet as a demented Brenda came into view carrying a can of yellow paint, some of it was smeared over hear face and hair.

'What have you done?' Margaret gasped in horror.

'That's put paid to your nice shiny floor, health and safety hazard it was,' Brenda swung the tin of paint around as she ground out the words, some of it dripped onto the blue plush carpet.

'Why are you doing this?' cried Margaret, 'it was your fault Nancy slipped, not the floor you stupid woman.'

'She was the love of my life,' Brenda put the paint down and rubbed her eyes, 'I told her how I felt and she told me to go away like I was some animal.'

'Was this before or after Dubai?' asked Mairead.

'After, when we got back home. Nancy needed a nurse and I said I would stay by her side forever.'

Margaret felt faint, this couldn't be happening, 'and she asked you to leave?'

'Yes and it's all your fault, this hotel is to blame. If we hadn't come here I would still be worshipping her and be in her life.'

'You need a doctor, shame he's been murdered,' said Mairead.

The glass doors slid open and Adele appeared looking horrified, 'oh my god, what the hell is going on?'

'Brenda's damaged the dance floor, I haven't had a chance to check it out,' Margaret told her, 'the woman is insane.'

'I'll go and have a look,' Adele walked briskly through to the lifestyle lounge taking in the recent dent in the wall where the door had damaged it.

'Brenda?' what are you doing here?'

Margaret and Mairead turned to the woman who had just appeared in reception, 'Karen, I didn't know you were coming here,' Margaret was stunned to see her.

'I didn't know myself until this morning, I had the urge to come back, is my job still going?'

'We don't know what's happening,' Margaret sighed, 'between this demented bitch and her two sidekicks, they've cost us thousands of pounds.'

'How's Nancy?' Brenda stumbled across towards Karen.

'Bill is looking after her, why are you here?' Karen replied.

'Getting revenge on the hotel of course,' Brenda said slowly as if no one was getting the point, 'and now I'm going for a good old paddle. Aggie and Ellen are waiting for me on the beach, so while I'm here I might as well get changed.'

'She's caused a lot of damage,' Adele had returned, 'the floor is a mess of yellow paint.'

'Shall we lock her in the loo?' asked Mairead.

'The guards won't do anything, what's the point?' said Margaret in despair.

'She's lost the plot,' said Karen. 'Nancy said she had made a pass at her and had been very upset when she knocked her back.'

'Why are you really here?' Margaret asked her in suspicion, 'you were working for Nancy Butcher.'

'I missed it here and I didn't like the way the company was going over there, it's all brown nosing and favourites.'

'I thought you were a favourite,' stated Margaret.

'I was in the beginning, but a new girl started two weeks ago and Nancy is fawning all over her.'

'That must have been horrible for you,' said Margaret with a hint of sarcasm, 'after all you've done for her.'

'I didn't do that much,' Karen said, 'just inputting and phone calls. Brenda was the deputy.'

'Surely you would be able to take over the role.'

'No, I thought so too, but the newbie got the job.'

'I'm going for a swim,' Brenda had emerged from the toilets wearing a bright green and yellow swimming costume that clung to her ample curves, 'are you going to come with me?' she asked Karen.

'Not now Brenda, I'm trying to get my old job back.'

'You don't want to work here,' Brenda stormed, 'I'll pop around later to see you.'

'Okay Brenda,' Karen grimaced.

Margaret and Mairead looked at each while Adele glared at both women.

'Get out of this hotel,' Adele told Brenda, 'and if you dare to show your face here again you will be very sorry.'

'Where's your body guards?' Brenda taunted, 'I don't see anyone that can help you.'

The glass doors slid open and Margaret screamed, 'Lou, you're home.' She ran up to her cousin and hugged her tight, tears sliding down her cheeks.

'What's going on?' Louise asked as Margaret finally released her.

'This bitch has ruined the dancefloor and Karen is hoping to get her job back,' Margaret explained in gulps.

'I'm going now,' Brenda told them, 'I won't be back and I've made my point.' With her clothes tucked under her arm and her large backside wobbling from side to side, she left the hotel.

'Where's the lads?' Louise asked.

'Down under,' said Adele before grabbing her daughter in a hug, 'I'm so glad to see you. Where's Jack?'

'I left him at the cottage having a snack,' she told her. 'When did you get back, Karen?'

'Yesterday, my aunt agreed to rent me the cottage for a while.'

'Brodie isn't here,' Louise stated, she had lost faith in her friend and didn't know if she could trust her anymore.

'I gathered that,' Karen smiled, 'when will he get back?'

'Not for a while, they only left a couple of days ago, Ebee's gone with him,' Margaret sat down on a chair in reception, her legs were shaking after the rampage, 'they wanted to bring their trip forward,' she explained to Louise.

'I wonder if the evil sisters knew that they weren't here,' Mairead mused, 'I mean, we were defenceless against them.'

'We will have to hire a doorman,' sighed Louise, 'bloody great homecoming this is turning out to be.'

'We can't afford to hire anyone at the moment,' Margaret sighed heavily. 'Bookings have dropped off and the restaurant has been quiet for weeks. It's just the yurts and chalets that are bringing in any money.'

'What the hell's been going on?' Louise asked her.

'Those bastards have posted negative reviews on trip advisor, I've asked for a press release to let people know it's all rubbish, but meanwhile we are losing money.'

'What about the regulars?' Louise was upset, she had been gone less than four weeks and in that time they stood to lose everything they had worked for.

'They come for meals at the weekends,' Margaret told her, 'but most people don't eat out during the week. We've got a dance due next month but if we can't get the floor repaired we will have to cancel.'

'I'll give Brendon Coyle a ring,' Adele walked briskly behind the reception desk and googled his number from local tradesman. After a brief discussion, Adele agreed that a team should come out as soon as possible and repair the damage.

'How much will that lot cost?' Louise asked.

'I'll get onto the insurers,' Adele told her, 'go and have a coffee and catch up with Margaret, Mairead, go and have a break,' she looked at Karen, 'we will get in touch if we need more staff.'

'Oh,' said Karen, 'okay. I'll pop up in a day or so for a swim.'

'Are you a member of the gym?' Adele asked.

'No, but I can join,' Karen was feeling out of place, she was expecting to be welcomed back with open arms.

'Come back tomorrow and Mairead will fill the forms out for you, obviously our prices will have to go up now to cover damages caused by your friend.'

'She isn't a friend, I used to work with her,' Karen explained, 'I was a valuable member of staff until I was kidnapped and tortured.'

'Yes, Louise told me all about it, terrible. How are your parents by the way?'

'Very well thank you, they didn't want me to come back here after what happened.'

'I'm not surprised, but I am that you decided to come back anyway. I mean, you left behind a man that adored you,' Adele said, 'if you'll excuse me, I'd better contact our insurance company.'

'Of course, I'll come back tomorrow,' said Karen slowly.

'Yes, okay,' Adele pressed the numbers on a card for the insurers and noticed Karen was still standing there, 'can I help with anything else?'

'No, I just wondered if you needed any help with clearing up or anything.'

'No, we're good thanks, bye Karen.'

Karen walked slowly from the hotel. That bloody Brenda had caused nothing but trouble for her, she had managed to conspire against her at the last job and now she had ruined any chances of returning to her job at The Cheyanne. As she headed down the road towards the cottage she was renting from her aunt, she muttered that she hoped the woman would drown.

Margaret had told Lou about Gerard's visit with his mother.

'What did he want?' Louise had asked.

'I don't know,' Margaret confessed, 'I suppose I didn't give him much of a chance, I told him to clear off.'

Louise laughed, although she didn't think it was funny really, 'Jack still wants to see his dad.'

'Of course he does, but that doesn't mean he can hurt you again.'

'He won't get the chance,' Louise said firmly and meaning it. 'Let's go back and see how mum's doing with sorting out the mess.'

Brendon and his team arrived shortly after the insurers, which meant that the damage could be seen and witnessed and the work was given the go ahead.

'How long will it take to put right?' Louise asked.

'We should have it as good as new in two days,' Brendon told her, 'then the floor will need to dry out.'

'What about our dance at the weekend?' Margaret said, 'will it be ready for then?'

'Highly unlikely,' said Brendon, 'I'd postpone till the weekend after if I were you.'

'Great,' Margaret sighed, 'I'd better get on to it. I could kill those bastards.'

'Join the queue,' said Louise, 'I'm going to the cottage to check on Jack, I'll see you later. We've still got loads to catch up on, for example, how's Finn?'

'I'll tell all when I come home,' grinned Margaret, hoping that Lou would be happy about the new build at Brian's.

As Louise walked across to the cottage, she noticed a helicopter hovering over the beach and an ambulance pull into the car park down the road, its lights were flashing blue. She jogged the rest of the way and was relieved to see Jack talking to his friends through the X Box.

'What do you fancy for dinner?' she shouted.

Jack moved his headphones, 'what did you say?'

'Dinner?'

'Spag bol would be great,' he grinned and put the headphones back on.

Louise got to work cooking enough pasta and mince for everyone. The dish was one of her specialities but her mind wasn't really on it. After all the doubts of running away and moving back to England, fate had stepped in and they could lose everything.

For months they had been working on an even keel, all expenses and salaries were looked after with the money coming in from the bookings and events, but now they had dried up they were in big trouble. Talk after dinner was going to be serious.

Just as Louise was putting garlic bread in the oven, she heard a loud knock on the door and wondering who it could be, she went to answer it.

Chapter 58

'Do you know Brenda Armitage?' it was one of the guards from the village, Louise didn't like the man.

'You mean the bitch that has caused massive damage to our hotel?' she replied sarcastically.

'I don't know about that, but her body was recovered from the sea an hour ago. Ellen and Aggie Duffy said you were to blame.'

'How the hell am I to blame?' Louise fumed, 'I've just arrived back home after a long journey with my son to find that not only has the two Duffy sisters and Armitage caused us long term damage online, but have also destroyed our floor.'

'Where were you during the last two hours?'

'At the hotel with my mother and cousin and then here cooking dinner for my family if you must know.'

'Yes, I must know,' the guard snarled.

'If you did your job properly people like them twisted beings wouldn't be allowed out on the street.'

'Carry on like this miss and I'll have to arrest you.'

'Clear off,' Louise shouted, 'I haven't done anything wrong, yet you persecute us and side with villains.'

'That's not true,' the guard stuttered.

'It bloody well is true, in fact, I'm going to contact a friend in Dublin and get someone up here to investigate you lot.' Louise was panting with anger.

'Calm down, Missy,' he patronised, 'we just need some answers.'

'I can't give you any.'

'If you think of anything that could help, give me a call,' the guard gave her a card.

'Oh, there was a helicopter hovering earlier,' she smiled sweetly, 'and an ambulance pulled into the carpark.'

'We know that,' he spat.

'There you go then, now I must check on dinner, I don't want that spoilt too,' Louise slammed the door in his face.

Her legs wobbled like the proverbial jelly as she went back to the kitchen to stir the sauce and just as she replaced the lid on the saucepan a feeling of nausea washed over her, she made it to the bathroom just in time.

'Jack, can you give me a hand please?' she took his headphones off his ears, 'I'm not feeling very well. Can you stir the sauce while I drain the pasta?'

'Okay,' he said reluctantly, 'you do look white, mum. Have you got that bug that's going around the school? Fergal said most of the class have had it while we've been away.'

'It's a good job it was during the holidays then.' Louise told him weakly. 'I think it's the shock of everything since we got back,' She didn't want to tell Jack about that woman drowning.

'What kind of things?' Jack asked, 'stuff at the hotel?'

'Yes, stuff at the hotel, nothing for you to worry about.'

Adele and Margaret arrived shortly before Frank and Brian. Louise just managed to serve up the spaghetti bolognaise when she had to make another dash to the bathroom.

'Are you okay, Lou?' Margaret asked with concern, noting her cousin's waxy pallor.

'The guards came to the door earlier informing me that Armitage is dead, ding dong the witch is dead,' she quipped without humour.

'They came up to the hotel afterwards,' said Adele, 'I tried to show them the damage she had caused but they weren't interested.'

'I've threatened to let the guards in Dublin investigate them,' said Louse with a smile, 'I had them running scarred.'

'You don't know anyone in Dublin,' said Adele.

'I do now,' she grinned, 'I got talking to a lovely couple on the ferry. Their son Phillip is a guard, I told them about the murders in Clodbury and they are going to ask him to come up here.'

'We stayed with them for a night,' Jack joined in, 'and the next day we went to the zoo.'

'It sounds as though you've had a great time.' Adele ruffled his dark curly hair.

'Yes, but it's good to be back,' he smiled at his adored Nan.

'How did that woman drown?' Frank sat at the table and took a piece of garlic bread to dip in his bolognaise.

'She was swimming by the river, apparently,' said Adele, 'she'd told the terrible sisters that there were too many stones and rocks down the other part of the beach.'

'Paul from down the road tried to save her in his fishing boat, but by the time he dragged her out of the sea it was too late.' Margaret wiped the corner of her mouth, 'his brother Kev told me. He'd come to see what damage the bitch had done to the floor.'

'How's the house coming along?' Adele asked Frank and Brian.

Margaret glared at her aunt, 'I haven't told Lou about it yet,' she glanced at her cousin, 'I was going to tell you later, when we had some peace and quiet.'

'You're not going to get that in Clodbury,' Brian sighed, enjoying his meal. It was the first time he'd joined the family at the table in many months. He was having a quick break before going to do more work on the house with help from Frank.

'Tell me now,' said Louise, 'you might not get a chance later.'

'Finn's designed a house, its being built on Dad's land for us to move into when we eventually get married. You and Jack can have the cottage to yourselves.'

'That's great news,' Louise told her warmly, 'it makes sense to be near your dad and it's only across the field.'

'So you don't mind? I've been so worried.'

'Silly, we can still have our girlie chats by the range,' Louise grinned.

'You bet, God, I've been so worried about telling you.'

'We've got more pressing problems,' she sighed, 'like cutting expenses and tightening the budget. We should hold a meeting tomorrow with the staff and directors,' said Louise, 'we may have to lay a few people off.'

'Ebee won't be back for a while, but I can email him,' said Margaret.

'No, don't spoil his holiday, the lads have worked hard and need this break.'

'I wonder what Brodie will make of Karen turning up.'

'I don't know what to make of it,' said Louise.

'She was great when she worked reception, but now Mairead does most of her shifts,' Margaret sighed, she hated not being to help Karen but didn't like the way she had gone to work for the enemy.

'We can't plan anything yet, we should get a financial advisor in too,' Adele suggested.

'Good idea, mum,' said Louise, 'but if you'll all excuse me, I'm going to have a lie down. I don't feel that great.'

'How long have you been sick?' Adele was worried, her daughter was normally bouncing with good health, 'have you seen a doctor?'

'I ate some dodgy fish in Wales,' she explained, 'the sickness keeps reoccurring, but I'll be okay when it flushes out of my system.'

'Not good enough,' said Adele, 'I'm booking you an appointment to see Doctor Fleming in the morning, everyone raves about how good he is.'

'If I don't feel well tomorrow, I'll go,' Louise sighed, 'I just need a couple of hours rest,' she got to her feet, 'Jack don't stay on the X box longer than an hour.' She went into her bedroom with the four adults staring after her with concern. Something wasn't right and it didn't seem like food poisoning.

Chapter 59

Louise felt considerably better the next morning and together with Margaret and Adele called a crisis meeting with all the staff and directors. They were not looking forward to it. The financial advisor was going to go through the books and offer constructive advice but warned that it could take several weeks to collate facts and figures.

The atmosphere in the conference room was tense, rumours and speculation had been buzzing around for days and each member of staff was apprehensive on the safety of their jobs.

Karnjit was the first to speak, although in the background keeping events ticking over, she was a valuable member or the team. 'I don't mind a cut in wages she offered.

'We don't know yet how we stand financially,' said Louise, 'we will know more next week. However, we did agree that you all needed to know the state of affairs.'

'Yes,' said Margaret, 'the hotel has been running well and the bookings for the chalets and yurts have exceeded our expectations, but because of the hate campaign against us by certain people, we are losing bookings hence money.'

'What can we do?' asked one of their young chefs, 'the restaurant has been quiet for weeks.'

'We need a massive marketing strategy,' said Louise, 'flyers and posters. The ball room floor is under repair so we are having to cancel the forthcoming dance. We need to focus on what we can do. Spa packages,' she looked across at Jan and the team, 'meal deals, anything you can think of.'

'But we also need the rooms booked, maybe special weekend rates or offer a health farm retreat so that we can use the pool, gym, spa and restaurant.'

'That's brilliant, Margaret,' Louise smiled at her cousin.

'I thought about it last night when I was lying in bed.'

'Great,' sighed Finn, 'and here I am thinking that you were dreaming of me.'

Everyone laughed and dispelled the tension, they were gathered to bring ideas and commitment, and to fight to keep their jobs.

'Why don't we run an aqua aerobics class?' asked one of the instructors.

'I could advertise personal training,' offered another.

The ideas ran thick and fast and the girls felt optimistic.

'We will call the press in to offer up your ideas,' said Louise, 'hopefully we can turn things around.'

Margaret, Louise and Adele were the last three to remain in the room, the men had work to do.

'What do you think?' asked Margaret, 'if we can carry out even some of the ideas it will make a difference.'

'I'll get in touch with those voucher companies, they could offer our hotel for a two night break with an evening meal included,' suggested Louise.

'That would even work for meals and spas,' said Adele, 'now I understand how they work.'

They were just about to get up when Finn came back, breathless from running, 'I've just heard some news from Paul; he said Edward is selling his land to a rich American guy.'

'Could that affect us?' Margaret said worriedly.

'He thinks it could, the guy is planning to keep a stud farm, or ranch, so could offer accommodation too. Paul reckons he could be stiff competition for us.'

'All we can do is wait,' sighed Louise, 'we will do what we can to get the bookings up.'

Margaret went to relieve Mairead on reception while Adele and Louise walked back to the cottage, Adele was worried about her daughter; she was pale despite assuring her that she was feeling better.

'How are, love?'

'I'm fine,' Louise assured, 'just a bit tired, I'm still getting over that sickness bug and the travelling.'

'I'll make you a nice cuppa when we get in,' Adele linked arms with Louise, 'and a bite to eat.'

Louise didn't want to worry her mother by saying that the thought of a cup of tea made her nauseas. 'I think I'll have a glass of juice, I need to get my fluid levels up.'

Chapter 60

Over the following weeks things began to slowly improve although the financial advisor warned them to be cautious. Ebee and Brodie returned from their overseas trip and both were shocked to discover that Karen had come back to her aunt's cottage. They were also horrified to learn of the antics of Brenda and the sisters. They both agreed that a doorman at the entrance to the hotel was a must and they would take it in turns to cover the shift until they could afford the salary for someone else to take on the role.

'Have you been down to see Karen?' Margaret asked as Brodie dropped by reception to check on the duty list.

'No,' he sighed, 'to be honest I wouldn't know what to say to her. So much has happened since she went away. We were so close, but now, we're like strangers.'

'Go down and have a chat with her later, you might be able to sort things out.'

'I'll see, I suppose we would need to clear the air if she's going to be staying here.'

'Did you notice all the building going on up the point? Edward has taken Sadie away while they do all the digging.'

'I've heard the rumours,' Brodie pulled a face, 'it seems to be one thing after another.'

'And that evil pair are still at large,' Margaret said, 'why can't the guards do anything about them?'

'Because they are useless. Is Lou really going to get a guard from Dublin up here?'

'She said she was, his name's Rory Connor,' Margaret smiled, 'you know Lou, if she says she's going to do something, she will do it. She's not been feeling too good lately though, it can't still be that dodgy fish she ate in Wales can it?'

'Has she been to the doctor's?' Brodie asked.

'No, but do you know what,' Margaret picked up the receiver and dialled a number,' I'm going to book her in for the morning.'

After a few minutes the line was picked up by a harassed receptionist, apologising about the delay but because of the sickness virus sweeping the county they were inundated with calls and appointments. Margaret sighed, 'I was making an appointment for that very reason, have you got any advice?' The receptionist told her to go to the local chemist and get an over the counter remedy, it was a virus and would have to run its course,' she continued, before saying in a rush that another line was beeping and she had to go.

'So that's that then,' Margaret told Brodie with disappointment, 'it's a virus and will have to run its course, Lou has good days and bad days so hopefully it shouldn't be too long before she's back to her normal healthy self.'

'All you can do is keep an eye on her then,' he smiled.

'Yes, how was your holiday down under? What with one thing and another we haven't had a chance to catch up with you or Ebee.'

'Fantastic, but we only got to see a couple of states, New South Wales and Victoria, so we are planning to go back next year,' realising he might be insensitive at the way the hotel business was going they might not even be working here he added, 'we are going to save for it at least.'

'I'm sure you will get there,' Margaret assured him guessing why he was trying to spare her feelings.'

'Yes, we will, you should go there for your honeymoon.'

'We need to plan the wedding first,' Margaret laughed.

'It could be a great advertising deal,' he joked.

The phone buzzed and still smiling, Margaret answered it. Her face had drained of colour when she hung up.

'What's wrong?' asked Brodie with concern.

'That was Adele, Lou had gone down to see Karen, you'll never believe it, but Aggie Duffy has died.'

'No loss,' said Brodie seriously. The woman was a witch and not a white one.

'I'm going to have to go, can you take over reception for a bit? Karen is in a real old state by the sounds of it.'

'Do you want me to go?' Brodie offered.

'That might be a better idea,' she agreed reluctantly. 'As soon as Mairead comes on duty I'll come down, Adele is looking after Jack.'

Chapter 61

Louise was comforting Karen and trying to make sense of what had happened when Brodie knocked on the door. Louise asked, 'shall I answer it?'

Karen nodded her head and clasped her hands together, her body was trembling and her whole demeanour was jittery.

'Brodie!' Louise was never so grateful to see anyone, 'maybe you can get some sense out of her.'

While Brodie sat next to Karen on the small sofa, Louise put the kettle on and warmed the tea pot. She had managed to eat a dry biscuit and sip small amounts of water when the phone had rang. Her mum had answered and explained that Karen had found Aggie's body on the beach while going for a short walk. Louise was the first person Karen had thought of to help, but Louise had found the sight of the corpse on the beach too much and had thrown up the small amount of digestive that o she had managed to nibble on. Using her mobile, she had phoned the Guarda station in Clodbury and reported the findings and assured the officers that they would wait near the body until they arrived. Officer Riordan was accompanied by two other guards and his eyes were sly as they took in Louise's presence.

'Trouble has a way of following you, Miss Lavender,' he stated.

'Karen found the body, I came to keep her company,' she told him, 'and now that you're here, we are going back to the cottage over there,' she pointed to the house Karen was renting. 'So that where you will find us should you want to know anything else.'

'Oh, indeed we will need you to answer some questions,' he snarled.

'He's an unpleasant bastard, isn't he?' Louise had said to Karen on the way up the sandy dune.

'He gives me the shivers,' said Karen.

Louise had just poured the tea when there was a deafening knock on the door.

'I'll get it,' said Brodie as Louise carried the tray through to the small sitting room.

'Did you see anything?' Riordan asked Karen, who was still shaking.

'No, how could I? I was going for a walk and a paddle. I thought at first that it a black bag had blown across the fields by that strong wind last night.'

'How do you think her face got so badly damaged?' he demanded.

'I don't know, I didn't look too closely at her face.'

'Have you taken the body away?' asked Brodie, thinking about the children that were staying in the chalets and yurts.

'You don't need to tell us how to do our job,' Riordan snarled.

'Maybe if you did a better job there wouldn't be so many murders then,' Brodie replied.

'Any more of your insolence I'll have you arrested.'

'He's not worth it,' said Louise as she handed a cup of tea to Karen, she had added extra sugar for shock.

'It was well known that you didn't get on with Miss Duffy,' Riordan snapped, 'I will be keeping a close eye on all of you,' he turned on his heels and slammed the door behind him.

'That does it,' Louise pulled out her mobile, 'I'm calling Rory.'

After the tea was drank and the cups washed and put away, Louise begged Karen to lock up and come up to the cottage with her for a while, 'you should really see a doctor,' she added.

'No, I'll be fine,' Karen assured her, 'I'll have an early night, thanks Brodie, it means a lot that you came down, especially when I treated you so badly.'

'Don't worry about that for now,' he told her, 'I'll visit tomorrow and see how you are.'

Louise linked her arm through Brodie's as they made their way up the road, 'How are you feeling?'

Brodie asked her.

'Not great to be honest, the sight of that decaying face will haunt me for a long time.'

'I wonder what happened to the old crone,' he mused.

'That's three deaths on the beach since I've been here, there must be a connection somewhere.'

'Brenda's drowning was an accident,' Brodie assured her.

'Denton's certainly wasn't,' Louise shivered, 'they've never caught who done it.'

They were nearing the gate when Louise noticed an enormous limousine parked outside the cottage, 'a visitor, that's all I need,' she sighed.

'I'll leave you to it, I must go and relieve Ebee for a couple of hours.'

Chapter 62

'Ah, one of the owners returns,' drawled a man sitting in her usual chair by the range. At first, Louise thought it was Eustace Doherty, with the white hair and long matching beard, but when the man got to his feet, she could see that it certainly wasn't their friendly, if not eccentric lawyer.

'Your mom has been keeping me entertained,' smiled the man, 'I'm Davie Lee, pleased to make your acquaintance.'

Louise looked quizzically at her mother, 'is Margaret still at the hotel?'

'Yes, she phoned about an hour ago, Mairead was delayed but she shouldn't be too long.'

'How can I help you, Mr Lee?' Louise asked politely.

'Please call me Davie,' he had an enormous smile of white teeth.

'It's been quite an eventful day, Davie, would you mind if I got a glass of water?'

'No of course not, your mom was kind enough to make me a cup of your English tea.'

Louise ran the tap for a few seconds before filling a glass, she took a few gulps and refilled it. She was suddenly so tired that she longed to go and lie down on her bed for a while, was it only just after 4pm? She sat opposite Davie Lee and waited for him to state the reason for his visit.

'I would like to wait until your cousin Margaret gets here, if that's okay,' he said it in such a way that there really was no choice in the matter.

'I don't know how long she will be,' Louise told him, 'would it be possible to come back another time perhaps?'

'No, the matter can't wait much longer I'm afraid, I've heard about the death of that woman, news travels fast in a small village.'

'Her death has nothing to do with me or Margaret,' Louise told him.

'I know, my dear, but it does make my plans more, how can I put it? Pending, yes, that's the word, pending.'

'I'm not sure I follow you, Davie, how are your pending plans anything to do with us?'

'All in good time, your son is a little charmer isn't he? Handsome and intelligent.'

Louise felt a chill travel up her spine, 'when did you meet Jack?' she asked.

'Just an hour ago, he is doing his homework now I believe.'

'Yes, that's right,' Adele confirmed, 'he's had his tea,' she smiled at Louise.

'Thanks mum, god it was horrible,' she took a long drink of water, 'the body was in a bad way, Karen was in deep shock, I tried to get her to come up here, but she wanted to stay put.'

'She was an evil woman, that Aggie Duffy' Adele said, 'she tried to ruin my life and along with her sister was the reason I fled to England.'

'I always wondered,' Louise sighed, 'I knew there was something you were holding back from me.'

'I'll tell you about it one day,' she promised.

'So, Davie, where are you from?' asked Louise.

'Texas,' he smiled, 'well, originally I came from the west of Ireland, but I've lived in the good ole US of A for many years.'

The strange man looked familiar to Louise but she couldn't quite place him. Her first instinct that he was a paedophile was dispelled, he was just showing an interest in her son. She couldn't blame her imagination for running wild though after what she had just witnessed on the beach.

'Is Lee an Irish name?' she asked.

'My father was English and they moved to Ireland when he married my Irish mother,' he explained.

'I see,' Louise took another sip of water wishing that Margaret would hurry up, 'I might give Margaret a ring and see what's keeping her.'

It appeared that Mairead couldn't get away and Margaret was having to man reception until Natasha got there.

'Shall we walk up to the hotel?' Louise asked him, 'you can explain the reason for your visit then.'

'That would be mighty fine,' he got to his feet, 'thank you Adele for your kind hospitality and I'm sure we will meet again very soon.'

Davie was very sprightly for his age, although Louise was finding it hard to guess what age he could be. He matched her swift pace equally and within minutes they were walking through the glass sliding doors, where Louise was pleased to see Brodie standing just inside, guarding the hotel against intruders. Although there was only one of the culprits left.

Margaret looked up as she saw her cousin walk towards the desk with a white haired man, 'hi Lou, sorry, I meant to leave an hour ago. Natasha should be here soon.'

'We really need more cover,' Louise sighed, 'maybe we should give Karen a few shifts.'

'We can't afford it,' Margaret sounded defeated.

'Oh, sorry, Mr Davie Lee meet my cousin, Margaret.'

'I'm pleased to meet you,' Davie shook her hand. 'I need to speak to you both, maybe if Natasha is arriving shortly we could wait until then and talk in private.'

'Sounds ominous,' muttered Margaret.

'I sincerely hope not,' smiled Davie charmingly.

Natasha arrived ten minutes later, 'I'm sorry I couldn't get here earlier, there's been a bit of a crisis at home,' she apologised.

'Is your mum okay?' Lou asked with concern.

'Yes, she's fine, she won't be able to make it in tonight but I can cover her shifts.'

'Thank you, we need to have a word with Mr Lee in the office, if you need us give a shout,' said Margaret.

Louise led the way and once in the office, Margaret closed the door, 'take a seat Mr Lee.'

'Davie,' he smiled taking a seat in one of the plush leather seats the girls had invested in when they had begun their journey into hotel management.

Once seated, Louise asked, 'you have our full attention, Davie, so please, explain what you want from us.'

'It's more about what you want from me,' he paused and took an envelope out of his jacket pocket, 'I don't know if you are aware of the fact that I purchased the three farms at the point,' he looked at the girls and waited for their reaction.

'We're not for sale,' said Louise firmly, 'we may have to make some cutbacks due to circumstances beyond our control, but we will recover.'

'I have every faith in you both,' he opened the envelope, 'I've been keeping an eye on your business and I must say, I'm very impressed. So much so that I would like to invest in you,' he passed the contents over to the girls and they gasped at the amount he was suggesting.

'Forty million pounds?' said Louise.

'Euros,' Davie contradicted, 'but if you need more, the funds are there for you.'

'But why?' asked Margaret in a daze.

'Potential my dear, and that's not me being patronising. I'm going to run the best breeding stables in County Donegal and your hotel being so close by will be an asset that would be foolish to deny. I've got a contract with the riding school to supply horses for lessons. Imagine, people coming from all over the world to stay at your hotel and spa and then go for a gallop across the beach. The advertising will put you back where you should be.'

'It sounds exciting,' said Louise, 'what's the catch?'

'That you turn my investment into a profit,' Davie replied.

'And if we can't?'

'You will, I have every faith in you.'

'As you can imagine, it's an amazing offer, but we need to put it forward to the board of directors,' Louise explained.

'Of course,' he agreed, 'and I'm hoping to earn a place on that board in due course,' he got to his feet, 'when would you like me to attend the meeting?'

'Shall we say 10am the day after tomorrow? That will give us time to let the others know,' said Louise, walking towards the door.

Davie shook hands with first Louise and then Margaret, 'it's been a pleasure, see you both real soon.'

After Davie had left the office, Louise collapsed back into the chair she had been sitting on.

'I can't get my head around it,' she spluttered.

'Me either,' agreed Margaret, 'forty million euros! That will put us back where we should be like he said, we could hold other weddings we still have the one for the actress to finalise.'

'I know and Ebee and Brodie can relax and stop worrying about their jobs.'

'There is still a catch, I can feel it in my bones,' said Louise.

Chapter 63

The following morning, Louise was making tea while Jack got ready for school, Margaret had taken a walk up to the hotel to check on Natasha. It was a long shift for her and the girls had decided to give a few shifts to Karen. She hadn't made an appearance since the night Aggie had died and there had been no sightings of her deranged sister, Ellen. A knock on the door made her jump, she was so lost in thought.

'Shall I get it?' Jack asked.

'No, sit at the table and help yourself to cereal, I'll go.'

Louise opened the door to find a dark haired young man smiling at her, if it wasn't for the fact that he was wearing a Guarda uniform she wouldn't have known the handsome stranger.

'Hi, you must be Rory,' Louise opened the door wide to let him in, 'thank you for coming all this way.'

'I like a chance to solve a mystery,' he gave a cheeky grin, 'my parents told me all about the strange goings on in Clodbury and then when you called I couldn't pass up the opportunity to try and help.'

'I'm very grateful that you have, would you like a cuppa?'

'I'd love one and could I be cheeky and ask for a slice of toast? I'm starving, I decided to come straight here instead of stopping in Monahan.'

Once Jack had gone to school on the local bus, Louise related everything that had happened starting with the death of Denton. Rory took notes and asked relevant questions, although Louise explained that she didn't know anything. She did tell Rory about her doubts about Riordan and how little faith she had in the local Guarda.

'I've arranged for a mate to come up tomorrow and work under the pretext of obtaining more experience, our chief wasn't too happy about it, but if there's a corrupt officer on the beat we need to find out.'

'Karen found Aggie's body, she lives down the road in the small cottage overlooking the bay, it's taken its toll on her. Before she went back to England, Karen was kidnapped by a retired doctor Swain, Aggie Duffy and her strange sister, Ellen.'

'Were they charged?' Rory asked.

'No, unfortunately when Karen was rescued, Aggie sustained injuries, so Riordan said it cancelled out the kidnapping.'

'It doesn't work like that,' said Rory.

'Well, it does here. Shall I take you down to meet Karen when you've had your cuppa and toast?'

'Maybe later. I'd like to talk to some of the people living around the area where Denton was murdered, I feel he is the key to all of this.'

'He was a horrible man,' stated Louise.

'Did he have many enemies?'

'I would think so, he stole land from a few people around here and I believe he built two houses on land that didn't belong to him because Riordan allowed him to.'

'I've certainly got a lot to get my teeth into,' Rory said ruefully.

'Would you mind if I left you to it then? I need to sort out some business at the hotel.'

'Aye, that's fine, is it okay to use your cottage as a base?'

'Of course,' Louise told him, she reached for a key on the hook, 'here's the spare. Treat the cottage like your own. Jack can sleep at his grandparents for a while.'

Margaret had already started the business of organising the meeting with Davie Lee. Louise still had a feeling in her gut that he wasn't all that he seemed, but when she had googled him the previous night, she discovered that he was a multi billionaire ranch owner, and the picture matched the man, so at least he was genuine. It was also true that the farms at the point had been sold to a rich American guy who was going to turn the land into a stud farm and ranch. Most people she had mentioned it to were excited about the new venture and jobs that would be on offer.

'Hi Lou, what kept you?' asked Margaret as Louise passed her a cup of coffee that she had picked up from the café.

'Rory arrived, you know, the guy I told you about. He is literally going to get on the case of the murders. I'm not fussed about the dead bodies, just getting one over on Riordan.'

Margaret raised her cup, 'to justice.'

'And prosperity for the Cheyenne,' Louise tapped her cup against Margaret's. 'Is everyone okay for the meeting tomorrow? I know Finn was trying to plan the last part of your new house.'

'Yes, he can spare two hours, Dad and Frank will be here of course, your mum and Ebee.'

'Do you think it's dodgy? I mean, why us?'

'We will all be there tomorrow to listen to what he has to say,' reassured Margaret, 'I've given Robbie the financial advisor a ring too, I thought it might be a good idea if he listened to the proposal.'

'Good thinking,' Louise said thoughtfully, 'it will make an enormous difference though, if he's not a crook. We can go ahead with those weddings we've been promising for months.'

'It's exciting really,' Margaret grinned, 'maybe me and Finn should get married here.'

'I thought you would anyway,' Louise laughed, 'freebie wedding.'

'Are you going to make my dress then? And the bridesmaids?'

'Okay, smart arse, free venue then.'

They were both giggling like school girls when Natasha came through the doors in a rush.

'Are you okay pet?' asked Margaret.

'No, not really,' Natasha burst into tears, 'it's Mum.'

Louise felt her stomach clench, not the lovely Mairead who wouldn't hurt a fly, 'what's happened?' she asked in a shaky voice.

'Mum has a guest in the house, a secret person and she won't let any of us see them. She looks dreadful and hasn't slept for ages,' Natasha sobbed.

Louise could have collapsed with relief, but something was going on that needed looking into.

'Shall we get Ebee and Brodie to go and check on her?' offered Margaret.

'No, she wouldn't let them in,' Natasha cried.

'Sit down,' Louise ordered the young girl, 'I'll go and get you a hot drink.'

Moments later, Louise put a cup of steaming tea with plenty of sugar in front of her saying, 'I'll be back in a while, I've things to do in the cottage,' she looked at Margaret before running out of the hotel.

As luck would have it, Rory had just made himself a cup of coffee and was dunking a biscuit into it when she let herself into the cottage.

'Hope you don't mind,' he said sheepishly, 'I felt a bit peckish.'

'Of course not,' Louise sat at the table, 'how did you get on?'

'Not great, nobody wanted to talk about Denton and most said that they didn't see anything.'

'I've got a problem I need a bit of help with,' said Louise, 'something weird is going on with my friend Mairead. Will you come out to her house with me please? After you've finished your coffee.'

Mairead's car was parked around the back of her house so Louise knew that she couldn't be far away. Rory banged loudly on the front door and looked through the letter box, 'I can't see any movement.'

'We will try around the back,' said Louise.

The back door was locked as she had guessed it might be, so she banged on the door and then again on the large glass window in the kitchen. She could see dishes piled up in the sink, which was very out of character for her friend.

'Something is badly wrong,' Louise told Rory worriedly.

He went back to the front door and opened the letter box, 'open up Mrs Devlin,' he shouted, 'I need to speak to you urgently.'

They waited for several minutes and then finally the door was opened. Mairead looked dreadful, her fair hair was thick with grease and her face was drawn.

'What's up?' Louise asked forcing her way into the house.

'Nothing,' said Mairead, 'I'm not feeling very well.'

Rory followed Louise into the house and closed the door, 'you need to tell us what's going on.'

Reluctantly, Mairead went up the stairs and they followed her to one of the bedrooms where the door was closed tight.

'I had to help her,' Mairead confessed, 'she has no one.'

To Louise's disbelief, Ellen was asleep in the bed, her wild hair tangled and spread out on the pillow.

'Why you?' Louise couldn't get her head around it.

'I don't know,' said Mairead softly, 'she was cowering by the back door when I'd finished my shift. She told me that Aggie was dead and that she had killed her.'

'Why didn't you phone the Guarda?' asked Rory.

'Riordan? He couldn't help,' said Mairead with derision.

'Tell us what you know,' he said gently.

Mairead looked at Louise and she nodded her head, 'Rory's come to help.'

Chapter 64

'Doctor Swain had created an ointment that would make you appear younger,' Mairead began, 'and Aggie wanted to use it. Swain had locked it away telling the sisters that it wasn't proven to be safe, and last week Aggie had found it.'

'Surely it wouldn't have made much difference to that old crone's face,' stated Louise.

'What it did do was burn right through her flesh like acid. It was a slow process and as they had walked along the beach gathering sticks for the fire, Aggie had slowly dissolved, her skin had peeled away leaving bone and sinew exposed.'

Louise remembered the rotting corpse on the beach and shivered.

'When it was obvious that Aggie had died,' Mairead continued, 'Ellen ran off in a blind panic. She was uttering those strange words like Gumden and other stuff and then she had clung onto me crying like a baby. I felt sorry for her but knew that I shouldn't. I didn't want the wains involved so I've kept it quiet.'

'She needs medical help,' soothed Rory, 'both mentally and physically I'd say.'

'She knows about Denton and Swain, that's why she's so petrified,' said Mairead.

Louise and Rory looked at her with interest.

'How?' Louise asked.

'She was a witness to Denton's death and she seems to think that Karen was too, that's why she was kidnapped by Swain. But that's all I know, it all came out in a load of rambling nonsense, but I managed to piece it together.'

'I'm going to phone for an ambulance,' said Rory, 'the woman needs proper help and you need some rest. At least we have something to work with now,' he looked at Louise.

'Go and have a shower, I'll sit with her,' Louise told Mairead, 'you need to get something to eat and get some rest. I can't believe you didn't tell us what was happening.'

'I felt guilty helping her, yet I couldn't not, it was like helping an injured seagull, they're a pain in the backside but you don't want to see them suffer.'

'I get that, but we could've helped, poor Natasha was in a real state.'

'I've been stupid,' Mairead sighed, 'but at least Ellen will get help and my conscience will be clear.'

'It would've been clear anyway, you are too kind hearted. I don't think I would have been so generous towards her after everything Ellen did.'

'She has been manipulated, first by Swain, who fed her fantasies, seduced her even, while Aggie was pure poison, using her own sister to get what she wanted, which was vengeance and spite.'

'Wow, how did you figure all that out?'

'Ellen has lucid moments, she can even talk normally, but then it's like a shutter comes down and she's an imbecile.'

'Why did she attach Ebee? It was totally unprovoked,' asked Louise, 'and all the harm she caused years ago to my mum.'

'I don't know, that's a mystery.'

Rory popped his head in the door, 'the ambulance is on its way. Do you want to meet me at Karen's when they've taken Ellen to hospital, Lou? She will be committed to a psychiatric ward while the assess her.'

'Yes, I'm quite enjoying playing Miss Marple,' she grinned.

Mairead gave Louise a lift to Karen's on the way to do a shift on reception duties, Ellen had been taken away to a secure unit at a hospital in Letterkenny. Because of the unprovoked attack on Ebee, Ellen was deemed not safe to be out amongst people, even if someone had come forward to look after her. It was highly unlikely that she would be released any time soon.

'Do you still feel sorry for her?' Louise asked as Mairead slowed down and pulled up outside Karen's cottage.

'Not really,' Mairead confessed, 'especially after the injuries to poor Ebee.'

'She could also have had something to do with Swain's death, we will never know,' Louise jumped out of the car, 'I'll see you later, there's a few things to sort out before the meeting tomorrow.'

Rory was sitting in a chair opposite Karen when she walked into the small kitchen. The atmosphere was tense and Louise wondered what had been said before she had arrived, 'cuppa anyone?' she asked.

'I'd love one,' said Rory with a smile that didn't quite reach his eyes.

'Are you okay, Karen?'

'Yes, I will be,' she shivered, 'I shouldn't have come back here, but things were going pear shaped at home. I thought it would be okay now that Swain was dead.'

'What happened with Swain? Asked Rory, 'what hold did he have over you?'

'It wasn't quite that, he terrified me, he seemed to think that I'd witnessed Denton's death, but I hadn't, I really hadn't,' Karen sobbed into a tissue.

'Why did he think you had?' he prompted gently.

'I don't know, I couldn't make sense out of it, he warned me that if I told anyone about Denton he would cause serious harm to my family.'

'Where was Denton's body found?' Rory turned to face Louise who was pouring boiling water into a tea pot.

'At the top of the sand dune,' Louise pointed out the window towards the car park, 'just over there, throat slit and a bullet through his head, I guess he didn't feel the seagulls pecking his eyes out.'

'You didn't like him,' it was a statement not a question.

'No, he was a horrible man, always threatening us,' Louise sat down while the tea brewed, 'he wanted our land, but we were not having any of his shit, but then the guards pulled us in for questioning, bloody joke.'

'Do you have any ideas of who would want to kill him?'

'Most of the village,' sighed Louise, 'he wasn't a loss to anyone.'

'Was he the reason you were kidnapped by Swain?' Rory asked Karen.

'It must have been, Ellen, or Aggie, I can't remember who, was hitchhiking along the road, I thought it was a little old lady otherwise I wouldn't have stopped, if only I had kept on going. Swain was abusing Ellen, I remember that, but a lot of that time is a blur, Swain had drugged me.'

'I'll get one of the lads to look into his background,' Rory told them.

'Aggie was an evil crone,' Louise spat out so savagely that Rory winced.

'You can fill me in on her later,' Rory jotted a few notes in his pocket book, 'shall we have some tea?'

Louise poured and stirred, adding milk and sugar to Rory's when a thought occurred to her.

'If Swain was worried that Karen had witnessed Denton being murdered, it must have happened around here, so maybe,' she paused a feeling of excitement building up, 'so just maybe, Teresa might have the deed captured on tape.'

Chapter 65

Teresa was at work until six, so they had to wait, her husband Dave was on a trip to Essex and wouldn't be home until the following day, the children were at university in Dublin.

'It's so frustrating,' said Louise. They were in the cottage with Margaret and Adele.

'We've waited this long,' Margaret touched her shoulder, 'it's a shame we didn't think of it when we watched the tapes before.'

'Tell me about it,' she sighed.

'Tell me about Aggie Duffy,' Rory asked, warming his toes by the range.

'She was the devil incarnate,' said Adele, 'a wicked, spiteful crone that took joy out of hurting others. She made my life a misery when I lived here years ago.'

'In what way?' Rory asked gently, 'only if you want to tell me, though.'

'I went swimming one day with a group of friends,' Adele sat near Rory, 'she hid my clothes and towel, I had puppy fat in those days and was highly embarrassed. I had to walk home in just a clingy wet costume that showed up all my lumps and bumps.'

'How did you know it was her?' he asked.

'I heard her cackling as I walked past, she was sitting at the side of the road, on my towel, to add insult to injury. I asked her for my things but she began to taunt me, calling me fatty and other cruel jibes. I ran home and sobbed in my bedroom. I never went swimming on that beach again.'

'You've got a lovely figure,' Louise told her, 'you should be proud to show it off.'

'Cruel remarks cut deeply when you're a child,' Adele said sadly.

'Yes,' Louise agreed, remembering the hateful things Aggie had said to her over the years, and the way she taunted Jack. 'I'm glad she's dead, it may be wrong to say it, but I am.'

'Are you staying for dinner,' Adele asked Rory, 'I'm doing a full roast, it's our last supper,' she laughed, feeling better after telling them about Aggie Duffy.

Rory raised an eyebrow and Margaret laughed, 'Adele is exaggerating,' she explained, 'she just wants a full table to cater for,' she smiled at her aunt, 'we can go to yours anytime you invite us,' she said cheekily.

'It won't be long before you move to your new home,' Adele added.

'The cottage is going to feel pretty strange,' said Louise sadly, remembering the cosy chats by the range.

'I'm sure we will be knocking on the door every five minutes,' Margaret laughed.

'Maybe I should get a cat,' Louise said, 'it can keep me warm on a cold winter's night.'

Rory blushed as he said, 'I'm sure there is someone special out there for you, Lou.'

Frank, Brian and Finn joined them just as Adele was dishing up, she wanted to cook the meal with little assistance but she allowed Jack to lay out the knives and forks. Margaret and Louise were sipping their favourite wine letting her get on with it.

'I wouldn't want to cramp her style,' Louise sighed, taking another sip of wine and then putting the glass down on a small table, 'since I've had that food poisoning I've lost the taste for alcohol.'

'I'm sure it will come back, Margaret chuckled.

'Margaret hasn't lost the taste,' grinned Finn.

'Nope,' she picked up Louise's almost full glass of red wine, 'waste not want not.'

The men agreed to clear away while Louise, Margaret and Rory went down the road to see if Teresa was home from work. As they neared the impressive house that was surrounded by tall bushes and hedges, they noticed that a light was on in the kitchen. As Teresa saw them approach, she quickly opened the door and let them in.

Rory explained the reason for their visit and Teresa was soon ushering them into the back office at the rear of the house.

'We've added more camera's since the last time,' she said proudly, 'and we have everything backed up on a stick, all dated and in order. Dave is thinking of moving away.'

'No! That would be a terrible shame,' said Louise.

'It's getting like Columbo around here.'

'There's only been three murders,' said Margaret.

'Yes and most of them just over the road,' Teresa exclaimed.

'I see your point,' said Rory.

It took over two hours to find the information they were looking for and they were all shocked.

'To be honest,' said Louise, 'if you think about it we shouldn't be too surprised.'

'It does answer a lot of questions,' said Rory, 'but gives us one hell of a headache, can I have the backup stick?'

'Yes, of course,' Teresa opened the drawer on the desk and passed it to him.

'Thanks, please don't show anyone else the footage, it will put their lives in danger.'

'That does it,' Teresa shook visibly, 'I think we will start looking at houses away from F' ing Clodbury.'

Rory was invited to stay another night before heading back to Dublin where he had serious work to do, 'until this is sorted out the village of Clodbury is not safe,' he declared solemnly.

'What about Karen?' asked Margaret.

'We might need her to play at being prey,' suggested Rory, 'but she won't be happy about it.'

Chapter 66

Louise had mixed emotions as she made her way up to the hotel, Margaret had gone up an hour earlier to sort out a complicated booking. Mairead had promised to cover reception and housekeeping for the duration of the meeting and Karnjit had happily taken on more duties. It was agreed that Karen wasn't yet ready to come back to work and Brodie was keeping his distance from her, stating that the separation had caused major differences. It was a shame as they had been a cute couple, but it certainly had been a case of out of sight out of mind. Karen wasn't the same person any more, but Louise could understand after everything the poor girl had been through and it wasn't over yet.

'How's it going?' she asked Margaret, noting the flushed cheeks and glinting eyes.

'I've just checked in a woman called Nikki Walker. She was sneezing all over the place and told me to remove any plants out of her room,' Margaret chuckled, 'as if we have plants in the room!'

Louise laughed, 'we certainly get all sorts,' she agreed, 'but it's good that things are picking up.'

'Nikki explained she was looking for a venue to hold seminars in the area, she said we ticked all the boxes.'

'Seminars for what?'

'Motivation and confidence,' Margaret explained, 'maybe we should go along.'

'Why?' Louise spluttered, 'do we need confidence?'

'No, I mean to give a talk, silly.'

'Hi girls, sorry I'm late,' Mairead took her coat off, 'the car wouldn't start and I had to get Kevin to give me a lift.'

'Do you want to grab a coffee before we leave you to it?' asked Louise, 'we could be a while.'

'In that case I will, do you both want one?'

'No thanks,' smiled Margaret, 'we need to get the room ready, one of us will order drinks through during the meeting. I don't want to be rushing to the loo half way through.'

'Are you nervous?' Louise asked as they set out glasses around the table in readiness for the meeting.

'A bit, it's a massive thing, isn't it?'

'And we need to make the right decision. I'm glad the financial advisor is joining us along with Eustace.'

Adele, Frank, Brian and Ebee arrived together quickly followed by Finn and Eustace. The financial advisor, Robbie followed Davy Lee into the room and they all took their seats. Adele had agreed to take minutes leaving the girls to fire questions.

It was remarkable how much Eustace and Davy looked alike, with their white hair and long beards, Louise thought they belonged in an episode of Lord of the rings, but then felt mean, although it would be handy if Eustace was a wizard and could cast a truth spell around the room.

Margaret made quick introductions to Davy and the meeting began.

Davy outlined his plans for his investment, he would put up the vast sum for the hotel and spa to work alongside his stud farm. It seemed too good to be true and Louise voiced her concerns.

'What's the catch?' she asked.

'There is no catch,' he told the room firmly, 'I will be returning to the states in a few weeks and I will expect you to keep me up to date with how everything is going.'

'Who is going to run the stud farm? Asked Ebee, wondering if he would get a chance to learn to ride the horses.

Davy picked up on a kindred spirit and gave him a dazzling smile, 'I've got a manager coming in tomorrow, but if we could share staff on occasion that would be wonderful.'

'We are short staffed at the moment,' Louise told him, 'due to lack of cash flow.'

'But that will change when I invest,' Davy assured her. 'I will put up 40 million euros, and there's more if you need it, however, I'm expecting you to turn things around.'

'Now that the evil duo are out of the picture we shouldn't have anymore conspiracies against us,' Margaret told him.

'I'm looking at a bigger picture, too,' Davy got to his feet, excitement seemed to ooze out of him like bolts of electricity, 'American's love Ireland, add to that the spa, yurts, cabins and now my stud farm, they will come here in droves.'

'It's going to take one hell of a publicity campaign,' said Ebee.

'Yes son, but that will all be arranged, fancy a shot at it?'

Ebee grinned widely, 'I would love to.'

'What do you think, Eustace?' Louise asked their lawyer.

'I'm thinking Arthur would approve,' he told them as he twisted strands of his beard into a peak, 'you wouldn't be here now if he hadn't speculated and dabbled in stocks and shares.'

'That's true,' Margaret nodded her head.

'Have you got a name for your stud farm?' Ebee mused.

'Yes,' said Davy, but didn't elaborate.

'It's an amazing offer,' Robbie added his voice to the meeting. 'Eustace can draft up the agreement that both parties are satisfied with.' He got to his feet, 'I'll leave you to it if there's nothing more for me to add at this stage.'

'It still seems too good to be true,' said Frank, scratching his head.

'What have we got to lose?' asked Margaret, 'Eustace will draft up the paperwork and we can go over it then.'

'What percentage of a return are you looking at? Asked Ebee.

'I would expect in the early stages of growth that monies will be put back into the business. Salaries will be worked out and deducted of course.'

'That sounds fair,' said Adele, 'and I wouldn't mind working at the stud farm,' she grinned, 'I love horses.'

'Splendid,' said Davy, 'and the stud farm will also be subject to growth, we could begin training jockeys after we get established, race horses at the Grand National, the potential is enormous.'

'Oh my god,' said Ebee, 'I'm so glad that I didn't go back to Nuneaton.'

Everyone laughed.

'I'll go and get some drinks,' said Louise, 'tea? Coffee?'

'I think we need champagne my dear,' said Davy with a wink.

'It's only eleven thirty,' gasped Adele.

'I'd rather have a beer,' said Frank and Brian in unison.

'I think we should go across to the restaurant,' said Margaret, 'we can order some food and have a drink while we wait. Are you going to join us, Eustace?'

'I'll have a drink but I've got a pile of paperwork on my desk,' he sighed.

'You've always got a pile of paperwork on your desk,' laughed Louise, remembering their first day in his office eons ago.

'Great stuff,' said Davy,' it will give me a chance to check out my investment, and then I'll expect a guided tour.'

'A job for the lads,' grinned Margaret.

After a delicious lunch of cod and chips, the chef's special of the day as the fish had been caught that morning off Lenan Point, the women headed back to the hotel to call a staff meeting. Eustace had stayed for lunch after all and had left when he had consumed his coffee and mints. He promised to have the documents ready by the end of the week.

'I'll need an architect next month,' Davy told Finn, 'will you have time to come over and take a look before I go back to the States?'

'Yes, I've nearly finished our house,' he cast a loving glance at Margaret, 'I'll come over tomorrow morning if that suits you.'

'Yes, great stuff.'

'Will you be coming back?' asked Louise with concern.

'Of course, Lou. I just have a few things to sort out over the pond. I'm going to be juggling a bit over the coming months.'

'Do you need me?' Adele asked, looking at her watch.

'No, Mum,' Louise grinned, 'have you somewhere better to be?'

'I'm going into Derry for a few bits,' she explained, 'I would like to beat the rush hour.'

'See you later then,' Margaret said, 'come around later for a drink.'

'So our jobs are safe?' Karnjit was bouncing on the chair she was sitting on in the office.

'Yes,' Margaret laughed, 'so all suggestions welcome, we need to show Davy Lee that we are worthy of his investment.'

'Have you set a date for your wedding?' asked Karnjit.

'No,' Margaret looked at her quizzically, 'why?'

'Because I fancy being a wedding planner, and what better publicity for the hotel for one of the owners to get married in The Cheyanne.'

'That's a brilliant idea,' said Mairead, 'you have both said that the hotel would be ideal for weddings.'

'Don't forget the famous wedding,' said Margaret. 'The bride to be will be arriving next week to have a chat and maybe perform,' she smiled.

'Things are really looking up,' beamed Karnjit.

'And Ebee could take the photos,' said Louise, 'have you seen his pictures from Australia? Stunning.'

'I think I'd better discuss this with Finn first,' Margaret was blushing, 'but you've got a point, we have said the hotel is an amazing venue for weddings, so we could get brochures drawn up and circulated.'

'Why don't we hold a wedding fayre?' said Louise, 'we can get people in to showcase their wares.'

'Great,' said Karnjit, 'Can I have the job of wedding planner?'

'You don't give up do you?' Margaret sighed and then laughed.

'What would my job be?' Mairead wondered, 'I mean, I run reception and keep an eye on housekeeping, but I would like something to get my teeth into.'

'Make notes of what you would like to do,' Louise told her, 'and we can work out a plan of action, how does that sound?'

'I'd like that. I do enjoy working on reception, but every day is the same.'

'Now we've got a cash injection we can plan and expand,' Louise pulled a notebook out of the top drawer of the desk, 'Point One, Karnjit wants the role of wedding planner.'

'Wants?' queried Karnjit.

'Yes, you will need to apply for the position,' smiled Margaret.

'Oh,' she said in disappointment, 'who else is applying?'

'We will need to advertise the post,' said Louise, tapping her pencil on the desk, then seeing the glum look on Karnjit's face relented, 'I'm only teasing, of course the job is yours, it's what you do best. We will also need input on filling up the ballroom at weekends, we need a crowd puller, a big, no a huge group. Any ideas?' she looked at the three women.

'Stavros and Flatly?' said Mairead.

"Ha ha,' chuckled Louise.

'No, seriously,' said Mairead, 'they are touring the north west, why don't we hold a Greek night with plate smashing?'

'I like that idea,' Louise chewed the end of the pencil, 'and I've just had an even better one,' she got to her feet and passed the notepad and pencil to Mairead, 'you can carry on, I've got serious plans with Margaret.'

'You have?' Margaret got to her feet.

Louise grabbed her arm, 'see you later girls.'

'Where are we going?'

'To the spa, I need a massage, my back is aching like crazy and we need a chat to Jan.'

'Sorry we haven't seen much of you lately,' Louise sighed as she lay face down on the lounger, she realised her stomach was beginning to bloat after all the stodgy cakes they'd been gorging on these past few weeks.

'I heard rumours that you were in trouble,' Jan rubbed oil into her hands and began to knead the muscles in Louise's shoulders.

'We're great now though, so after our massages, we will fill you in.'

Margaret was in the other treatment room with Olga, the cleaning lady had wanted to improve her skills and undertaken intensive courses in beauty therapy.

'Do you want a facial?'

'Why not, give me the works.'

Over an hour later, faces glistening with oil and rosy from the facial, Margaret and Louise sat sipping water and chatting to Jan about the future of the health centre.

'We need ideas,' Louise told her, 'we want to be the best there is and we want to be different. We want you to be in charge, are you up for it?'

'I'd love to,' Jan cried, 'my friend, Vikki, does reiki and aromatherapy, there seems to be a market for alternative therapy.'

'We could hold training classes,' said Margaret.

'I'd be up for that,' said Jan.

'I'm thinking aqua aerobics in the pool, too,' said Louise. 'We need to invest in the gym, make it bigger and better.'

'Do you want me to look around for an instructor?' asked Jan.

'No,' smiled Margaret, 'I think we will give that job to Mairead.'

Chapter 67

Louise dropped a large brick of turf into the top of the range, replaced the cover and sat down opposite Margaret, 'I'm sure I've got IBS,' she undid the top button of the black trousers she was wearing.

'It could've been the beer batter we had on the cod,' suggested Margaret.

'Don't mention bloody fish to me,' Louise pulled a face, 'although it was nice and I think I was very brave to face it after the last time. My stomach is really bloated, I'm going to cut down on carbs.'

'Maybe we could hold slimming classes during the week.'

'I'm not that fat,' Louise threw a cushion at her cousin, 'but I will be 30 in two weeks, can you imagine it?'

'Yes, because I'll be 30 the week after,' Margaret laughed.

'Shall we have a party? We could hold it in the ball room, it would be fun.'

'One of the perks of owning a hotel,' Margaret replied, 'it would make sense though, and it could be like a relaunch.'

'I'm going to miss our cosy chats by the range, although I think we should get an oil burner in before the winter, I'm sick of emptying out the ashes.'

'I usually do it!'

'All the more reason to get the central heating sorted then,' Louise giggled.

There was a knock on the door and Adele appeared with a large B and M bag in one hand and a bottle of wine in the other.

'You come bearing gifts Mother?'

'No, Lou, I wanted to show you what I've bought,' she passed the wine to Margaret, and took out a soft purple throw out of the bag, 'your dad isn't interested,' she moaned.

'He's a man,' Margaret went into the kitchen with the wine and after filling glasses with wine and one with a fruit cocktail for Louise, carried them through on a tray with a bowl of nuts.

'Thanks, Louise took her glass, pleased that she hadn't poured her wine, 'It's a bit bright, mum,' nodding her head towards the throw.

'That's the reason I got that colour, to liven up the living room,' sighed Adele, 'and I got cushions to match, they look great.'

'It's your home,' Margaret smiled at her aunt, 'you can put in it what you want.'

'So what are you girls talking about?'

'Getting old,' Louise looked at Margaret, 'but we are going to have a party in two weeks to commiserate that fact.'

'Can I help with organising it?'

'To be honest, mum, you can organise the whole thing, we are going to be snowed under. We have interviews to do for the concierge job and a new caretaker for the yurts and cabins, Ebee and Brodie will be needed more at the complex.'

'Free reign then?'

Margaret cast a worried glance at her cousin and in a hesitant voice said, 'free reign within reason.''

'Where's Jack? I haven't seen much of him this week.'

'He's stopping over at the twins' house tonight, then they are staying here at the weekend,' Louise took a sip of wine and put the glass down on the small table, 'they are all studying for exams.'

'Those were the days,' Adele shuddered and the girls laughed.

'They could stay over at your house,' Louise said, 'you have more room and can spend quality time with your grandson.'

'Nicely done,' Adele laughed with good humour, 'but of course they can stay at ours. Davy Lee seems genuine,' she added, and the offer of millions is amazing.'

'What I don't understand,' said Louise, 'is why us? There's potential up and down the country, and surely the south west is more relevant for a stud farm.'

'He doesn't appear to be a relevant kind of a guy,' said Adele, taking a big gulp of wine, 'did you ask him why he chose to invest in you?'

'Put it this way,' said Margaret, 'he knows what he wants and how to do it, and without his help we would have lost most of our business.'

'Don't look a gift horse in the mouth,' Adele said seriously, and then they all collapsed in tears of laughter at the aptness of the saying.

The next morning, Louise and Margaret were sitting at the big table eating scrambled egg on toast when there was a loud knock on the door.

'Good job we're dressed,' sighed Margaret as she got up to answer it.

Louise could hear some of the exchange and poured tea into another mug, 'good morning Uncle, have you had breakfast?'

'Yes, thanks Pet, I'll not refuse a cuppa though.'

'Sit yourself down and tell us what the emergency is.'

'Can you plan a wedding in the next couple of months?' he asked.

'Couple of months? That's pushing it dad, who's getting married?'

'Me and Maureen, you don't mind do you? Only, I was thinking, I'm not going anywhere and she's not either, so why not get hitched?'

'Why not indeed,' grinned Louise, 'what if we made you a special offer?'

They both looked at her waiting for an explanation.

'You could be our guinea pigs, I'll ask Mairead to get Natasha and Vincent to put brochures together and when we hold the wedding fayre, you can demonstrate the real thing.'

'That would be too public,' Brian protested.

'Not for the ceremony, or the reception, just a brief glance at the happy couple posing for photographs,' she explained further, 'and we would foot the whole bill.'

'Would we?' Margaret said.

'Yes, what do you think?'

'Could I talk it over with Maureen first and see what she thinks?'

'That would be a very good idea,' said Margaret, 'and no, Dad I don't mind, of course I don't, I'm happy for you both,' she wiped a tear that was rolling down her cheek.

Natasha and Vincent were only too happy to help and the girls decided to use one of the cabins as a work room for them, agreeing that they needed space to create.

Ebee had been asked to take photographs and take part at the wedding fayre, Natasha wanted a picture of the happy couple in the outfits they would be wearing and after a day of shopping in Derry and Letterkenny the bride and groom were kitted and booted out for the big day.

'We just need to wait for a sunny day,' said Natasha, 'then we can get to work.'

The day produced itself as if by magic, clear blue skies and a radiant sun gave the perfect lighting for the pictures they needed, the only people allowed to take part in the creative masterpiece was Natasha, Vincent, Ebee and the happy couple.

'We have a surprise up our sleeve,' Vincent explained, 'all will be revealed when it's ready.'

'Okay,' Louise surrendered, 'we will back off and let your juices flow.'

Margaret cast her a weird look that Louise failed to notice.

The stud farm was taking shape in a far more speedily fashion than their hotel had done, but then they had a massive work force and experience behind them. Stables had been erected and the existing house had been raised to the ground and rebuilt, Finn had been on hand to design the new build with specific instructions.

'It looks like Southfork,' said Adele when she returned from having a sneaky peak.

'What's that?' asked Louise, they were in the coffee shop having a quick break between interviewing.

'It was in television series in the 80's,' Adele explained, 'you were too young to remember the programme. It was called Dallas.'

'I think they did a re run a few years ago, or a revamp, whatever it was it didn't air for long,' said Margaret.

'That's because Larry Hagman passed away,' sighed Adele.

'Davy Lee is probably recreating his place in America,' said Louise.

'When does he get back?' Adele asked.

'The week of our party,' said Margaret, 'although he doesn't know about it of course.'

'He does,' confessed Adele, 'I emailed him an invite and he said he would be honoured to attend.'

'Bloody hell, Mum. Who else have you emailed?' Louise felt a tremor of fear creep up her spine.

'Eustace, of course,' Adele said flippantly, 'and proper invites have been delivered to friends and acquaintances.'

'Why couldn't you just keep it simple?'

'Simple is boring, besides, you need to network and showcase your wares.'

'How vulgar,' Louise sighed.

Margaret looked her cousin in the eye, 'what?' said Louise.

'You've asked my dad to showcase his wedding and now your put out because your mum has set us up?'

'I suppose you've got a point,' she said grudgingly and then her mobile beeped. Louise read the text from Rory, 'he's coming up tomorrow,' she pulled a face, 'it's all systems go.'

The young guarda arrived just as the tea was made and the bread was toasted, Louise let him in while Margaret poured the tea, 'Good timing,' she grinned, leading him through to the kitchen.

'Is toast okay or would you like a good Irish fry up?' Margaret buttered some toast and took a bite.

'Toast is fine, but could I be cheeky and ask for a fried egg to go with it?'

'You can and you have,' Margaret laughed.

He sat at the table and Louise passed him a big mug of tea, 'have you spoken to Karen?'

'Not really,' Louise confessed, 'I called down two days ago to see if she was okay, but I could see that she wasn't, she's still very jittery.'

'So you haven't told her about the tape?'

'No, I thought I'd leave that up to you,' he took a swig of tea and Margaret put a plate of egg on toast in front of him.

Karen looked bemused as she opened the door to find Rory and Louise standing there with serious expressions, Margaret had decided to stay behind and do some work, a group of people had booked in for a team building session and they both hoped that it would go better than the last time, although it couldn't go much worse they had both agreed.

'Can we come in?' Louise asked her gently.

'Of course,' Karen opened the door wide and after Rory closed the door they followed her into the sitting room.

'What's wrong?' Karen began.

'We've discovered who murdered Denton and Swain,' said Rory.

Karen clutched the arm of the chair, 'who was it?' she whispered, fear evident in every word.

'Riordan,' Louise told her, 'with the help of Swain.'

'They thought you had seen them,' Rory continued, 'that was the reason they kidnapped you.'

'But why did Riordan kill Denton?' Karen was confused, 'and I didn't see anything.'

'We've been doing some digging, Denton and Riordan had been involved in all kinds of scams, especially building houses on land that didn't belong to them. Denton became a loose cannon, he was fond of the drink and his mouth ran away with him. Riordan needed to shut him up.'

'How did you find out all of this?' asked Louise.

'A couple of the lads have been posing as tourists, it's amazing how much tongues are loosened by a drop of the good stuff.'

'Are you going to arrest Riordan?' asked Karen.

'We need more evidence,' Rory at on the sofa and Louise joined him, 'we need you to pretend that you saw something the night Denton was murdered.'

'But I didn't, 'emphasised Karen, 'how did Swain die?'

'We don't know that yet,' Rory ran his fingers through his dark curly hair, 'will you help catch Riordan?' he repeated.

'What happens if it goes wrong? I couldn't go through that again,' she sobbed.

'Don't worry, we will figure out another way,' Louise scrutinised Karen, taking in her shoulder length blonde hair and the attire she was wearing. 'Do you want to come to our party on Saturday? Mum is organising it, so I don't know if she's sent you an invite.'

'No, I haven't had one, but I'd love to go, what's it in aid of?'

'Me and Margaret are turning 30, scary isn't it?'

'Not really,' Karen giggled, 'I'll be 40 next month.'

'You're looking good for your age then,' Louise got to her feet, she had thought Karen was years younger, Brodie was 32, she had noted his date of birth on the job application form, 'see you on Saturday, oh, we are doing a kind of fancy dress, or fancy wig, so can you get your hands on a dark long one?'

'I've got a curly blue one if that's any good?'

'Perfect,' grinned Louise, 'the bigger the disguise, the better.'

'What was that all about?' Rory asked as they walked up the road towards the cottage.

'I've got a plan,' she told him, 'I'll tell you all about it over a cuppa.'

'I'm not sure I like it,' Rory told her firmly, 'it's too dangerous and Riordan is unpredictable.'

'Karen is too scared to do it,' she passed him a mug of tea, 'what choice have we got?'

'We could try and go with what we've got,' he took a sip and put the mug on the table.

'Do you really think it will hold up in court? The pictures are grainy, he could deny they are him.'

'I know,' he sighed, 'but we will have to trap him at the party, when there's a lot of people about'

'Hence the wigs,' Louise explained, 'I'll tell mum to inform people to wear a wig or disguise, but we need a plan to get Riordan there, he knows we intensely dislike him.'

'I suppose we could report a disturbance, but we can't let it slip that Karen knows anything until the night, after Karen has arrived at the party in her blue wig, we can't put her in danger.'

Louise phoned Adele and the wheels were put in motion.

Chapter 68

The night before the 30th ball as the cousins decided to name it, Natasha and Vincent summoned them to their utility cabin, 'bring Brian and Maureen,' Natasha added.

'It sounds intriguing,' smiled Margaret as she put a call through to her dad, 'the invites are amazing. The brochures for the wedding fayre must be ready.'

'I wish we'd known how talented Vincent was before,' Louise sighed, 'he's an amazing graphic designer.

'He's just finished university so its perfect timing, Dad's on his way over, he's going to meet us there.'

'Have you got your wig sorted out?' Louise asked as they made their way across the field towards the cabins.'

'Yes, I got it from EBay, it's a curly auburn affair and it will look great with my new red dress. What about you?'

'I got mine from Amazon,' Louise told her, 'but I don't want to describe it yet.'

'Spoil sport,' Margaret gently punched her arm,

Brian was waiting outside the cabin for them, 'where's Maureen?' asked Louise.

'She won't be long, she was just taking a bun out of the oven, and no, not that kind of bun before you give me a wise crack,' he was looking at Louise as he said this.

'Shall we knock?' he asked.

'Yes, let's give them a warning that we are here,' Louise rapped the door with her fist and then rubbed her hand on a denim clad leg, 'that bloody hurt.'

'You shouldn't have knocked so hard then,' Margaret scolded.

Natasha opened the door and invited them in, 'where's Maureen?'

'She's on her way,' grinned Louise looking at her uncle Brian and then sticking out her tongue.

'Oh my god,' Brian exclaimed.

Standing by each side of the window was a life size cut out of Brian and Maureen in their wedding finery.

'The school let us have the cardboard,' Natasha explained proudly.

'I can't believe how realistic they look,' Margaret gasped.

'You can keep them near the entrance to the reception area,' Vincent was adding strokes to something on his computer.

'Sorry I'm late,' Maureen burst through the door and stopped dead in her tracks, 'wow.'

'Do you like them?' Natasha asked shyly.

'We love them,' Louise went closer for a better look. On a small table just under the window, were stacks of leaflets and glossy brochures.

'You did give us free reign?' Vincent asked worriedly.

'Of course,' Margaret picked up a brochure and flicked through the pages, 'these are first class. Have you any idea how to circulate them?'

'A lad from the village has offered to deliver them to local shops in Clodbury and surrounding villages, we thought if they were posted through letter boxes or delivered to houses, they would end up in the recycle bin.'

'Also,' added Natasha, 'we have developed a website and the brochures can be requested. We have also drafted leaflets for afternoon tea, medieval banquets and themed party nights, is that okay?'

'More than okay,' gasped Louise, 'you have been busy.'

'Mum has had an input, she's full of ideas,' Vincent was serious.

'I hope you both will be at the party,' Margaret said warmly.

'Yes, we will come with Mum, Vincent can drive,' she gave him a smug smile.

'I love them,' Maureen couldn't take her eyes off the cardboard cut-outs.

'The next step is to contact Bridal wear, rings and cakes,' said Louise thoughtfully, 'Ebee will be in charge of photography, we could even dress Brodie in a chauffeur suit and hat to drive a swanky car.'

'I wonder if Davy could get his hands on one, or better still, a horse and cart, how amazing would that be,' Margaret was lost in a fairy tale.

'I can see you having that for your up and coming wedding,' chuckled Louise.

'I don't like horses,' said Brian.

'Tough.' Said Margaret, 'you will have to get used to them.'

Louise didn't want to make a grand entrance, she needed to mill around and be spotted at the right time, Margaret was blissfully unaware of the danger her cousin was putting herself in and she would have been horrified and tried to stop it had she known.

'How do I look?' Margaret twirled around causing the skirt of the gorgeous red dress to cascade around her and the curls of the wig to bounce wildly on her head.

'Stunning, let me take a picture,' Louise snapped open her phone and took several shots of her.

"Why aren't you ready yet?' Margaret queried.

'I'm going to sort Jack out first, he's putting on a Michael Jackson wig and dark glasses, he's been practicing his moon walk all day.'

'It's going to be a blast,' Margaret was excited, 'maybe my hen party will be next.'

'Or Maureen's, although I think she will want something low key.'

'Go on up,' Louise told her, 'I'll join you by the bar in a few minutes.'

As soon as Margaret had closed the door behind her, she quickly donned the dress and wig, making sure that she resembled Karen as much as possible, although close up, they were not alike at all. She down played her make-up and the dress was one that Karen would choose, not herself. In a way, Louise felt cheated that she couldn't shine like Margaret, she would have loved to have done up her big blue eyes and applied lip stick and blusher to enhance her natural beauty, instead of downplaying, but it had to be done.

'Bloody hell, Mum, what are you wearing?'

'Jack, stop using language like that,' she chastised.

'Stop evading the question,' he retaliated.

'It's fancy dress, remember.'

'Yes, but you don't look very fancy, you look like a cashier in a supermarket.'

'Thanks, Jack, I appreciate your honesty, now let's get out of here.'

Louise looked out for Rory as soon as she entered the decorated ballroom, banners and pictures of Louise and Margaret adorned the wall and the tables were beautifully done, Adele had found her vocation. She spotted her parents at the other side of the bar and sent Jack over to join them, she watched him until he was safely in their grasp and then moved next to Rory at the bar.

'How's it going?' she asked, 'did you drop some hints down at the station?'

'Not yet, I will ring the station to say that there is a prowler in the grounds, hopefully he will catch a glimpse of you and make his move, please, do not go far from my side,' he begged.

'I'll try not to, but I will want a dance,' she smiled cheekily at him.

'You look a bit frumpy,' he teased.

'Great, you sound like Jack.'

'You still look beautiful, Lou, even if you haven't made an effort,' his voice was husky and she felt a trickle of alarm, she wasn't in the market for romance, even if he was a hot policeman.

'Karen is an attractive woman,' she replied with a grin.

Adele had booked the young group they had used the year before and now older and more experienced, they wowed the crowd.

'They are set to go far,' Louise shouted over the music to Margaret.

'Is Karen here, yet?'

'I haven't seen her, and it wouldn't be hard if she was wearing the blue wig.'

'She might be a bit late,' shouted Margaret.

'Can I have this dance?' Finn was wearing fitted blue denim jeans and a black shirt which was open at the neck. He was also had a red clowns wig on his head which completely destroyed the look.

'Are you doing an audition for IT?' Louise yelled, just as the band stopped playing.

Finn laughed, 'I've got a nice balloon if you want to follow me.'

'Idiot,' Margaret laughed.

'I'll leave you love birds to it,' Louise smiled and went to get a drink from the bar.

She noticed a dark haired man watching her intently and she shivered, it couldn't be him, she told herself crossly and when she tried to cut across the throng towards him, he had disappeared.

'There you are,' said Rory with relief, 'what would you like to drink?'

'Lemon and lime, please, it's really hot out there,' she swept her arm towards the dance floor.

'Karen hasn't arrived,' he said slowly, 'maybe we should forget the idea.'

'No, we can't,' Louise stated, 'he needs to be locked up.'

'Are you sure you want to do this?'

'Yes, I'm sure.'

'I'll go and see if I can see her outside,' Rory went outside leaving Louise to glance around at all the people her mother had invited. There hadn't been an appearance of Davy Lee as yet, everyone present had come up to wish her and Margaret a Happy Birthday and to hand them gifts, although the girls explained that the ball was for fun and they hadn't expected gifts.

'I'm not going to open mine till the day,' Margaret had declared.

'I agree, although mine is only 2 days away,' Louise had replied.

'Done,' Rory was back in the room and Louise felt a moment of fear and apprehension, she would feel better if Karen was safely ensconced with Margaret and Finn.

'I wonder where she is,' Louise mused.

'Why don't we go and get her, we still have time before I put the call through to Riordan.'

'Okay, I'll just tell Mum so she can keep an eye on Jack.'

'He's fine, look at him doing breakdance to Thriller,' Rory laughed.

'We won't be too long,' Louise picked up her bag and tried to catch Margaret's eye, but she was watching Jack, along with all the other adults, 'I want to watch Jack first,' Louise moved closer to the edge of the dance floor and clapped loudly when he had finished. 'Right let's go and grab Karen.'

'So, Karen never saw anything?' Rory asked as they walked down the road.

'No, maybe she should've stayed in England,' Louise pondered, 'she doesn't leave the cottage except to go to the shop and she hasn't asked for a shift at the hotel, even though we've offered her some work.'

'This might push her over the edge,' Rory warned.

They walked the rest of the way in silence, Louise wondered if she should have left well alone, but then that wasn't in her nature. Riordan needed to be brought to justice.

'There's a light on,' Louise knocked the door and when there was no answer, pushed Rory to open it.

'Karen,' she called out, a chill running up her spine, something felt very wrong.

Rory followed her into the small sitting room and Louise gasped when she saw Karen sitting with her hands and feet tied with a torn sheet, a gag was around her mouth.

Louise spun round, 'do something Rory,' she told him. 'Here's your proof.'

'You just couldn't leave it could you Lou,' he looked sadly into her big blue eyes, 'and now we have no choice but to get rid of you both.'

'Oh my god,' she turned to run out of the cottage, but Rory gripped her arm and forced her to sit next to Karen.

She let out a piercing scream before he put a hand over her mouth. 'No one can hear you, Lou, they are all at your party, what a master stroke to play right into our hands.'

'I don't understand,' she managed to get out before a gag was placed firmly around her mouth.

'Ron here is my cousin,' he explained as he tied her hands together and then her feet after removing her shoes, 'we had a nice little business going on here until you put a spanner in the works.'

Louise couldn't answer now, and she felt weary and tired. It would be easy to close her eyes and go to sleep.

Chapter 69

'Where's Lou?'

'I'm surprised you're here,' asked Brodie, 'I though she never wanted to see you again.'

'She didn't mean it,' said Gerard, 'where is she?'

'She was at the bar with that cop from Dublin,' he told him, 'I don't know where she is now, there's Ebee over there, go and ask him.'

Gerard had a bad feeling in the pit of his stomach, he had been watching Louise for most of the night, waiting for the right moment to speak to her. He walked towards Ebee and shouted over the music, Abba were playing Money Money, which he thought was very apt, 'Have you seen Lou, Ebee?'

'Hi Gerard, great to see you, no sorry mate, what's up?'

'Something feels wrong,' he explained, leading the big guy away from the loudspeaker.

Brodie had gone to ask Margaret but she hadn't seen her cousin in a while. The bar man, over hearing the exchange, spoke up,

'She went outside with that dark haired guy.'

'Did you hear why they were going outside?' asked Gerard.

'Something to do with a Karen, I couldn't hear much else over Thriller.'

'What's going on?' asked Margaret, seeing Gerard and Brodie at the bar.

'We're looking for Lou,' Gerard answered, 'have you seen her?'

'No, and she wouldn't want to see you,' she glared at Gerard.

'We haven't got time for this,' he shouted, 'where is she? I got a bad feeling.'

'I really don't know, but she can't be far,' she reasoned.

'Really? The barman reckons she's gone down to Karen's with that cop,' said Brodie.

'Why would she do that? It's our party.'

'I'm going to find her,' said Gerard, 'are you coming?'

'On our way,' said Ebee.

'Count me in,' said Brodie joining them.

'I'm coming too,' Margaret started to follow.

'No, you stay and entertain your guests, do some networking or something,' said Ebee with authority.

They walked quickly down the road, almost running, 'they might just be sitting in Karen's having a drink,' Brodie reasoned.

'Do you know this Rory bloke?' Gerard asked.

'Not really, Lou was going to get him to come up and sort Riordan out. They were hatching some kind of a plan but she kept it pretty close to her chest.'

Gerard pulled his mobile out of his jacket pocket, 'can you send someone out to Clodbury,' he turned to Ebee, 'what's Karen's last name?'

'Brown,' he replied.

'This is the second time we've rescued Karen,' stated Brodie.

'Yes, your errant girlfriend,' stated Ebee.

'Not anymore,' Brodie quickened his pace to match the others, 'I quite like Karnjit now,' he smiled.

'They're going to meet us there, but it will be at least ten minutes,' Gerard finished his call and put the phone back in his pocket.

'Who?' asked a bemused Ebee.

'The Guarda.'

'Rory's a cop,' Brodie said.

'We will talk about that later,' spat Gerard, 'but meanwhile I want my Lou out of that house.'

The curtains were drawn but they could see a light through a small gap where they didn't quite meet.

'I'll knock first,' said Ebee, 'you two keep back.'

Gerard gave him a look and pushed past him, and then hammered on the door. They could hear the sound of a television but nobody came to answer the knock.

'Stand back,' said Ebee as he ran towards the door, although a big man, he bounced off the solid wood clutching his shoulder, 'I think it's broken.'

Gerard ignored his cries of pain and ran around the back of the house, he knew the kitchen overlooked the bay but hoped a window or a door on this side was open.

The kitchen was in darkness, which was odd if the two women were inside, Gerard could feel his gut tense and a sense of dread made him feel dizzy. He tried the back door handle and to his surprise discovered that it wasn't locked. Ebee and Brodie followed him inside being as stealthy as possible for three grown men. They tip toed to the door that led into the sitting room and listened out for voices, when none could be heard, Gerard carefully opened the door.

He almost cried out when he saw Louise and Karen on the sofa, both bound and gagged and asleep. He had just reached them when a voice told him to freeze.

Spinning around, he saw a man he assumed was Rory, pointing a gun at his chest.

'Is this a bad cop film?' Gerard asked, edging towards the women.

'It's a horror film, for you anyway,' replied Rory smugly. 'It's a shame you've stumbled on us, caught in the act as it were, but you do realise you can't leave.'

Smug Rory was soon prone Rory as Ebee hit him with all his considerable strength, despite the hurt shoulder, over the head with a cast iron frying pan. Brodie quickly retrieved the gun while Gerard took the gag off first Louise and then Karen.

'Call for an ambulance,' he barked at Ebee, 'good job by the way,' he smiled at the big guy.

They looked up as footsteps bounded down the stairs, 'what's keep you Rory?' Riordan said and then noticed the gun pointing at his head.

'Get over there,' Brodie ordered, 'and quick before my shaking trigger finger accidently presses it,' he demonstrated and a bullet shot up and into the ceiling, 'oops,' he chuckled, 'good job I changed my aim.'

'Bloody Americans and their guns,' said Ebee after the call to the ambulance had ended. He used the torn sheets to truss up Riordan while Gerard rubbed Louise's wrist and tried to wake her.

'They've been drugged,' stated Ebee, 'let's hope the ambulance gets here quickly.

The Guarda were the first to arrive and as Gerard explained the situation, one of the boys in blue checked the girls over, 'It looks as though they've been sedated,' was his diagnosis.

Karen began to stir and then panicked when she realised what had happened.

'What's Lou doing here?' she asked, and then saw Gerard, 'are you back then?'

'Lou was coming to see you, she was worried by the sounds of things, and yes, I'm back, and just like Take That, I'm back for good.'

Soon after, the ambulance arrived and because Louise was still in a deep sleep, they carried her out on a stretcher.

'I'm going with her,' Gerard declared, 'Let her family know,' he looked at Ebee. Brodie had relinquished, albeit reluctantly, the gun to one of the officers.

'Miss Brown, are you okay to walk to the ambulance?' the paramedic asked.

She got to her feet and Ebee helped her towards the waiting vehicle.

Once the ambulance had left for the hospital, one of the officers explained the situation.

'We've been watching this pair for months, but we didn't have enough evidence to go on.'

'What about the murders?' asked Brodie, 'after all that's happened this year we had lost faith in the Clodbury Guarda.'

'One bad apple up here and one in Dublin, I'm afraid,' he stated. 'We didn't know much about the murders or how they connected to Riordan, we will want a full statement from you all when you are up to it.'

'Teresa who lives opposite Karen has footage of Riordan killing Swain, Lou thought Rory was one of the good guys,' Ebee said sadly.

'Most of us are good, and we will do our best to restore your faith in the service,' the officer smiled.

Chapter 70

Louise slowly opened her eyes to see Gerard bending over her, 'what are you doing here?'

'Saving you,' he quipped.

'My head hurts,' she pulled a face, 'could I have some water please?' There would be time to question why Gerard was here later, when her head was clear and she could talk without her voice feeling as though it was coming out of a bird cage.

Gerard helped her to sit up and passed her the water, 'what happened?' she squeaked, then cleared her throat.

'Rory drugged you,' he told her. She remembered the lemonade and lime, he must have slipped something into it.

A young woman wearing a white coat and a stethoscope approached her bed, she had a chart in her hand and a solemn look on her face.

'Hello, Louise, I'm Doctor Travis. We took some bloods when you were admitted, how are you feeling?'

'Like I've got a raging hangover, and I haven't had a drop of alcohol for weeks.'

'You were administered a strong sedative, but luckily it causes no long term harm, and your baby is fine.'

If they were in a cartoon, Louise was sure her jaw would hit the floor, 'baby? What baby? My baby is almost thirteen.'

Gerard grabbed her hand, if his Lou was expecting another man's child he would deal with it, one thing he was sure about, he would never let her go again.'

'I don't understand,' she stuttered, 'how can I be pregnant? I haven't had a visit from and angel about an immaculate conception,' she tried humour but it didn't work.

'How far along is she?' asked Gerard, if Louise knew the dates it might jog her memory.

'We would need to do a scan to get a better picture, but I'd hazard a guess at around five months.'

'What?' Gasped Louise.

Gerard cast his mind back to what he was doing five months ago, he was working flat out on the farm with his father breathing down his neck. He had managed to escape for that brief wonderful evening with Lou and then returned home until he had come to his senses.

'Lou,' he gasped, 'remember that night we drank too much wine? I had to leave early the next morning to get back to the farm.'

'Of course I remember,' she felt like hitting him, then realised she was turning into her cousin.

'That must've been the night you conceived, it's my baby,' tears filled his eyes.

'So it's your bloody fault that two days before my 30th I discover that I'll be up to my eyes in nappes and bottles.' She burst into tears, it was all too much.

'It's a lot to take in,' the doctor soothed, 'so I'll leave you while I do the rounds.'

'This time it will be different,' Gerard stated firmly, 'I'm never going to leave you again.'

'How can you say that? The farm won't go away.'

'I've left the farm, it's up to dad what he does with it, but I'm not getting into that now, you are more important.'

'What happened to Karen?' she asked, 'is she okay?'

'Karen is fine, she will be in to see you before they discharge her.'

'Are you really my knight in shining armour?' she teased with glistening eyes.

'I hope so, although I did have my usual back up with Ebee and Brodie.'

'Those guys,' Louise chuckled and felt so much better.

Louise was kept in overnight for observation and Gerard went to tell Adele what had happened and to get her some clean clothes. They had agreed not to mention the baby, Jack should be told first.

The following morning, Gerard went to collect Louise from hospital, he refused to let anyone else do the journey of forty six miles each way, he was never going to let her go again.

'Where are you living?' Louise asked as they drove out of Letterkenny.

'I've found a room somewhere for now,' he touched her hand, 'Clodbury is my home now as long as you are here.'

'What about the baby? How do you feel about it?'

'We both missed out on Jack, didn't we? This time will be different. It's such amazing news Lou, I couldn't be happier.' Louise believed him, but there was still something bugging her.

'Your mum said that there had only been one love in your life, I was so hurt.'

'When was that?' he asked.

'The day I brought Jack to meet your family and say hello to you. There were pictures hanging on the wall of that grand house, I was angry that you didn't tell me you were rich.'

Gerard took a deep breath, 'the farm is my uncles, my dad only rents it, cheaply, but it's not his.'

'Oh,' she paused, 'and who was your one true love?' she had to know, they needed to be honest now.

'Yes, well, the girl was a beautiful, blonde haired nymph, from the moment I saw her my heart was lost forever.'

'Oh,' said Louise in a small voice, 'who was she? Did she die or something?'

'She lived overseas,' Gerard said slowly, 'it was like losing part of myself when she didn't return. Her name is Louise Lavender.'

'All that time wasted,' sighed Louise, although her heart felt lighter than it had ever done.

'We've come full circle,' he gripped her hand, 'and this time we will do it right.'

On the day of her birthday, Louise came down to breakfast to find the table laid and bacon and eggs sizzling in the frying pan, 'happy birthday,' Margaret gave her a hug and kissed her cheek.

'Don't expect this on your birthday,' she teased.

'Did you want toast or is your IBS still playing up?''

'I'll have a slice please, I quite fancy dipping it in my egg,' Louise grinned, knowing that she would have to tell Margaret very soon that it wasn't Irritable bowel that was bloating her stomach.

There was a knock on the door and Margaret went to answer it, 'only because it's your birthday,' she quipped.

'And I've just got out of hospital,' Louise added.

Margaret returned with Karen, who was looking a lot better than she did the last time they saw her.

'Happy Birthday, Lou,' she passed over a gift bag and card.

'Thanks Karen, that's sweet of you,' she reached up to give her a hug.

'I didn't make it to your party,' her grin was rueful, 'where's Jack?'

'Wrapping my present in his room,' Louise sat down, 'have you had breakfast?'

'Yes, thanks, but I'd love a cuppa if one's going. So, it's all over?'

'I hope so,' sighed Louise, 'what are the odds of me meeting Riordan's crooked partner in Dublin?'

'I know, it beggars belief,' agreed Karen, 'but your bravery ensured that they are both locked up.'

'And yours,' Louise touched her hand.

'How was Swain involved?' asked Margaret sitting at the table, she had poured tea for them all and bacon and eggs were waiting to be dished up.

'It's pretty sketchy,' said Karen, 'Swain was a perv, and that is bad enough but especially bad when he was a doctor. Riordan knew all about his sick secret of abusing female and sometimes young male patients and when Denton was shot, he blackmailed Swain to help him with the body. But then Swain had one over on Riordan, so he had to get rid of him. He thought the Duffy sisters would take the blame, but they had alibis.'

'And because Denton was murdered outside your house, Swain thought you was a witness,' added Louise.

'Yes, and he didn't believe me when I said I hadn't, but of course, by asking the questions he put himself in the frame anyway. Thank god for the boys, I thought I was going to die.'

'So did I, last night,' confessed Louise.

'What are you going to do now?' Margaret asked as she slid a plate of bacon and eggs in front of Louise.

'Nancy phoned this morning,' Karen took a sip of tea, 'I know you don't like her, but she needs me as her personal assistant, the other one didn't work out.'

'Are you going home?' Louise asked.

'I think that's for the best, Brodie has moved on,' Louise and Margaret raised their eyebrows and Karen sighed, 'I can't blame him after the way I ran off and abandoned him, but it still hurt when I saw him walking along the beach with Karnjit, they were holding hands by the way.'

'Oh,' said Margaret, 'I didn't see that coming.'

'Happy Birthday, Mum, Jack bounced into the kitchen and gave her a hastily wrapped present and a card.

Louise hugged her son tight, 'thanks Jack, sit down and have some breakfast, its hard work wrapping presents.' She tore off the bright red paper to reveal a pair of slippers.

'Nan said you needed some new ones,' he told her before shoving bacon into his mouth.

'They are very nice,' and useful for my stay in hospital she thought.

The door opened and Gerard appeared with a large box in his hand, 'happy birthday, Lou,' he dropped a kiss on the top of his head, 'Good morning everyone.'

'Hi dad, do you want some breakfast?' Jack asked.

'No, I'm good thanks, but I'll have a cup of tea if that's okay.'

Karen got to her feet and rinsed her cup under the tap, 'I'll see you later, enjoy your day, Lou.'

'Thanks for the present, Karen, it was very sweet of you.'

After she had gone and the breakfast was finished, Gerard ruffled Jack's hair, 'fancy a walk up the road after you've got dressed?'

'Okay, what about mum?'

'Your mum too,' he smiled, 'she can open her present when she gets back.'

After a quick wash, Louise cleaned her teeth and slipped on a pair of black leggings and a pale blue sweatshirt. Jack was already dressed and chatting to his dad when she joined them in the kitchen, 'it's a shame you can't be so quick on a school day, Jack,' she teased.

'Dad's wants to show me something, it's a surprise.'

'It's my birthday,' she stuck her tongue out and grinned.

'Have you had a look at the new stud farm? Gerard asked as the three of them walked up the hill to the point.

'No,' she confessed, 'I haven't been invited, apart from the fact I've been busy.'

'I'll give you a guided tour,' Gerard took her hand, 'Davy won't mind, and it's where Jack's surprise is.'

'You got me a horse,' Jack shouted, excitedly.

'Don't be silly, Jack,' Louise admonished, then to Gerard, 'how do you know Davy Lee?'

'I asked him for a job, so not only have I got the job of my dreams, I have also somewhere to stay, so Lou, I will never leave you again.'

'How long have you been here?'

'I arrived the night of your party, I was going to ask you to dance, but you disappeared,' he shivered.

'And you came looking for me,' she gazed adoringly into his eyes.

'Call it a hunch,' he said tightening his grip on her hand.

'It looks pretty amazing,' Louise stood at the wrought iron gates, 'the house looks American.' The homestead was built on a rise giving the owner spectacular views over the bay on both sides, the white picket fence separated the grounds from the stud farm, which was enormous, 'I didn't realise it was so big,' she exclaimed.

'Enter,' he swung the gate wide and they stepped onto the newly acquired Davy Lee land. Still holding Louise's hand and with Jack on his other side, they went over to the largest paddock where a stable hand was leading a horse around the track, 'this is the latest addition to the stock,' Gerard explained, he waved to the lad and he walked the horse over. It was a beautiful black stallion with dark brown socks.

'What unusual colouring,' Louise leaned over to stroke his head.

'Davy has high hopes for him,' Gerard fished around in his pocket and gave the horse a lump of sugar, and then he passed Jack a cube, 'he won't hurt you,' he assured his son.

'What's his name?' Jack asked as he held a trembling hand towards the horse, and then giggled as the sugar was taken carefully without biting.

'Snowy,' Gerard told him.

'Really?' Jack said with disgust.

'No, not really, his name is Monty, or the full Monty,' Gerard laughed.

'Why?'

'Because the owner is hoping he is,' Gerard explained, 'now come on over to the stables.'

There were twenty stables, most had a horse inside but others were empty. The last stable was larger than the others and inside was a mother and a young foal. The mother was pure white and the baby white with a streak of black along its back.

'Oh my god,' gasped Louise, 'they are beautiful, stunning even.'

'Did you learn to ride?' he asked.

'No, and I won't be able to for a while,' she said ruefully.

'I'll teach you one day,' Gerard said huskily, and then he turned to Jack, 'the foal is looking for an owner, are you interested?'

Jack screamed, 'really? He is mine?'

'As long as you promise to look after him and earn his keep,' Gerard was serious. 'You will need to get up early, help muck out the stables and feed the horses. In exchange you can have lessons at the riding school until you are good enough to ride here.'

'Does Davy Lee know that you are promising one of his foal's to a young lad?'

'Let's go and ask him,' said Gerard, taking the hand he had released when he took the sugar from his pocket.

Louise felt a chill of apprehension, she knew there was something about Davy that she couldn't trust and now the feeling intensified.

He was sitting in a rocking chair on the porch like a character from Gone with the wind and she couldn't help a chuckle escaping.

'Happy birthday, Lou, I'm glad you think I look amusing in my old rocker,' Davy Lee said seriously.

'I'm sorry, but the scene is so I don't know, American, Is your ranch called Tara by any chance?'

'I'm so glad you get it, Lou. Most people don't, and I like your thinking. Tara would be a bit cliché though, don't you think?'

'Oh, definitely,' she said straight faced. 'How did you know it was my birthday, by the way?'

'Your mom sent me an invite to your party and Gerard told me it was today, and how are you, young Jack? Do you like the foal?'

'I love him, is he really mine?'

'Of course and hopefully one day he will run in the Grand National.'

'Why?' asked Louise, 'I mean, you've been most generous investing in the hotel, and now this? It doesn't make sense.'

'It makes perfect sense my dear,' he got shakily to his feet, 'come on in, the kettle has boiled.'

Inside, the massive kitchen was very Irish, an enormous black range sat along the back wall and comfortable chairs around it for them to sit on, on the other side was a large oak table three times the size of the one in the cottage, with six high backed chairs to match. 'Sit down,' Davy invited and as she sat on a large sofa, Gerard sat beside her and jack on the other. Davy made tea while Louise tried to get her head around it all.

'Tea or juice?' Davy asked Jack.

'Could I have lemonade please?' he answered.

'Sure you can,' Davy filled a glass of the tradition Irish cloudy kind that Jack was keen on and handed Louise a mug of tea, 'sugar?'

'No thanks,' she took the mug and had a sip. She was relieved that she could drink the stuff now after months of it making her want to throw up.

'Has Gerard told you why he is here?' Davy passed Gerard a mug of tea and sat in an armchair facing them.

'That he arrived the day of the party and works for you,' she looked at Gerard, 'I'm guessing that he has a room here.'

'Indeed he does, Lou,' he smiled. He took a deep breath and a big swallow of tea.

'Shall I explain?' Gerard looked at the old man for guidance.

'It might be for the best,' Davy Lee said.

'Remember when you went back to England after the misunderstanding?' he took Louise's hand. 'My heart was broken, I know that's not possible, but it was,' he paused. 'Dad had just took over the farm so I decided to go to America.'

'I remember you telling me that,' Louise said, wondering where this was going.

'I went to work for Davy, and I realised that riding horses, breaking them in, was my vocation, I loved it and while I worked hard and grew up, I came to realise that one day I would return to Ireland and find you.'

Louise gasped, she didn't want to return to Clodbury because of him, how could she have got it so wrong?

'I was there a few years, I even had a visa, but one day, out of the blue, my mum phoned to say that dad needed me back on the farm.'

'I only gave him the bloody farm so that he would release Gerard,' Davy bit out, and then realised what he'd said.

'I don't understand,' said Louise, although she was getting a glimmer of light in her brain.

'Davy is my mother's brother,' Gerard confessed, 'he was due to inherit the farm, but wanted to travel to America to make his fortune. When his father passed away, he came back for a while, but the stud farm in America was in his blood. My dad offered to run the farm, he had just been made redundant from a factory and wanted a new direction.'

'So the big house with the pictures on the wall belong to Davy? Louise asked.

'In law, yes, but I will sign it over to my sister and brother in law. I should have done that years ago, but I knew that Gerard wasn't cut out for farming and I wanted to give him a way out.' Davy sighed.

'When you came out to the farm, and then my visit with my mother to the cottage, I realised that things had to change,' Gerard thought back to that fateful day. 'I was putting the farm before you and Jack and I realised how stupid that was, maybe it was fear of retaliation by my father, but it got to the stage when he pushed me too far, and I'm glad he did.'

'What made you invest in the hotel?' Louise asked, 'was it pity for us?'

'No, of course not,' Davy assured her. 'We had watched from afar, me and Gerard, at your progress then the attacks by those Duffy sisters. We could see what would happen if people stopped booking rooms, so I decided to step in. I didn't realise that I would fall in love with the place. This spot is ideal for a stud farm, I've always had vision, Lou.'

'I was always going to come back Lou, but I needed Davy's help,' Gerard confessed.

'Gerard is my heir,' said Davy, 'he's more of a son than a nephew and one day the stud farm will be his.'

'What about the hotel?' asked Louise, 'the investment in the hotel, how do we stand with that?' It was too much to take in, she was feeling dizzy.

'I've had an agreement drawn up,' Davy looked at the three of them sitting together on the sofa, 'my share of the investment will pass to Jack and any subsequent brothers or sisters.'

Louise looked at Gerard sharply and he shook his head.

'I don't know what to say,' Louise felt her eyes fill with tears.

'Finish your tea and I'll show you around,' Davy said proudly.

'Who is looking after your stud farm in America?' she asked.

'I've got men to run things, and I'll be going over from time to time to make sure they're doing a good job,' he got to his feet and put the mugs in the sink, 'follow me,' he commanded.

The kitchen led into a wide hallway with three doors leading from it. The first room was a sitting room or lounge, all the floors were highly polished wood, and in this room there were plush deep piled rugs and heavy curtains of a rich shade of blue. The suite was soft white leather with cushions that matched the curtains, adding a splash of colour. Against a back wall was a white grand piano and Jack eyes up with interest.

'You can have lessons, if you would like,' asked Davy, noting his interest.

A television, the size of the living room in the cottage, hung against the opposite wall, 'it has 3D if you want to watch a film sometime,' his new found great uncle informed him.

'Can I bring some mates up to watch?' Jack asked.

'Don't be so cheeky,' Louise told him.

'I want this to be your home,' Davy told her and meant it. Louise didn't know what to say.

He opened the door to another room, it was the same size as the large sitting room but completely devoid of furniture, 'this is yours to do as you wish,' he told her.

'I live at the cottage,' Louise said gently, 'with Jack and Margaret.'

'Yes, well, follow me,' he opened another door at the back of the large room cleverly disguised as a bookshelf, albeit devoid of books. 'The stairs are this way.'

'Magic,' said Jack in awe, running up ahead.

'Be careful,' Louise cried, the stairs were rich mahogany although a stair carpet covered the centre part of the step.

The six bedrooms were identical in that they were all double en-suite with a window that opened out on to a balcony, each with a different view of the bay. Only two were in use, Gerard had the room at the back of the house, overlooking the back bay and the hotel, Davy the one they were presently standing in, the bed was made and various cushions gave the room an expensive look.

'Who looks after the house for you?' Louise asked, 'the house is shining.'

'My indispensable, Lizzie,' Davy sighed, 'I don't leave home without her.'

'It must be hard work keeping the house this size in order.'

'She manages, in fact, she has practice back home at the ranch,' he chuckled, 'I'll introduce you to her later, she's just gone into the village for supplies.'

Louise burst out laughing, 'I love it,' she stated, and then looked at Gerard, 'are you going to show me your room?'

'Another time,' he grinned, 'I didn't get a chance to tidy it and Lizzie draws the line at doing mine.'

'Please dad,' said Jack, 'I want to see your bedroom.'

Gerard's face turned crimson, but he led the way to his room and once he opened the door, Louise could see why he was so embarrassed, although he shouldn't have been.

On the bedside cabinet was a photograph in a frame, taken when they were both teenagers, before she had discovered that she was pregnant, she went over to pick it up, 'God we were so young, and we were so happy back then.'

'And in love,' he added, 'I take it everywhere, like uncle and his Lizzie.'

'Shame the picture couldn't tidy your room,' she teased, although he had not told the truth, his bed was made and clothes put a way.

'Time to get back,' Louise ushered Jack out of the room, 'I need to get a shower.'

'Have you plans for this evening?' asked Davy.

'We are going out for a family meal, why don't you join us?'

'I'd love to,' he gave her a flashing smile, 'can I bring Lizzie?'

'Of course, I'll make a reservation for 7pm, thank you for showing us your lovely home.'

'You can both visit whenever you want,' he offered.

'It's certainly a day of surprises,' Louise said as they walked back down the road towards the cottage.

'I love my foal, thank you, dad. Can I name him?'

'Of course,' Gerard ruffled his hair.

'We have another surprise for you, Jack,' Louise took him to the side of the road and put her arm around his shoulder, 'before we go inside, we need to tell you something.'

'We're not going back to Oxford?' it was a statement rather than a question.

'No,' Louise laughed, 'we are staying put, especially now that you will have a baby brother or sister in a few months.'

'Really? I don't know if I should be disgusted or happy,' he exclaimed.

'Settle for happy, cheeky,' said Gerard, 'we are going to be a proper family from now on.'

'There you are,' Adele exclaimed when they walked into the cottage, 'Happy birthday, Lou.'

'Thanks mum, we've been up to the stud farm.'

'It's amazing,' said Jack, 'and I've got my own horse.'

'Really?' Adele raised an eyebrow.

'It's a long story,' she picked up a present from the stack on the table, 'I want to open my gifts.'

With a selection of body lotions, jewellery, perfume and chocolates on one side of the table and a pile of wrapping paper on the other, Gerard's box was the last to open.

'Is it another pair of slippers?' she grinned.

'Open it and find out,' he passed her the box and stood by her chair while she tore off the paper.

Inside the shoe box was another box, she opened the lid to find a smaller box, 'is this a Russian present?' she pouted, 'or a new spin on pass the parcel?' She continued opening boxes until she finally found a small box nestled in pink tissue paper. She held it in the palm of her hand and looked at Gerard, who took the box and opened it.

'Will you marry me?' he asked, as Jack, Margaret and Adele watched her reaction.

He opened the box to reveal a solitaire diamond ring, 'I love it,' she gasped, she looked into his beautiful blue eyes and saw the love shining in them. 'Yes, of course I will marry you.'

Gerard slid the ring onto the third finger of her left hand and kissed her for so long Jack made the sound of retching, forcing them to pull apart, laughing.

'When are you going to move into the cottage?' asked Margaret as they sat around the table drinking tea and eating birthday cake. A table had been booked for them all, including Davy and Lizzie. Brian and Maureen were on their honeymoon and Margaret had sent them a text to let them know the happy news.

'I'm hoping Lou will move into the house that will be mine one day,' he said looking first at Louise and then Adele.

'But that wouldn't work,' said Margaret angrily, 'you can't travel 46 miles each way every day.'

'No, I totally agree,' smiled Louise, 'Gerard, that wouldn't work,' she teased.

'And we'd never get to see you,' joined Adele, 'this is your home.'

'Lou?' he asked softly, 'will you come and live with me?'

'I'll have to ask Jack first,' she looked at her son, seeing the gleaming eyes and being in on the teasing, 'bloody right I will,' he grinned.

'Jack,' they said in unison, 'mind your language.'

Adele had booked a function room at a hotel in Malin for the family, 'it's a birthday and engagement celebration,' she told the girl who took the booking.

'What's wrong with our function room?' Margaret asked as she got ready.

'You know mum, she would want to organise it, and besides, we have a booking tonight, an anniversary party. The couple have been married for fifty years, can you imagine?' Louise applied mascara to her long lashes.

'I wonder if me and Finn will last that long,' Margaret sighed.

'Of course you will, he adores you. Tonight is about us, lets enjoy it while we are still single.'

'It's good that we can leave our hotel in safe hands,' Margaret brushed her hair, Is Jack meeting us there with Gerard and Davy?'

'Yes, I think he will be spending a lot of time up there in future.'

'Are you still suffering with IBS?' Margaret noticed the swell of Louise's stomach.

'It's a pain,' smiled Louise, patting her tummy. She was going to tell them all about the baby later.

Frank gave a short blast of his horn to let them know he was waiting outside, 'shame dad and Maureen can't be here,' sighed Margaret as she clambered into the back of the car.

'We can face time him later, pet,' said Adele.

The round table was set for eight and they were the first there, they had just sat down when the other half of the party arrived.

After the main course was eaten and the plates taken away, Louise looked at Gerard and he got to his feet.

'First of all, happy birthday Louise and Margaret,' they all raised their glasses in a toast and chorused happy birthday to the girls. 'Thank you Lou for agreeing to marry me, it should've happened a long time ago, but better late than never,' he leant down and kissed Louise on the lips. 'Now it's your turn Lou.' He sat down and she got to her feet.

'Happy birthday, Margaret and thank you for being there these past few years,' a tear slid down her cheek, 'thank you all for being here tonight, it's amazing that we are here tonight,' she shot Adele a look, and watched as her mother opened facetime on her iPad. 'Hello Brian and Maureen.'

Adele turned the screen around so that everyone around the table could see the beaming faces of the absent newlyweds.

'Before you go and enjoy the rest of your honeymoon,' Louise continued, 'we have some exciting news to share with you all,' she turned to Gerard who got to his feet and put his arm around her shoulder, 'we are going to have a baby.'

'Oh how wonderful,' Adele got to her feet and hugged her daughter and then her future son in law.

'So you haven't got irritable bowel?' Margaret felt hoodwinked by her cousin.

'Sorry, Margaret, we only found out at the hospital, and we wanted to tell you all together, after we had told Jack of course.'

Chapter 71

A few weeks later, the girls were sitting in their chairs by the range, drinking hot chocolate. They had argued about who should be the first to get married, or even if they should have a joint wedding, but with the help of Adele and Brian, who advised strongly that it should be their special day, had decided that Louise should get married first, as not only was it a long time coming, but with the baby only a couple of months away, it made sense.

'Our last night of cosy chats by the range,' Margaret sighed.

'I know and I can't believe I'm getting married tomorrow, dad is a nervous wreck.'

'Will Gerard carry you over the threshold?' Margaret chuckled.

'I hope not, I weigh a ton.'

'Have you spoken to Ebee?'

'Yes,' Louise smiled, 'he asked if he could move into the cottage, I said he would have to ask you too. It makes sense.'

'It does,' Margaret agreed, 'he wants to make it his home. His room at the hotel is far from that.'

'I don't think he will be living here alone either,' Louise smiled, 'he got a letter from someone on the film crew that had been chasing him around for ages.'

'Not Shirl with the pearl?' asked Margaret. Ebee had told her last year when they were both in a melancholy mood over lost loves that his heart had been broken by a girl called Shirley who was a belly dancer in one of the films he was working on.

'Yes, that's the one, and she's been trying to locate him for years, how's that for a misunderstanding?'

'We could make a list of them,' Margaret quipped.

'Brodie and Karnjit are going to rent a house in the village, it will give them space from work,' Louise told her, 'oh and Ebee has got Vincent an interview with a producer, it's an exciting opportunity for him.'

'He's been a great help here,' Margaret said thoughtfully, 'and Natasha is an amazing designer, it's wonderful that she's designed our wedding dresses.'

'And the way she has disguised my bump is so clever, although I've warned Ebee he'd better catch me at the right angle.' She finished her chocolate and pulled herself out of the chair, 'I think we should have an early night,' she yawned, 'it's going to be a long day tomorrow.'

Chapter 72

A year later

'How are you feeling?' Louise asked, patting Margaret's baby bump.

'Tired, aching legs, heartburn, did you feel like this?'

Louise gazed lovingly at the baby girl in the pushchair, the thick black curls fanned out on the pillow and her rosebud mouth relaxed in sleep. 'I can't remember,' she laughed, 'but if I did, it was all worth it.'

'Rosie Lea is gorgeous, and Jack is besotted isn't he?'

'Slightly less than her father, although with her being a mini me helps,' she laughed.

'Yes, it's uncanny,' agreed Margaret, 'she even has your blue eyes.'

'And my hair,' Gerard laughed as he entered the box at Aintree they had booked for the day. Being owners of one of the favourites running in the race meant that they had a perfect view of the racetrack.

'Where's Jack?' Louise lifted her face for Gerard's kiss.

'With Davy and your parents, Brian and Maureen have gone for refreshments.'

Finn was behind Gerard and moved to sit by his wife, 'are you feeling any better?' he asked with concern.

'No, but Lou assures me it will be worth it.'

Rosie Lea opened her eyes and sat up, and then noticing her daddy gave him a sleepy smile.

'Hello my baby girl,' Gerard crooned as he undid her safety straps, 'come to daddy,' he lifted her out just as the race was about to start and she chuckled happily. He sat her on his knee and they all watched and screamed as their horse romped home first.

'I quite like owning part of a racehorse,' grinned Margaret.

Gerard carried Rosie Lea while Louise pushed the stroller towards the beaming group standing by the winner. Davy was congratulating the jockey, Cody Ray on a job well done.

'The perfect end of a perfect day,' Adele sighed happily, 'Ebee just phoned, everything at the hotel is good, Mairead has finished her shift and Karnjit is taking over.'

'Did you know that Brodie proposed to her last week?' said Finn.

'Yes,' said Louise, 'I know everything.'

'Do you know how much I love you?' asked Gerard.

'I do now,' she sighed folding into his arms.

The End

Or is it…………

L - #0201 - 191120 - C0 - 210/148/17 - PB - DID2956025